FORGED

FORGED

A NOVEL

DANIELLE TELLER

PEGASUS BOOKS
NEW YORK LONDON

FORGED

Pegasus Books, Ltd.
148 West 37th Street, 13th Floor
New York, NY 10018

First Pegasus Books cloth edition May 2025

Interior design by Maria Fernandez

ISBN: 978-1-63936-943-0

10 9 8 7 6 5 4 3 2 1

Printed in the United States of America
Distributed by Simon & Schuster
www.pegasusbooks.com

For the best dad in the whole world,
Robert Arthur Dyck,
who told me my first stories

PROLOGUE

T. R. Madden, United States Treasury Department, Custom House

I will never forget the first time I saw Mrs. Catherine "Kitty" Warren, sitting demurely in the empty grand saloon of the SS *Great Northern*. Of course, I knew of Mrs. Warren's suspected criminal activity prior to 1902, in my capacity as a special agent of the Treasury Department; she was already quite notorious by then.

I had boarded the steamer at quarantine to take the declarations of passengers en route to the steamship pier. This was merely a courtesy, to speed the work of the deputy collector so that weary passengers were not overly delayed; I had no mandate to investigate smuggling or enforce fines. While the vessel was being tied up, I was informed that all the passengers, save one, had left the saloon in preparation for disembarkation.

The saloon seemed deserted except for a morose deckhand sweeping the tiled floor. Despite bright sunshine pouring through the domed skylights, I nearly missed the woman in a wingback chair. She had perfectly erect posture, her hands folded neatly in her lap—like a deer standing stock still in the woods, she disappeared into the sumptuous surroundings.

I approached. "Pardon me," I said. "I am Special Agent Madden, of the United States Treasury Department. May I ask if you have made your declaration?"

With a serene smile, she said, "I am unfamiliar with the preliminaries, sir, and I find myself quite at a loss."

She was approximately thirty five years of age, conservatively dressed in a gown of gray satin and lace, her hair impeccably coiffed. Her features were too strong to be considered pretty, but her mien was pleasant. Her most striking attribute was, without doubt, her eyes: bright, clear, and sea green; I was impressed by the frankness and intelligence of her gaze. Her aspect conveyed a genial approval, as though she saw me as I most wished to be seen.

I noticed the brooch pinned to the shawl in her lap. It was shaped like a butterfly, with a body of black pearls and wings of concentric precious stones; rubies in the center, ringed by sapphires, emeralds, and an outermost layer of brilliant diamonds. "That is a spectacular piece," I said.

Her cheeks dimpled. "It's only glass, but pretty, isn't it?"

"I have never seen glass that looked so much like real stones," I said.

Mrs. Warren laughed and touched the back of my hand with gloved fingertips. "The French are so clever," she said.

"May I ask your name?"

"Mrs. Catherine Warren."

I was electrified. She was near legendary at Custom House for her jewel smuggling—and her ability to avoid our detection. "Are you expecting someone?" I asked, certain that she was waiting for an accomplice to help her sneak goods onshore.

"Oh, no," she said. "I am quite alone." She smoothed her skirt. "You seem very kind. Perhaps you could help me?"

So as not to raise her guard, I went along with the pretense that she was unfamiliar with import rules. I described the tariffs in simple terms and conducted her to the deputy collector for her official declaration. I confess that I relished witnessing the end of her putative criminal career. I may even have been thinking about the credit I would bring to our department for nabbing her.

The collector looked seasoned and gruff, with his heavy brow and full white beard, and I was sure he would make a thorough inspection.

Mrs. Warren smiled with what, for all the world, appeared to be delight at the prospect of making her declaration. "I have received such expert counsel from this gracious gentleman," she said, placing her hand on my forearm. She spoke softly, forcing the collector to lean close.

"I understand that you wish to know about my new jewelry," she said. "But I am no aficionado. I have a few cheap pieces, my tiny vanities, worth nothing at all, really."

"Where is your luggage?" the collector asked.

"The porter has already taken my trunks for me."

"What did you buy during your stay in France?"

Mrs. Warren looked to me, as though I knew. "So little that it is hardly worth mentioning." She shrugged her shoulders expressively, like a European. "Some linens for my own use. Old secondhand pearls that have not even been strung." Her laugh was charming, conveying both amiability and modesty. "I have listened carefully to Special Agent Madden here, who has advised me on the import rules, and I'm sure I have nothing of value to declare."

I fully expected the collector to scoff at her description of pearls as "secondhand." Yet to my astonishment, he thanked her and waved her on without further questions or comment. After waltzing through customs without paying a penny, Mrs. Warren raised a hand in adieu. Dumbstruck, I did not return the gesture.

"Why didn't you order a search of her trunks?" I demanded of the collector.

"A woman like that is harmless," he said dismissively.

"But that was Mrs. Kitty Warren, a known jewel smuggler!" I was almost sputtering.

"Not known to me," he said, looking for other stragglers. Seeing none, he began to pack his bag.

"The one person you should have detained is her!"

The collector's smile was condescending. "You are young," he said. "It's good to have enthusiasm for your work. But you will learn in time to pick out true suspects. The lady was no crook."

After that first encounter, I took personal interest in this woman who had so long evaded us. We put Mrs. Warren under surveillance in Paris after discovering that she engaged the services of a jeweler on Rue de la Paix. Major Peterson, chief of the Paris office, made an arrangement with one of the shop's employees. Whenever Mrs. Warren commissioned the jeweler to set precious stones or acquire rare jewels, the clerk would place her items in the display window, using a coded layout. Then one of our men would photograph the items and send images and descriptions back to New York.

In this manner, we developed a catalog of Mrs. Warren's foreign jewelry acquisitions, which were many, all valued at princely sums. Customs inspectors studied the photographs in hope of recognizing the pieces when they were smuggled into America. There were sapphire rings and black pearl ropes, emerald necklaces and diamond bracelets, all of the highest quality. Unfortunately, detailed accounting was not enough—even when we were tipped off about her movements, she eluded us. She would not arrive on the steamer she had booked, or when her baggage was searched, nothing would be discovered. Then, months or years later, a wealthy socialite at the opera would be spotted wearing one of the extravagances we had documented in what we called "Dragon Kitty's Treasure Catalog."

In 1905, just before Mrs. Warren's financial schemes were exposed to the world, I was perusing an *Evening Telegram* and saw a photograph of her emerging from the Fifth Avenue Hotel in New York City. I marked the plainness of her features with some surprise; in my memory, she was a handsome woman. She wore an evening gown and fur stole, but what caught my attention was the elaborate diamond necklace encircling her throat. At its center: a heart-shaped stone of some twenty carats. Just the month before, I had seen that necklace in Dragon Kitty's Treasure Catalog.

The photograph had been taken the previous night. It was already past suppertime, but I hastened to the hotel. I had even more motivation than before, having endured my colleagues' ribbing about letting Mrs. Warren slip through my fingers.

The hotel clerk confirmed that Mrs. Warren was indeed still in residence and gave me her room number. I rapped smartly on the door, and a neat young woman in a black dress answered. She looked at me warily as I proffered my official card.

"What is it you want?" the maid asked, none too politely.

Her coldness heightened my suspicions. Serendipity had brought me near my quarry, and I could not miss my chance. Unobtrusively, I moved my foot into the doorframe, preventing the door from shutting on me. "Please convey my card to your mistress," I said. "I am here on the business of the United States Treasury Department."

The girl narrowed her eyes but moved aside to let me enter the foyer of the luxurious suite. She disappeared for a full five minutes before the woman herself appeared, clad in an exquisite silk kimono, holding my card. "To what do I owe the pleasure, good sir?" She gazed at me levelly; the angles and planes of her face were exotic in the lamplight, the air tinged with jasmine perfume.

Unaccountably, I felt awkward and jittery, like a boy in a spelling match. In an exaggerated, languorous motion, she brushed curls back from her milky cheek. It was clear that she had no recollection of our prior meeting.

"I am with the Treasury Department, madam," I said.

"This much I already knew." She handed my card back nonchalantly.

I pulled the *Evening Telegram* from my overcoat pocket; I had folded the paper so that the incriminating photograph faced outward. "I saw you in the society pages."

"An admirer from the Treasury Department?" Mrs. Warren's smile was conspiratorial.

"This necklace." I tapped the page for emphasis. "We have reason to believe that you purchased it in Paris."

"Oh, that thing." She laughed. "Flashy, I suppose. I borrowed it from a jeweler. It is good advertising for them when my photo appears in the newspaper."

"We have evidence that you bought it from a shop on Rue de la Paix."

Her shrug was elegant. I could not help notice that her silk robe slipped minutely lower down her shoulder.

"I could search your rooms right now, madam, and if I found the necklace, you would be subject to heavy fines."

Mrs. Warren tilted her head. "You have a warrant?"

If I'd had any doubt that she was expertly versed in the requirements of the law, it was erased. From her playful smile, it was apparent that she did not fear me. I fumed at the toothlessness of my office—I had no right to enter her rooms, and the police in New York did not take customs matters seriously. Our department relied on the honesty of good citizens, while dishonest lawbreakers made sport of defrauding the United States government.

"I *will* obtain a warrant," I said. "If I must spend the night in the corridor outside your door to be sure that you do not flee before I have obtained it, I will."

Mrs. Warren looked amused. She touched my arm gently. "Never fear, Mr. Madden," she said. She had registered the name on my card. "There is no need to guard my door; I won't scurry off into the night."

She treated me like a child who had said something absurd; I was shamed for my zealousness. I knew that someone of her notoriety would not go into hiding over a dispute about a necklace. Nevertheless, I resolved to obtain a warrant as soon as the judge was in his chambers. Either Mrs. Warren would produce the necklace, or I would find it in her suite. I had her cornered—she would not escape.

The hotel clerk let me use an unoccupied guest room that night, as I planned to go to the courthouse just after sunrise; it made little sense to travel home, to the upper part of Manhattan, so late in the evening.

I slept fitfully, fully dressed, awaiting my wake-up call at any moment. It was still dark when the bellboy knocked on my door. I jumped to my feet and splashed water on my face, tidying myself as much as I could without comb or razor.

I expected the lobby to be deserted at that hour, when dawn barely brightened the windows, and was taken aback to see none other than Mrs. Kitty Warren, perched on a settee.

"My dear Mr. Madden," she said, clasping my fingers between her gloved hands. "It is a lovely morning." She was different from the night before, with rosy cheeks, a brisk manner, and a scent like clean laundry. "I hoped we could take breakfast together." She cocked an eyebrow at the surprise on my face. "You do recall our rendezvous?"

"Of course, madam," I said, recovering myself. "But what of the diamond necklace?"

"Oh, I sent a boy to pick it up at the jeweler's. The owner will open the shop early as a favor. Come, I have already ordered; I trust that eggs Benedict will please you? I took the liberty of requesting a side of caviar."

Mrs. Warren removed her gloves and folded them neatly, tucking them into her bag. "You see, Mr. Madden, the European fashions are always ahead of ours, and my friend, Michael Younge—you may know his jewelry shop on Union Square West—he asks me to bring him new designs."

She paused, and when I looked up from stirring my coffee, I glimpsed an expression of intense observation, like a raptor surveying its prey. The moment passed, and with a smile, she continued, "I don't buy gems in Europe, you see. I gather all of the stones here in New York or, if Mr. Younge advises, Cleveland or Pittsburgh—it is important to match them carefully. I only bring them to Paris for settings. That's all right, isn't it? I do hope I haven't done anything wrong."

"According to the revised statutes," I interrupted, "all merchandise taken from the United States and conveyed to foreign countries to be reconstructed is dutiable upon return at the regular rate of sixty percent." Whether or not Mrs. Warren knew of this regulation—and she almost certainly did—she would be liable for import duties.

Mrs. Warren smiled at me, then leaned forward, speaking in confidence, though the dining room was deserted at that hour. "All I got from the French jewelers was advice, and surely we are not required to pay money for a few friendly words of guidance, maybe a drawing or two."

A tow-headed boy rushed in, carrying a blue velvet box. He came straight to the table and plunked it down in front of Mrs. Warren, his expression like a retriever dog, worshipping its master.

"Ah, Henry," Mrs. Warren said. "Thank you so much for bringing this little bauble." Oddly, she introduced me to the boy, saying, "This is Mr. Madden, a diligent and honorable employee of the government of our great country. Mr. Madden, this is Henry."

The boy ducked his head, then drew himself up, puffing out his small chest. I was at first offended by this eccentric elevation of an errand boy, but when I saw what pride Henry took in the introduction, I grew magnanimous. "Nice to meet you," I said, and offered my hand. He shook it with a soft, shy grip, then darted away again.

Mrs. Warren opened the box. There was a letter written on thick, cream-colored paper inside, which she handed to me. It was from Younge and Co., signed by Mr. Michael Younge himself. The letter attested that the necklace had been assembled in the United States from gems purchased within our national borders.

"It is really lovely," Mrs. Warren said, tilting the box up so that the light through the windows sparkled on the diamonds' many facets. She snapped the box shut and handed it to me. "If you like, you may return this to Mr. Younge yourself."

I had no riposte. It all appeared to be perfectly legal, though I knew it was not. "I must beg your leave," I said. I had failed in my duty and was unable to stomach taking breakfast.

Mrs. Warren stood, smiling. "I'm sorry you can't stay. It was such a pleasure, Mr. Madden," she said. "I admire the work that you do."

God help me, I smiled in return. "The pleasure was mine, madam," I said, like a fool. A part of me actually meant it. When I looked into her luminous eyes, I almost believed her to be innocent. I wanted her to be innocent. I could scarcely have guessed then that smuggling was the least of her crimes.

PART I

PART 1

CHAPTER 1

Scratching her shin with a calloused heel, Fanny pushed the tip of her pencil across the slate with concentration. A bulbous upper case *B* was followed by six cramped letters, spidery and backward-slanting, barely legible in the feeble light of the shack's only window. She leaned down to peer at a scrap of paper by her elbow, then methodically wrote the same name again, immediately below the first; the pencil made the faintest squeak. With the slate in one hand and the paper in the other, she held them nearer the window, appraising her work. She still hadn't managed to make a perfect replica of the signature.

Ignoring the rain that hammered against cracked panes and leaked across the rough pinewood sill, Fanny set the tablet down and wrote the letters again, then again. When her pencil bumped against the bottom of the frame on the downstroke, she wiped away the dusty script with a rag and started over at the top.

Cold seeped into Fanny's bones; stillness stiffened her limbs. The gray light hadn't noticeably dimmed, but she could feel dusk gathering in the woods, like wolves converging. Soon, Father and the boys would be back from partridge hunting, expecting their supper. She stood and glanced outside, through the warped glass. A thick, gnarled branch of the apple tree took up most of the view; withered brown leaves, battered by rain, still clung to its underside. She had told her father that the tree needed to be cut back to keep the rats off the roof and out of the loft, but he never listened.

Fanny hid her slate and the scrap of paper in the dusty, cobwebbed gap behind the storage chest. She knelt by the hearth, tucking a wayward strand of tangled hair back under her kerchief. Beside the woodpile was a whiskey barrel filled with kindling; she grabbed a handful, and as she blew on the embers, she dropped in dried grasses and twigs, little nibbles to coax the fire back to life. Before she left home, Fanny's sister had given advice about housekeeping. It was important, Betsy said, to have the water boiling before Father got home with partridges. She had looked earnestly into Fanny's eyes as she made her point, making sure that she understood.

Fanny fed sticks to the licking flames, and when those caught fire, spruce logs. A nutty fragrance and snapping filled the air as sap pockets cracked open. She hauled the blackened pot filled with water from the hearth to hang it by a thick hook over the fire, her arms trembling under the weight, heat burning her hands. Betsy had made it look easy, but then she had been full grown, nearly five years older and several stone heavier than Fanny. With a curse, Fanny lifted the pot higher, the water sloshing erratically. Just as she thought she might drop it, the iron handle slid onto the hook with a clang. Fanny snatched her hands back and pressed them to the cool stone of the mantel. Next time she would hang the pot first, then fill it with water.

Fanny set a chipped enameled bowl on the table next to a burlap bag, from which she scooped out a pile of bush beans. The tips of the long-stored legumes had gone soft, and some were slimy; they smelled of must and rot.

The wind picked up, driving rain under the door and through the broken window. Fanny chewed on her lip as she shelled the beans, throwing seeds into the bowl with a *thuck, thuck* that was drowned out by a sudden downpour thundering on the roof.

Just as the rain lessened, there came shouts in the distance, then the pounding of boots on the porch. The door was flung wide. Fanny's brothers jostled each other, laughing and hooting; the smaller one, John, shook his head like a wet dog, spraying water in every direction.

"Stop it!" Fanny snapped, wiping droplets from her face with the frayed sleeve of her dress. "Take your boots off, both of you! You're tracking mud."

John tossed his soaking glove at her; it struck her shoulder, leaving a damp patch, then fell to the floor.

"Here you go," Billy said, laying a brace of fat partridges on the table. His wobbly adolescent voice broke on the word *go*, shifting to a higher register, which made John snicker. Billy paid him no heed; though he was bigger than his younger brother, he lacked John's appetite for battle.

The door opened again. John hushed, and Fanny went back to shelling beans, glancing at her father from the corner of her eye, trying to divine his mood. Daniel was a tall, sinewy man with a ruined face; he had lost an eye in a bar fight, and his left cheek was knotted with a scar from an accident with a harrow. He leaned against the doorframe, pulling off his boots; the cold rain blew in around him. Fanny shivered.

When Daniel stepped forward to set down his rifle, water dripping off his crooked nose, Billy quietly closed the door behind him.

"What about supper?" Daniel said. His flat tone gave nothing away.

"Ready soon." Fanny kept working; she heard the rustles and clunks of her father and the boys shedding their outerwear. With chapped fingers, she tore open the fibrous pods, hastily digging out seeds. "I'll pour you a dram of whiskey."

The blow to the side of her head was hard enough to make her stagger.

"I'll get it," her father said. "Seems you're too busy."

A brief, bright flare of anger obscured Fanny's sight, but she returned to her task as though nothing had happened. Her temple throbbed, and she tasted blood where she had bit her tongue.

John snorted. He stood dripping by the fire, his feet spread wide in the posture of a grown man, taking in the spectacle with a smile.

Daniel picked up a dusty jug from the shelf and hefted it, weighing its contents. "Girl!" he barked, a guttural report. It wasn't as threatening as when he drew the syllable out, savoring it. But it wasn't good, either. "You were supposed to go up the creek for more whiskey!"

"There's plenty there." Fanny drew up her shoulders; the back of her neck felt naked, a snail unable to retract into its shell.

Billy cleared his throat and made a humming sound, his prelude to speech when he hadn't yet thought of what to say. He was gentle, always the peacemaker. God only knew how he ended up in their family; Fanny wasn't sure he would survive it.

"Snow's coming soon," Billy said finally. "We should kill that pig."

Daniel grunted. He filled a cup with the amber liquid and drank it down in long gulps.

The water over the fire burbled and spat. Fanny grabbed the partridges by their legs and plunged them into the pot. She wasn't careful enough, and a wave splashed over the edge, sizzling on the hearth. Fanny flinched as flying drops burned the underside of her forearm, but she didn't let go of the wizened claws. *Just a minute in boiling water,* her sister had said. *Then the feathers come off easy.*

John crowded the fireplace, standing too close behind Fanny, getting in her way. Though he was a year younger, he had grown taller than Fanny and was feeling his oats. She pulled the birds straight up by their feet, letting hot water stream back into the pot. "Move," she said to John.

John came even closer, taunting her. It took effort to hold the wet birds high, arms extended over the steaming pot; she could feel pricks of sweat beading on her forehead. The partridges were pathetic things, their feathers plastered to their little pink bodies. Fanny could hear her brother's raspy breath, felt it stirring the hairs at the nape of her neck. Swiftly, she lifted her foot and smashed her bare heel into John's toes. He yelped and hopped back.

"You little bitch," he said, in a perfect imitation of his father.

Fanny turned her head slowly, saw his raised fist. She allowed the full force of her fury to flood her expression.

John glanced away. He lowered his skinny arm and picked at a scab on his chin, as though that was what he had intended to do all along. "You'd better get supper ready, little bitch," he hissed. He slouched over to Billy, who was drying the rifle with a rag.

When the partridges stopped steaming, Fanny sank to the floor to pluck them. She crossed her legs, tucking her dirty feet under her skirt. It was hard to see what she was doing; the window had become a black square in the wall, dully reflecting flickers of fire. "We might light a candle, Father," she said.

"I'm not made of money." Daniel was on his second or third cup, and his words came out rounder, fuzzy-edged. He sat in the shadows; Fanny could make out little more than the silhouette of his slumped shoulders and bent head. "You just hurry up," he said. "Seems your sister didn't teach you too good."

Without thinking, Fanny tossed a handful of feathers into the fire, where they sent up a thick smoke and foul odor.

John coughed. "That stinks like dogshit!"

Fanny glanced quickly to where her father sat; he was still hunched over his whiskey. To John, she said, "Since when's your nose so delicate? You smell worse." Fanny was embarrassed by her mistake, but wasn't going to show it.

"You're not just too stupid for school. You're too stupid to live."

John's accusation was a jab at a fresh wound. School had been the only bright spot in Fanny's life, and John knew it. The teacher had said that she was the smartest student she had ever taught, and had Fanny been a boy, she might have gone to college.

Fanny tried to shake the clinging wet down from her fingers, then gave up and wiped her hands on her skirt. She went back to plucking, depositing the feathers in a neat pile on the floor. When she was done, she laid the floppy, naked partridges side by side on the hearth. The room was silent except for her father's sighs and the crackling fire. The rain had stopped. Billy and John were sitting idle, waiting to be fed. Fanny gathered up the large pile of feathers in two hands and dumped it into the fire. She watched the thick black smoke billow and coil up the chimney. She held her breath against the stench.

The kick to her back forced the air from her lungs. Later, a deep purple bruise would bloom over her bony spine.

"Stupid bitch," her father said, coughing.

Moving fluidly, as though she felt nothing, Fanny got up and threaded the birds onto the spit. She went back to shelling beans.

"We should kill that pig," Billy said. "When it comes the first of sleighing, we'll be glad of salt pork." He made a little humming noise.

After supper, the room was illuminated by little more than cloud-veiled moonlight from the window. Daniel hauled himself unsteadily up the ladder to the loft. Within minutes, he was snoring. John climbed up next, once he was sure that his father was asleep.

"That was a good feed," Billy said. He cracked his knuckles.

The fire had died to glowing embers and starved orange flames that flicked like snake tongues; Fanny could scarcely make out her brother's face, hovering beside her. She scrubbed a greasy plate in a tub of tepid water. "Goodnight, Billy," she said.

"Goodnight." He sounded relieved to be dismissed. The rungs of the ladder groaned under his feet.

Fanny stacked the plates, wet and still slick with fat despite her efforts, then took the dish tub outside to empty it. She had to rest the metal bottom of the tub on her sore hip bone; she wasn't strong enough to carry it with her arms alone. She slid on a pair of soggy, oversized boots, probably her father's, though she couldn't tell in the darkness, and kicked open the door.

The meadow was drab in gray light cast by the moon. Bats darted erratically; there came a doleful hoot of an owl, then silence. The rain barrel was full to the brim, but the sloping ground had shed most of its water into the creek. Fanny set down the tub and tipped it up, letting the contents slosh into the drainage ditch that surrounded their shack. Shadowy crabgrass bent under the greasy deluge, then slowly picked itself back up. She looked to the hulking black woods. There was nothing beyond the boundaries of their property but more poor farmers, immigrants who had fled the Old World in hope of taming the Canadian wilderness. They squatted in shanties on jagged clearings, scraping what they could from the earth, plagued by ravenous black flies and mosquitoes during the good months, deadly cold and hunger during the bad. Her father, like all the farmers, pretended that dirt held a better future, that one day they would be more than frightened animals in a hostile wilderness, scurrying outside just long enough to drag provisions into their squalid holes. Pretending that each day was building a future and not just staving off death until the dirt claimed them, inevitably, indifferently.

Fanny was tired, and there was a sharp smell of winter in the night air, but she was reluctant to go back inside. She leaned against the splintered doorframe and pictured her sister on the train to Cleveland, a new hat perched on her head, gloved hands clasped in her lap.

Betsy, ever the obedient daughter, hadn't even yearned to escape. She had seemed content with the burdens of housework, the company of her few friends, the prospect of eventually becoming a mother herself. It was Fanny who obsessed about leaving, the way a famished man dreams of food. And yet, Betsy had left. And she was here.

She picked up the empty tub and looked in the direction of the distant train station. The wall of the forest was pitch-black; it swallowed the feeble light of the moon and gave nothing back.

CHAPTER 2

Three years after Betsy left, in the dead of winter, Daniel, Billy, and John were sickened with ague. They moaned, drenched with sweat, woolen blankets piled over their shivering bodies. A harsh wind drove snow through chinks in the door. Fanny kept the fire low, nursing the dwindling wood pile. She slaughtered a scrawny old hen to make soup and carried steaming bowls to the loft.

"Big Ned sent word he's taking his sleigh to town tomorrow," she said, placing the last bowl and spoon next to John's mattress. "Should be quick travel with all this snow."

Daniel grunted. Billy, who seemed the least sick of the three, propped himself up on an elbow and reached for his soup. The musk of unwashed bodies and illness hung over the loft like a malignant fog.

"Thought I'd go with him to fetch medicine." Fanny strove to keep her voice neutral as her heart pounded and her breath quickened. In the years since she had been forced to quit school, she had only twice been allowed to go into town, and never alone. Her father said that "bitches and slatterns" couldn't be trusted with money. He relied on John, who was only fifteen, but not on Fanny, a year older.

11

Daniel rolled heavily onto his back and squinted at his daughter. His face was red and slick with sweat, except for the nacreous ridges of his scars. "What medicine?" he rasped.

"Laudanum to help you rest and ease your sore throat. Brandy for your tea." She balled her fists behind her back. "Besides, it's time someone checked on the mail. I would be back before dark."

Daniel turned away, exhaling with a hiss. It was the closest Fanny would get to permission. She climbed back down the ladder without another word.

Fanny stared into blackened rafters as the fire died, ignoring snores, moans, and coughs from the loft. She didn't sleep at all that night, with a moth-wing quiver in her stomach and an ache in her chest. To strengthen her resolve, she allowed herself to take a mental inventory of injuries—the bruises, the lump on her thrice-dislocated elbow, the thick scar on her thumb, the insults she had absorbed about her soft, bleeding girl's body, her feeble female brain. Betsy had escaped, and she would too.

When the geese honked, rousing themselves, and the window appeared as a faint, opalescent square floating in blackness, she swung her feet onto the cold floor. Out of habit, she knelt, shivering in her nightgown by the hearth to start a fire. Then she remembered that she wasn't coming home again. If her father or brothers wanted a fire, they could make their own. Certainly Billy was already well enough to get out of bed.

There were only two dresses to choose between, both wool. Fanny quietly pulled on her Sunday best, which was no more stylish than her workaday dress but had no patches or tears. Her coat was hopeless, grimy, with threadbare elbows and seams repaired so many times that the fabric shredded like cheesecloth. She wrapped a knitted shawl around her shoulders, knowing it was meager protection against the cold. From the high shelf, she took down her mother's quilted bonnet. She didn't know why her father had kept it; he had traded or repurposed everything else belonging to his wife after she died. Fanny had tried on the cap countless times over the years. She coiled her braided hair beneath the crown and fastened the ties.

The sun was rising pink and gold when Fanny stepped outside. It was a windless, mild winter day. Chickadees chirped and whistled to one another; the burble of the stream was muffled by a roof of ice. A sagging pine bough released its burden of snow with a soft *whump* and powdery plume.

Fanny heard the jingle of Big Ned's sleigh before she saw it round the copse of aspens at the edge of their property. He waved a gloved hand as he pulled near; the horse pranced to a stop, snorting and tossing its head. Fanny was fond of the spirited mare, and she patted her sturdy neck before climbing up beside Ned.

"So kind of you to bring me," she said.

Ned pulled the coarse wool blanket from his lap and extended it to Fanny. "You're not dressed for winter," he said gruffly.

He was a bear of a man, brusque and unkempt, but Fanny knew him to be good-hearted. He had tilled and planted their field when her father had broken his arm, and he always brought shortbread from his wife at Christmas. Fanny draped the blanket loosely over her legs. "It's not cold."

"You're too skinny." Ned slapped the rawhide reins against the horse's haunch and clicked his tongue. They lurched forward, gliding smoothly over the wet snowpack. He glanced at Fanny. "There's salt pork in that bag."

Fanny opened the burlap sack he had indicated with a jut of his chin and pulled out a greasy package. She unwrapped the meat; the briny scent provoked a flood of saliva. "You want a piece?"

Ned nodded. She handed him a chunk of pork and tried to savor hers slowly, but instead tore into it with a bite too big to chew with her lips closed. She felt foolish with her cheek bulging, sucking in air so that she wouldn't drool.

"Guess hunger's good sauce for any food," Ned said. "My old lady stashed pritters in there too, if you don't mind 'em cold and soggy."

Fanny ate, and they traveled in silence over hilly, well-cleared country. Deep snow filled depressions in the land, covering up swampy muck that trapped wheels of wagons and corduroy roads that rattled bones. It felt like magic, the swift skimming over a slippery blanket, riding toward town at double or triple summertime speed. It reminded Fanny of dreams of flying, swooping over forests and fields like a hawk.

As they passed a barnyard, Fanny nearly jumped out of her skin. From just behind her right shoulder, a shrieking cock's crow shattered the quiet. On and on it went, like the squall of a baby, and it was answered by fainter crows in the distance. Big Ned laughed, the sound nearly drowned out by raucous squawking, and then Fanny joined him. For all its bluster, the rooster's call was comical.

"Didn't know you had a bird back there," Fanny said.

"Ah, he thinks he's king of the hill." Ned chuckled. "You heard all the angry hollers he gets back, but he knows he's safe in his basket."

Tall woods arose on both sides of their path, and Fanny tried to relax into the rhythm of their journey. Even at the quick speed they traveled, it was an hour-long ride into town; an hour during which Fanny had nothing to fear. She had a warm blanket across her lap, a full stomach, and a plan. Yet her mind would not still.

As they passed wooden shacks on the outskirts of town, Fanny said, "Will you drop me at the general store? I should start with my shopping."

"You'd best leave the big items for last," Ned said. "Don't want to lug them around all morning."

"Not to worry, I haven't much to buy." Fanny lifted her straw bag, implying that all she needed would fit inside. "And I like to look at the shoes and hats, even if I can't afford them. I'm hoping there are velvet ribbons in the store, too—I would adore a pink one."

Ned grunted, dropping the conversation, as Fanny had known he would.

The snow thinned and turned a dingy gray as fields gave way to roads, then the sleigh's runners dug into a sludge of melting ice and mud. The tired mare slowed, her coat mottled with patches of sweat. When they reached the brightly painted storefront, Ned pulled to a halt. "I'll meet you back here at noon," he said.

Fanny felt a stab of guilt as she thanked him with a sunny smile. She pulled her shawl tighter around her shoulders and descended to the street; mud oozed around her boots. The flaking white paint on the steps up to the front porch of the store was stained dark with footprints, and Fanny added her own, walking nonchalantly, a hand trailing on the banister. A pair of middle-aged customers in sensible wool coats strolled past, chatting. Fanny dawdled, pretending to look at the display in the big picture window. She watched Ned's reflection in the glass until he tied up his horse and lumbered away, then she cleaned her soles on the iron boot scraper and took a deep breath, trying to settle her nerves. She stood straighter and opened the door with an assertive sweep of her arm. The bell in the doorway tinkled, and the shopkeeper, a hollow-cheeked man with thinning gray hair, glanced up from his ledger on the counter. He dismissed her immediately, dropping his eyes back to his sums.

Fanny's stomach clenched, but she marched up to the counter. The shopkeeper ignored her still. She reached into her bag and pulled out the piece of paper she had worked on so carefully the previous day. She knew that the forgery of her father's signature was perfect, with its lumpish B and backward slant, but she could feel her fingers tremble. She laid out the check, smoothing it with both hands, though it wasn't wrinkled. "My father gave me five dollars to buy a suitable travel outfit," she said.

The shopkeeper raised his head, the lenses of his pince-nez glinting in a ray of light from the window. "What's that?" He appraised her skeptically.

"I am going to Cleveland to meet my fiancé, and my father wishes for me to be suitably dressed."

He rubbed his cheek with his knuckle. "Five dollars is a lot of money."

Fanny lifted her chin and looked directly into the shopkeeper's close-set brown eyes. "My fiancé is a wealthy member of my cousin's family, and I cannot arrive at his American mansion wearing the clothes of a poor farmer's daughter." The stiltedness of her speech made her cringe, but she did not let her gaze waver.

The shopkeeper appeared unconvinced. "Rich relatives, eh?"

Fanny plunged on. "I'm to take the balance in cash to pay for the train. My father wouldn't send me away penniless. I'm sure you would do the same for your child."

He held up the check with ink-stained fingers and examined it closely.

"You know my father's notes; he has been shopping here for years."

The man cleared his throat. "He never sent you before."

"I have never been engaged to be married before." She forced herself to maintain her pose; she could feel the thud of her heart against the hand that clutched her shawl to her chest.

He pursed his lips and inhaled deeply through his nose. She continued to watch him with an expression that she hoped was pleasantly expectant. The shopkeeper gestured toward the back of the store. "Women's ready-to-wear is against that wall there. Alterations cost extra."

Fanny sauntered self-consciously in the direction he had indicated, trying to slow her breathing. She paused to observe the way another shopper rifled through the dresses, checking tags and touching fabrics. When the woman drifted on, Fanny took her place and mimicked her motions. Even the small selection seemed like a treasure trove, with so many colors and trims to choose from. Fanny settled on a blue dress with a velveteen bodice and high neckline. Not knowing how to judge the size, she furtively held it against her body, assessing the position of the seams. It would do, she decided. She selected a bonnet with satiny blue ribbons, hoping that it would match the dress; she had no experience with fashion.

The shopkeeper raised an eyebrow when Fanny placed her items on the counter. "Aren't you going to try it on?" he asked.

Fanny's face grew hot. She hadn't known that this was an option. "There is no need," she said with feigned hauteur. "I know it will fit." She hunted for more words that would make her seem older and more sophisticated, but he was already bent over his ledger, scribbling. He reached beneath the counter and produced dollar bills, which he counted out, though there were only two. He added some coins, then pushed the money to her across the counter.

"Your father must be uncommonly generous or uncommonly eager to be rid of you," the shopkeeper said.

Fanny smiled shakily as she scooped the stupendous bounty into her bag. "Thank you, sir," she said. "Good day to you."

Outside, Fanny breathed in cold air in great gulps, waiting for her heart to slow. The new dress was wrapped in paper and clenched tightly under her arm. She looked around to get her bearings. The town was quieter than she remembered; there were no carriages passing by, no wind in the trees, and the few pedestrians she saw went about their business in silence. An old wooden bench, slats half-rotten and over-grown with dead ivy, powdered by snow, looked sadly forlorn. The train station was two blocks away; she could see its stubby clock tower peeking over the squat brick buildings across the street, silhouetted against a horizon of corrugated clouds. A child wailed in the distance, and a woman shouted. Already, the village that she had thought of as bustling seemed achingly plain and small. Fanny, hugging her bag to her chest, set out for the station. She would go to Cleveland and somehow find her sister, Betsy. There, she would start her real life.

CHAPTER 3

The series of train rides to Cleveland took a greater toll on Fanny than she had anticipated. In fact, she had not truly anticipated any of it—she had run away from home in spite of her ignorance about the world and its workings. If any image of the train ride had come to mind, it was the one she had conjured of her sister, sitting calmly with a pert hat and clasped gloved hands, watching pleasant scenery float past.

Instead, Fanny was squeezed to the corner of her seat by a large man who smelled of sweat, Florida Water, and stale cigar smoke. She curled herself up to keep out of the way of his thick, sprawling limbs. Her new dress didn't fit as well as she had hoped; the bodice gaped open over her thin chest, so even though she felt hot, she kept her shawl wrapped tightly around her shoulders. Her skirt was too short, exposing her ugly, scuffed boots, and she pulled at it compulsively, as though she could make it lengthen. Chewing on her lip, she stared blindly out the window, her legs crossed tightly, trying to ignore the increasingly urgent calls of her bladder.

When she disembarked at the grand Italianate station in Toronto, streams of briskly moving passengers rushed past her like schools of fish toward a lure. The numbers and variety of people were astonishing; she had never heard a foreign language before, and now they were all around her, in trills, guttural vowels, crisp consonants. There were tall black hats on the men and enormous bustles on the women, making them look like hens with swishing, fluffy behinds. The shades of complexions startled her—the darkest she had ever seen was the village butcher's, who was Métis, and his skin was only a smidge darker than her own in summertime. The building itself made her dizzy, with its impossibly high ceilings and fortress-like walls.

With watering eyes, Fanny darted through the crowds, looking for a place to empty her bladder. The signs were mysterious, the urgency unbearable. She ducked into a stairwell, lifted her skirts, and shamefully discharged the urine that she could no longer contain. It splashed on the cement and spread in a dark pool, smelling faintly of ammonia. When a door on a lower level creaked open, she dropped her skirts and fled.

In the tributaries to the great marble station building, there were food vendors. The scents of fried dough and grilled meat made Fanny's mouth water, but she was fearful of missing her next train and didn't want to wait in line. Just finding the ticket counter and the correct platform made her vibrate with anxiety; everyone but her seemed to know exactly what to do and where to go.

Once on the platform, she thought she saw women glancing at her sidelong, and felt out of place in her ill-fitting dress, ragged shawl and worn boots. She made herself small in the corner of a bench, pulled a book from her bag, and pretended to read sentences that she had already read a half dozen times before, blocking out her surroundings and her grumbling stomach.

The train to Buffalo chugged and wheezed into the station. Fanny moved toward the back of the line to watch how other passengers boarded and arranged themselves, and as a consequence, she had few options for seating. An elegantly dressed middle-aged woman sitting across the aisle from two young women, whom Fanny understood to be her daughters, reluctantly made room for Fanny next to her. She fastidiously tucked her travel blanket over her lap, as though Fanny might contaminate her by touching her. Fanny, chilled through, eyed the fur longingly. Listening in on their conversation, She learned that they were visiting a dying relative who had a substantial inheritance to bestow. She also learned from an offhand remark that there were toilets onboard the train, which caused her to blush in private shame at her own ignorance.

The woman bent toward the bag at her feet, but seemed constrained by an overly tight corset and thick waist, the reach of her hands falling short. She gestured to one of her daughters, who pulled out three neatly wrapped sandwiches from the bag. Soon, the smell of onion and fish filled the air, making Fanny's stomach churn. She read the book she knew nearly by heart, then softly hummed tunes that she and her sister used to sing when they were alone together, trying to will her mind back to sweeter times.

Fanny followed the woman and her daughters as they disembarked, completely focused on buying food and drink, but when she stepped off the train at the small Buffalo station, everything was closed.

By the last leg of her trip, Fanny was stupefied by disorientation, worry, hunger, thirst, and exhaustion. She stared out the window at passing warehouses, then farmers' fields and forests. As the sun set and the view turned sepia, then black, she could see nothing but her own pallid reflection by gaslight in the window. She thought about what might happen at her journey's end. She had planned to seek out Betsy and her husband in Cleveland, but had no idea how to find them or whether they would be pleased to see her. In the years since her sister left, Fanny had heard no news from her; she had told herself that this wasn't surprising, given their age gap and the fact that Betsy had never taken to reading or writing. But as she approached her destination, Fanny could no longer ignore the voice in her head whispering, *Betsy wouldn't forsake me.* Had something happened to her? Or had she decided to put her entire past behind her, including Fanny? And now that Fanny had some notion of the alarming size and complexity of cities, she realized that wandering about and asking after her sister was not a sound plan.

As the train pulled out of the station at Erie, the conductor announced that they would be in Cleveland in approximately three hours. She leaned her forehead against the cool window, her breath fogging the dark, cold glass. Her head ached with every beat of her heart.

The seat jiggled as someone sat down heavily beside her. From the smell of stale tobacco and damp wool, she guessed it to be a man. She glanced over and took in his closely cropped gray beard, hawkish nose, and bowler hat glistening with beads of melted snowflakes. He was looking at his pocket watch and paid her no attention.

Fanny went back to gazing dully outside. She leaned her head into the corner between the headrest and window, rocking gently with the motion of the train, lulled by the rhythmic *clack-clack* of wheels on the track. She dozed fitfully, dreaming of finding a gold coin in a bushel of dried beans.

Fanny woke to silence. The train had stopped. She could see nothing but darkness outside, and most of the passengers around her were asleep.

"A problem with the signal, I expect." The man beside her had a deep, rumbling voice. He was tall and portly, but kept carefully to his side of the seat. "It's not uncommon."

She considered pretending that she hadn't heard him, but he was looking right at her. The whites of his eyes gleamed in the dim light. "I know, sir," she said with feigned nonchalance.

"Where are you headed?"

The question seemed innocuous. "To Cleveland. To meet my sister."

"Ah. She may have a long wait at the station, I'm afraid. These delays are sometimes lengthy." He offered the statement like a test, regarded her with interest. When she didn't reply, he nodded slightly, as though she had confirmed something he already knew. "Where are you from?"

Fanny quickly considered. "Toronto."

He made a sound in his throat that conveyed skepticism. "And in which part of Cleveland does your sister live?"

Fanny's shoulders tensed. "I don't know the neighborhoods, sir."

"Hmm. And how do you propose to find her?" He said this casually, scratching his beard, but his gaze was steady.

She twisted the worn fringe of her shawl between her fingers. His attention unnerved her, and like a dousing with cold water, she was jolted into the realization of how callow she had been. "I suppose I will ask around," she said weakly.

For some time, the man was silent, and Fanny hoped that he had forgotten about her. He sighed and pulled a card from the pocket of his vest, then lifted his briefcase to his lap and removed a pen. Without having to dip the pen in ink, he wrote an entire line of script on the back of the card. Fanny wondered at the mechanics of this magic.

The man blew on the glistening writing and handed her the card. "My brother lives in Cleveland," he said. "This is his address. He might offer you employment."

Fanny nodded mutely, though she didn't think that she should trust this stranger. "Thank you, sir."

His brow furrowed. "You *can* read?" He looked chagrined to have to ask.

Fanny nodded again stiffly, vexed. Even Betsy knew how to read, and she had quit school years earlier than Fanny.

"Our family name is Garth," he said. "My brother lives on Euclid Avenue, not too far from John Rockefeller's house. He's done well for himself. Coke ovens."

She had no idea what he was talking about. "Thank you, Mr. Garth." Fanny held the card carefully so as not to smudge the ink. "Much obliged."

He smiled benevolently and settled back into his seat, closing his eyes. "Good luck to you, young lady."

With a cotton mouth and foggy brain, Fanny woke to the sound of the train's whistle and squealing brakes. The seat next to her was empty. As the train slowed, passengers crowded the aisle, pulling bags down from racks. It was still dark outside; a hum of murmured speech enveloped her like a blanket, and she yearned to go back to sleep. She forced herself to rise and shuffle out of the car, into the stinging night air. Numbly, she followed the crowd down the platform, lit by the sulfurous glow of gas lamps, something she had never seen before this trip through Toronto and Buffalo. It was an alien world suffused by strange light. Once out of the station, the crowd melted away, climbing into carriages, calling out directions, slinging baggage to boys in woolen mufflers. The brisk clop of hooves faded into a chill wind that sighed in Fanny's ears and blew puffs of snow from the roof behind her. A snowy gust licked the nape of her neck with its cold tongue.

"Need a place to stay, missy?" said a voice from the darkness.

Fanny started. She hadn't seen the pair of men sheltering under the stairs; they were hulking shadows marked by the pinpoint orange glow of cigarettes. She took a deep breath and walked swiftly away, toward a beckoning light, a ghostly gleam a half-dozen blocks in the distance. Where the snow had been shoveled and the sidewalk was bare, her lone footsteps echoed forlornly from close-set brick buildings. The distant whistle of a train merged with shouts of laughter from a single lit storefront that read "Kelly's Pub" in peeling paint. Fanny veered to the opposite side of the street and quickened her pace.

As she approached the artificial light that mimicked daylight, Fanny felt even more disoriented. Before her was a deserted public square surrounded by tall poles that beamed astonishing white brightness onto the crooked silhouettes of barren trees and an expanse of trampled snow. She blinked. None of it looked real to her.

Fanny shivered and pulled her inadequate shawl closer, considering what to do. She guessed from the position of the gibbous moon that dawn was still a few hours away. There were benches in the park, and the eerie light seemed safer than the darkness. She spotted a chestnut tree and raked her freezing fingers through the snow at its base, turning up a handful of nuts that were past ripe but still edible. She opened the soft shells and ate the musty contents greedily until the clench in her stomach uncurled. When she wasn't eating, she melted snow in her mouth to try to slake her thirst. On the closest bench, she lay down, clutching her small bundle in her arms, tucking her shawl tightly, trying to ignore the slats that dug into her hip and shoulder bones and the cold gusts that made her long to be back on the train. A bat swooped and darted overhead, reminding her of home. Fanny thought of the stream full of speckled trout, the lingering snow in the shade of pines, the soft wind, and the plow churning through earth for fall wheat. She drifted in and out of sleep until the sun rose and a man in uniform shook her.

"Get on your way!" He sounded offended. "You know the park is off-limits!"

Fanny sat up, stiff and chilled to the bone. She straightened her bonnet. "I'm sorry," she said. "I had nowhere to go."

The man glowered at her. "Get on with ye."

Instinctually, she made herself childlike, touching her hand to her forehead, as though checking for fever, then she brought her hands to her breastbone, prayer-like, and saw his blunt features soften. "Do you . . ." she whispered and ducked her head. "Do you know a Betsy Bartlett, sir?"

He looked away and sighed, his breath fogging in the cold. "I'm sure I know several."

"I'm looking for my sister."

"I wish you luck, lass." He did not seem entirely unsympathetic.

Fanny's hands and feet were numb with cold, but she kept herself still. "Do you know where I might find a room to stay?"

The man's eyes were sad, but his voice was brusque. "Move along, lass."

"I thank you for your time, sir," she said, but he was already walking away.

CHAPTER 4

In the weak light of winter dawn, Fanny re-counted her money, then tucked the bills into the bodice of her dress, returning the coins to the bag. Once shops were open, she would buy food and then look for a cheap place to stay. She examined the calling card from the man on the train; on the front were engraved the words *Paul O. Garth, Esq. 280 Front Street, Toledo, OH*, and on the back, handwritten, *Mr. Laurence Garth, 467 Euclid Ave*. She put the card away and wandered from the park, not knowing which direction to take. The city streets were forsaken, with shuttered merchant stalls. Cobblestones were mottled with smears of frozen horse manure, and the smell of urine wafted from alleys. Lines of laundry flapped stiffly in the frigid breeze, defiantly bright flags on a backdrop coated with layers of industrial soot, everything else dreary gray.

Fanny passed a man pulling a coal cart and a boy lugging a big burlap sack, but neither greeted or even acknowledged her. A skinny dog with matted fur approached at a trot; Fanny slowed her pace as she eyed it warily. It sniffed at her hand, its snout warm and slimy against her cold skin. She curled her fingers into the protection of her palm.

"Keep your dirty mutt out of my trash!" a woman yelled from the other side of the street.

Fanny jumped; the dog let out a low growl and loped away. From the direction of the voice, a door slammed shut.

Thirst was a fire in Fanny's brain that canceled some of the chill in her bones and hunger in her belly. She broke a carrot-shaped icicle from the side of an awning and sucked on it. The trickle of melt did little more than tease her thirst, but it soothed her mouth and throat.

As she rounded a corner onto a broad street lined by nondescript multistory brick buildings, Fanny saw a smartly dressed older woman exit a housing tenement, with curtained windows and flower pots filled with dead chrysanthemums flanking the entrance. She twisted her key firmly in the lock and stood for a moment, smoothing her skirt with gloved hands, adjusting the straps of her bag on her forearm. The flamboyant colors and fanciful cut of her outerwear held Fanny's gaze; she wore a high-collared fitted jacket of purple velvet that flared at the waist, a scarlet fur-trimmed wrap and broad-brimmed hat.

The woman glanced to her left and right, her expression blank. Her eyes fell on Fanny, and her rounded features warmed into a sympathetic smile. She descended three stairs from stoop to sidewalk, a drooping lavender feather in her hat trembling as she moved. When they were face-to-face, Fanny saw that she had a pale, powdery complexion crisscrossed by fine wrinkles, and her lips were strangely pink.

"You look like you might be lost, young lady," the woman said in a cheery voice.

Harsh words and cruelty had lost the power to make Fanny cry, but unexpectedly, the kindness of a stranger caused her to blink back tears.

"Poor dear." She stepped closer and reached out with a consoling squeeze to Fanny's arm. "Are you new to our fair city?"

At the sympathetic touch of a hand, Fanny felt even smaller. "Yes, ma'am." She swallowed, trying to steady her voice. "I have come to find my sister."

"Ah." The woman cocked her head, and the feather on her hat bobbed. "Sisters are so precious. Mine have always been such a comfort to me. In which part of the city does yours live?"

Fanny cleared her throat. "I am not certain, ma'am. I need to find out."

"Not to worry—I'm sure that your mother and father will help." Her voice was reassuring. "This isn't your responsibility alone, young lady." A little shake of her head—*Silly girl, you don't need to take this on.* "At which hotel are you all staying?"

What was left of Fanny's youthful confidence crumpled. In a tiny voice, she said, "I am here by myself, ma'am."

The woman seemed to contemplate this for a moment. She plucked at her glove, straightening a seam, then gazed at Fanny. "Well," she said, "as it happens, I am going to see a friend who always has the kettle on. I'm sure that she will have something warm and hearty to serve up. Why don't you join me, and we can chat more about how to find your sister." Her cheeks pouched out like a squirrel's when she smiled broadly, showing a crooked row of teeth.

Fanny felt weak with gratitude but also wary of such good fortune. "I wouldn't want to trouble you, ma'am." She hefted her bag, which had slipped down her shoulder. "I have a bit of money and could buy myself something."

"I could tell at first glance that you are a resourceful girl." Her eyes serious, she said, "It's not a good idea to associate with strangers, is it?" She put out a gloved hand for Fanny to take. "You may call me Mrs. Laporte. What is your name, dear?"

"Fanny, ma'am."

She squeezed Fanny's hand gently, then let go. "What a nice, sensible name." Her squirrel smile appeared again. "Now we are no longer strangers!"

Warmth suffused Fanny's chest. "I am so glad to have met you, ma'am."

With a delicate touch to the coiled hair at the nape of her neck, as though making sure it hadn't come undone, Mrs. Laporte said, "How old are you, dear?"

"Sixteen, ma'am."

A closed-lip smile this time. "Sixteen is a good age." Mrs. Laport bent nearer, lowering herself slightly to be closer to Fanny's height. "My friend lives only two blocks that way." She gestured and gave a little shrug: *It's no trouble at all.* "Come along!" She flicked her skirts, as though pulling loose of some obstruction, and strode down the sidewalk, glancing back encouragingly to make sure that Fanny was following.

Fanny jogged a few steps to catch up with the taller woman. "I do want to thank you so much for your Christian charity, Mrs. Laporte." Her stomach ached with hunger, a thing with claws.

They stopped at the corner to let a wagon go by. The slumbering city was waking; there were sounds of hooves and carts, voices calling out, children crying and playing. In the distance, a shrill whistle blew.

Mrs. Laporte turned to Fanny. "Well, my dear, when you get to know me better, you will understand that I make it my business to ensure that young women in Cleveland are safe." She sighed. "I understand how awful it is not to have a roof over your head or know where your next meal is coming from. I do what I can to help."

The clatter of wagon wheels on the cobblestones receded. Mrs. Laporte stepped into the street, careful to avoid a steaming pile of fresh horse dung. "Come, just over here." She pointed down the block to a long wooden sign that read "Black Dog Tavern ALE SPIRITS WINE." Once abreast of the sign, she walked past the pub entrance and led Fanny to the side of the building, down recessed stairs to the basement level. She rapped on a grimy, circular window embedded in a black-painted door.

There was a reluctant creak, and a thin-faced young woman poked her head out. "He's not here," she said.

Mrs. Laporte stepped her foot against the doorjamb, though the woman hadn't moved. "Molly, dear," she said, her tone both light and chiding. "I am here to see *you*."

Molly's neutral expression didn't change, but she pulled the door wider and stepped back to let them enter. The room was dark and smelled of smoke; a baby wailed, and Molly grimaced. "The cold must've woke her."

As if to prove her right, a gust of wind lifted a swirl of snowflakes from the entryway and pushed its way inside. Molly shoved the door closed, and the room was swallowed by shadows. The smell of coal smoke did not completely mask the animal fug of unwashed bodies and diapers. As Fanny's eyes adjusted to the gloom, she made out soot-stained brick walls and a hodgepodge of furniture: an unfinished table with crooked heads of bare nails protruding from the boards, mismatched chairs, a dented coal scuttle beside a squat potbelly stove. Molly had her back to a gaping fireplace in the far wall, hungry with disuse. She stooped over a cradle, rocking gently. The wails pitched higher, hoarse and angry; Molly lifted up a swaddled bundle, bouncing it in her skinny arms. Gradually the cries subsided.

Mrs. Laporte peered into a pan on the stove as she eased off her gloves and pulled out her hatpin. She sniffed. "Your broth seems past its prime, Molly." She laid down her hat, gloves, and wrap on a bench by the door.

"I got a good ox bone just yesterday," Molly said defensively.

Fanny remained awkwardly rooted near the entrance, clinging to her bag like a life preserver.

"My guest's name is Fanny, and she has just arrived in Cleveland." Mrs. Laporte undid the buttons on her coat but did not remove it. "The poor thing hasn't had any breakfast!"

"Welcome, Fanny," Molly said. Her voice was hollow.

"Come, you can put your things down here, Fanny, next to mine," Mrs. Laporte said warmly. To Molly, she said, "I think some tea and porridge would hit the spot."

Fanny took off her bonnet but kept her bag.

Molly shifted the baby to the crook of an elbow and continued to bounce as she went to the stove. With her free hand, she opened the cast iron door and poked inside with a pair of tongs, then added a scoop of coal. With balletic economy, she closed the hatch with her foot, took a kettle from the sideboard, filled it from a barrel of water, and placed it on the stove. Next came a pot, to which she added oatmeal and more water; the stovetop hissed as she set it down. "Should be ready soon," she said, wiping her palm on her skirt. Only then did Fanny notice that Molly's hand was missing the last two fingers.

"How is the little one?" asked Mrs. Laporte.

Molly nudged back the edge of the baby's blanket to expose her sleeping face. She had cream-puff cheeks and skin the color of caramel. "She's doing fine." Molly said this softly, but shot the other woman a guarded look. She returned the baby to the crib, tucking her in gently.

Mrs. Laporte put a hand on Fanny's shoulder, light as a sparrow. "Do sit," she said, waving vaguely at the cramped, low-ceilinged room.

Fanny selected a wooden stool. It wobbled as she sat, causing her to instinctively fling out her arms and drop her bag; her shawl slid from her shoulders.

Mrs. Laporte gave a tight-lipped smile to acknowledge the fumble but made no effort to help. "Tell me about yourself, dear," she said, taking a seat on the only upholstered chair in the room.

"There's not much to tell, ma'am," Fanny said, blushing. She reached for her shawl, which had fallen behind her, but the stool wobbled again, and she had to brace her feet on the floor to regain her balance. She sat up straighter, and spoke politely as her mother had taught her. "I grew up on a farm over the border. I want to better myself in the United States, and I came to Cleveland, because my only other family is here, my sister." Though she was still chilled, her cheeks burned.

Mrs. Laporte stood to remove her coat, and motioned Molly over to take it. Fanny seized the moment to hop up and gather her belongings.

"And what is your sister's name?"

Fanny stuffed her bag under the stool and carefully took her perch atop it once more. "Betsy Bartlett. Her married name is Betsy Smith." She balled up her shawl in her lap. "Her husband is a carpenter. He was said to be making a good living, what with all of the construction going on here."

Even through the competing smells, Fanny thought she caught a whiff of bubbling porridge, and the scent made her mouth water. Her stomach growled so loudly that she pressed the crumpled shawl to her waist, trying to muffle the sound.

Mrs. Laporte cocked her head, her small, dark eyes alert, making Fanny think of a squirrel again. "Your sister came from Canada to marry this man?"

"Yes, ma'am."

"How did she know him?"

Fanny thought about this. "There was a woman my father knew, some sort of matchmaker. She traveled around. I didn't hear anything until it was all arranged. My sister showed me a photograph—he was handsome." Worried that this might be an inappropriate detail, she glanced at her interlocutor, but Mrs. Laporte's expression of polite curiosity was unchanged. "She said he owned his own house in the city," Fanny continued. It hadn't occurred to her before that the marriage was unusual. At the time, she had been caught up in the turmoil of her own emotions—envy that her sister was escaping, misery that she was forced to quit school.

"I suppose you'll need a place to stay while you look for your sister." Mrs. Laporte tapped a finger pensively against her pink lips.

Across the room, Molly hissed and jerked her hand back from the stove, then resumed stirring.

"Yes, ma'am," Fanny said, trying to appear unworried.

Mrs. Laporte brightened. "I might be able to help with that."

Fanny's heart lifted.

Looking toward Molly and raising her voice, Mrs. Laporte said, "Dear, do you know if we have any room at the boarding house just now?"

The door banged open; a gust of cold wind swept in. The silhouette of a man filled the doorway. He was so tall that he had to duck his head to enter the room. He stomped his boots.

"Ah, Frank, there you are," Mrs. Laporte said.

The man grunted. He took off his hat and hung it on a peg by the door. His face was weather-worn, and he had a port-wine stain over the left side of his forehead and cheek.

"Frank, this is Fanny, and she is new to town."

Frank paused in taking off his coat and took a long look at Fanny. His bushy eyebrows and shaggy salt-and-pepper hair might have given him an avuncular appearance, but he had cold eyes.

"I was just saying," Mrs. Laporte continued blithely, "that I might be able to find a nice warm bed for her to sleep in until she finds her sister."

Frank examined Fanny a moment longer, then went back to removing his coat. "New girl?" he said.

Mrs. Laporte smiled, this time showing crooked teeth, but there was a burr of annoyance in her voice when she said, "I thought we should extend a helping hand." She rose abruptly and went to the stove. "Is this ready?"

Molly nodded. Mrs. Laporte brought down a dish from a shelf and served the porridge herself, while Frank sat down heavily to remove his boots. "I want eggs," he said. Fanny was familiar enough with bullies to pick up on the subtle threat in his tone. She watched him warily as he stood back up, stretching to his full height, flexing his fingers and making fists. Mrs. Laporte was suddenly in front of her, holding a steaming bowl and cup of tea. "I added some honey," she said. "To both." She set the tea on a nearby table and handed Fanny a spoon.

Fanny ate the gruel with a voracious appetite; she had never been so hungry. It had a musky taste, but it was warm and hearty, and she was glad that everyone left her to gobble in peace. Molly and the baby disappeared down a corridor. Mrs. Laporte and Frank moved to a corner of the room and spoke in low voices. Fanny caught the occasional word; from what she gathered, someone was sick. She scraped every last bit of oatmeal from her bowl and set it down reluctantly.

In the quiet and warmth of the dark room, tension drained from Fanny's body; murmured conversation and the ticking sound of the cooling stovetop soothed her. A shaft of light from a high window fell across the flagged floor. In its greasy rays, a haze of smoke floated, writhing. A strange feeling came over Fanny, a glittering dreaminess and lightheadedness. She sipped her tea, waiting to be revived. Mrs. Laporte drifted back into her vision, picked up the empty bowl. "Can I get you more?" She smiled.

"Yes, please, ma'am." Fanny inadvertently loosened her grip on her cup, splashing tea onto her lap. She wiped at it with her shawl, then lost her balance on her crooked stool, only just avoiding a fall by pitching her weight forward, hands braced on her knees, dregs of tea dripping from the cup she'd nearly dropped, head hanging.

"Are you all right, dear?" Mrs. Laporte stood over her. The heavy scent of her perfume made Fanny queasy.

"I think perhaps I ate too fast, ma'am."

"You poor thing," Mrs. Laporte said, taking her by the elbow, encouraging her to rise. "No wonder, you were famished. Perhaps you should lie down for a moment."

Fanny struggled to stand, but her legs wouldn't obey. A gray veil descended over her vision. She felt herself lifted by strong arms as she sank into blackness.

CHAPTER 5

Fanny woke in the dark to the muffled sound of piano music, voices, and laughter. She was lying facedown, her flesh pressed against rough linen. She tried to turn over, but her hands were tied above her head, pulling her aching shoulder joints into an unnatural position. Her temples throbbed, and a dull pain in her groin caused her to curl her knees in toward her belly. The movement only made the pain worse.

A drip of saliva trickled from the corner of her mouth, merging with the dampness of the cloth beneath her cheek. To her left, light seeped around a closed door, dimly illuminating the small room. She could make out patterned wallpaper, a nightstand. Gingerly, she shuffled to a crouched kneeling position, feeling dizzy. The pressure in her shoulders eased, but she faltered under a wave of nausea, pausing to take deep breaths. With numb fingertips, she probed the bristly rope that bound her hands, following its short length to cold, twisted bands of wrought iron, a headboard. She picked at a thick knot, clawing at the bits she could reach; her fingernails bent backward from the effort, but the rope didn't give.

Fanny's skin crawled—she became aware that she was naked, and she heard herself whimper, an involuntary reflex. She was puzzled that the sound of a wounded dog would come from her own mouth. The nakedness was bewildering; she had almost never been completely undressed before. Even when she bathed, it was with a basin and cloth; there was no need to take off all of her clothes.

"Help!" she croaked. She tried again, louder, "Help!"

The sounds of carousing continued.

Her yelling seemed nightmarishly muffled, but she tried again, panted, catching her breath.

The door banged open, and Fanny blinked in the jaundiced light. She felt the stirring of the air before she saw the bulky shadow moving toward her. "Shut up, or I'll shut you up." The words were perfunctory, but the blow to her head brought shards of pain, spangled lights, and a deep, woozy sickness. She made herself small, as she had learned to do when her father beat her, burrowing deep into the center of her body, where nothing could touch her. When she emerged, her head still ached, but the man was gone.

A crash, shattering glass, and cawing laughter surged from somewhere nearby. Farther away, men were shouting. There came a clanging of church bells; Fanny counted, one, two, three o'clock. A curtained window was dimly illuminated with a spectral glow that could not be moonlight.

Fanny's last memory was of tea and feeling faint. Her mouth was dry, her tongue sticking to her palate as if glued, and her eyes stung. Circulation began to return to her bound hands, a thousand piercing needles. She resumed picking at the knotted rope, but she could gain little purchase no matter how much she contorted her fingers. Her useless nails were too soft.

Floorboards groaned outside the room, and there were murmured voices. She smelled cigar smoke. There was a phlegmy cough and gravelly snicker. Fanny held her breath. The footsteps moved away.

A faint, spasmodic creaking filled the air. Fanny realized that her whole body was shaking so hard that the bedframe was rattling. She attacked the rope with her teeth; sisal splinters made her lips bleed, but the knots wouldn't budge. Despair rose like a viscous tide, choking her. She slumped, her cheek against her forearms, gasping. She could make no sense of the dark room; her bondage; her sore, chilled, trembling, exposed body. Sobs escaped her raw, constricted throat into the indifferent silence. She cried like a small child, bewildered and abandoned. If anyone heard, she was ignored.

Fanny settled into exhaustion, a void. Her heart thudded dully against her ribs. The church bells rang four times. Then five. The sounds of carousing dwindled, gradually replaced by street noise, the clatter of horse-drawn carts on cobblestones, the calls of merchants. Weak morning light filtered through curtains that Fanny discovered were scarlet; an unwelcome bold, warm color.

When the door scraped open, she responded listlessly, a turn of her head. Molly stepped across the threshold and carefully closed the door behind her, her gaunt features impassive. She carried a bucket and a wicker basket; the scent of fresh-baked bread wafted through the stale, gamy air of the small room like a caress.

Molly set her burdens down and removed her cloak. "Morning," she said.

The absurdity of the casual greeting sparked the dead ashes of Fanny's anger into a flickering flame. From a painful crouch, she drew herself up as much as she was able. "Untie me." Her voice was hoarse.

Molly pulled a paring knife from her pocket. The carbon steel blade was rusty and razor-thin. "Palms up," she said. Fanny held very still as Molly slid the knife between the pallid underbelly of her blue-veined wrist and the bracelet of coarse rope; she sliced outward with a practiced flick. The rope fell away. She repeated this on the other side.

Finally able to turn over, Fanny sat, pulling in her legs and arms to cover her nakedness. To her horror, her thighs were smeared with blood, and there was a bright red stain on the mattress. Her mind tried to expel the thought of rape as the stomach vomits up poison. Though she willed it to stop, her body quivered like a plucked string.

Molly pulled a coiled sheet from the foot of the bed and shook it out, letting it settle over Fanny. She set the bucket next to the nightstand. "For washing up." She lifted the sponge and squeezed it, letting water run back into the bucket, as though Fanny couldn't speak English or was an imbecile who didn't understand the use of a sponge. She shook her three-fingered hand, flicking off droplets, then wiped it on her skirt, leaving a wet mark.

"Where am I?" Fanny pulled the sheet all the way up to her chin, hugging herself with trembling arms. "What—" Her voice wobbled; she squeezed her eyes shut.

"I brought food," Molly said, rustling through the basket. "Milk." There was a thunk on the bedside table, then more rustling.

Fanny opened her eyes and watched the sallow little woman calmly slice a chunk of cheese with the same paring knife she had used to free Fanny's hands. It seemed that a naked, bloodied girl tied to a bed was an everyday occurrence. Molly spread a napkin next to the milk bottle and placed a bread roll and slices of cheese on top. Fanny's stomach churned.

"Where are my clothes?" Fanny moved to stand up, but Molly put a hand on her shoulder, pushing her back down. Her pincer grip was surprisingly strong.

"You won't be allowed out," Molly said. "You could yell and scream, but nobody will come." She wiped the blade on the edge of the napkin and put the knife back in the pocket of her skirt. "Except maybe to—" She bit at the side of her nail, then sighed. "Just do what you're told."

Beads of cold sweat dripped from Fanny's armpits and slithered over her skin. Molly followed her gaze to the door. "Don't try to run," she said.

From the basket, Molly pulled shiny, rose-colored fabric. She tossed it on the bed. "Put this on after you clean up."

Fanny pulled the sheet tighter around her shoulders.

Molly put a hand on the doorknob. "Be back later. I'll bring some medicine. Makes it easier for new girls." She opened the door, then glanced back. "Get yourself clean."

Fanny lay still with her eyes closed for a long while after Molly left, pretending that when she opened them, she would see the soot-stained rafters of her father's cabin. The sounds of the city would not leave her in peace, though, and panic nudged at the corners of her mind, even as she tried to quash thoughts of what might happen next.

Pulling back the sheet, Fanny took a long look at herself. Bruises were nothing new; blood wasn't either, but it wasn't her time of the month, and from the ache she felt, Fanny knew that damage had been done. She got out of bed carefully and squatted over the bucket, washing away the outward evidence of injury with shaking hands. When she was finished, she used the sheet to dry herself. She picked up the dress Molly had left behind; it was more flimsy than the underclothes she normally wore, but she put it on, then checked under the bed, the only place in the small room where anything could be hidden—only a bedpan. There were no shoes or stockings, none of the clothing she had been wearing. The money she had tucked into her bodice was gone, then, too.

She didn't want to accept Molly's food, but Fanny forced herself to finish it; there was no telling when she would be able to eat again. The milk only sharpened her thirst, and the bread and cheese were gone in a few bites. She shook crumbs from the napkin into her palm and pressed her tongue to her salty skin to collect them.

Fanny eyed the door but went first to the window to get her bearings. There were bars, disguised as decorative latticework, but no less a cage. Through the metal and warped, grimy glass, she could make out blurry figures on the sidewalk below, gliding silently by like slow-moving fish. She was not more than ten feet above the pedestrians, but escape through the barred window was impossible.

Fanny crept to the door and turned the brass doorknob haltingly. She felt the latch release—it wasn't locked from the outside. Inch by careful inch, she opened the door, stopping when she heard the hinges creak. Once the opening was wide enough, she put her head through and peered down the narrow corridor. It was empty, dimly lit, with a faded Oriental-style carpet and plaster cornices. The noise and commotion of the previous night had died out entirely; a stagnant hush hung over the building. At the end of the hallway was a window. It too was barred. In her bare feet, she tiptoed in the opposite direction, past closed doors, until she reached the top of a stairway.

Fanny crouched down, her breath catching at the pain the movement caused. She could see into the parlor below, which was darkened with heavy curtains. A single blade of sunlight pierced the shadows, lighting swirling dust motes. There were lumpish couches, tasseled lampshades, and a green-tiled fireplace disgorging ashes onto its neglected hearth. A rancid miasma with sweet overtones of alcohol and stale smoke was its own distinct presence in the room. Beyond the parlor was a foyer. A burly man wearing a black greatcoat hulked in the adjoining doorway, his back to Fanny. He toyed with the nightstick in his hand, swinging it, a slow pendulum.

Her heart hammering, Fanny retreated into the hallway. She was brought up short, startled, face-to-face with a girl with long black hair and pretty, almond-shaped eyes. She wore a stained satin dress with torn lace at the neckline. Her gaze swept from Fanny's head to her feet. "You seem pretty lost, Dolly." She held a cloak in her arms, which she donned, wearing it untied and loose.

Fanny tried to smile, her fear receding before this delicate, fawn-like girl. "I'm Fanny," she said. "Who are you?"

The girl smirked. "You planning on running?"

Fanny hadn't thought that her agitation was so obvious.

"Honey, you know it's worse out there than in here." She fixed a twisted strap on Fanny's dress.

The brush of fingers on her shoulder and the echo of Molly's earlier warning made Fanny's bare arms prickle with goosebumps. "Can you tell me about this place?" she said.

"What's to tell?" The smirk again. "It's a whorehouse." She swept hair back from her face, gathering it in her fist, and let it fall, smooth and shining like satin, down her back. "You let them do what they want, and you get food and a roof over your head."

The girl's manner was casual and relaxed; there was no dread in her expression, nor hopelessness. She seemed at home. For a moment, Fanny questioned her own horror at being trapped in such a terrible place.

"What's goin' on up there?" The bellow came from downstairs, from the man at the door. His voice was irate, but Fanny recognized the Irish accent, the same as her mother's. There was some small comfort in that recognition.

"Nothin' at all, Mack!" the girl called out, imitating his cadence. "Just comin' down to use the privy." There was a flounce in her step as she walked away.

Fanny watched her disappear down the stairs. There was a muffled exchange between Mack and the girl; her laugh floated up from the foyer. A door slammed. Fanny shrank back down the hallway into the awful room with scarlet curtains. She kept watch on the hallway through the keyhole.

After several long minutes, there came the sound of the door opening, letting in a surge of street noise that died when it slammed shut again. She heard the girl whistling a tune off-key before she saw her, now in stockinged feet, carrying her boots in her hand.

Fanny stepped out, whispering, "Wait! Can I talk to you?"

The girl stopped walking but kept whistling, trying to get a note to the right pitch. Tiny flecks of spittle glistened on her pursed lips. With a flick of her fine-boned wrist, she gestured for Fanny to go back into the room; Fanny didn't know if it was a dismissal or invitation, but she obeyed. The girl stepped in behind and closed the door, dropping her boots unceremoniously on the floor, where they dribbled muddy, melting snow. She wrinkled her nose. "You have to open the window a little bit in the morning, even if it's cold." She sat primly on the edge of the bed.

Fanny was nauseated as she thought about the previous night. She had only fragments of memory—her head crashing into metal bars, being pressed down so hard that she could barely breathe, a choking animal stink, her body shoved about like a side of meat. The parts she remembered were nightmarish, but what hid in the dark, what her mind could not quite conjure, was worse. She went to the window and tried to pull it open, but it was painted shut with careless glops, the brushstrokes still visible in the dried paint.

"Where d'you come from?" the girl asked without much interest. Her eyes had a glazed look.

"Canada." Fanny reached for a tone of composure. "I'm looking for my sister."

"We see girls from Canada sometimes." She flopped back onto the bed. "What's her name?"

The words chilled Fanny. "She came here to get *married*." Her voice did not convey the certainty she was trying to summon within herself.

The girl laughed mirthlessly. "Married? Is that what they call it?"

The queasy feeling in Fanny's stomach turned to a trickle of ice water.

"Her name is Betsy," Fanny whispered.

The girl fluttered her feet slowly, a dreamy swimmer. A hole in the heel of her stocking sprouted woolen threads like spider legs. "Betsy's a common name," she said to the ceiling. "She might've been here, before my time. There was at least one Betsy." She sat back up. "Mrs. Laporte would know."

Fanny held her fear tight to her breast. She did not let herself know what she knew. She thought only of how to get her own boots and stockings; how to get away. "What if I have to use the privy?" she said. "Where is it?"

"Around back, in the alley. But they won't let you out," the girl said matter-of-factly. "Use the bedpan." She rose with a loud exhalation and picked up her boots, frowning at the wet footprints left behind. "Best clean that up," she said. "They don't like messes." She waggled her fingers in a sardonic farewell. "Good luck." Once through the doorway, as she was pulling the door shut behind her, she paused and added, "You should get some rest—it'll get busy once the sun goes down."

CHAPTER 6

As the day wore on, the angle of the sun shifted, slowly pushing a slab of winter light across the floor and up the opposing wall. The rectangle faded, shadows closed in, and the building seemed to wake—creaking footsteps in the hallway, voices calling, sounds of dragging and thumping from overhead.

Fanny paced, her breath shallow. A crowd of emotions jostled for primacy; she nurtured anger as her best protection. It was no use being angry at herself—though she was, deeply, fiercely, disgustedly—so she focused on her captors. Peering out the warped window, Fanny watched for Molly's return, but the people passing by were mere faceless smudges of color against the muddy road. She kept her eyes averted from the bed, with its stained, blood-smeared sheet.

Fanny started when the door opened, but she hid her sudden intake of breath with a cough. Molly looked as she had before, face pinched, a basket dangling from her arm. She set it down with a doleful sigh.

"I'm glad you have returned," Fanny said in a low voice, her head bowed.

Molly replaced the empty milk bottle on the bedside table with a full one and dropped a greasy newsprint-wrapped packet next to it, a mechanical repetition of her earlier actions.

Fanny sank to the floor and hugged her knees; she shivered, on purpose this time. From the corner of her eye, she could tell that Molly had stopped what she was doing to look at her.

"Couldn't I get something warmer to wear?" Fanny said. She pulled her knees tighter to her chest. "It's so cold in here."

Molly went back to emptying her basket. "You earn your comforts."

"What—" Her voice quavered. "What do you want from me?"

"Me? Nothing." Molly held out a dented flask. "Take the laudanum. You'll feel better."

Fanny grasped it hesitantly and unscrewed the rusty cap. She tilted the container back but blocked the flow of bitter liquid with her tongue. She pretended to swallow, then handed the flask back to Molly, wondering what she could say to soften her disposition. "What's your baby's name?" she asked.

Molly's face was stony. She wiped the mouth of the flask with her skirt, then took a swig, grimacing. She twisted the top back on and dropped it in her basket. "Janey," she said flatly.

"That's a pretty name."

Molly pulled bundled linens from her basket and dropped them on the floor. "Guests will be arriving soon. Put dirty bedclothes under the bed. Someone will collect them." She lifted the basket and turned to the door. "They'll probably send in Frank or Mack to teach you the ropes. Mrs. Laporte likes new girls to be broken in right." She turned the doorknob. "They won't beat you unless you act stupid."

"Don't leave me here!" The outburst was too pointed, not beseeching as Fanny had intended. She covered her face with both hands and hunched her shoulders, as if weeping. She needed to appear as a fearful animal, a little bunny that could be soothed with gentleness. She could feel Molly's attention on her, could imagine her wavering. With effort, Fanny lowered the bright, hard shield of her anger to lay bare her softer underbelly. She reached for thoughts about her mother, frail by the end, so weak that she couldn't cough, her breath rattling through the phlegm and blood in her windpipe. When a sob escaped her mouth, she clasped her hands to her breast. "Please!" She shuffled forward on her knees, clutching at Molly's skirts. "You must help me!"

Molly backed away sharply, but not before Fanny grabbed the knife from her pocket. She uncoiled, using her whole body weight to pull Molly away from the door. Fanny's years of defending herself against her brothers had prepared her well; toppling the young woman was easy as wrangling a baby goat. Molly collapsed onto the bed with a squawk, and Fanny leaned over her, a forearm across the young woman's throat.

Fanny leaned her arm harder into Molly's neck and held the tip of the knife to the place where the convulsions of the woman's heart made her skin flutter. Fanny thought of the pulsing opening in the soft skull of a newborn, and she felt a twinge of pity. She also felt surprise: Molly looked at her with wild eyes. Fanny hadn't known that she had that power.

"You could scream." Fanny mimicked Molly's statement. "Nobody would come."

Molly's breath scraped in her throat, so Fanny took her arm away, keeping the knife in place. A bead of bright blood had appeared at the tip of the blade; it trembled as Molly panted.

"Take off your clothes," Fanny said, pulling the knife back several inches.

"What?" Confusion joined the fear in Molly's face.

Leaning close, Fanny repeated in a slow hiss, "Take off your clothes."

With shaking hands, Molly undid her buttons; one was broken, another missing. Tears leaked from the corners of her eyes.

"Off!" Fanny yanked the skirt up hard with her free hand, and Molly squirmed out of the dress, gasping.

Molly's underclothes were stained and worn to thin gauzy patches over her shoulders and breasts. Eyeing the knife, she hunched forward and crossed her arms protectively over her chest.

Again, that flicker of pity. Fanny thought of a dying calf mauled by wolves; how she had to shoulder the gun and not flinch. "Your boots and stockings," she said.

Molly went limp with a mewling sound. How many beatings and rapes had she endured to make her such a broken thing? Fanny set down the knife, which no longer seemed necessary, and unlaced Molly's boots herself. She would not let herself be broken like that. She wrenched the boots off by the heel, holding her breath against the smell of decaying leather and foot odor. Reaching up to Molly's thighs, her fingers brushed soft private skin; she winced as she peeled off garters and wool stockings.

The same piano music from the night before swelled from the floor below, along with talk and laughter.

The rope Fanny had untied from the bed frame lay on the floor; Fanny picked up the longest section. "Clasp your hands together," she said. Molly was still limp; Fanny looped her wrists and trussed them with a sure knot, then used another section of rope to tie her hands to the bedpost.

Molly's clothing was too small; the seams groaned over her shoulders, and the boots pinched her feet. She donned the cloak, pocketed the knife, and returned the food and medicine to the basket. With her hand on the doorknob, basket in the crook of her elbow, she glanced back at Molly, who lay half-naked and prone on the bed, still as death. She had an impetuous impulse to offer help, as though she was a bystander who had happened upon this sad scene. Instead, she pulled up her hood and took a deep breath. She told herself that she was Molly, leaving to go back to her infant child. She knew the building, the people; nothing would distract or surprise her. She was just a woman doing her job.

Fanny stepped through the doorway, closing the door firmly behind her; she strode purposefully down the hallway to the stairs. In the parlor, a piano tinkled, lamps glowed red under draped crimson fabric, cloying incense mixed with the smell of smoke and spilled wine. A woman dressed in what looked like a pink corset and petticoat leaned on a newel post, looking down at the parlor, giggling. As she descended, Fanny saw that a fire blazed in the hearth; on the couch, a woman perched in the lap of a stout, mutton-chopped man like a little girl hoping for candy. A couple of heads swiveled her way but didn't linger, returning to more interesting sights. When Fanny reached the landing, she saw that the man guarding the door had changed, and she recognized the port-wine stain on his face. A bilious dread rose to her throat; Frank would remember her. Was he the man who had struck her the night before? In her clouded memory, the cold voice came back to her; something about it seemed familiar.

Fanny pulled her hood lower, and at the base of the staircase, she stepped to the wall, pretending to check the contents of her basket while glancing around the room. She saw the girl with the long black hair lounging against the armrest of an oversized chintz-upholstered chair near the fireplace, folding and unfolding a lace fan. She was alone, the nearest couple absorbed in an embrace, bowler hat knocking against peacock-feather headdress. Without allowing herself to second-guess the wisdom of her actions, Fanny set her basket down and sidled up to the girl. When she was close enough, she reached out a hand to touch her shoulder. The girl looked up with unfocused eyes, her features slack. There was no recognition in her gaze.

"Could you show me the way to the privy?" Fanny asked softly.

The girl's head lolled back, like she was falling asleep, but then she pushed herself upright, hanging on to Fanny's arm for balance. "I'm going to be sick," the girl said. Her face was slick with sweat. She lurched, raised a hand to her mouth.

"Whoa, there." Fanny put her arm around the girl's waist to steady her.

The man who had been kissing the feathered courtesan looked over in annoyance. Fanny smiled apologetically.

The girl set off, leaning into Fanny as they walked behind the piano and its tired player, toward a door opposite the foyer. Fanny didn't dare look around to see if Frank had noticed them. They stepped into a dark corridor; the air was cold and smelled of rotting food. Fanny tugged the door closed behind them. The girl was already stumbling down the hallway; Fanny followed, placing her feet carefully on an uneven floor buried in shadows. Ahead was a small square, glowing faintly, blue-black. As she approached, the square resolved into a window in a door that the girl flung open; she disappeared out of sight, leaving the door gaping. A bitter wind blew in, bringing tears to Fanny's eyes.

Stepping outside, Fanny could see that they were in a courtyard surrounded by brick buildings on three sides; a tall iron gate with spear-like pickets blocked the fourth side of the yard. The wind blew the door shut behind her with a bang, and she flinched. It was brighter outside by the glow of streetlamps than it had been in the corridor. Fanny knew that the moon was nearly full, but it was hidden by the smoke or clouds she could see in the patch of sky above. A pair of wooden outhouses, one gap-toothed with a missing plank in the door, the other listing like a drunkard, squatted in the enclosure.

The girl leaned against the brick wall and vomited on the trampled snow. She coughed, wiped her mouth with the back of her hand. "I feel better," she said. She swayed to her feet, yanked the door open. She disappeared back into the building without another word.

Fanny shivered, her exposed skin already going numb from the cold. She went to the gate; it was locked with a heavy chain. She jumped, but the top rail was too high for her to reach; her pinched toes hurt when she landed.

She realized that she had left the basket inside. Someone might recognize it as Molly's, an indication that something bad had befallen her. Fanny's heart beat erratically. They might already be looking for her. She could almost feel the door opening at her back, Frank lunging at her.

A shout, laughter—three men came into view through the gate, strolling down the street. One paused to stuff his pipe while the others called out jocular insults. Fanny shrank to a crouch beside the building, watching them pass. She looked up at the sheer wall overhead; the nearest handhold, the lip of a window opening, was yards above her head. She scanned the area. There was nothing but the outhouses and a silhouetted heap between them which, from the rancid smell, Fanny assumed was decomposing garbage.

She approached the privy that was missing a board and kicked at the snow to find the piece that had fallen out. It wasn't there, or was buried too deep to find. She yanked on the board next to the gap, and it wiggled. Bracing a foot against the base of the structure, she pulled, leaning back and jerking hard. A sharp pain lanced her palm, and she gasped. A fat splinter was lodged there, causing a hot trickle of blood.

Nearby, a horse and carriage rumbled noisily; Fanny froze, flattening herself against the wall. A long shadow swept across the courtyard as the carriage passed, the rattle and hoofbeats tapering into the distance.

Fanny's palm stung. She held it up, and was struck by how clearly she could see by the eerie orange glow of the hazy sky. As she eased the splinter out and blotted her bleeding hand on the snow, it occurred to her that the carriage driver probably wouldn't have noticed her. He was in the streetlight looking ahead, not into darkened courtyards. Even if he had bothered to turn his head, had seen her, it wouldn't have mattered—she was just someone using a privy.

As quietly as she could, she went back to pulling on the board until the nails on one end released their purchase. After that, it was easy to twist and pry the other end away. Fanny dragged the board over to the wall nearest the gate and probed the veins of mortar with her fingers, seeking a crack, a space between bricks that wasn't properly filled. When she found a sizable one, she leaned the board against it, creating a ramp from the ground to the edge of the protruding brick. She tested it by pushing downward; her makeshift ramp scraped down the wall and thumped onto the snow.

There was a banging noise, and Fanny glanced sharply toward the door—it was still closed. The sound came from an upstairs window shutter that had come loose and was flapping in the wind.

Dragging her feet from side to side, Fanny swiped away snow and felt for irregularities in the ground. A deep divot provided a brace for one end of the board; she leaned the other end against the wall. This time when she pushed on it, the ramp gave only a little, then held.

Her heart pounding, Fanny stepped onto the board, gripping the icy metal pickets of the gate for balance. Rough wood provided better traction than she could have hoped. She climbed until she could reach the top rail of the gate with both hands. She swung a leg up and hooked her heel over the bar like she was climbing a tree, but from there she was stuck, hanging like a baby opossum. She couldn't roll her body up over the fence, as she had done hundreds of times on a tree branch, without impaling herself on the sharpened pikes. With fingers numb from the pressure and cold, she held on tightly and slowly slid her leg over the top rail, squeezing her skinny thigh as far as it would go between the pickets until she was almost straddling the rail. When she was upright and able to hold on to the pointed tops of the pickets, she awkwardly lifted a foot to a half crouch and vaulted over the gate. She landed on her feet but stumbled, falling forward, sprawling on the road, her palms stinging. As she pushed herself up, a couple, arm-in-arm, bore down on her. She hurried to stand, but they were already crossing to the other side of the street with a grumble of disgust, like the contents of a bedpan had been strewn at their feet. Fanny didn't care—she was free.

CHAPTER 7

F anny picked herself up and ran. *Far* and *fast* crowded out any other thought. Heads turned as she darted down the road, but she ignored them. She followed a street with a long, straight row of gaslights, smeared by smog in the distance, because it was an arrow pointing away from where she had been—no risk of confusion, no doubling back. The densely packed inner city fell behind her; she entered a residential area, passing houses with lawns and walkways. The staccato beat of blood in her ears and her ragged breath were loud in the slumbering neighborhood; the occasional distant wail of a train horn, rattle of cart wheels, or bark of a dog only emphasized the growing silence. She slowed with fatigue, gasping for air, and for the first time noticed the throbbing of her feet in too-tight boots. Bent forward, hands on her thighs, her nostrils flared with each inhalation, like a horse that had been driven too hard. When she caught her breath, she felt the frozen tears that had tracked down her cheeks and into the corners of her mouth.

The streetlamps around her were few and far between, the nocturnal air sweeter with the scent of cedar and pine. Fanny took in tidy lots, swept sidewalks, deserted roads. There was less smoke, and she could see the moon. Her panic receded; her breath slowed further.

As she cooled from running, her damp skin chilled by a sharp winter breeze, fits of shivering set in, and the pain in her feet became a misery. She looked for a sheltered place to stop, but around her were only dark houses glaring back with glassy eyes. Behind her in the city were sheltered doorways of shuttered businesses, the train station, or even an alley where she could get out of the wind, but the idea of returning sickened her. She limped on.

Ahead, a narrow church spire rose into the moonlit sky. Fanny's family hadn't been churchgoers since her mother died, but she had comforting memories of singing hymns and reciting prayers. As she got closer, she could see that the building was massive compared to her little country church, with multiple spires and three doors facing the road, each large enough to admit a horse-drawn omnibus. The building was intimidating, but weren't churches meant to be refuges? She climbed the stairs to the nearest door. When she pulled on the wrought iron handle, it swung open easily.

Inside the church, moonlight turned the stained-glass windows inky blue but left much of the nave veiled in blackness. It made the space feel limitless. The vaulted ceiling rose to a dizzying height before fading into shadows. Rows of pews stretched forward, swallowed by gloom.

Fanny pulled the door closed and stepped into the silence. The air smelled of camphor and linseed oil; her cautious footsteps echoed. She felt along the wall near the entrance for a bowl of holy water, hoping to slake her thirst even at the price of blasphemy, but found nothing.

Sitting on the nearest pew, Fanny unlaced her stolen boots. Her hands shook. The relief of freeing her feet from the tight binding was so intense that it was almost pleasure; she sighed, cradling her toes gently with her fingers. There was a damp spot at the tip of one of her stockings that she assumed was blood.

Fanny took a deep breath and pressed a cool palm to her forehead. She was safe for the moment, but without Betsy as a beacon, she had no path forward. Hot tears welled up; she squeezed her eyes tight to stop them. How could she have been stupid enough to believe the story about a wealthy suitor? Their father must have known or suspected the truth. Betsy had been sold like a farm animal; Fanny understood that now.

Her head ached and her stomach cramped. She stretched out on the pew, careful not to put pressure on the swollen lump on her scalp where she had been struck. Thinking about the immediate future caused a bitter, choking feeling, so she tried to imagine a more distant time, when she will have saved up enough money to open a shop like Miss Snell's back home, the bakery in town with fluffy biscuits. She could find Betsy, and they could live together in a house with window boxes full of petunias and an apple tree in the backyard.

The wood was hard against Fanny's bony frame and her body groaned with complaints, but she closed her eyes and took deep breaths. Soon, she plummeted into the merciful abyss of sleep.

Sharp prickles against her arm jerked Fanny from her dreams. The church was bright with sunshine, the jewel-toned windows glowing; she blinked against the light. An old woman with a round face scowled down at her. Her small, cloudy eyes were widely spaced, her pert nose that of an ancient doll.

Fanny sat up, groggy, pulse bounding. The woman poked her again with the straw bristles of her broom. "You get on out of here, now," the woman squawked. "This is no hobo stop!"

"Ma'am," Fanny said, flailing for a response. Although she spoke at a normal volume, her voice echoed in the empty nave.

"Out, out!" She shook the broom vigorously at Fanny.

"I am here—" Fanny looked around as though the answer might be found in the unoccupied pews. "I am here for a purpose." *What purpose?*

"Balderdash!" the old woman said, sniffing.

"Ma'am," Fanny repeated, patting down her hair, which was doubtless a rat's nest. "I, uh, I—" The man on the train, the offer of help—the words on the card came back to her. "I am going to visit a Mr. Garth!"

The woman lowered the broom and frowned skeptically. "What does a bit of street trash like you want with Mr. Garth?"

"You know him!" Hesitantly, Fanny smiled; she felt her chapped upper lip crack as it stretched. Putting a hand to her mouth, she noticed the fuggy stink of her breath.

"I know every family in this congregation." The woman's bosomy chest puffed further out, pigeon-like. "That pew there belongs to Mr. Rockefeller himself, who is the leading member of this church." In her pride, she seemed to have forgotten that Fanny was beneath her notice. "The Garths aren't nearly so grand, but they are pious folk."

Fanny primly plucked lint from the skirt of her dress; the fabric looked shabbier and dirtier in the bright light. As she had suspected the night before, the toe of her left stocking was dark with blood. "Well," she said, "I need to find Mr. Garth, at his brother's request." She slid the boots from under the pew. "If you will set me in the right direction, I plan to go there now. I was only resting a moment because I hurt my foot. And of course I had heard that this church is so lovely." She bit down on the inside of her cheek as she eased the boots back onto her sore feet, keeping the laces loose. With a little gasp, she said, "Mr. Garth is expecting me."

The old woman shook her head. "Can't imagine what they would want with the likes of you."

"Do you know how I can find his house?" Fanny cast her mind back to the train. Picturing the cardstock, the neat handwriting, she could read it as though holding the original in her hand, a trick that used to astound her teacher.

The woman pursed her puckered lips, opened them for a retort, but Fanny smoothly continued, "He lives on Euclid Avenue. Number four-six-seven." She tilted her head, arranged her face in a pleasant expression. "Do you happen to know the way?"

With a grudging air, the woman said, "I suppose that would be Millionaires' Row."

Fanny resettled the cloak on her shoulders, waiting.

Pointing toward the door Fanny had entered, the old woman said, "That there is Euclid Avenue. If you go out to the left, then straight on, that's toward the rich folks' mansions." She leaned on her broom. "Never had a reason to go there myself."

"Thank you kindly, Mrs.—?"

"Foley," she said curtly.

"Thank you, Mrs. Foley." Fanny stood to leave. "I will be sure to mention how helpful you have been when I speak to Mr. Garth."

The morning was bright and cold; Fanny pulled up the hood of her cloak. The houses that lined the street were small and orderly, with neatly painted trim and snow-covered square lawns like freshly ironed handkerchiefs. Down the cobblestones of the quiet street came a quick tap of hooves; Fanny looked back to see a glossy black brougham with thin wheels bearing down on her. She stepped aside and watched it speed past. It was drawn by a big roan with a bouncing mane; the driver wore a high-collared, gold-trimmed overcoat. The carriage was gone before she glimpsed the passengers, but she imagined they must be very fine indeed.

Fanny's feet hurt, but less than the night before. She took a handful of snow from a low bank and let it melt in her mouth; the cold made her teeth twinge. Though she knew it would ultimately make the chapping worse, she held a second handful of snow to her irritated lips as she walked.

A few children in the front yard of a brick house were making a snowman. They had rolled up a snaking swath of snow, baring dead grass beneath and giving their creation a dingy hue. One of them waved with a mittened hand, wet wool drooping, as she walked by.

The farther Fanny went, the larger the houses were, and the more spacious the lawns. The air was clearer and the buildings less soot-stained than downtown, where an ashen veil had hung low, blocking views of the sky and dimming the brightness of the sun.

Fanny hadn't grown up with house numbers, but she understood the concept. The larger homes didn't have mailboxes, at least not near the street, so she couldn't see any addresses. She approached one of the houses down a long sandstone walkway that had been cleared of snow, trying to get a closer look. When she was still twenty paces away, a boy wearing a bright red muffler exited the front door. He seemed startled to see her there.

"Hello, what can I do for you?" The boy's tone was polite but wary, as though she could be threatening. He kept a gloved hand on the door handle.

"Excuse me," Fanny said. "Can you tell me where to find 467 Euclid Avenue, please?"

"Oh, I don't know." The boy looked puzzled, like her question didn't make sense. "We are number 224. Who lives there?" His cheeks had turned rosy with cold or discomfort. "You might go around back and ask at the servants' entrance."

"A Mr. Laurence Garth."

Under the brim of his cap, his eyebrows twitched. "Mae Garth's family?"

Fanny hugged her arms closer. "I don't know. I just know it's Mr. Laurence Garth."

"Well, if it's Mae's house, you have half a mile to go yet. There are elephants and pineapples on the gate." He still hadn't let go of the door.

Fanny ducked her head. "Thank you." She fled back down the walkway.

Fanny hobbled along, keeping an eye on the gates. She didn't know what a pineapple was, but elephants would be hard to miss. The houses she passed were ever bigger, spaced ever farther apart and set back from the gently curving road. As she rounded a bend, the vista opened into a broad promenade lined by elm trees, their bare branches scratching the sky. A white five-story mansion looked like a fairytale castle with battlements and parapets, twisting spires and dainty quatrefoil windows. A more somber but no less grandiose home was built of dark stone and boasted three rows of tall arched windows with decorative tracery below a steeply pointed roof with cupolas. Beyond the properties on the north side of the road, Fanny caught glimpses of sparkling water.

Fanny almost missed the elephants. The wrought iron gate was small, flanked by sandstone pillars carved with shallow bas-relief figures, including the elephants she sought. In the distance, beyond grounds dotted with trees and shrubbery, sat a sandstone building with a plain facade, diamond-paned windows, a decorative cornice at the roof's edge that alternated spherical and pyramidal elements. The effect was of a bland, friendly face topped by a shaggy fringe.

By the time she stood before that gate, Fanny was lightheaded with hunger, thirst, and exhaustion and sick from what she had endured. Numb to grandeur after all she had seen on the long walk, she pushed through the unlocked gate without thinking and started up the long driveway.

She heard the baying of the mastiffs before she saw them, bounding toward her, spraying snow with their broad, swift paws. After a quick intake of breath, she gathered herself. "Ho, lovies!" she called in the most cheerful voice she could muster. She put her fingers to her mouth and whistled.

The dogs were upon her, barking; she clapped playfully but waited to see tails wag before she extended a hand. She thought about Daisy, the mongrel retriever her father had brought home for partridge hunting. She and Betsy had loved that dog; they had taught her tricks when she was a puppy and made a bed from rags for her in the barn. Daisy would walk Fanny to school in the morning and find her own way home. When Daniel started training her, he did so with "kicks and licks," the same as he did with his kids. Daisy turned skittish, then ran away. It was maybe why Fanny refused compliance to her father; she didn't want to be like that cowering dog. But then again, she did run away.

The three hounds competed for her attention, butting ponderous heads against her legs, shoving their companions away with muscled shoulders. With difficulty, she waded through the churn of dogs as one might negotiate choppy surf, and when she broke free, Fanny struck out across the lawn, ankle-deep in snow. She shied away from the front entrance, circling around the massive building, the dogs trotting at her heels. There were no fences or barriers to impede her; no human footprints besides her own. A squirrel zigzagged crazily across their path and scampered up a nearby weeping conifer. The dogs charged after it, baying at the base of the tree, scrabbling their nails against the rough bark. Safe in the high branches, the squirrel chattered. Fanny kept walking, thinking she was rid of her convoy, but the mastiffs soon tired of their losing game and caught up to her.

Behind the mansion was a carriage house and stable. Fanny could see that the driveway curved in from the opposite side. She passed a series of terraces bordered by balustrades and urns to the driveway's trampled snow and muddy wheel tracks; there she found a modest door that she assumed must be the servants' entrance. She lifted the wreath-shaped brass knocker and rapped hard several times while the drooling hounds squirmed back and forth, threatening to topple her when they bumped against her, their wagging tails thumping against the door.

The woman who answered was young; she wore a white apron and cap. Her skin was light umber, and when she opened her mouth in surprise, Fanny could see that her teeth were flawless.

Before either of them could speak, one of the mastiffs tried to push past, into the hallway. The aproned woman quickly pulled the door to, blocking what remained of the ingress with her body. "You know you can't come in here!" She sounded more exasperated than angry. "What kind of guard dogs are you?"

Fanny grabbed the hound's collar, belatedly helpful. The dog pulled away, but good-naturedly, as though it was only playing at getting inside.

"I have never seen these beasts so friendly with a stranger." The woman shook her head. "How can I help you?"

"Mr. Garth's brother sent me, miss." Fanny pretended to check her pockets. "I have his card here somewhere." She patted and clutched with increasing distress, even reaching underneath her cloak to check her bodice. "I can't believe I lost it!"

"What's it about?" Her tone was guarded.

"He said Mr. Garth would have a job for me."

"Oh. I don't believe we have a position open." She was still holding the door mostly closed, peering out, and now her expression looked like a door closing, too.

"I am a hard worker," Fanny said quickly. "And a very fast learner!" One of the dogs knocked her too hard, and she fell forward, catching herself on the doorframe, her face inches from the other woman's. Fanny was flustered, but on an impulse, she did her best comic impression of a pleading orphan. She got a small smile in return.

"Well, get those beasts out of here—you seem to at least be good with them—and I'll let you in. I will make an inquiry for you."

CHAPTER 8

Fanny dashed back in the direction she had come, whistling for the dogs, and to her surprise, they bounded after her. She stopped to make a snowball, threw it as far as she could. While the mastiffs chased it, she ran back to the house, and the woman let her in.

As Fanny closed the door, the woman was touching the back of her wrist to her forehead, smiling broadly. "Whew!" she said, dropping her hand, which was dusted with flour, and left a smudge. "My name is Grace."

"Fanny." She bobbed her head. "Fanny Bartlett."

"You sure have a way with dogs."

Fanny was about to explain that she had grown up on a farm but thought better of it. "It was my fault they nearly got in here. I'm really sorry."

"Well . . ." Grace continued to smile. "No harm was done, and it was actually somewhat amusing." She gestured for Fanny to follow. "You can take a load off your feet while I find the housekeeper."

Fanny could smell the kitchen before they entered; her mouth watered at the scent of baking bread. The room was cavernous; there were at least two cast iron stoves that she could see, with clusters of pots and pans hanging over them. In addition, tiered brick ovens gaped in the wall.

Behind a sturdy wooden table, a matronly freckle-faced woman was dividing biscuit dough with capable swipes of a knife. She glanced up, barely lifting her chin, and returned to her task. "What is it, Grace?" Her words were as clipped as her movements.

"This is Fanny, ma'am." Grace indicated a stool for Fanny to sit on. "She came about a job." To Fanny, she said in a low voice, "This is Mrs. Campbell, the cook."

"No jobs here." Mrs. Campbell began scraping up the raw biscuits with the flat of her knife and depositing them with mechanical efficiency on a blackened sheet pan.

"I know, ma'am. But I thought I could still ask Mrs. Williams."

The cook shrugged her broad shoulders. "Don't be long."

Grace rinsed her hands in a bucket standing just outside the entrance hall and straightened her cap. "Just wait here," she said to Fanny. Grace's dark eyes had a liquescent softness that caused a strange pang in Fanny's chest.

Mrs. Campbell slid the pan into an oven and shut the door with a clang. She riddled the grate, then puffed on the bellows until the fat iron kettle roosting on the hotplate began to sing. She poured steaming water into a chipped teapot, ignoring Fanny all the while, and set a plate piled high with straw-colored biscuits on the edge of her work table.

Fanny leaned against the wall and let the dry, alimental heat of the kitchen seep into her bones. A wholesome, slightly sweet, yeasty aroma enveloped her like a blanket.

"Best eat those fresh," the cook said, pointing to the plate of biscuits with a knobby finger.

Fanny blinked, sat up straight. "I can have one?"

Mrs. Campbell was already walking away; she returned carrying teacups. "Eat up," she said, placing a chipped cup next to the plate. "Tea will be done steeping soon."

Fanny hesitated, hardly believing her luck, and quelling her suspicions after the last bit of "charity" that had been extended to her. Mrs. Campbell brushed up crumbs of pastry dough, humming tunelessly. Taking a seat on the low, rough-hewn bench, Fanny felt like a child, as the edge of the enormous oak table came up nearly to her armpits. She breathed in the floury warmth of the biscuits and took her first bite. She had never imagined a more lovely taste; it broke apart in her mouth with buttery softness. The cook poured tea without comment, her hands liver-spotted, her knuckles red and chapped. Fanny didn't know if it would be rude to take a second biscuit, but as the other woman paid her no mind, she thought that it couldn't be forbidden. It was as delicious as the first, and as she took the last flaky bite, she decided that three or four biscuits surely wouldn't be too many.

"Mrs. Williams says we aren't hiring." Grace stood in the doorway, looking downcast; Fanny wondered why she cared about the fate of a homeless girl she had only just met. "She said if you leave your references, she would think of you should a position open up."

Fanny had expected this; as she filled her stomach, she had come up with a response. "My former employer was a spartan but godly spinster," she said. She didn't know if she was using the word *spartan* correctly, but she hoped that her audience wouldn't know, either. "She belonged to the same church as Mr. Paul Garth, this Mr. Garth's brother, in Toledo." She clasped her hands together and looked from Grace to Mrs. Campbell and back again. "When she knew she was dying, she begged Mr. Paul to look after me, and he sent me here."

Grace glanced timidly at the cook. "Fanny could sleep in my room for tonight, anyway," she said. "It's the Christian thing to do."

The cook sighed. From her furrowed brow and closed fist on her aproned hip, the verdict did not look good; Fanny's heart sank.

"It's settled then." Grace smiled, beckoning to a bewildered Fanny. "Let's get you a bath."

Mrs. Campbell clucked her tongue. "I need you back down here in two shakes of a lamb's tail to get supper started," she said.

Grace was already leaving, tugging on Fanny's sleeve. "I'll be back in one shake, Mrs. Campbell!"

Fanny followed on Grace's heels, hoping to get away before the cook had a chance to change her mind.

"It's fine for you to sleep in my room," Grace said in a lower voice. "Our housekeeper never goes in there."

Grace led Fanny up the narrow servants' staircase, four flights to the attic. There was a long corridor with a low ceiling and identical oak doors at regular intervals. The lintels were so low that Fanny instinctively, though unnecessarily, ducked her head as they entered Grace's room. It was an austere cell, painted white; the only wall decoration was a crucifix above the head of one of the two narrow beds neatly made with plain blue quilts and matching pillows. Between the beds was a gaily colored rag rug and a wobbly-looking nightstand that held a stack of books and a candlestick. Light came from a small window that looked out onto part of the steeply slanted roof; a shallow closet with no doors held only three dresses on hangers and a hatbox on the shelf above. The little room smelled of rosewood, wax, and lye.

"You can sleep in Dena's bed." Grace pointed to the one without a crucifix above it. "She went back to Twinsburg for a spell." She sat on the edge of her bed. "You can leave your boots and cloak here."

Fanny's feet were numb; when she pulled off her boots, pins and needles soon turned to pain.

"Your foot is bleeding!" Grace stood over her.

"My boots rub my toes sometimes." Fanny smiled in a way she hoped was sprightly.

"I should show you to the bath." Grace put a hand on Fanny's elbow to help her up, as if she was an old woman in need of assistance. "Nobody comes up here this time of day, so you won't be bothered." She walked her to the room at the end of the corridor.

For Fanny, bathing meant a bucket and rag or, in the summer, a jump in the pond. She hadn't known what to expect—certainly not a copper bathtub and a pair of marble sinks. When Grace turned on the faucet and water poured out, Fanny marveled.

"I'm sorry we can't bring hot water up here," Grace said apologetically. "At least it's nice and toasty on the top floor. Just let the water sit for a while to warm up, and it'll feel fine." She opened a cupboard and took out a lump of soap, a cloth, and a towel. "Put the soap back in the dish with my name when you're done." She gave Fanny a quick smile. "I will bring you something to eat. I would tell you to join us in the kitchen for supper, but I don't think Mrs. Williams, our housekeeper, would approve." She glanced over her shoulder, as though she half-expected someone to be there. "Be sure to clean up after yourself, stray hairs and the like." With a curt nod, Grace was gone.

Fanny ran her fingers under the water flowing from the faucet, then filled her cupped hands and drank until she could no longer even imagine feeling thirsty, stopping only when her stomach was bloated. She dried her hands on the towel Grace had given her and shut off the faucet. While the water sat to warm, she wandered around the bathroom, touching the smooth marble of the sinks, grimacing at herself in the huge, gleaming mirror. Before, she had only seen her face in her mother's handheld looking glass, dim and distorted. She examined every angle up close, admiring the crispness of the image created by expert silvering—she could see the pores in her skin. She backed up to assess her appearance. There were ashy smudges under her eyes, and her complexion was blotchy. The face staring back at her from the extraordinarily shiny surface had a pointed chin, a wide mouth, and slightly hooded eyes. She looked nothing like her pretty mother or sister.

Fanny struggled out of the tight dress, taking care not to rip the straining seams. She was glad to get it off; without underclothes, the wool had scratched against her skin. In the mirror, she could see purple bruises on both of her shoulders. She probed them gingerly, and found they weren't too tender—she had had worse. Her collarbones protruded sharply, and she could see the corduroy bumps of her ribs when she took a deep breath. She let out the air with a long hiss and played with her hair, piling it on top of her head, coiling it at the nape of her neck, letting it fall over her shoulders. She wasn't ugly, really—just plain.

Fanny went to the bath and lowered herself in the cool, clear water, her flesh goose-pimpled and her teeth clenched. Slowly, she adjusted to the temperature, and then the gentle lapping against her neck felt like a benediction. When she rubbed the soap between her slippery hand and the wet cloth, it lathered to a froth, unlike the lumpish, chicken-fat colored soap she used at home. The suds smelled of lavender and lifted dull layers of dirt, until her skin was pink and squeaking under her scrubbing fingers.

Despite the luxury, it occurred to Fanny that there was a parallel to her imprisonment in the brothel; once more she was isolated and entirely dependent on someone else for food and shelter. But what choice did she have?

She thought, *I have to find a way to make money.*

I have to convince them to let me stay.

Fanny pinched her nose and lowered her head beneath the surface, moving slowly from side to side so that her hair billowed and undulated like seaweed, washing away the filth of the last days, cleansing her mind for what was to come.

CHAPTER 9

Grace appeared earlier than Fanny had expected with the promised plate of food and cup of sweet wine. Fanny was sitting on the foot of the bed still wrapped in a quilt, because she couldn't bear to put back on the ill-fitting and dirty wool dress after scrubbing herself so clean in the bath.

Grace didn't seem scandalized; in fact, she appeared to immediately comprehend the situation. "Dena keeps clothes in the chest under the bed," she said. "I'm sure she wouldn't mind if you borrowed some. You could also borrow mine, but she is closer to your size." She moved the books from the nightstand to her own bed, and set down the plate and cup. "I'll be back later. You can read if you want."

"Thank—" Fanny's voice snagged on something sharp, a needle prick of shame at being the recipient of undeserved charity. "Thank you, Grace."

Grace's departing look of pity was too much, and Fanny's sight blurred with tears. She picked up a book from the top of the pile, flipped blindly through it, batting back a swarm of fractured, intrusive fragments of memory. She was safe, she told herself, but she couldn't rid herself of the feeling that she was perched on a precarious ledge, given a fleeting and false sense of refuge.

The hours wore on, and in the quiet, distress seeped out of Fanny's body. Despite its precariousness, she settled onto her ledge. She put on the borrowed clothes, untangled the snarls in her damp hair with her fingers. Lying on the bed, she allowed herself to luxuriate in the comfort of a real mattress with clean sheets and soft blankets.

The book Fanny had chosen was imposingly titled *Middlemarch, A Study of Provincial Life, Volume II,* but she was drawn in from the first sentence. She lit a candle when the sun set and kept reading. Though she was at first distracted by occasional footsteps in the hallway, the murmur of feminine voices, the sound of water running in the bathroom, that became background noise. When the door opened, she was snapped out of deep absorption in a fictional world.

"I'm ready for some shut-eye." Grace shut the door behind her and put her hands on the small of her back, arching. She regarded Fanny, and with a smile said, "I see Dena left a nightdress behind. That's good." She pulled off her cap, revealing a coiled braid of black hair with a few stray curls poking out. "How do you like *Middlemarch*?"

A thought occurred to Fanny. "How did you know I could read?"

Grace sat and began to unlace her boots. "You used some big words." She slid off a boot and let it fall to the floor with a *thunk*. "And I could tell from the way you stared at my books."

Fanny felt suddenly too shy to hold the other young woman's amused gaze. "You have so many. Did you buy them yourself?"

"You mean why does a girl with my complexion possess literature?" She drew out the last word, each syllable distinct.

Fanny heard the bitter edge in Grace's tone, but didn't understand it. The sensation of standing on a cliff's ledge returned; Grace was her only tether to safety, and she was inexplicably annoyed.

"Oh, don't worry." Grace continued to undress unselfconsciously, hanging her clothes in the closet. "I'm sure you mean well."

Fanny had no idea how to undo whatever harm she had caused. She glanced at Grace, in her white undergarments, dimly lit by the flickering candle. "That is your natural complexion?" she ventured.

Grace scoffed. "You're even more peculiar than I thought."

Fanny kneaded the knot at the base of her neck. With no apparent signpost in sight, she floundered on: "I only had two books at home that my teacher gave me as a gift when I left school, *Gulliver's Travels* and *Oliver Twist*. I don't know any of these ones. I wasn't sure which one to read."

Grace picked a volume from the stack and handed it to Fanny. "This one."

Fanny read the title: *Narrative of the Life of Frederick Douglass, an American Slave, Written by Himself.* In school, she had learned about slavery and the American war, but it was abstract to her; something that happened in another place and time. Her throat clenched at the magnitude of her ignorance. "You—" Her voice was small and strangled. "You weren't a slave?"

Grace's laugh was incredulous. "You seem clever—and yet you know so little." She pulled on a nightdress and got into her bed, turning her back to Fanny.

Fanny held her breath, trying to think what to say. She let out her breath quietly. "I don't actually know much about the United States." The seconds went by slowly as she waited in vain for a response. "I grew up on a farm in Canada," she added softly.

Fanny kept her unfocused gaze on the book in her hands. Finally, Grace said, "I don't know much about Canada."

"Oh, there's not much to know." Fanny hoped that she didn't sound overly eager. "Snow, wolves, black flies."

There was a huff from the other bed that Fanny hoped was amusement, followed by, "Here it's millionaires, factories and poor folks."

"Are your people from here?" Fanny ventured.

The narrow bed creaked as Grace turned onto her back. She pushed the quilt down to free her arms and clasped her hands over her waist, staring at the ceiling. From her profile in the dim light, Fanny couldn't make out her expression, but her body seemed relaxed.

Grace sighed. "In a manner of speaking," she said. "My mother was a tutor for Mae, the only child of Mr. and Mrs. Garth." She yawned. "Mama was a white woman." She said this as though it explained some mystery.

"And your father?"

"He was a lawyer. A big deal, apparently. I don't remember him. He moved to Washington. Then he died." Her words strove to be casual, but had hard edges. She pulled her arms closer, crossing them over her chest.

Fanny waited to see if more was coming, then said, "Mine only almost died when he got drunk as a skunk and fell out of the loft and onto the woodstove." She paused again. "He's not good at much, not even kicking the bucket." She threw this out in the same offhand way Grace had spoken. Without looking, she could feel Grace's smile.

"My mother taught Mae during the day, then came home to my grandparents' house in the evening and started her lessons all over again, teaching me." Grace seemed to be warming to the subject. "I went to school, too, but it was a pretty terrible one, and she wanted to make sure that I learned everything that a rich little white girl could learn."

The image of Grace nestled against her mother, reading by the hearth, books strewn about them, made Fanny envious. To change the subject, she asked, "When did you start working here?"

"Part-time when I was twelve. My mother wanted to keep an eye on me, and we needed the money." Grace laughed cynically. "Of course nobody knew I was her daughter. She told them I was some sort of charity case, and because everyone adored my mother and the Garths are charitable people, they took me on." She sighed. "So, yes, this is where my mother's dedicated tutelage brought me."

"But you are smart, and educated, and still young," Fanny said, feeling defensive on Grace's behalf. "I am sure there are other things you could do."

Grace lifted herself on her elbow and fluffed her pillow. "Oh yes, I could marry a prince one day." She lay back down and wiggled to find a comfortable position. "Can you blow out the candle when you're done reading?" After a beat she muttered, "I won't be staying here forever." She closed her eyes and turned away.

The sight of her settling into sleep, the blanket gently moving with each breath, made Fanny think of Betsy. "Goodnight," she whispered, as much to her lost sister as to Grace.

Fanny extinguished the candle and lay down, too. She was exhausted but still wide awake, her mind turning over all that she had learned in such a short time and all that remained inscrutable.

From above came a muted scrabble of claws, squirrels or roof rats. Something mechanical-sounding juddered and whined briefly. Fanny peered into the darkness, but all she could make out were murky shadows. She listened for the sound of Grace's breathing, wondering if she was already asleep. A shutter knocked in the wind. In the next room, someone coughed. Fanny pulled the quilt up to her neck, pressed her ear into the understuffed pillow.

"Why did you really come to Cleveland?"

Grace whispered this so quietly that Fanny felt like the voice was inside her head, reading her mind. Unbidden, childhood images of

Betsy, sentimental pastels, flitted past—Betsy with her woolen cap and pink cheeks, digging tunnels in the snow; Betsy with a tiny foal, sunlight pouring through the slatted fence behind her; Betsy swinging down from the blossoming apple tree. "I came to find my sister," Fanny whispered back.

"You didn't find her."

It hadn't been a question. Fanny bit her lip. She could hear the rustle of bedclothes as Grace turned over in the dark. There was a long silence. Grace breathed out, "I'm sorry."

It was said with such gentleness. Fanny wanted to say, *I will find her*, but she was too ashamed. "Thank you," she said softly.

There was more rustling as Grace resettled herself. Fanny waited, but there was no more.

Fanny jolted awake, disoriented, when Grace poked her in the belly with a hairbrush.

"Get up, sleepy." Grace was already dressed; she set down the brush and started braiding her hair. "You need to find something to wear."

Fanny swung her feet out of bed, bracing for a cold floor, but the rag rug had a soft, pleasant bumpiness under her calloused soles. She pulled the bin of clothes from under the bed; in the dawning light, it was hard to tell one item from another, but she knew from the night before that there was only one dress, which she identified by texture. "I have no underclothes," she said.

"Well, that's where you're wrong." Grace dropped a ball of cloth onto Fanny's bed.

Fanny picked it up, and it fell apart into two soft, silky pieces that she held out toward Grace in puzzlement.

"Mae has dozens of these things—she won't know they're missing."

"Mae? But what are these?"

Grace pinned up her braid. "Underclothes, silly."

Fanny examined them skeptically; they were so insubstantial. "That you stole? For me?" She felt herself flush.

"I don't consider it stealing," Grace said. "We're just borrowing from someone who has far more earthly possessions than she needs." She adjusted the edges of her cap. "And I think you should have something nice."

"You feel sorry for me." Fanny didn't like the way that sounded and amended it with "If you think it won't cause trouble, well, thank you very much." Though she wasn't sure that she would like to wear anything made of such scanty fabric.

"I don't feel sorry for you. I get the sense that you can take care of yourself. But you still need underwear." Grace glanced toward the window, the apricot glow of the rising sun. "It's getting late. Come down to the kitchen as soon as you're ready and help me prepare for breakfast. Maybe Mrs. Williams will keep you if she finds you useful."

Fanny paused her hurried dressing to run her hands over the smooth undergarments and decided maybe they weren't so bad. She threw on the dress and borrowed Grace's hairbrush, doing her best to imitate her hairstyle with the few hairpins she had left. The boots were left for last—she had no choice but to put them back on. As she laced them up, though, she almost welcomed the pain. She had been so lucky over the last day—her good fortune surely couldn't last. Irrationally, this small suffering felt like a talisman protecting her from falling back into the despair that she knew all too well was out there. If her feet hurt, maybe the fates would ignore the undeserved blessings of a full belly, warm clothes, and help of a kind soul.

The cook welcomed Fanny with a nod and set her to work on cutting paper-thin slices of apple. The knife was so sharp that it made the job easy.

When she was almost finished with the apples, Grace joined her at the counter and began arranging the slices on a silver platter. "Help me make a layer like this," she murmured. "Then we put the stewed plums and cherries on top."

The kitchen was busy. A young woman wearing a black dress with a lace collar and long white apron was rolling golden brown balls of dough in powdered sugar and carefully stacking them to form a pyramid. Another woman, darker-skinned than Grace, was at the sink, up to her elbows in dishwater. Mrs. Campbell seemed to be everywhere at once, stirring pots, kneading dough, pulling a tray of bacon from the oven—the kitchen filled with a delectable aroma. Her moon face was red from the heat of so much burning coal, and she kept a rag tucked into her apron to wipe her forehead, as she flitted about like a robin in a tree. Nobody spoke except the cook, and then only to give orders. Fanny did as she was told and kept her mouth shut.

The woman who had been making a pyramid of fried dough was joined by two younger girls wearing similar black dresses and white aprons. Together, they silently ferried full serving dishes upstairs. On their third trip, Mrs. Campbell said, "Last ones, duckies." She heaved a great sigh and mopped her brow. Then, with a smile, she turned to Grace and Fanny and said, "You girls get our breakfast on the table. I made extra bacon today, so there should be enough to go around."

Like a lid lifted from a boiling pot, the tension in the kitchen was released.

Grace showed Fanny to the cupboards, where they collected dishes and cutlery; together, they set the long, rough-hewn table with mismatched chipped porcelain and tarnished silverware.

"Did you sleep well, Fanny?" Mrs. Campbell asked, filling a kettle.

"Oh, yes, ma'am, thank you. Best sleep in a long time."

Grace moved about their task with an ease that was almost languid, but she had three places neatly arranged before Fanny had finished even one.

"How is Moses doing, Phoebe?" Grace called out.

The servant at the sink turned and wiped her creased face with the rolled-up sleeve of her dress. Her graying hair was close-cropped, something Fanny had never seen on a woman before. Her smile was broad and lit up her whole countenance. "Better, Miss Grace, praise the Lord."

"I'm so glad to hear that. I know it was tough going for a while." Grace adjusted the cutlery she had just set down, making sure that they were evenly spaced. "Please tell him that he is in my prayers."

"We are all so grateful," Phoebe said. "God is merciful." She plunged her hands back into the sink, scrubbing a pot with vigor.

Fanny wondered why an old woman would call a young one "miss." The cook paid no attention to the exchange, humming as she poured a cup of tea for herself.

"What happened to Moses?" Fanny whispered to Grace.

"Factory accident. He lost his foot."

"Oh no! Her husband?"

"Son. Phoebe is a widow."

Fanny had more questions, but she sensed that she should hold her tongue.

As they brought platters of food to the table, the other servants began to gather, both men and women, all of them white except Grace and Phoebe. The tenth and last to arrive was a tall, thin woman dressed all in black, her hair pulled back severely in a tight chignon. She had a long nose and close-set eyes. From the deep grooves between her brows, Fanny could guess her usual expression. The others made room for her, taking their places at the table only after she had sat down.

"Good morning, Mrs. Williams," one of the men said.

She nodded to him, then said, "Now we bow our heads for grace." Her voice was dry and papery, her accent British. Eyes shut, she intoned piously, "Lord, bless this food and grant that we may be thankful for thy mercies be. Teach us to know by whom we're fed."

Fanny closed her eyes.

"Bless us with Christ, the living bread," Mrs. Williams continued. One of the men tried to stifle a cough. There was a hitch in the monotonous recital, and a sniff. "Lord, make us thankful for our food," she said more loudly. "Bless us with faith in Jesus's blood; with bread of life our souls supply, that we may live with Christ on high."

Fanny stole a glance around the table, and when her gaze returned to Mrs. Williams, she saw that she was scowling at her. "Amen," the housekeeper said pointedly, accusingly.

Fanny closed her eyes. "Amen," she said with the others. She kept her eyes shut until she heard the others moving and beginning to speak in low voices. She peeked at Mrs. Williams, who was carefully straightening the knife and fork beside her plate, her antennae doubtless still quivering, monitoring activity.

There was quiet conversation and clinks of metal against porcelain as the food was served. Grace, who was sitting next to her, whispered, "Take this basket, pass it down."

Fanny saw that the food was being passed around the table clockwise. Grace held out a bread basket, and there was a bowl of boiled eggs to her right as well. Fanny took a roll and quickly handed the basket to the man on her left, then pushed an egg onto her plate and handed off that platter, too. She could still feel Mrs. Williams watching her. The kitchen heat felt suddenly oppressive.

"So who do we have here?" the housekeeper asked, her eyes fixed on Fanny.

Fanny wasn't sure whether the question was directed at her, or someone else. Fortunately Grace spoke up, saying, "Ma'am, this is the girl I told you about earlier who is applying for a position as a domestic."

"I told you that we are not hiring right now."

"With Dena gone, we are short-handed, ma'am. I thought just until she gets back?" Grace spoke deferentially, but she did not appear to fear the woman.

Mrs. Williams rubbed the bridge of her aquiline nose as though it were silver in need of polishing. "What references did you bring?"

Fanny clasped her hands together and bowed her head briefly, squeezed her eyes and gullet closed. This was a method she had learned to make her eyes misty. She looked to Mrs. Williams, but kept her chin tilted down, like a submissive dog. "Ma'am, I was formerly employed by a Miss Maude Somerset of Toledo," she lied. She let her gaze fall, then return. "This saintly gentlewoman belonged to the same church as Mr. Paul Garth, this Mr. Garth's brother." She paused, letting her words settle over the hushed group. "When Miss Somerset grew ill, knowing she would die, she begged Mr. Paul to look after me, and he sent me here." Drawing a mournful sigh, Fanny added, "She was so kind to me, and she wrote a beautiful reference, and gave me a letter from Mr. Paul to bring with me, but I was robbed of my trunk and every scrap of my belongings as I left the train station." Fanny took in the looks of pity around the table. "It was so charitable of Grace to let me stay here. If I can make myself useful until Dena returns, that would give me great pleasure. You wouldn't need to give me anything but the roof over my head."

Mrs. Williams cleared her throat. "What were your duties for this former employer?"

Fanny had not prepared a response to this question, and she didn't know how the duties of servants were divided.

Grace jumped in, saying, "She worked as a parlor maid, like Dena, but she also took over for Miss Maude's personal maid when needed."

"She did a nice job in the kitchen this morning," Mrs. Campbell added, spearing a slice of bacon with her fork. "A good worker."

Mrs. Williams tapped her fingers against the edge of the table, brow furrowed. The silence around the table was palpable. "Well, all right, then," she said. "The girl can stay." Her mouth puckered sourly. "Just until Dena gets back."

CHAPTER 10

A t bedtime, Grace gave Fanny a primer on the duties of a parlor maid. As she unpinned her hair, she said, "Dena always starts by laying the fire in the drawing room."

Fanny, alarmed by how little she knew, asked, "How will I know which one is the drawing room?"

"It's the one decorated in red." Grace brushed her hair, which puffed up with each stroke, like cream being whipped. "Then lay out the table in the breakfast room." She raised an eyebrow, anticipating Fanny's question. "Yellow. It's my favorite room, sunny and cheerful." Grace's slender fingers deftly rebraided the glossy curls. "If there are flower deliveries, Arthur will bring them to you to arrange. You replace the bouquets in every room." She laughed at Fanny's expression. "Just do what looks nice." Her plait fell in a rope down her back. "Anyway," she said, tying off the end of the braid, "I doubt the Garths really notice the flowers anymore."

"But how can there be flowers in winter?"

"Oh, dear girl, have you never heard of greenhouses?"

Fanny hadn't, and Grace put a hand to her mouth, covering her smile. "Never you mind," she said. "It's a grand and peculiar thing." She went on to explain the other duties, such as making the beds, cleaning the floors, setting out the morning and evening newspapers, bringing afternoon tea, waiting at the dinner table, clearing up after the meals, answering the sitting room bell, trimming the lamp wicks, cleaning the pantry, making sure that towels were washed and available in abundance, maintaining the drawing room fire, polishing silver, dusting the rooms with particular attention to the windowsills, which needed to be dusted at least twice per day; more in the summer when the windows were open, because of the accumulation of fine soot from the factories. "The air may seem clear here," she said, "but if you leave the sills alone for a week, they will turn black."

The bewildering list made Fanny queasy with anxiety, but she strove to keep an outward appearance of calm as she asked Grace for clarifications. They spoke until there came the faint sound of clocks downstairs chiming midnight.

Grace fluffed her pillow with a shake. "If we don't get some sleep, we'll both be flagging tomorrow." In a higher register, with a passable British accent, she said, "Tired hands make for shoddy work, girls!"

Fanny laughed. "Well, I think I have asked every question I could imagine." She didn't know what to do with the rush of gratitude she felt. She wished that she had possessions, or money, or a service she could offer in exchange for such kindness from the other girl, who was tucking up the blanket below her chin. She blew out the candle and fervently whispered, "Thank you, Grace."

Grace mumbled something back; within minutes, she was snoring softly.

They rose early, while it was still dark and there was no stirring from the other women in the servants' quarters. Fanny lit the candle and donned Dena's uniform, a long black dress and white apron with a bib. Grace helped her pin a white cap to her hair.

"You will need to blacken those boots," Grace said. "They are looking shabby."

Fanny wasn't feeling as pinched by the boots anymore; they had stretched.

"Do you need me to go over your duties again?"

There was a flutter in Fanny's stomach, and her palms were damp, but she shook her head. She had memorized Grace's instructions, playing them over in her head as she fell asleep.

Grace patted her on the shoulder. "Find me if you run into trouble."

On an impulse, Fanny pulled her into a quick hug. Grace stiffened, but then gently returned the squeeze. When they moved apart, she was smiling shyly. "Time to work," she said.

Grace helped Fanny gather a sack of wood and kindling from the pile behind the pantry. The servants' staircase was gloomy after leaving the well-lit kitchen; Fanny held the candle high and placed her feet carefully. When she reached the landing, she pictured the layout of the floor as Grace had described it. She turned right at the base of the servants' staircase, then left and left again. Fanny could feel the vastness of the space and the solidity of the walls, floor, massive doorframes—the bones of a giant. The cool air scented with indoor greenery reminded her of the breath at a cave mouth in the forest.

Fanny pushed through a heavy silk portiere, maneuvering her candle so as not to singe the cloth. She entered what she hoped was the drawing room, which Grace had said was decorated in red. Fanny held the candle closer to the wall; in its light, the wallpaper was deep crimson, flocked with fleurs-de-lis.

She looked for the fireplace, but didn't see one. That couldn't be right—the red walls belonged to the drawing room, and her first task of the day was to lay the fire. Chewing her lip, squinting in the dim light, she stepped farther into the room and walked along the perimeter. Her candlelight fell on gilt chairs, lamps with engraved globes, a cabinet laden with ornaments. A tall filigreed screen in the shape of climbing rose vines jutted into her path; Fanny peered closer, saw nothing but blackness behind it. She lifted her flickering flame higher, took in the colossal carved mantel, realized that she was facing a firebox large enough to fit an armchair. The overmantel, made from highly polished mahogany, stretched from floor to high ceiling. Fanny approached it with awe; putting down her bundle of wood, she cautiously pulled at the filigreed screen. It moved easily on its curved feet.

She had thought that Grace had loaded her up with a ridiculously large amount of wood, but as she set the fire, she saw that she would need it all, and even then the pile would be dwarfed by the size of the firebox. She worked efficiently, setting it as she would at home, but on a much larger scale. Grace had told her that the matches would be on the mantel, but there were so many strange silver and glass ornaments to search by candlelight that it took some trouble before she discovered that the head of a painted wooden statue of an English setter popped off to reveal a trove of matchsticks in its belly. By the time the fire caught, a pale light was leaking around the edges of the tall red damask drapes that covered the room's many windows.

Fanny tugged at the drapes gently and then more forcefully; the heavy fabric barely budged. The rods were so far above her head that she could gain little traction, so she resorted to a billow-and-pull maneuver that coaxed the curtain rings to move. Only when she was finished with the last one and was tucking the final swag of drapery into the gold curlicue holdbacks did she pay any attention to the mullioned windows. Some panels were engraved with oval emblems twined with flowers; the glass was clear as still water, free of distortions. Outside, the clouds were pearlescent gray, softly molded like meringue dropped from a spoon. They made a blanket enfolding the city, except in the east, where a sliver of pink peeped over the horizon.

The milky light of pre-dawn brought details of the room into focus. Beside Fanny was a grand piano, a round lace covering on its glossy surface, underlying a silver vase of orchids. There was a gilt sofa upholstered in carmine plush, a table made of bird's-eye maple, with an openwork silver basket filled with bonbons at its center. A jade jardiniere with primroses stood in front of the bay window, where a bronze reproduction of the Venus de Milo gazed sternly, her amputated arms disquieting to Fanny. Settees and armchairs of floral brocade were grouped around small tables with ivory dishes, porcelain animals, and miniature rosy-shaded lamps. Fanny gaped, until the distant sounds of human activity returned her to the moment.

The breakfast room was as yellow as Grace had described; by the time Fanny found the dishes and cutlery and set them out in what she hoped was the right pattern, the clouds had partially dispersed, and morning light was streaming through the windows, brightening the room further.

As instructed, Fanny fetched the newspaper from the mudroom downstairs, where it had been pushed through the servants' mail slot. She ran into Grace, whose sleeves were rolled up, hands slick with greasy wash water. Grace *tsk-tsk*ed at the ashes on Fanny's apron, and reminded her to change it for a fresh one before bringing up the tea service.

Back in the breakfast room and slightly breathless, Fanny laid out the newspaper at the head of the table. Dusting came after breakfast. The house was so spotless that it felt to Fanny like some sort of charade, swiping the feather duster over pristine surfaces, but she was fascinated by each shiny bauble she encountered. The rooms kept unfolding, one upon the other; a ludicrously vast space for one family. The dining room had a carved ceiling, chandeliers dripping with crystals, high-backed chairs upholstered with purple velvet. The back drawing room was a bramble of chartreuse satin and malachite. Even the smallest privy was hung with miniature paintings in gold frames and had a Persian-style carpet.

When the clock struck ten, Fanny took the servants' stairs to the third floor, to make up beds and tidy the guest rooms. Seeing that none of those had been disturbed, she descended to the second floor to make up the bed for the Garths' daughter. The parents had their own attendants, Grace had explained, but Dena was responsible for Mae's room. Mae's door, painted with mayflowers, was open, and Fanny entered with the expectation that the room would be vacant. When she saw her, she froze.

A teenaged girl with creamy skin danced in a white nightdress, a tangle of golden hair down her back, her leg lifted in an arabesque. She was framed by a bay window, the casements pulled wide open. Pale curtains billowed in the chill breeze like sails; shadows rippled across the hardwood floor. Outside, the clouds had scattered, leaving cerulean patches between, but snowflakes still drifted down, glinting in the sunlight. The girl leaped in a grand jete, then twirled, her skirt twisting around her thighs; a curtain, puffed up in the wind, dropped a sprinkle of glittering snow at her bare feet. She smiled, eyes closed, and, buoyed as though on the crest of a wave, leaped again to silent music.

Fanny pressed herself into the wall, transfixed. She was arrested by the sheer beauty of the moment, but also by the sensation that she had stumbled upon something private, almost sacred. She prepared to scurry away, but the girl opened her eyes.

"Oh, hello," she said. Her cheeks were flushed, her smile ecstatic. "Isn't this glorious?"

Fanny sucked in a breath of cold air. "Yes, miss," she said. "Excuse me."

The girl advanced, her eyes excessively bright, like robin's eggs after a rain. "Who are you?"

"My name is Fanny, miss. I'm a new parlor maid." She shivered and wrapped her arms around her chest. "I just came to make up the bed."

"Oh, are you cold?" She spun around, slammed one window shut, then the other. The curtains deflated, inanimate objects once more. "I'm Mae Garth." She held out a hand.

Fanny, confused, looked at the doll-like hand with tapering fingers, one adorned with an opal ring. She wondered if she was meant to take it, and how she might do so politely.

Mae drew her hand back, still smiling. "Yes, Mother does say that I am too chummy with servants, but I don't see what the fuss is about." She laughed, as though she had said something witty.

"I will come back later to make up the bed, miss." Fanny edged away.

"No, stay! You can do it now."

With a despairing glance back at the beckoning open door, Fanny approached the unmade bed. She had never seen such an elaborate confection of satin and lace, decorative pillows and duvets. The hairs stood up on the back of her neck as she imagined the other girl's gaze upon her; with flustered, hurried movements she pulled at sheets and blankets.

From the corner of her eye, Fanny saw Mae come closer. She slowed, listening for instructions or a reprimand, but to her surprise, Mae pitched in, pulling her side of the sheet taut. Disconcerted, Fanny looked to Mae to discover the reason for her intervention, but Mae was humming to herself, paying little attention to her.

"I haven't seen Dena in a while." Mae's voice was low and melodious, filled with a casual confidence and warmth. She turned back the top of the sheet inexpertly, leaving it rumpled. "They sent the mulatto, who always does a nice job, but she is so *phlegmatic*." She enunciated the last word with care, a pretty furbelow at the end of her sentence.

Fanny did not fully understand; she kept her mouth shut, following Mae's lead on sloppily throwing the bedspread over the pillows, piling cushions on top.

"Do you dance? You look like a dancer." Mae tossed the last silk throw onto the bed. "There. I think that looks perfect."

It wasn't clear to Fanny whether she was teasing or being sincere about the dancing. "I've never been taught," she said uncertainly.

"If you have any talent, you can learn." Mae gave her a friendly smile, and Fanny tingled with pleasure. After a few moments, Mae said, "I've begged for more ballet lessons, but Mother says ballet is for little girls and not proper young ladies." She crossed her eyes, and stuck her tongue out the side of her mouth. Then, deadpan, she said, "And I am a proper young lady."

Fanny was so surprised that she couldn't suppress a laugh.

"Oh what lovely dimples you have!" Mae exclaimed. "And such beautiful eyes. What color are they? Gray? I wish that I had gray eyes. Blue is so boring."

Heat crept up Fanny's neck and along her scalp. "I can't imagine prettier eyes than yours." Her tongue felt thick in her mouth.

"Well, we all must make the most of what God gives us." Mae sat and bounced on the edge of the bed.

Watching her, Fanny felt her blush grow deeper.

Mae grabbed the open book that lay sprawled on her nightstand and flopped back on the bed, holding the pages close to her face as she scanned them. Fanny waited awkwardly, shifting her weight from foot to foot, until she finally realized that she had been dismissed.

After that encounter, Fanny's heart didn't stop thumping until she was done cleaning the breakfast room, scrubbing the pantry, trimming the lamp wicks, and setting out tea in the sitting room. She did not cross paths with Mr. and Mrs. Garth, though she saw their lip smudges on the crystal glasses and crumbs on the porcelain. She followed Grace's instructions carefully; a clock in every room had seemed like another strange extravagance, but she discovered them to be indispensable for keeping track of the day. She sped or slowed the pace of her tasks to be where she needed to be at the appointed time. When it was nearly suppertime, she tucked her rag into the pocket of her apron and dashed downstairs to join the line of girls waiting to ferry food upstairs to the dining room.

"Just leave them on the sideboard," the plump one, named Cora, whispered.

"What should I do about serving?" Fanny whispered back.

"Whatever Mrs. Williams tells you to do." Cora took a bowl of aubergine and cherries and a tureen of sauce from the cook, and mounted the stairs with slow, even steps.

Fanny looked for Grace, but she was nowhere to be seen. She took the covered dish that Mrs. Campbell placed in her hands and followed Cora. The dining room was transformed by the glow of candlelight and soft illumination of gurgling lamps. In the shadows, the row of family portraits on the wall seemed foreboding, staring down coldly. Mrs. Williams was inspecting the table, frowning, a knobby finger rubbing the bridge of her nose. With only three places set at the far end, the expanse of white tablecloth stretched out forlornly, a snowy tundra. The housekeeper looked up and noticed Fanny.

"You will just observe tonight," she said. "Stay out of the way, and learn the protocols for serving."

Fanny nodded, relieved, and hurried back downstairs to get the last platters. When she returned, the Garth family members were taking their places at the table. Cora and Ethel, in their newly laundered white aprons, were standing by the sideboard like soldiers for inspection. Mr. Garth was mutton-chopped and cleft-chinned; his starched collar

pressed into his pouchy neck. He sipped from his brandy glass even as
he sat down; wet-lipped, he smiled genially at his wife and daughter. "I
should not talk politics with the fairer sex, but I do say that I am pleased
to have seen in this evening's paper that Harry Bowler is predicted to
top the ticket in our district."

He received no response as his companions took their seats. Mrs. Garth
was older than Fanny had expected, given the youth of her daughter. Her
mousy hair was streaked with gray, and her face was crisscrossed with fine
lines, like a piece of paper that had been crumpled and smoothed out. She
had a placid manner, folding her hands neatly in her lap, keeping her head
slightly bowed. Mae was lovely in a pale muslin dress with fabric roses
along the neckline, her hair swept up with sparkling combs.

"I should think that Bowler will keep those electrified lights away
from our streets," Mr. Garth continued. "We live in the most elegant
neighborhood in this United States—how could they deface it with
those ugly things?" He took another sip of brandy; the pink tip of his
tongue flicked across his top lip. "Did you know that there are more
millionaires here on Euclid Avenue than anywhere else in the world?
New Yorkers and Parisians think they're so grand." Mr. Garth sat back
as Ethel leaned in, offering him a tray of oysters. He slid a few onto his
plate with the silver tongs. "Paris put in arc lighting, I heard. Imagine
those ugly lights on the Champs-Élysées." He snorted.

"When will you take us to Paris, Papa?" Mae asked, signaling to
Ethel that she didn't want oysters. "I am dying to go. You promised
to take me before I turned seventeen, and I'm already seventeen!"

Mrs. Garth glanced at her daughter but said nothing. She speared
a mollusk with a two-pronged fork. Cora offered a dish of macaroni
au gratin, from which Mrs. Garth spooned out a generous portion.

"Paris is overrated." Mr. Garth lifted his empty cup and peered
shortsightedly, squinting, into the corners of the room. James, the valet,

came forward with the decanter of brandy and refilled the glass. "All that *parlez-vous* and hoity-toity fancy handkerchiefs and pointy shoes. You're better off here with good, wholesome folks."

"I'm not a child anymore, Father." Mae took a helping of green beans and chicken from the proffered platter. She smiled prettily and set down the serving spoons. "I've already had my debut. You will be needing to find me a rich husband soon," she said teasingly.

"Why would you rush into marriage?" Mr. Garth took a gulp from his cup and a big spoonful of macaroni. With his mouth full, he said, "You have everything you need right here, and you should be grateful." He coughed, and a particle of food flew out.

Mrs. Garth flinched and dabbed her thin lips with her napkin.

"Oh, dear Papa." Mae's voice was syrupy. "Just because I will someday be married doesn't mean that you will lose me."

He grumbled but looked pleased. "Don't you hurry things. You're still my chickadee."

Mae tucked a loose curl behind her seashell ear. "Well, at the very least, I should have a lady's maid."

Mr. Garth shook his head. "You know how hard it is to find good domestics. And we have plenty of help."

Mae sliced into her chicken. "Melanie Crane has her own maid, and she's even younger than me." With the tines of her fork, she peeled back chicken skin and pushed it to the edge of her plate, where she poked at it, rolling it up.

Her mother made a disapproving sound and admonished her with a scowl, but Mae ignored her. She gave her father a coy look and said, "A lady's maid isn't too much to ask for your *favorite* daughter, who loves you so dearly, and who always goes walking with you when you ask."

With a fond chuckle, Mr. Garth said, "You certainly know your way into your Papa's heart. I will speak with Mrs. Williams."

CHAPTER 11

Fanny, pacing the floor excitedly, nearly pounced on Grace when she entered the room. "You will not believe what I heard!"

Grace, with a laugh, put out a hand to fend her off. "What lit your skirt on fire?"

"Mae told her parents that she wants a lady's maid!" Fanny clasped her hands tightly and bit her lip.

"Fascinating," Grace said dryly. She removed the hairpins that kept her cap in place.

"I don't know what will come of it, of course." Fanny tried to calibrate her tone to better match Grace's placidity. "But Mr. Garth said that he would speak with Mrs. Williams. I was thinking that perhaps you could take that position. And as they would need someone to fill yours, I might stay." She pulled on Dena's nightdress, then shimmied out of her underclothes. "This could be good fortune for both of us."

Grace's back was to Fanny, a wall.

Fanny paused. Her news was not well received. "I think it would be easy work, being a lady's maid."

Grace proceeded to pull off her boots, then her stockings.

"Just—I don't know. Helping with her wardrobe, bringing her biscuits."

"I will never be a lady's maid. Certainly not *hers*." Grace tossed her stockings into the laundry basket, then took a deep breath. "But of course I would be glad if you could stay."

Her dourness quashed Fanny's hope. "I thought Mae was quite lovely."

"Well, I suppose you might think that." Grace examined a blister on her finger, pushing at its pearlescent edge.

Fanny was annoyed, but she tamped the feeling down. "You could at least ask Mrs. Williams about taking the post."

Grace shook her head. "You really did grow up in the back of beyond, didn't you? You're so innocent."

Innocent felt like an insult to Fanny. She certainly was not ignorant of the brutality of men. She did have gaping holes in her knowledge, however, and her survival depended on learning fast. "You're right," she said. "I need you to teach me."

The following morning, Fanny found Mae in her room again. She was reading, still in her nightdress, one with pink trim. Fanny wondered how many she owned, and what it might be like to lie abed well into the day, with nothing to do. Mae glanced up. "You can clean later." She pushed tangled hair back from her face. "I'll be out this afternoon."

Fanny was nervous, but she didn't want to have to leave. "It's so dark in here, miss." She went to the windows, opened the curtains. "So you don't strain your eyes."

The sunlight fell directly on Mae, and she glowed, her skin flawless, her eyes impossibly blue. Fanny's breath caught.

"It's too bright." Scowling, Mae turned her back to the windows.

Fanny's heart gave a hard knock. "Would you like me to close them again?"

Mae sighed and flopped onto her stomach. Her voice muffled by the duvet, she said, "It's fine."

For an uncomfortable moment, Fanny debated what to do. Her eyes fixed on the froth of yellow curls. It was a sight that belonged in fairy tales. She didn't know if she longed more to touch the curls or to have them as her own, to toss over her shoulder and shake them down her back or pile onto her head into a beautiful confection. "Miss," she said, feeling lightheaded. "I could help you fix your hair."

Mae groaned.

"I did my sister's hair. I'm quite good."

What she muttered was unintelligible.

Fanny waited, unsure what to do next.

Mae sat up. "Fine," she said again. She scooted to the edge of the bed and jumped out. "Come with me." Her silk nightdress clung to her like a bat wing; the hollows and curves of her body made Fanny think of the armless statue in the parlor.

In an adjoining room, Mae made a sweeping gesture. "Voici mon boudoir!" There was floral wallpaper and a wedding-cake ceiling; the moldings looked like they were made of white frosting. An oval mirror in an ornate gold frame dominated the far wall; in front of it was a spindly-legged table, its surface cluttered with toiletries, and a velvet upholstered stool, upon which Mae perched and waited expectantly.

"I will need some water," Fanny said.

"You can fetch it in the powder room." Mae handed her an enamel bowl and waved her delicate hand toward another doorway in the boudoir.

In the small powder room was a toilet encased in white painted wood, carved with fleurs-de-lis, and a pink marble sink. Fanny fumbled with the bulbous gold faucet, trying to divine how to turn it on; when she succeeded, a forceful spray of water splashed back at her, so that the front of her dress was wet and her face dewed with drops. She quickly shut it off, then eased the faucet back on until she had a gentle flow. When the basin was full, she carried it back, taking small shuffling steps so as not to spill any.

"Put it here," Mae said, indicating the vanity in front of her. The surface was spread with hairpins, decorative clasps, vials of straw-colored liquids, miniature crystal jars with silver lids. Fanny had to nudge aside some clutter to make room for the bowl. She scanned the items on the vanity and picked up an ebony horsehair brush that was bigger than both of her palms put together.

Standing behind Mae, she gently gathered her hair, so that it all fell behind her shoulders. It was soft and heavy in her hands, and she could feel the heat radiating from Mae's skin. Gently, Fanny ran the bristles over the wispy outer surface of the golden halo, trying to untangle the first layer.

"You have to go at it a lot harder than that," Mae said, laughing. "Otherwise we will be here all week!"

Fanny pushed further into the pillowy tangle, solicitously holding the hair near the roots, so that Mae wouldn't feel the tug on her scalp.

"Here," Mae said, tipping her palm up. "Give it to me." She took the brush and attacked her hair with long, ruthless strokes. The bristles rasped harshly, their rhythm halting briefly as they caught against a recalcitrant snarl, then resuming energetically. "Like that." Mae handed the brush back with a flourish. The section she had brushed lay in surprisingly tame waves.

Fanny held the brush out in front of her, like it was a relic being blessed, summoning the courage to do as she was told. Taking a deep breath, she started in with as much vigor as she could muster.

To Fanny's surprise, Mae didn't so much as tense up. Her plump lower lip thinned and her eyes narrowed, but she offered up not the smallest sound of complaint. Within minutes, her hair was a smooth cascade down her back with only a faint nimbus of frizz.

"We need rag wrappers," Fanny said. Back home, she had made ringlets for her sister on the weekends Betsy went into town for Cousin Hettie's parties. Fanny had been too young to go, and after their mother died, nobody spoke of the parties again.

To her relief, Mae pulled out a drawer full of rags. "I never get these to work properly," she said.

"Not to worry, miss." Fanny separated a shaft of damp, rosewater-scented hair and carefully bundled it with a scrap of fabric, tying it neatly. "This will come out nicely for your afternoon appointment, I promise."

Mae looked at her reflection approvingly.

"You could have your maid do this every day, miss. It really isn't so much trouble." Fanny said this quietly, respectfully, implying that it wasn't her place to say. She began spooling up another shank of hair.

A cloud passed over Mae's expression. "I don't have my own maid."

Fanny paused, as though shocked. "I'm sorry, miss. I didn't mean to presume."

"I am more than old enough to have one," Mae said. "But my parents are so provincial."

Coiling hair around another rag, Fanny said, "You really ought to have help." She paused, as if considering. "You know, when Dena returns, there will be one maid too many. You might mention this to your parents."

Mae sat up straighter. Regarding Fanny in the mirror, she said, "It's Letty, isn't it?"

"Fanny, miss." She continued her work on Mae's hair.

"Have you ever been a lady's maid?"

The question took Fanny by surprise. She, not even qualified to be a parlor maid, would never be selected for the post—it was impossible with Mrs. Williams in the way. Nevertheless, she was suddenly filled with a fierce if cautious hope. "I know what the position requires," she said slowly.

Mae toyed with an ivory comb, the slightest furrow between her brows. "My maid would need to know what being a lady entails." She glanced at Fanny again in the mirror. There was doubt but also interest in her eyes.

Fanny scarcely dared to breathe. Mae's interest was a little bird she had to try to coax into her hand. Since she didn't know what it meant to be a lady, a different approach was needed. "The first requirement of a lady's maid is complete dedication to the role," she said. With her fingertips, she gently brushed a loose strand of hair up from the back of Mae's neck. "I can tell how spirited you are, and how expressive in your dancing—"

"I have the heart of an artist," Mae interjected with a sigh. "But my parents don't care. All they think about is propriety."

"I can see that you are passionate, miss," Fanny said. She didn't have to pretend at admiration. "You shouldn't be surrounded by nay-sayers or have a maid who might tattletale to Mrs. Williams." She stopped, letting Mae make the logical next step on her own: Mrs. Williams would report to her parents.

From Mae's expression, it was clear that she had understood the implications.

Fanny gave the dressed hair a final pat with a towel. "There, all done."

May examined Fanny's handiwork, then studied her own face in the mirror. She rubbed her cheeks, grimaced to examine her teeth, which were just crooked enough to be charming, the incisors almost imperceptibly overlapping. She turned her face to see her profile. "Do you think I look like Mrs. William Waldorf Astor?"

Fanny didn't recognize the name and couldn't tell whether the comparison would be favorable or not. "You are far more beautiful, miss," she said.

"Do you really think so?" Mae cocked her head, looking pleased.

Fanny tidied, emptying the bowl of water, straightening up the vanity.

"What's your favorite time of day?" Mae asked.

Fanny was worried about being late for her other tasks, but she felt that rushing out would be a mistake.

Mae laughed. "You look frightened, silly goose!"

Fanny forced herself to relax and smile. "I suppose I like evening best."

Clapping her hands together, Mae beamed. Fanny had answered correctly.

"Evening is enchanted." Mae stood, and performatively stretched her arms overhead, arching her back. Instead of her long hair swaying behind her, she had a lumpy corona, like a rag doll. She turned her face and winked so quickly that Fanny wasn't sure if she had imagined it.

Like a dancer on a stage, she swept her arms back down balletically and paused for several beats, waiting for her audience to focus its attention.

"At night, when dark has fallen . . ." she said in her low, melodious voice, her chin lifted, hand to her breastbone. She paused, adjusted her stance, then, as though reconsidering her delivery, continued more dreamily, "Night is the magic time. When darkness blots out all that is ugly in the world and enfolds me in its mystery, I feel that anything is possible. I feel that I might climb to the top of the roof and jump off, flying, spiraling high above the lights of the city, out over the darkling lake." In imitation of flight, she raised her arms again, their undersides so pale as to seem translucent; fine blue veins showed beneath the white surface like tracery on Delft pottery.

Fanny was entranced. She had never been whimsical, but she felt a deep longing to join this peculiar flight of fancy.

"I would swoop in the moonlit sky to New York, to the poshest hotel." Mae paused, seemed to picture the scene. "I would take a table by a dining room window, watching ladies in yards of watered silk and diamonds come and go on the red carpet. There would be nattily-dressed waiters, white linen, sweet-smelling lilies, popping corks, an orchestra playing a gay, lively tune." She breathed deeply, her gaze unfocused. "I would take all the pink champagne I wanted, watch it bubbling and foaming in my crystal glass." Mae touched the tip of her tongue to her lips as though she could taste the champagne.

There was a knock at the door.

"Come in," Mae called, all playfulness gone.

Ethel, in her white cap and apron, entered bearing a tray. "Good morning, miss." She gave Fanny a curious look. "Mrs. Garth asked me to bring you up some eggs and toast since you missed breakfast."

Mae wrinkled her nose. "Set it on the desk, please."

"I should be going, miss," Fanny said.

Mae waved to Fanny, thanked Ethel, and went back to her book.

When they were out of the room, Ethel said, "Odd one, isn't she?"

Fanny thought Mae was extraordinary, but she just shrugged and repeated something Grace had said, "The rich are different."

Fanny couldn't bring herself to tell Grace about what had happened in Mae's chambers. Instead, she said, "What did you mean when you said that you wouldn't be working here forever? What will you do?"

"I want to start my own business."

"Really?" Fanny helped Grace untangle her apron strings.

"Thank you," Grace said, hanging her apron in the closet. "I want my own hair salon." She pulled a jar from behind the hatbox on the shelf, opened it, and smeared yellowish cream on her hands and forearms. "I've been saving money, and on my days off, I help out at Miss Rose's." Grace mutely offered the cream to Fanny, who shook her head. "Miss Rose has three hairdressers working for her, and she sells her own products as well."

Fanny rolled off her stockings, looking thoughtful. "Do you suppose there is real money to be made? So that a woman could be independent?"

"Unmarried, you mean?" She replaced the jar, concealing it behind the hatbox once more.

Fanny nodded.

"Miss Rose is married, though nobody calls her by her husband's name. I want to get married. Don't you?"

"What men do to women—" Fanny stopped herself. "I don't want a husband."

Grace looked at her thoughtfully. "Perhaps we could go into business together." She paused, then added, "It wouldn't have to be hairdressing. I'm open to other ideas."

Fanny saw the two of them poring over a leger, side-by-side, in a room of their own. The thought was immensely comforting, yet somehow, after her vague but magical fantasies in Mae's room, even the distant dream of running her own small business with a friend felt lacking. "Perhaps," she said. Then, "That sounds wonderful."

CHAPTER 12

Fanny dedicated herself to learning as quickly as she could. In the evenings, she peppered Grace with questions, and she kept a close watch on the other girls as they did their work, picking up on ways to be more efficient. Her tasks felt lighter each day, and the luxurious surroundings that had first bewildered her became familiar. She was emboldened to examine the statuary, softly press down on a piano key, peek into a book left on a side table. She kept the discarded morning newspapers and tucked them away in the pantry for later reading, should she have time during the day.

When Fanny crossed paths with Mae, she was respectful but managed to make a pleasantry about imaginary New York dining that turned into an ongoing amusement between them. If Mae caught Fanny's eye in passing, she might mimic drinking champagne, and Fanny would subtly feign disapproval, or if she thought nobody would notice, raise an invisible glass in return. She always left these brief encounters feeling elated.

The Garths rarely had overnight visitors, but once, a young man by the name of Joseph Carrow came to stay. Through the servant gossip vine, Fanny learned that he was an older cousin of Mae's. He was clean-shaven and shaggy-haired and had an earnest manner that set him apart from the Garths. Something about the way he spoke reminded Fanny of home, maybe the flatness of his vowels or the frankness of his speech. As she silently served meals, or tidied, or built fires, Fanny observed him with Mae, the way he smiled at her coquettish remarks but also gently challenged her opinions and views. In one exchange, Mae declared her intention to live in New York at the finest hotels and to dine out every evening.

"That sounds expensive," Carrow said dryly.

Mae smoothed a ringlet that draped over her shoulder. "Papa is rich."

He regarded her fondly but offered a rebuke. "Not infinitely so. You might do well to temper your aspirations."

"Then I will marry an infinitely rich man," she said with faux petulance, pouting prettily.

Carrow, unsmiling, shook his head. "A marriage without love or friendship can be like a prison cell," he said. "Promise me you won't be impetuous, cousin."

Mae rolled her eyes. "Don't be dreary. What would you know about marriage anyway?" Then she seemed to have a sudden realization. With a small, mischievous curve of her lips, she said, "Why, Joe Carrow, are the rumors true? Are you engaged to a girl back home?"

His cheeks colored, and his eyes slid away from Mae. His gaze landed on Fanny, who was arranging the silver more meticulously than necessary; she cringed, worried that she had been caught eavesdropping. But he started talking without averting his gaze, and she realized that he saw her as no more than part of the furnishings; he stared vaguely in her direction as he would at a painting on the wall.

"It's not an engagement," he said with mild irritation. "I wish busybodies would mind their own business."

Mae appeared eager to stay on the subject, but Fanny heard no more, as she could no longer delay her next task. She left with a new understanding: Being rich was not the opposite of being poor. Rich people also wanted more money to buy happiness.

One morning, as Fanny was dusting in the parlor, Mrs. Williams appeared in the doorway. From the way she sucked in the flesh of her wrinkled, onion skin cheeks and pursed her meager lips, her annoyance was abundantly apparent. "It seems that Miss Garth has set her heart on you being her lady's maid," she said tartly.

Warmth spread through Fanny; she felt her joints loosen, her body grow lighter.

"I explained to Mr. and Mrs. Garth that you have no relevant experience, and there are many more qualified women he could hire."

The lightness vanished. Fanny was unaware that she was nervously smoothing the feathers of the duster until Mrs. Williams slapped her hand away. "You will get oil on the feathers!"

Fanny bowed her head. "Sorry, Mrs. Williams."

"Finish up in here, and I will have Ethel take over. Miss Garth is upstairs; report to her when you are done with the dusting."

It took a moment for the meaning to sink in. *She was to be Mae's maid.*

Mrs. Williams sniffed. With a long-fingered hand, she brushed the white apron at her waist, expunging a miniscule speck. Turning abruptly, her skirt flaring out behind her, Mrs. Williams muttered something about *these Americans.*

"Yes, ma'am," Fanny said to her retreating back.

That night, Fanny was equally anxious to share her news with Grace and worried about Grace's reaction. After washing and changing into nightclothes, she perched on the edge of Dena's bed, bouncing her knee, chewing her nails, waiting for Grace to finish work. Creaking footsteps shuffled, sauntered, or strode by in the corridor, but the bedroom door did not open. Fanny picked up the book she had started, scanned a page without absorbing the words, set it back down on the wobbly nightstand. She paced the narrow area between the beds, six steps to the wall, then back again. She tried to replicate one of Mae's arabesques, but her back foot caught on the hem of her nightdress, and she tottered, blushing at her clumsiness. She smoothed out her nightdress and sat back down on the edge of the bed, flipping through a new book.

When Grace finally arrived, sighing and kicking off her boots before she even sat down, Fanny blurted out what she had to say.

"So that is why I saw so little of you today," Grace said. "And why you are already prepared for bed."

Fanny was distressed. "It must seem terribly unfair that I was given this position instead of you."

Grace gave her a strange look. "Unfair," she said quietly. She gave a cheerless half smile. "Unfair, indeed." More briskly, she said, "Don't worry yourself about that. I would not have accepted had the position been offered to me. It's not my aspiration to be a lady's maid."

Tentatively, Fanny said, "I think it's a good posting. Miss Mae seems lovely."

"Don't tell me that you are taken in by her." The words were tinged with amusement but also disdain.

"I don't understand what you have against her. She's charming. It is not her fault that she's rich." Fanny sounded more heated than she had intended.

"The wealth is not her doing. She was born to it."

Cutting her off, Fanny said, "What is so wrong with being rich, anyway?"

Tartly, Grace said, "The point isn't the money, Fanny. It's that having money makes some people feel like they are better than everyone else." With a raised hand and lowered brows, she seemed ready to continue her lecture, but instead Grace exhaled slowly, audibly, and visibly deflated. "I *am* happy for you," she said. "And truly glad that you will be able to stay."

Unable to stop herself, Fanny muttered, "It's no crime to be born under a lucky star."

Grace grimaced and turned her face away as she started to take down her hair. Silence, thick and stifling, filled the room.

Fanny, contrite, slid back on the bed to lean against the headboard and pulled up her knees. She gripped her shins, plucked distractedly at the coarsening hairs that grew there. "It was a hard day?"

Grace made a sound in her throat signifying the affirmative. She kept on unbuttoning her dress.

"Mrs. Williams seemed to be in a state when I saw her at supper."

There was no response.

Fanny pulled her knees in further. "Was she on you all day today?"

"It was a day like any other, just longer." Grace climbed into bed. "I'm so tired." A moment later she said, "Will you blow out the light." There was no upturn in inflection at the end of the sentence, but firm closure that did not invite further dialogue.

Fanny wet her thumb and finger with her tongue to snuff out the candle the way her mother had; the wick sizzled briefly, a last gasp. She didn't close her eyes in the darkness but stared into the shadows, trying to make out ceiling moldings by the faint, eerie glow of distant gaslights that leaked through the window. She could feel her heart beating uncomfortably; she wanted to whisper to Grace, to find a way to end their evening on a better note.

When Fanny did close her eyes, an unexpected tide of misery washed over her. Loss and loneliness—her dead mother, her missing sister, even timid Billy was precious, precious and lost. The floodwaters of remembrance could be perilous, but with a roof over her head and food in her belly, Fanny allowed herself to cry silently into her pillow, wallowing, wiping her snotty nose on the edge of the pillowcase. When her thoughts turned to the brothel, however, Fanny slammed the floodgates shut. Sadness could be cleansing, but monsters were not allowed out of their cages.

Once settled, Fanny envisioned Mae on the roof, her skirt rippling in the breeze like a white flag, goosebumps on her exposed flesh. It was an inky night sprinkled with stars, a misty blue cloud scudding over the shining face of the moon. She imagined herself standing next to her, linking their hands together. She would warm Mae's hand in her own, gently clasp the birdlike bones, sense the tumultuous passage of blood beneath soft skin. They would jump together into the sky.

CHAPTER 13

A bright slice of sunshine already shone through the high window and splashed merrily across the cedar floor. Grace was gone, her bed neatly made. Fanny rose in a panic, dressed as quickly as she could. Why had Grace not woken her? The clocks chimed the top of the hour: nine o'clock. Her stomach flopped.

Creeping down the servants' stairs, Fanny prayed that she would not meet Mrs. Williams. She went straight to Mae's room and knocked timidly on the door. As she waited in the sunlit hallway, she felt exposed, a hare far from its burrow. There was no response. Fanny knocked again, a bit louder. Hearing the resolute tread of boots on the servants' stairs, she could bear to wait no longer—she opened Mae's door, flinching at a creak of the hinges, and slipped inside.

The room was a dim gray except for a diffuse glow that seeped around the edges of heavy damask curtains. Fanny pushed the door closed slowly to muffle the hinges' complaint, and paused to let her eyes adjust. Soft, snuffly breaths came from the canopied bed. Fanny inched forward until she could see Mae's sleeping form, splayed out like a statue of a dancer caught mid-flight, one leg extended, an arm flung back, skin like white marble and hair streaming, the bedclothes twisted around her waist. There was something untamed about Mae, even in sleep.

Fanny stepped further into the floral-scented air of the bedroom while the clock on the bureau ticked its *tsk, tsk, tsk* at a girl lying abed so late in the morning. The hollow above Mae's sternum deepened as she took in a long, sighing breath; she rolled fully onto her back and stretched her slender arms overhead, her eyes still closed. Not wanting to bother her, Fanny moved slowly toward the divan to sit and wait, secretly relishing the chance to watch Mae in repose.

"Fetch my mauve satin robe from the closet, will you?" Mae said, her voice husky with sleep.

Fanny was shaken from reverie by this unexpected utterance. "Yes, miss," she said, snapping to attention.

The enormous wardrobe swallowed her whole; surrounded by tightly packed racks of clothing, she searched in the dim light. Everything looked like a shade of gray, so she rifled through the clothing using her sense of touch, seeking out soft textures. Her agitation rose as she pulled garments out, but failed to identify a robe.

"It's on the hook. To the left of the door," Mae called out.

Fanny unhooked it with relief.

Mae was still lying with her eyes closed. "You can open the curtains, but slowly, because I don't like the light to come in all at once." She extended a hand blindly.

"Yes, miss." Unsure what was expected, Fanny offered the slippery robe to the outstretched hand.

Mae sighed, draping it over her face like a loose blindfold.

As Fanny edged a curtain along its rod, blinking in the glare, she said, "Should I bring you some breakfast?"

"I don't eat breakfast."

Fanny was disappointed; she had hoped to get a bite to eat for herself in the kitchen.

Once the windows were open, the room was suffused with sunlight, the walls azure as a summer sky, white accents gleaming. A fresh bouquet of coral roses stood on the dresser, and Fanny realized it was the source of the scent she had noticed.

"Look at the clothes I left on the divan, and see if there are any you like." Mae was sitting up against a cluster of pillows, squinting and pointing. "I'm going to get you new boots, too. What size do you wear?"

"Oh—I don't know." Fanny had always worn her sister's hand-me-downs. "These boots I have are fine." It was true that they didn't pinch much anymore.

Mae snorted. "Those boots are *not* fine. They are the ugliest, most tattered things I have ever seen. A barefoot Federal straggling home from Virginia would turn up his nose at those."

Fanny stared at her feet, wondering what a Federal was, and why a servant would need new boots. She was swimming in strange, murky waters, her nose barely above the surface.

"Well, tell me what you think of the dresses."

Mae was so much smaller than Fanny; there was no way that one of her dresses would fit.

As though she had heard the thought, Mae said, "They used to belong to my tutor."

The dresses were made of dark-colored wool and sensibly cut, but of far higher quality than any Fanny had ever owned. She picked one up and examined the stitching. "Why do you have your tutor's dresses?"

Mae, snugly wrapped in the satin robe, came to Fanny's side and inspected the garment with her. To Fanny's surprise, she leaned into her, a hand on her shoulder. The crown of Mae's head came just above the level of Fanny's chin; a blond curl tickled her cheek.

"She died and left some of her things here." Matter-of-fact.

Grace had spoken so wistfully about her mother, Mae's tutor. "Didn't she have any family to give her belongings to?"

Mae shrugged. "I wouldn't know."

Fanny held the dress at arm's length, trying to imagine Grace's mother. Mae's indifference chilled her. "What did she die from?"

Pushing lightly on Fanny's elbow, Mae said, "You should try it on."

"Did you like her?"

"She was fine, I suppose." Mae pulled away, crossed her arms. She looked out the windows with a bored expression.

Fanny draped the dresses over her arm. "Thank you, miss. This is so kind of you." She moved toward the boudoir, but Mae stopped her with an imperious clap of her hands.

"You can change right here," Mae said. "After all, I have to change in front of you. Turnabout is fair play." On the last phrase, Mae twirled, her robe flaring.

Fanny wasn't opposed to undressing in front of others; she'd had little choice at home. She undid the buttons of her dress, but remembered that she was wearing undergarments stolen from Mae's laundry, and she froze.

"Go on!" Mae bounced on her toes like a child impatient to reveal the gift she had brought.

Hesitantly, Fanny shrugged one arm out of a sleeve.

"Oh, for the love of Saint Christopher, I will look away if you are so shy." This was followed by an amused huff.

Fanny got into the new dress as quickly as she could. Mae was looking at her with anticipation when she turned around; she took Fanny's hand, making her twist from side to side, smiling her approval.

The other two dresses came next; when Fanny shed the first, Mae showed no sign of recognizing the pilfered underwear. Fanny felt like a doll being clothed to please her owner, but her heart thumped happily at the attention she was receiving, and she played along, spinning when asked, admiring the cut of the dresses in the gilt-framed mirror. When they were done, Mae declared the russet frock with a v-shaped waist to be her favorite. "You must wear this one today," she said, "and after you do my hair, I will do yours. You look too dowdy with it coiled up like that."

Fanny didn't properly understand her duties, but she was certain that being fussed over by Mae wasn't one of them. "Miss, I should make up your bed and fetch you some food, as you haven't broken your fast yet this morning."

Mae rolled her eyes. In the bright light of the windows, her near-invisible lashes glowed, revealing their sweeping length. "It is almost lunchtime. And we need to sort out where you will sleep—now that you are my personal maid, you must be near me."

Fanny cradled her sharp elbows with her hands, not quite hugging herself. Her feelings were unfocused—a flush of warmth at Mae's friendliness, uneasiness about Grace catching her wearing her mother's clothing, concern about Mrs. Williams's displeasure, and, snaking beneath it all, a vague feeling that this was somehow all wrong. "Can I not continue to use Dena's bed?" she said.

"She's coming back soon. The housekeeper told me when she brought roses this morning. Of course that was just a pretext to wake me up and get me down to breakfast for Mother. I told her that *I* was staying in bed, and *you* were staying on the staff."

Fanny felt a jolt of fear—so Mrs. Williams was still working to have her dismissed.

"She says it's not proper to elevate you to lady's maid when you are so young and have no experience. I told her that I was keeping you."

Mae sounded jaunty, but Fanny was not convinced that she had the power in the household that she seemed to think she had. She was only a seventeen-year-old girl.

"It's her British snobbery," Mae continued. "She thinks Americans don't know anything about servants." She shook her head and pursed her lips disapprovingly. In a poor imitation of Mrs. Williams's accent, she said, "I don't give a fig what that woman says." She poked Fanny's shoulder with a finger, smiling. "Now let's make my hair pretty."

When Mae went down to lunch, Fanny continued to tidy the bedroom, trying to ignore her hunger pangs. She wanted to sneak to the kitchen to get some food and to see Grace, to know that Grace had forgiven her for her crossness the night before. She couldn't bear the thought of running into Mrs. Williams, however, who was apparently itching to be rid of her, and she was embarrassed to be seen wearing Grace's mother's dress, her hair styled in a bouffant by Mae's nimble hands.

The door banged open, and Mae burst back into the room, her cheeks pink. "Come, Fanny! We're going shopping!" She went to her wardrobe and selected a fur-trimmed coat.

Fanny hurried over to help.

"I tried to convince Mother to let you have the guest room next door to me," Mae said as she shimmied her arms into the coat Fanny held. "I should never have brought it up with Mrs. Williams within earshot. Of course the old biddy was *horrified* by the idea." She brushed off Fanny's silent offer to do the buttons.

"Miss, my cloak is up—"

"And Mother is so cowed by her own housekeeper. Ridiculous." Mae cinched the belt.

"I should fetch—" Fanny gestured toward the door.

"But no matter," Mae said, tossing Fanny a bright red coat from her wardrobe. "The divan in here is so comfortable that it can be used as a bed."

Mae walked briskly to the hall, glancing over her shoulder. "Well, come along! The carriage is ready!"

Thus, Fanny became Mae's roommate.

It was the first time Fanny had taken the front stairs, with its cabbage-rose garland carpeting and heavy mahogany railings, lines of curved and glossy balusters. Mae trotted quickly down, her skirt softly ballooning, her ringlets bouncing. She led Fanny to a back entrance that opened toward the stables.

The periwinkle sky was cloudless, and a fresh layer of snow blanketed the ground, intensifying the dazzling sunlight. A gray stepper hitched to a brougham shook its mane and snorted, its breath fogging in the wintry air. It pawed at the gravel, and the driver shushed the horse in gentle tones. Mae hopped into the carriage, waving at Fanny to follow. They drove out the side entrance, past gateposts topped by cast iron lamps.

"We are going to the 'busy store,' the new one, Crow and Whitmarsh." Mae removed a pair of gloves from the pocket of her coat and wriggled her hands into them, then took up the strings of her purse once more.

Fanny tucked her reddened, calloused fingers into her palms, willing her hands to be daintier.

The carriage bumped over cobblestones, and the girls swayed in unison in the cushioned seat. Mae stretched out her legs and crossed her ankles; the patent leather toes of her boots peeked out from under her frilly petticoat. "Mother brings in all of our clothes from New York, of course," she said. "But Whitmarsh is good for the basics."

Euclid Avenue looked different when framed by the windows of the brougham—less overwhelming, more like a fanciful painting. Mae sat with a straight back, her chin slightly lifted; her hair had the warm tint of honey in the sunlight, and the garnets in her ears glinted. Fanny saw her as a princess riding through her realm, surveying her lands.

"If I can convince Papa to take us to Paris, you will have to come, too," Mae said. "We need you to be properly dressed."

Fanny was overcome. Her life had been surreal since stepping across the threshold of the Garth mansion, but at the mention of foreign travel, it burst into a kaleidoscopic dreamscape. She thought, *Why me?* and then realized that she had said it out loud.

A tiny crease surfaced and vanished at the side of Mae's mouth as if she were suppressing a laugh. Fanny's cheeks burned.

"You have potential," Mae said, her eyes bright with amusement. "And I didn't want some old biddy the housekeeper chose for me, someone *proper* and *sensible*. You're not some timid, boring calf like the other servants."

Fanny thought of Grace, who was neither timid nor boring, with a twinge of guilt.

The driver took a corner at a brisk trot, and the radial force sent Fanny sliding helplessly toward Mae, jostling against her, while Mae braced her gloved hand against the carriage door. For a moment they were pressed together, the thick wool of their coats muffling the troublesome intimacy of accidental touch. Fanny imagined that she could feel the rise and fall of Mae's breath, slight as a butterfly wing against her side. The turn slackened, and Fanny scrabbled back to her former seat on the bench. Mae dropped her arm and went on as though nothing had happened. "Remember when you first came to my room, and you said that I had beautiful eyes?"

Fanny, mortified, could remember no such thing.

"You watched me dance with such a canny look, just one of your dimples showing." Mae touched her own cheek with her index finger and smiled. "You looked like someone with mischief up your sleeve."

Fanny felt like a fraud. Nevertheless, she realized that she was smiling too, and that realization brought new confidence. "I can help you in any way you need, miss." She looked Mae directly in the eye, intuiting that it was the moment required. "Especially if that involves mischief."

Mae laughed with delight.

CHAPTER 14

Crow and Whitmarsh was palatial, teeming with customers, the clothing and household items arranged in color-coordinated displays of tasteful opulence. The chandeliers were lit, casting a lead crystal shimmer, even though sunlight streamed through the windows. Counters were rose marble, potted plants tropical, attendants solicitous, the air filled with tinkling piano music and perfume. Mae knew the store well, and led a disoriented Fanny from department to department, cooing over pretty clothes and notions. She bought cream puffs at the tea counter, and even if Fanny hadn't been famished, they would have seemed like clouds angels gamboled upon. Her tongue had seldom tasted sweetness, let alone tender pastry oozing with luscious custard and whipped cream, powdered with sugar and magic.

It quickly became clear that the beneficiary of this shopping excursion was principally Fanny. Though Mae bought herself some hair ribbons, almond bark, and French-style hosiery, for Fanny she purchased nightclothes, underclothes, boots, stockings, and a warm coat and hat to match. Fanny carried a tottering pile of boxes into the Garth mansion, numb from excess.

Back in Mae's room, Fanny was jubilant, helping Mae tear apart tissue paper wrapping, throwing it into the air like streamers. At her mistress's insistence, Fanny modeled the new clothing, paraded jauntily as Mae laughed and clapped her hands. Fanny made a deep curtsy, then fell theatrically to her knees. Mae beckoned Fanny closer, indicating that she wished her to lean her chin on her lap; the velvet skirt was soft against her throat. Mae held out a piece of almond bark, teasing her like a pet, snatching the treat back whenever Fanny tried to take a bite. Finally she relented, sliding to the floor, an arm slung around Fanny's waist. They gobbled up the box of almond bark, so sugary sweet that it hurt Fanny's teeth; when Mae requested milk to wash it down, Fanny rose and trotted down to the kitchen, the pert heels on her new boots clicking prettily.

Mrs. Campbell was pounding a sinewy leg of lamb with a meat mallet, her round face flushed, and only grunted in response to Fanny's greeting. Fanny breathed in the oniony scent of a stew bubbling on the stove. She opened the first of three iceboxes, looking for milk. An unwrapped chunk of dry cheese appeared neglected, so she stuffed it in the pocket of her skirt. In the second icebox she found a row of milk bottles beaded with condensation, a thick layer of cream on top; she grabbed one and went in search of cups.

As Fanny opened the cupboard, Grace emerged from the pantry, a basket of potatoes balanced on her hip. Grace stopped abruptly, her eyes wide but her face stony. Fanny's spirit plummeted, knowing what a sight Grace was taking in: Fanny, with her newly styled hair, cheeks powdered with strawberry rouge that the shopgirl said was the "natural look everyone nowadays wants." Grace's mother's dress, the skirt flaring over a new rose-colored crinoline.

Fanny felt the surge of Grace's sadness rise up to swamp her. "It wasn't my idea," she mumbled. Too late—Grace had moved on, asking Mrs. Campbell what was needed for the potatoes.

A dull pain clamped around Fanny's heart and lungs. She stood with one hand on the cupboard, following Grace with her eyes; her neat back in the plain black dress was a rebuke. *Never mind*, she thought. If Grace couldn't be happy that she had found stable employment and a convivial mistress, then perhaps she had never been Grace's friend. Still, the pain did not relent. Fanny took the milk and cups and mounted the steps, careful not to trip over her swaying skirts.

Fanny's days and nights were a strange mix of servitude and companionship. At times, Mae kept her close, bantering and giggling, sharing her food. Other times she ordered Fanny about or pushed her away. The cloistered, humid nature of their existence in a closed suite of rooms, combined with Mae's fickle temperament, kept Fanny obsessed with Mae's moods. Even when she took meals in the kitchen with the other servants, Fanny didn't listen to the gossip or brood about Grace giving her the cold shoulder; instead, she reviewed in her mind every recent interaction with Mae, scanning what she remembered of her words, inflection, posture. In her thoughts, she tried to edit out her own clumsiness, her faux pas, and focus on those moments when Mae was like sun glitter on water. She blamed the poor treatment she sometimes received on Mae's sheltered life; a lack of hardship could, she supposed, lead to a lack of empathy, and any time Fanny betrayed hurt feelings, Mae was quick to shower her with attention. Mae was, she told herself, a good person.

Fanny learned about fashion when she helped Mae dress for her outings, and she heard the details of the dinners and soirées Mae attended. She grew to understand who held power in the upper-crust society of Cleveland, who was considered modish or foppish, and who had social convening influence and who did not. Mae had a startlingly good memory for colloquy, and repeated whole conversations back to

Fanny in a way that sounded verbatim, as she brought in individual verbal tics and word stylings.

There wasn't enough work to keep Fanny busy all day and evening, so she asked Mae to lend her books from the family's library. To be funny, Mae brought some of her father's driest tomes, along with novels and romances. Fanny grimaced and slid the gold-lettered albums away to make Mae smile, but when Mae was gone, she pulled the spurned books back, studying them with dogged determination. She didn't understand everything she read about finance and business, but it made her feel like she was peering through curtains into a smoke-filled, deep-voiced, belly-laughing realm of powerful men. To hold the reins of a financial empire—how exhilarating that would be! She was particularly enthralled with a book called *On the Principles of Political Economy and Taxation*; the idea that competing and common interests didn't need to be at odds was a revelation to her. It was possible for both parties to get what they wanted, as long as they were clever about seeing the full picture and understanding one another's true interests. A queer little story called "Bartleby, the Scrivener" also struck Fanny, though for very different reasons. The absurdity of life as a menial clerk on Wall Street made her see that the gold dust of success did not come from merely brushing shoulders with the prosperous.

At night, as she lay in bed, Fanny imagined that she had been born a boy, one with an inheritance and a powerful father to help her climb the ladder to heady heights of influence and wealth. The dreams were so real that she sometimes woke to the surprise of her doughy girl body, the scratchy linen of a cheap nightgown, menstrual cramps auguring an uncomfortable few days of blood-sodden rags. It was the lot she had rolled, as her father might say, but Fanny did not want to accept it.

Wintry gusts gave way to soft breezes, and snow, slumped and soiled, melted away. From the tall windows in Mae's room, Fanny watched a dense embankment of clouds, muddy gray, building on the horizon, while Mae jumped out of bed and padded over to her. She leaned her head against Fanny's shoulder; her hair tickled where it touched Fanny's neck, and she had a babyish milk scent of sleep.

"I had a dream," Mae said. She put her hand on Fanny's back; her thumb pressed lightly into the hollow at the edge of Fanny's shoulder blade, and Fanny felt that place loosen.

Mae continued, "I had a dream that you were by my side walking down a grand staircase, and everyone below looked up with wonder."

Fanny breathed out a sound of amusement.

"I was wearing the dress we saw in the magazine, a silvery satin with pale blue side panels, an empire waist with a diamond clasp." She touched a finger to the base of her sternum. "You had an ostrich-feather fan. There was lovely music." Mae hummed a few bars and waltzed in a circle around Fanny. She smiled in a self-satisfied manner. "Oh!" Mae said, her blue eyes widening. "Wouldn't it be fun if you attended the party tonight, the Lollie Berwick affair?"

Fanny blinked, uncomprehending.

"You could pretend to be my second or third cousin, come from Pittsburgh or Toledo or somewhere like that?"

The blank brilliance of possibility filled Fanny's mind.

"It will be dull, a tea party, really. But having you there would be so amusing!" Mae's laugh had the subtle huskiness conferred by cobwebs of sleep. She gathered up her hair and coiled it on the crown of her head. "You must come. It is decided." She was a princess, high in her white palace.

Fanny studied the hangnail on her smallest finger. She pressed on it so that it hurt, but even the pain was sweet. Gloves could hide her work-worn hands.

"None of my dresses would fit you," Mae mused, "but I could take one of Mother's, and she would never notice. A bit short on you maybe, but ample room in the seams."

Could she pass? She badly wanted to try.

"They won't know anything. This is just for Lollie's so-called friends, and her parents won't pay any heed to who comes and goes."

Mae's sense of adventure lifted Fanny's spirit further; she was soaring. She was too exultant to speak calmly, yet somehow her voice was steady. "If you're certain that I won't get you into any trouble, miss, I'm happy to oblige."

Mae chose to wear one of her more sedate gowns that evening, crêpe de chine with puffed sleeves and a high collar. With a flourish, she presented a green moiré for Fanny to wear.

"Mother can't squeeze into it anymore," said Mae. "She probably doesn't even remember she owns it." She held the dress against Fanny's body, pressing the fabric against her hips, estimating the fit. "Still, you will need to cover it with your coat when we go downstairs."

Fanny nodded solemnly, her heart jumping.

"Oh!" said Mae. "How it complements your eyes."

Mae draped the dress on the bed and revealed the bottle of champagne in her bag. "Snuck it from the wine cellar." She grinned.

Fanny had difficulty removing the cork, and when it popped, Mae squeaked with surprise, then laughed as froth gushed from the neck of the bottle, ran over Fanny's fingers and splatted onto the floor. As Fanny cleaned up the spill with her handkerchief, Mae poured champagne into china teacups. "Don't you love how the bubbles tickle your nose?"

Fanny stuffed the wet handkerchief back in her pocket. It was all so strange, this frothing mess. She just smiled.

"Come, time to toast!" Mae picked up the teacups and handed one to Fanny. "To my dear cousin." She lifted her cup high. "What shall we call you?"

Fanny held her cup aloft. She said the first thing that came to mind. "If we are to get up to mischief, perhaps I should be Brontë's Catherine. She never follows the rules."

Mae stepped closer. "To Catherine." The corner of her mouth curved up. "I shall call you Kitty." She tapped her cup against Fanny's and took a sip. Her plump lower lip glistened with champagne. "Tonight will be so amusing."

They left in the gloaming, the murk of a mud-scented early spring twilight. The clop of the horse's hooves sounded lonely as they made their way farther from the city, down Euclid Avenue to its pastoral reaches. In the carriage, Mae held Fanny's gloved hand, as though they were indeed cousins. Fanny felt transformed by her costume, a rope of pearls around her neck, the light, silky texture of the dress against her skin. Mae had loaned her jeweled combs for her hair and fine stockings with lace garters.

Mae leaned close and spoke in a low voice, as though someone might overhear. "You're from Pittsburgh, and you have come to stay with me because your fiancé jilted you." Her breath was sweet with wine. "That way, if you are quiet, everyone will understand."

Fanny closed her eyes; champagne fizzed in her veins. With a stab of boldness, she squeezed Mae's hand. "Dear cousin," she said.

Mae laughed.

The house they approached in the gathering darkness was many-peaked and cross-beamed, warm light spilling from the windows. The drive took them past marble lions and bare elms, stiff as a line of soldiers. A servant in a black suit opened the door and ushered them into a hall with an ebony and straw-colored parquet floor, walls covered with flocked paper, and a ceiling with cherubs frolicking on cottony clouds. Fanny held her arms close to her body, feeling unworthy to touch even the air that surrounded her.

In the parlor, about a dozen young men and women were scattered, leaning against the mantelpiece, stretched out in divans, perched on footstools. Many of them sipped a tangerine-colored drink from cut-crystal coupe glasses that glinted in the light from the chandeliers. In one corner, a scruffy-haired boy with acne was having a heated discussion with a bespectacled, tall lad whose waistcoat gaped as if it was made for a larger man. A trio of girls on a settee, all dressed in pastel satins ornamented with lace, leaned their heads close together, ringlets bobbing. A card game was being played at one of the tables, where evidently a witty comment was made, because all of the players burst into laughter.

The French doors to the adjoining parlor were wide open; blue cigar smoke curled out. A group of older men were conversing there and no doubt providing disincentive for misbehavior by the youths.

"Mae, you are always late!" An attractive girl with wide-set eyes approached, smiling broadly. She was plump, and Fanny was startled to see the tops of her breasts spilling from her decolletage, a pair of glowing crescent moons. "Well, I'm glad you came." She held out a hand to Mae.

"I would never miss one of your lovely soirées." She took the girl's hand and turned slightly to include Fanny. "This is my cousin Kitty, visiting from out of town. Kitty, this is our hostess—or, I should say, hostess's daughter, Lollie Berwick."

In the looks exchanged between Mae and Lollie, it was evident that Mae had the upper hand. Lollie's expression verged on worshipful. She broke away and said to Fanny, "So glad that you could join us this evening. Just a little congregation for young people." She covered her mouth as she tittered sociably. "Very casual."

Fanny noted how many heads in the room had turned toward Mae. A young man with a self-consciously proper bearing and fashionably cut tailcoat brought glasses of cordial to present to the pair of them. With a little bow, he held out the coupes, his attention beaming in Mae's direction. "A drink for the ladies, and cheers to your good health," he said.

Mae smiled imperiously as she took her cup. Fanny curved her satin-gloved fingers around the graven crystal and watched desultory bubbles break the syrupy surface of the strange-colored liquid. She found herself saying, "Where is your glass, gallant sir, so that we may toast to your health as well?" She had so convinced herself that she was Mae's cousin that she spoke with jesting familiarity, in a voice she hardly recognized as her own.

The boy blushed but looked pleased.

"Also," Fanny continued, "this will give you time to think of a nice toast for Miss Mae. But remember: women are never disarmed by compliments. Only men are. That is the difference between you and the wiser sex."

Mae let out a throaty laugh.

"Gregory, may I present my silver-tongued cousin, Kitty. Kitty, I present Gregory Peabody." Mae bestowed another glowing smile on the boy.

"Charmed to meet you, Gregory," Fanny said. "You should fetch your drink forthwith. 'Tisn't polite to keep ladies waiting to toast, particularly when they are parched, as we are."

As the boy scurried away, Mae grabbed Fanny's arm and put her mouth so close to Fanny's ear that her breath tickled. "This will be even more amusing than I had hoped," she whispered delightedly.

When Gregory returned, he brought several other youths in tow. A young woman in a sapphire gown stepped forward, a lopsided grin on her plain, snub-nosed face. "Hello, Mae," she said with a sardonic raise of her glass.

Mae tensed, gripped Fanny's arm more tightly.

"I hear you suddenly have a new cousin," the girl said. She didn't bother to look at Fanny. "How very strange. I will have to speak with your mother to learn all of the particulars."

"Isabelle." Mae's enthusiasm had vanished. "How lovely to see you."

Fanny's unmerited confidence also evaporated. They had been found out, and it was clear from Mae's expression that she feared her parents' reactions to her hijinks. It would be worse for Fanny, who would lose her job.

"You were always fond of playing childish games." Isabelle commanded the space around her in a way that, even in her queasy apprehension, Fanny couldn't help but admire. Isabelle spoke in a low register with clear, unhurried diction. "I should think that you are too old for such things now, Mae."

The small group watched with anticipation, but Mae seemed frozen, apart from the clenching and unclenching of her hand on Fanny's forearm. It was up to Fanny to protect them both. She heard herself say, "Time for our toast!" in a surprisingly enthusiastic voice. She touched her coupe to Isabelle's glass, still raised at half-mast, more firmly than necessary, then to Gregory's and Mae's.

Isabelle looked sour. She addressed Fanny directly. "You are not my relative, and I know for a fact that Mr. Garth's brother does not have a daughter."

Fanny could feel the blood drumming in her temples. As most of her notions of polite society came from novels, she said, "If you are Mae's dear cousin, you are therefore my cousin also." Why hadn't she and Mae come up with a more precise cover story? She took a drink of her sweet cocktail.

Isabelle watched her with half-hooded eyes, Mae with overly wide ones.

"I am a second cousin on the Garth side of the family," Fanny said more smoothly than she had thought possible. "My mother grew up mostly abroad, so she didn't see much of Mae's father in her childhood." She smiled at her little audience, noting that she had their full attention. "I won't bore you with a long story, but after my father left us, we fell on hard times. Mama had to work in a garment factory, and she died of consumption." She paused on this sad note, observing the sympathetic looks she was getting. "It's a painful subject for Mr. Garth, who feels that he should have done more to help." She patted the hand that gripped her arm. "Isn't that so, Mae?"

Mae let go of Fanny's arm and set down her cocktail. "Kitty is right, we never speak of it," she said quietly, her expression mournful. "Poor Papa can't forgive himself."

Fanny felt a rush of pleasure at how well Mae played her part.

Though Isabelle still looked skeptical, Fanny could tell that the murmured condolences of others were having an effect. She decided to press her advantage. "I am so very happy to meet you at last, Isabelle," Fanny said.

At this unexpected turn, there was a subtle rearing back of Isabelle's head and shoulders, like a horse spotting a hazard.

Fanny plunged on. "Mae has told me so much about your accomplishments." She stepped closer, as though she had something to confide. "I sometimes wonder if she is envious of you."

Isabelle seemed off-balance, unsure how to react. The rest of the group was losing interest and resuming conversation among themselves.

"You absolutely *must* tell me about that—oh, I am so stupid, what did Mae call it?" Fanny gave a self-deprecating shake of her head. "She said that you received ever so many compliments . . ."

Isabelle said, "The painting?"

"Yes!" Fanny nearly spilled what was left of her drink in her eagerness.

Isabelle smiled at Mae, almost fondly this time. "Don't tell me you've been talking about my art."

"You are so talented!" Mae sounded so genuine that Fanny almost believed her.

"She brags about being your cousin," Fanny said. "And though we aren't blood relatives, I am going to brag about you, too." She linked her arm through Isabelle's. "Come, cousin, let's refill that glass for you."

"Excellent idea," Isabelle said, apparently mollified. "Do you paint, Kitty?"

As they walked away, Fanny caught Mae's eye and winked.

CHAPTER 15

Mae and Fanny returned from Lollie's sorée tipsy and giggling, leaning on one another as they traversed the rain-slippery flagstones to the back door.

"Isabelle's face when you complimented her . . . It was too funny!" Mae's foot skidded out from under her, but Fanny steadied her.

"Of course women are *never* disarmed by compliments," Fanny said.

A sudden gust of wind caused them both to clamp their free hands down on their hats, which set off another fit of giggles.

"And when you said to that boy, 'Of course Pittsburgh is within walking distance . . . as long as you have a couple of weeks to spare,' I laughed so hard, bubbly nearly came out my nose!" Mae hugged Fanny's arm. "You really are witty. Did you see the way Walter Firth looked at you? I think he is raaahther"—drawing out the vowel—"enamored of you."

Since winning over Isabelle, Fanny had been floating, the warmth of alcohol coursing through her veins. "Pish posh," she said with a flick of her wrist. "Everyone is enamored of *you*. You have them aaahl in your thraaahll."

With an amused groan, Mae bunted with her shoulder and took Fanny's hand in hers. They opened the back door a crack and peeked in; all was quiet and dark. They had stayed out past curfew, so Mae wanted to creep up the servants' stairs to avoid detection on the front staircase.

"Mother wakes at the slightest creak," she whispered.

In the hallway leading to her room, Mae showed Fanny which parts of the floorboards to sidestep in order not to make noise. With the bedroom door firmly closed behind them, they laughed like scofflaws finally safe in their lair, peeling off gloves and doffing coats and hats, heedlessly tossing them on the floor. Mae threw her arms around Fanny, then twirled away.

"Help me out of my dress," she said.

Fanny could make out little more than Mae's outline in the darkness; she lit the lamp on the bedside table, which bathed her in soft light, but a writhing column of smoke smudged the space between them. Mae approached her with a crooked smile. "My maid hasn't kept the wick properly trimmed." She picked up the lamp and examined it, her fingers pausing on the key while she gazed at Fanny. Slowly, she turned down the wick, removed the globe and blew out the flame. "'We waste our lights in vain, like lamps by day,'" she murmured.

Fanny was unfamiliar with the quotation, but it made her shiver. By the faint glow of the moon and streetlights, Fanny carefully undid the tiny covered buttons on Mae's gown, then unlaced her stays. She could not make out the pink lines the boning must have made on such pale skin; in the darkness, she imagined how those shallow furrows would feel under her fingertips.

Mae heaved a sigh of satisfaction. "I am so content here," she said. "This quiet, just the two of us." She covered Fanny's hand with her own, pressing it to her shoulder, where Fanny had been lifting off her gown. "So much better than plebeian chatter in a vulgar drawing room."

The meaning of *plebeian* was lost on Fanny, and she didn't care for Mae's pretensions, yet the tone of her voice was like warmed honey on buttered toast.

Fanny helped her step out of her gown and undergarments, and tenderly lifted a fresh nightgown over her head. Like a sleepy child, Mae obediently pushed her arms into the sleeves, and Fanny released the bunched satin, let it slither over Mae's slim body until the hem came to a stop, brushing against her ankles.

"I'm so tired." Mae took the pins from her hair and handed them to Fanny. "I will leave washing up for the morning." She yawned, stretched languorously and turned toward bed.

"Your jewelry, miss." With those words, Fanny felt the last vestige of Kitty leave the bedchamber.

Mae made a small sound of recognition and removed her necklace and earrings. "Thank you, Fanny," she said. "Be sure to hang my hat where it can dry. It got quite wet."

The jewels were heavy in Fanny's hand, still warm from Mae's skin. "Yes, miss." There was no sparkle in the darkness, but the gleam of gems and gold was all the more compelling, moonglow instead of sun brightness. Before laying them away in the mahogany jewelry box, she draped the necklace over her inner arm, twisting slightly this way and that to observe the craftsmanship. Each small diamond was surrounded by a corona of perfectly matched amethysts. She found herself hesitating to return them to the box.

The flop and cough of Mae arranging herself in bed brought her back to the moment. She carefully placed the jewels in their velvet nest. In the boudoir, Fanny undressed as quietly as she could, pulling on the linen nightgown Mae had given her. The excitement of the evening leaked from her body along with the agreeable fizz of alcohol, leaving her feeling dull. She went to her makeshift bed and lay under the blanket, listening for the sound of Mae's breathing.

The rain started up again, pelting loudly against the windowpanes when the wind gusted. The onslaught raged and abated haphazardly, like a drunken bully. Fanny tucked her blanket tighter and burrowed into her pillow, trying to keep intrusive thoughts from dispersing the gathering fog of sleep.

"Kitty?" Mae's whisper was tentative.

Fanny didn't answer right away. She wasn't Kitty anymore, was she?

"Are you awake?" The whisper louder.

A burst of rain pounded against the window; wind groaned in the chimney. Fanny raised herself up on her elbow. "I'm awake," she said.

"Could you come over here? Please?" This was uncharacteristically soft, even pleading.

Fanny slid her feet to the floor, and wrapped herself in a quilt. She went to Mae's bedside and stood uncertainly, trying to make out her form in the darkness.

The bedclothes rustled and the frame squeaked. "Here, lie down a moment."

Fanny edged onto the mattress, careful not to jostle. She lay stiff-limbed, wrapped up in her quilt like a mummy.

"Get under the covers, silly." Mae's voice was still hushed, but she sounded more imperious, more like herself. She pulled back the bedclothes, and Fanny shed her blanket, abandoning it on the floor. She slithered cautiously between the sheets, aware of the trapped heat from Mae's body, someone else's cocoon. The pillow was so downy that Fanny had the dreamlike sense of falling, as she had, when a child, into a pile of freshly cut hay.

"I was thinking you could come with me to my great-aunt Millie's house. In Newport." Mae was lying on her back, her arms stretched over her head. "Once we get there, we could pretend that you are my impoverished cousin who is in need of my patronage." She turned to her side, toward Fanny. A flash of lightning illuminated her features, still as a graven statue, but when thunder rolled, she reached for Fanny's hand. She touched her forehead to Fanny's shoulder. "I'm not really afraid of thunder," she whispered.

Fanny believed her. As for Mae's vision of Newport, she held her tongue in mute anticipation.

"I go for the whole summer, and my parents only come for two weeks, if at all." Her mouth was close to Fanny's ear; though the rain spattered loudly, her words were clear. She squeezed her hand. "Aunt Millie is doddering and pays no attention. We could have such a merry time!"

Fanny tried to imagine what this might mean. "Would we be companions, then?"

There was a brief silence. Fanny could feel the coldness of Mae's nose through the fabric of her sleeve.

"I fancy that it would be like tonight! We would deceive all of those boring people into believing that you come from excellent stock but have fallen on bad times. We could make up any story we wished." She paused, sucked in air through her teeth, something she did when she was thinking. "Well, maybe we even try to find you a suitor."

Fanny stiffened, but Mae laughed. "Just for our own amusement, of course. We could have such an enchanting summer, both of us, scheming among those tedious people."

Mae snaked her arm around Fanny's waist and burrowed her face into the crook of her neck. Another peal of thunder rolled across the heavens, but Mae did not flinch. Fanny felt so light, a dandelion seed spinning in the breeze. She wanted never to land.

The next morning, Fanny woke with a start when Mae, still asleep, kicked her. As her memories gathered like a flock of starlings landing by ones and twos, and then by the dozen, she relished the nearness of Mae and the satiny feel of the sheets against her bare arms. She raised her head to gaze at Mae, but the other girl flopped away with a soft groan and covered her face with her pillow. Fanny came to her senses and slinked out of bed.

Mae would welcome tea and apple juice, Fanny knew, and probably not biscuits, but she brought those from the kitchen, too. She set up the meager breakfast on a side table and proceeded to tidy the room, conscious of every movement and sound Mae made.

"I'm so thirsty," Mae rasped finally.

Fanny rushed to her side with the watered-down juice she liked. Mae propped her head on her hand and took a long draft, then coughed and dropped back down, eyes closed. She seemed ready to fall back asleep, but then shoved and kicked off her bedcovers in an irritated way. "My head hurts," she said.

Fanny sat down gently on the bed beside her, thinking she might press a soothing hand to Mae's forehead the way her mother used to.

"Stop jostling me. Get off," Mae whined. "Get me a cold compress."

The loss Fanny felt was in proportion to her joy the night before. It was like stepping from the most glorious garden on a summer's day into the cold gray of winter, like taking a starving bite of fresh bread only to have it snatched away. Her whole body felt heavy and numb as she prepared the compress.

By the time Fanny returned to Mae's bedside, Mae had fallen asleep again. She slept for hours more, then woke with a luxurious stretch. "There you are," Mae said to Fanny, who was sitting on the window seat;

she had been turning the pages of a book, not really reading, nervously wondering what she was meant to be doing. Fanny rose hesitantly.

"What's wrong?" Mae asked, her pretty brow furrowed.

"Are you feeling better, miss?"

"We're not back to this 'miss' thing again, are we?" Mae smiled, stretched again with a happy sigh. "We did have great fun last night, didn't we?"

Fanny's heart thudded almost painfully; she was caught in a snarl of strong feelings she could not untangle. Mae went to her, took both her hands, and squeezed them gently. Her skin felt so soft. Mae beamed at her. "I'm so grateful to have found you," she said.

When Fanny encountered Grace during the course of her workday, Grace was always polite but too busy to talk. Fanny considered going to her room in the evening to try to reestablish their rapport, but she had to attend to Mae at bedtime, and the more time passed, the more awkward she felt. On the eve of their departure to Newport, Grace stopped her in the servants' staircase and pulled her to the side, into a corner of the landing. The sweet scent of her hair conditioner gave Fanny a pang of wistfulness.

"You're off to spend the summer in Newport," Grace said matter-of-factly.

"Mae asked me to go with her . . ." It was a weak start, and Fanny was about to amend it when Grace started speaking again, evidently in a rush to get back to her tasks.

"I want to say something to you before you leave." The little crease appeared on Grace's forehead, as it often did when she was concentrating. "I supported you in your lies so you could be hired here," she said in a hushed voice. "I don't regret it. But Fanny, I hope you don't carry on down that road."

"I don't really—I'm not on a road of any kind."

Grace put a hand on her shoulder and looked into her eyes. "I don't think God minds if you tell a little fib now and then, just to get by. But if you follow Mae Garth into any trouble, she will skate away free, and you won't. That's all I'm going to say."

There was no point in protesting, Fanny realized, so she just nodded. "Perhaps we can do something together when I get back?" she said. "Maybe go rowing on the lake?"

Grace gave her a tight smile. "I wish you safe travels."

CHAPTER 16

Aunt Millie's house boasted three stories and twenty rooms—a humble structure, by Newport standards. Mae didn't hide her disdain; she had announced to Fanny before leaving Cleveland that they would spend as little time as possible under that roof.

Summer was in full swing when they arrived, with yachts swanning off the coast and lilac-perfumed garden parties buzzing—flounced, beribboned little girls chased by boys in straw hats, champagne-soaked nights, revelers reeling giddily under winking stars, orchestral strains floating on the sea breeze.

On the first day, Mae went alone to greet her aunt. She reported to Fanny that Aunt Millie was still in her chambers, wearing her morning wrapper. Confusion over Fanny's "mistaken" identity as a maid was swiftly cleared up; Mae assured Aunt Mille that Fanny was family, claiming that since her mother had written, travel plans had changed. She hadn't expected her poor cousin to show up on her doorstep, after all.

Mae proposed a stroll to Fanny, and the pair ventured out under matching pink parasols. Mae's white dress rippled in the soft July breeze; her face shone with morning freshness.

"We'll go first along the shore, which is a lovely walk, and I will point out all of the best summer homes." There was a smile in Mae's voice that delighted Fanny.

Down the drive, fine gravel crunched beneath their neat low-heeled shoes; a pair of chimney swifts darted across the spotless sky. Mae took Fanny's hand and swung her arm like they were little girls. "We will have such fun," she said, prancing for a few steps.

They rounded a corner onto a sparsely populated residential street; a small barouche passed them by, the horse clopping wearily along the bricks, its neck drooping. From farther down the street, a pair of casually dressed male pedestrians approached, one speaking and gesticulating energetically, while the other, head inclined forward, appeared to listen intently. Though the listener's face was partly obscured by the brim of his hat, something about him was familiar to Fanny. Mae followed Fanny's line of sight, glancing at the two men. She slowed, dropped Fanny's hand. "That's Joe," she said.

Fanny remembered then the earnest young man with floppy hair who had visited the Garths earlier in the year. "But that's your cousin," she said in a low voice, her joy giving way to alarm. He would know that Fanny wasn't a family member, and worse, he might recognize her as a servant from Cleveland.

Mae had already recovered from her surprise, however, and the spring came back to her step. "He's my mother's nephew," she said. "He doesn't know anything about Father's side of the family. Besides, we're just girls. He won't give us much thought."

Indeed, even though Mae walked straight toward him, Joseph didn't notice her until she called his name. He looked up abruptly, and his companion cut short his monologue, frowning.

"Why, Mae, what a pleasure!" Joseph said. "I didn't know you were in Newport." He tipped his hat toward Fanny, turned back to Mae. "Where are you staying?"

"At my great-aunt Millie's," she said in a chipper voice. "As usual. I come every summer."

He seemed slightly flustered. "Of course. I don't think I know your aunt." He gestured toward his companion. "This is Chauncey Cooper," he said. "He's invited me to stay."

"Charmed," Mae said, with a slight bow of her head.

"Likewise," Cooper said, sounding bored. He checked his pocket watch.

A pause ensued. Joseph smiled at Mae, looked back toward Cooper.

"We were just going to the fishermen's path," Mae volunteered.

"A beautiful walk!" Joseph had found his exit. "I hope that you both have a lovely time." He tipped his hat again. "I hope you come visit us soon, Mae."

"So nice to run into you, Joe," Mae said.

The girls walked on. "I never visit that part of the family," Mae said when they were out of earshot. "They are so bourgeois."

Fanny acknowledged her distractedly. She was thinking about how being unimportant is the same as being invisible.

The fishermen's path took them along steep bluffs, shining ocean on one side, palatial mansions with verdant, soigné lawns on the other. Fanny contemplated the imposing facades of what Mae called "the villas," wondering what went on behind the flashing windows. The ornamented casements and sky-reflecting glass gave her the impression of picture frames awaiting their subjects; there was something lonely about those empty reflections, but she could imagine the glow of chandeliers and tantalizing glimpses of occupants at night, a sense of mystery and possibility. Bathed in oyster sea-light, the mansions seemed more romantic than those in Cleveland, and in the murmur of waves sloshing at the foot of the cliff, Fanny heard the sound of money. Even in her dreams, she had not imagined herself in such a place, keeping such company. It made her dizzy, and like the best narcotics, it erased the pain of her past and made the future seem infinite.

Mae gave an account of the families who inhabited the summer villas. She had been visiting Newport ever since she was a toddler, and through osmosis, she had absorbed the history of the town. A shingle-and-stone-clad Queen Anne belonged to a famous Egyptologist known for exploring the tomb of Ramesses II. A multi-gabled house with piazzas and a grand porte-cochère belonged to Bostonians who threw an enormous gala every August—the lady of that manse was a devoted customer of Charles Worth in Paris. Worth, Mae explained, was a tyrant of high fashion who snubbed anyone he didn't fancy, but he was said to have a soft spot for American millionaires, who never asked about prices. The lady from Boston wore provocative, low-cut gowns and was inordinately proud of her "avant-garde haute couture."

Mae was most enthusiastic about an enormous Italianate villa called Château-sur-Falaise; she said that it had the best ballroom in Newport. The owners occupied the pinnacle of New York society, and Mae was determined to gain invitations to their soirées. "I won't be truly out in real society until I attend my first ball at the Scott villa." She tossed her curls. "I will *astonish* with my talent in the quadrilles." Her grin was impish.

The path descended from the cliff until they were near the ocean's edge; late-morning sun turned the sand to pale gold. A gull, bleached by dazzling light against a cerulean sky, coasted, then plunged into the ruffled belly of the sea. Fanny longed to follow it, to jump into the cool water.

But Mae wrinkled her nose. "I do so dislike the smell of rotting seaweed. We should stay away from the beach."

In Mae's bedroom, Fanny was back to being the maid, sewing loose buttons on one of Mae's traveling ensembles. It didn't bother her to take orders; in fact, she was glad of it. Since she could not often predict what she could do to make Mae happy, she appreciated direction in the form of commands. The switch from servant to companion and back again was disorienting, however. She didn't know how to address Mae, or what manner to take with her.

"You will of course take dinner with Aunt Millie and me tonight," Mae said. "We should go through your closet and decide what you will wear."

Fanny had been assigned a room of her own, and in the closet hung her few day dresses and the evening gowns that Mae had pilfered from her mother's storage trunks.

"Mother's old clothing is quite out of fashion, and won't fit you perfectly. You're taller and thinner."

Fanny had tried on one costume early that morning, and had been surprised by how well she filled it out. She had gained a good bit of weight in her short time at the Garth house.

"But that would be expected for my distant, orphaned cousin who has fallen on hard times," Mae continued. "You will be an object of curiosity, I am sure."

Fanny pricked her finger with the needle, and a tiny crimson bead appeared on the whorls of her fingertip. She sucked it away and watched to make sure it wouldn't reappear. It occurred to her that Mae had never asked about her past or her family. She glanced toward the bed, where Mae was sprawled out, petting one of Aunt Millie's fluffy Persian cats. "How can you get an invitation to Château-sur-Falaise?" Fanny asked.

Mae rolled to her back, ignoring the insistent pawing of the cat. "It's all a matter of ingratiating yourself with the right people," she said. "You can think of it like a ladder. We will get invited into the less desirable homes, but there will still be a gradation in the desirability of the guests." She fanned herself lazily with a hat box lid. "My cousin

Angelique explained it all to me. She lives in New York now, though she only married a lawyer." Mae hiked up her skirt to cool her legs. "You use the top layer of the lower rungs to get yourself invited into the next higher level of parties. And so on."

The cat jumped from the bed, landing on the floor with a light thud. It sauntered over to Fanny, curling itself around her ankle. Fanny pulled Mae's traveling frock into her lap to keep it safe from cat hair. She wished that she had a hand free to pet the purring creature. "How do you know who belongs to that top layer?" she asked.

Mae laughed. "Everyone knows. And if there are faces you don't recognize, it takes one conversation to clear everything up. Newport is really very small."

"But if you've been here previous summers, don't you already know all the people who matter?"

"Oh dear." Mae sounded amused. "You really have so much to learn."

Fanny tugged on a brass button to check the soundness of her work as she waited for Mae to elaborate.

"You *have* heard of a debut, have you not?"

Nodding, Fanny pretended to be absorbed in stitching in the next button.

"Have you?"

Fanny cleared her throat. "Of course." From the corner of her eye, she could see Mae sit up on the edge of the bed.

Mae bounced off the mattress and came toward her. The cat, which had been lounging at Fanny's feet, startled and ran out the door. Mae stood over Fanny, who was working on a low stool. She put her small hand on the crown of Fanny's head, entwining her fingers in her hair. "So, then," she said. "What is a debut?"

"A beginning." This was the sum total of Fanny's knowledge, from the little bit of French she had learned in school.

To her relief, Mae ruffled her hair and made a satisfied sound in her throat. "Indeed. And my beginning was just last autumn, so I am now, officially, a real person, according to Newport society. I intend to make the best of it."

Fanny was nervous about her first dinner with Aunt Millie, about eating at a fine table with an array of tableware and fussy, arcane rules. Mae reassured her that her aunt was blind as a bat and nearly deaf, too. "Well, not quite blind or deaf," she amended. "But close enough." She reminded Fanny about the rules of etiquette, and said that it would be the perfect place for her to practice, in case they attended an event that included a sit-down meal.

A figure was partially visible near the entrance of the dining room as they descended the stairs. From the skirt's bustle and train, Fanny assumed it was Mae's great-aunt. She again adjusted the bodice of her satin gown so that the gap at the top was less pronounced. She stood straighter, taking careful but quick steps as Mae had taught her, so that she seemed to "glide downward, like gently falling snow." Mae had delivered this instruction in a humorously arch tone, fluttering her fingers.

The old woman wore lace from head to foot, including what looked like a black doily on top of her thin gray hair. She extended both arms as she approached them. "I am so glad to have you young ladies here with me." Her voice was reedy and her hands, when they clasped Fanny's, were powder-soft and warm. She held on for a long moment, and Fanny tamped down a growing urge to squirm away. Aunt Millie squinted at her with watery pale blue eyes, the whites stained yellow like old porcelain. "I am so sorry for your troubles, my dear." She patted the back of Fanny's hand, then let go with a kind smile. "You are most welcome in my humble home."

Fanny ducked her head with shame at deceiving the old woman. Then she reminded herself that she did, in fact, have troubles aplenty—even more than Mae's fictional cousin. The gold-tinged giddiness of her seashore walk was receding, laying bare the cold reality of her dependence on the good will of others. Good will, Fanny knew, was not to be trusted. "Thank you," she said. "I am so grateful for your generous hospitality."

"Auntie"—Mae spoke loudly and slowly—"we should sit down to dinner."

Aunt Millie had just extended a hand to her great-niece, which she withdrew, looking flustered. "Of course, dear." She glanced toward the polished mahogany table with three gleaming place settings. "Where is Winnifred?"

A woman carrying a crystal decanter filled with tawny liquid emerged from a doorway at the far end of the dining room. She was neither young nor old, her apron grease-stained, her hair messily pinned up under a white cap.

"Ah, there you are," Aunt Millie said.

"You are ready to sit, then, are you, ma'am?" Winnifred's accent had a singsong quality that reminded Fanny of her mother's, but it wasn't Irish. The servant pulled out the chair at the head of the table and unceremoniously plunked down the decanter. She turned abruptly and exited the room, leaving a lingering whiff of animus in her wake.

Aunt Millie shuffled to her seat, lowering herself laboriously, hands braced against the armrests, shoulders trembling. Once seated, she blew out a long breath, smiled, and indicated that the girls were to take their places on either side of her. "Dearest Mae, would you do the honor of pouring our aperitif?"

Mae made a face at Fanny, indicating mock disapproval at her aunt's request. This made Fanny uncomfortable, as Aunt Millie didn't strike her as all that blind.

"Auntie is quite the reformist; she doesn't believe in having servants work." Mae poured the port into their glasses, filling hers and Fanny's to the brim. "There is only the cook, Winnifred, and a cleaning girl who comes during the day."

Aunt Millie sipped her drink and smacked her puckered mouth in appreciation. "I am just an old spinster, living alone. I don't need much." She glanced at her great-niece with narrowed eyes. "But I do have a gardener, dear. And a handyworker."

"Auntie had a companion living with her here for ever so many years." Mae turned to her great-aunt and raised her voice. "How long has it been since Frances died, Auntie?"

The wrinkled face seemed to deflate, the grooves deeper, the jowls drooping. "Five years already." She sighed, set down her glass. "It's so quiet here without her. You girls do my heart good with all of your youthful energy."

"Frances was quite something. She wore her skirts so short that her bloomers showed." Mae laughed. "She would rant about women's suffrage and organize letter-writing campaigns." She took a giant swig from her glass and refilled it. "She came from a prominent family, but it's no wonder she never married."

Aunt Millie's gaze lifted; she blinked. "Frances was a dear friend," she said softly.

"She was nice, but odd." Mae delicately licked the shine of port from her lip, catlike. "Do you suppose you might have married, Auntie, had Frances not radiated so much suffragette zeal in your house? I'm sure she made men afraid to call."

Aunt Millie shook her head with a rueful smile. "Even in my youth, I was never a beauty like you, dear Mae. And I do believe that spinster-hood suits me. We aren't all cut out to be wives."

Winnifred reappeared with a silver tureen. "Soup," she announced curtly as she set it down. She ladled the chowder into their bowls, but not the way Fanny had seen it done at the Garth residence, unobtrusively and with discretion, the servant leaning in slightly past the left shoulder of each diner, working silently. Winnifred stood beside Aunt Millie and reached across the table, seemingly unconcerned about her arm blocking her mistress's view, the metallic clang and scrape of her serving utensil, or the fine spray of fishy broth she sent up from the bowls by pouring from a height. Aunt Millie sat with her hands clasped over her belly, a contented smile on her face.

As Winnifred filled her bowl, Fanny lifted her brimful glass with utmost care. She watched Aunt Millie lean over her chowder and inhale appreciatively. To live in such a place with a dear friend, to not need a man or worry about money—the old woman's life had been one to envy.

"Kitty, dear," Aunt Millie said, "how long has it been since you and Mae last saw one another?"

Fanny had rehearsed her story with Mae, but the question provoked a slight jolt; port spilled onto her hand and dripped down her forearm, where it soaked into the sleeve of her dress. Hoping that neither of her dinner companions had noticed, she took a sip before setting the glass back down. "Three years ago, I traveled to Cleveland, ma'am," she said. "To attend the wedding of Theodore Garth."

"That's my cousin Teddy, Auntie," Mae said, enunciating clearly.

"Teddy is only my second cousin once removed." Fanny wondered if she should speak more loudly, but Aunt Millie's polite smile and attentive gaze did not suggest that she was having trouble hearing. "My mother was close with his mother when they were younger, though, so it was important to her that we go." She picked up her spoon, then noted that the other two weren't eating and set it down again, her cheeks warming.

Aunt Millie blinked her rheumy eyes and looked down at her place setting as if she had forgotten it was there. "Of course, we must eat the soup before it gets cold!"

To Fanny's surprise, the old woman slurped unselfconsciously as she took a spoonful of chowder.

"I hardly knew Kitty before the wedding," Mae said. She didn't touch her soup, but she refilled her glass and Fanny's so that they threatened to overflow again. Fanny frowned, and Mae twirled a ringlet around her finger, opening her beautiful eyes wide with fake innocence. She had noticed the spill earlier, Fanny realized, and was teasing her.

"We hit it off right away," Mae continued. "Within hours, Kitty had all of those boring Cleveland boys dancing to her tune." She released the ringlet, which bounced back into place by her shell-like ear. "And we had such fun commenting to one another on all of the different fashions. I couldn't stop laughing!"

Aunt Millie coughed, covering her mouth with a shaky, liver-spotted hand. She set down her spoon. "But dear Mae," she said. "It must have been so sad to see Kitty back on your doorstep, having lost first her mother, and then her home."

"Oh yes." Mae dipped her chin, sighing out a heavy breath; she lowered her hands to her lap and shook her head slowly. When she lifted her head, her eyes were bright. "Poor, poor, Kitty. It was so unfair, the way her brother's new wife put her out of the house. She gave Fanny a tremulous little smile. "I'm only glad that she had the good sense to come to us for help."

Fanny would not have imagined that Mae could be such a compelling actress. She realized that Mae was thoroughly enjoying herself, while she felt squeamish about the lies they were telling the old lady. It had been fun to deceive the rich young highbrows in Cleveland—a harmless game—but it seemed mean to take advantage of Aunt Millie. "You have been so kind to me," she said, directing her words to the room at large.

"Dear girl," Aunt Millie said, reaching a wrinkled hand toward Fanny. "How long has it been since your mother died?"

Fanny eyed the old woman's hand on the white linen, unsure whether she was expected to reach back to her. Tentatively, she put her hand on the table; Aunt Millie squeezed it gently, shook her head, softly clucking her tongue. "Poor dear," she said.

"It has been just over a year, ma'am," Fanny said. This was the story that she and Mae had agreed upon.

Mae watched them, idly pushing her spoon around in her soup. "Kitty's mother was very frail," she said.

"I lost my mother when I was about your age," Aunt Millie said, still holding Fanny's hand. She had a subtle, slow tremor, and her bones felt fragile, but her grip was firm. "There is no greater loss for a young woman who is only just embarking on an independent life." She squeezed once more and let go.

Unexpectedly, Fanny felt the weight of true grief about her mother's death. She longed to tell this kind stranger about how hard it had been to lose her; how little love she had received afterward. Instead, she said, "I miss my mother very much, but Mae has been a great consolation."

Mae smiled cheerfully. "We will make sure that Kitty is distracted from her troubles while she is with us here in Newport." She winked at Fanny.

"Yes, I do hope that you will find some consolation here, dear," Aunt Millie said. "You seem like a strong and brave girl."

"You give me far too much credit," Fanny said, wishing that she could go back to being Mae's maid in Cleveland, where expectations were simpler. Then she remembered the chilly farewell she had received from Grace, and reminded herself that she no longer fit in there, either. "But I do thank you," she said. "I will do my best to take in what Newport has to offer."

CHAPTER 17

Fanny's first social event in Newport as Cousin Kitty was a small gathering hosted by one of Aunt Millie's elderly friends. Mae tucked Fanny into a beribboned bonnet and pulled her around by the white lace-gloved hand to meet luncheon guests, spreading Dickensian tales of Kitty's misfortunes. Met with polite nods and murmured sympathies, Mae quickly became bored. She yawned theatrically when she thought no one but Fanny was watching, and teased a young waiter by standing overly close when taking glasses from his tray; he blushed crimson when Mae blew him a kiss behind her aunt's back. Mae preened and kept their champagne coupes full, but declared the whole event a criminal waste of time.

A few days later, Fanny heard Mae's light feet running up the stairs. She flew into Fanny's room, breathless, waving an envelope. "You will never guess!" She landed on the bed with a bounce, rumpling the bedclothes that had been so neatly smoothed and tucked. Fanny, who had been reading in the bay window seat, obeyed Mae's eager, beckoning hand and sat at her side. Mae bounced performatively on the mattress again, jostling against Fanny with a giggle. "We've been invited to the Marshalls' garden party!" She threw her arms around Fanny and gave her a quick squeeze, then showed her the invitation, gilt lettering on creamy stationery. "Auntie talked to her friend, the hostess of that luncheon—" She paused dramatically. "Who just happens to be the secretary of the Newport Garden Association!"

Fanny smiled uncertainly.

"Mrs. Marshall is awfully proud of her gardens," Mae added.

"I see," Fanny said, though she didn't.

"Auntie had her friend speak with Mrs. Marshall after the Garden Association meeting—she told her all about your misfortunes, and how kind and generous I have been to take you in for the summer." Mae beamed proudly, as though she believed her own stories. "So we have been invited to one of the most exclusive garden parties in Newport!"

Fanny warmed to the glow of Mae's excitement, but like an alpinist overlooking a precipice, suddenly realizing how high she has climbed, she felt vertiginous. "Is Aunt Millie going, too?" she asked.

"No, of course not." Mae handed Fanny the note that had been tucked into the envelope. "She doesn't like to go out. Aunt Millie did this for us, and it seems that Mrs. Marshall likes to be charitable." Mae poked Fanny's ribs with her elbow. "I am sure it doesn't hurt our cause that we are such pretty young things!"

Fanny was pleased to be included in the plural pronoun, but she had no illusions about her beauty relative to Mae's. She read the neat, loopy script, cordially inviting them. "How can you tell all of this from such a little note?"

"Dear cousin, you are so sweet and naive," Mae said, patting Fanny on the cheek. "Luckily, you are a quick study." She jumped up. "The party is only a week away! We must decide what to wear. My ivory muslin, I think."

Fanny doubted that any of the few dresses in her closet were appropriate for a garden party.

"And you will do my hair like you did for Patricia's soirée in March. I received so many compliments." Mae was already on her way out the door, her voice trailing behind. "Bring my tea in an hour."

The Marshall mansion was a white marble colossus styled after a French chateau, complete with Corinthian porticos and arched windows flanked by fluted pilasters. As their carriage climbed the curved ramp, sunlight casting rainbows in spray from a fountain, Mae let out an excited chirp, and Fanny's stomach fluttered.

Liveried footmen helped them down from Aunt Millie's hired carriage; stern men in long coats held open Baroque iron doors embellished with the monogram *CM* set in ivy-wreathed medallions. The girls were ushered through a cavernous entrance hall, past a grand staircase of tawny marble with a bronze banister. The ceiling gleamed with gold friezes separating paintings of cavorting scantily clad gods and goddesses. Fanny craned her neck, dizzily taking in the images.

"Don't gawp," Mae whispered, tugging her arm.

At the far end of the hall, honeyed sunlight poured through French doors, pooling on the glassy parquet floor. The doors let out onto a marble terrace overlooking a verdant sea of manicured grass and, beyond that, the ultramarine glitter of the sea itself.

White tents were pitched on the lawn, streamers fluttering from stiff peaks, benches and garden seats sprinkled about at polite distances and garlanded with flowers. A bed of blue hydrangeas edged with red geraniums lined the whole width of the terrace; between garden paths were tufts of sweet violets, nodding dahlias, and candy-colored begonias. A crowded rose bed with low picket fencing was partially visible beyond the south-facing wall of the mansion.

Throughout the grounds, ladies in pastel dresses gathered like displays of confectionaries, chatting, parasols aloft. Gentlemen in gray frock coats and tall hats lounged at tea tables; girls in starched muslin dresses promenaded by the cliff's edge. Threading their way through archery and croquet games, waiters bore drinks and canapes on flashing silver trays.

Mae paused before the scene of the party, one gloved hand resting on the balustrade, the other gripping Fanny's arm. She seemed to hold her breath as she scanned the crowd. "I don't know anyone here," she said in a tight voice. Her posture was more than usually erect, shoulders back, her delicate collarbones emphasized by faint mauve shadows. "We will have to introduce ourselves." She lifted her chin.

Feeling bold on behalf of her friend, Fanny waved down a waiter striding past them toward the lawn; she snatched two bubbling flutes, misty with condensation. She handed one to Mae. "To future alliances," she said. The smile she received in response made her heart soar.

Mae tapped her glass against Fanny's. "New alliances."

Fizz tickled Fanny's nose; in trying to suppress the sneeze, she let out a little mousy squeak. Mae laughed, the tension evaporating. She linked her arm through Fanny's. In silent accord, they descended the stairs to brave *le beau monde*.

Mae was used to attracting attention; from the way her look of expectation faded to disappointment, Fanny could tell that she was disconcerted when gazes slid blankly past her, seeking a spark of recognition elsewhere. Though the partygoers gathered in loose clusters, every conversation or game felt like a closed circle excluding Fanny and Mae. They wandered for a time in the periphery, Mae keeping Fanny near. Without understanding the hierarchy, she could tell that Newport society had its own ecology, that she and Mae were as inconsequential in their environment as the sea birds floating high overhead in the salt-washed sunshine.

Mae was more beautiful than ever—wind-loosened blond curls, clear blue eyes, her dancer's body wrapped in snowy muslin. She was gold and silver, precious and cool; a world apart from the sweat and toil Fanny knew. Mae belonged in Newport, even if Newport did not yet realize it.

"I am sure that you will leave here triumphant today," Fanny said. "You are absolutely flawless, and it will not take long for others to appreciate your qualities."

Mae slowed to a stop. "That is Tabitha Marshall," she said softly. "The one in lilac and green."

Fanny followed the direction of her gaze to a sour-looking young woman standing alone by the rose garden, watching a croquet match. The mint ribbon about her waist matched a wreath of ivy on her hat, which was anchored to her head with many windings of gauze, guaranteed to foil any effort by the wind to snatch it away. A little purple parasol on a carved ivory handle hovered absurdly over her much larger hat brim.

"She is the granddaughter of our hosts." There was awe in Mae's voice.

Fanny thought it great luck that Tabitha was unoccupied and thus approachable. "We should introduce ourselves," she whispered.

Mae was uncharacteristically quiet and still; Fanny sensed a shyness in her. Yearning for Mae's happy smile gave Fanny courage and being laughably out of her own depth made her as reckless as a drunk. "Come with me," she said.

With a sharp intake of breath Mae registered protest, or perhaps merely surprise—still, she allowed herself to be guided forward.

"Miss Marshall?" Fanny said as they drew close.

Tabitha looked toward them, but said nothing. Her mouth was compressed to a hyphen, shadows bracketing its corners. Fanny persisted.

"My name is Kitty Davenport, and this is my benefactress and cousin, Miss Mae Garth."

Tabitha's eyes were cold, lids slightly drooped, like a lizard in repose. Fanny could feel Mae's tension.

"I want to thank you for inviting us to your garden party." Fanny pushed on. "It is a great honor for me to be here, and Miss Garth was kind enough to change her plans in order to accompany me."

"It is lovely to meet you, but I cannot take credit for inviting you," the woman said dryly. "This is my grandparents' summer cottage."

"We didn't mean to intrude on your solitude," Mae said in a small voice, her discomfort palpable.

The word *cottage*, the bizarre little parasol, the unearned disdain only made Fanny feel more like Alice in Wonderland, offended by absurdity. "Oh, of course," she said with a smile. "It is only because of Miss Garth's charity that your grandmother so generously extended an invitation." She stepped slightly to the side, allowing Mae to draw a greater share of attention. "Miss Garth is the kindest and most modest person you could ever wish to meet," Fanny said with increased confidence. "Miss Astor says that she is an angel."

Subtly, Tabitha's expression shifted, as a breeze alters the surface of a pond.

"And Miss Garth was practically a big sister to the Rockefeller girls in Cleveland." Fanny nodded to Mae, who was blushing. "She doesn't like me to speak of it, lest people think she—well, I don't know if you are familiar with the family, as they are rather new on the scene."

Tabitha looked at Mae with interest; she appeared to be trying to place her. "How old would the Rockefeller girls be now?" She touched the bridge of her long nose with a manicured finger and rubbed thoughtfully. "They must still be quite young."

Mae's wide blue eyes were fixed on Fanny's.

"Bessie is nearly our age," Fanny said, glad that she could remember the gossip. "And as you know, quite unostentatious and pious." This was not quite how Mae, who had no personal knowledge of the Rockefellers, had put it. She had sniffed mean-spiritedly about the fact that the Rockefellers lived on the unfashionable south side of Euclid Avenue, without any views of the lake, and that they had bought an existing home, as if they couldn't afford to have one built. "Miss Garth is likewise quiet and unassuming—doubtless, the Rockefellers recognize in her a kindred soul." Fanny gave Tabitha a closed-lip smile. "But of course you can surely sense that yourself."

Tabitha angled her stance toward Mae, further pushing Fanny to the sideline. "I have never been to Cleveland," she said. "I hear that it is being built up at a tremendous pace."

Mae was still looking to Fanny, who raised her eyebrows slightly, making it clear that she expected Mae to answer.

"It's nothing like New York," Mae said. She cleared her throat with a delicate cough and continued more assertively. "But you must visit one day. They say that Euclid Avenue is the Champs-Élysées of America." She smiled and shrugged. "Of course nobody who has been to Paris would agree." She included both herself and Tabitha in those *who have been to Paris*, ending with an amused, self-effacing moue.

Fanny put a hand on Mae's elbow and murmured, "Excuse me, I think I see Miss Riley. I won't be long."

Mae nodded, and with a sweet bloom of pride in her chest, Fanny left her to plant a dainty foot on a higher rung of the social ladder.

Fanny wandered the lawn, slowly sipping mint water, pretending to be looking for a friend. When Mae caught up with her, she spoke with clipped breathlessness. "Tabitha invited me to dinner next week!" Her small frame seemed to thrum with excitement. "She made a point of telling me that her brother Charles will be there!"

Though an author of Mae's triumph, Fanny received the news unenthusiastically. The froth of pride had subsided, leaving a curdled, slightly bitter aftertaste.

"Charles is the eldest son, and not yet married," Mae trilled, falling in step with Fanny.

"But surely you aren't looking for a husband!" Mae had spoken of independence, adventure, perhaps finding a flat of their own, just the two of them.

Mae laughed. "Of course not. But think what it means that she invited me!"

"Your entrée into New York society." That's what Mae had called it.

Mae sighed happily.

"Did Tabitha ask you more about the Rockefellers?"

"Not really." The breeze ruffled her skirt and tugged at the ribbons in her hair; Mae looked dreamily out to sea. "It was all very pleasant." She turned her gaze back toward Fanny. "You did well to think of those girls. They keep entirely to themselves, so nobody could contradict you."

Fanny relished the praise. She *had* done well.

"You really were wonderful." Mae seized Fanny's arm, causing her to halt. "The way you spoke with Tabitha. You are so gifted."

The sunlight that shone on Mae's upturned face was matched by the warmth in her voice. Behind her, on the horizon, silver ocean-glint met the deep blue of sky, stretching beyond sight toward the storied old world—London, Paris, Rome. Inside Fanny something stirred, a gossamer dragonfly wing of genuine hope.

CHAPTER 18

That night, Mae padded into Fanny's room on bare feet. The full
moon had risen; in its light through the open window, Fanny
could make out the white folds of Mae's nightgown, her pale
face haloed by a bumpy corona of rag-tied hair. She stopped, hovering,
backlit by moonbeams.

"Kitty?" Mae held her hands out uncertainly, grasping at shadows.

"Yes, I'm awake." Fanny wasn't sure why they were whispering. "I'm
right here." She flung back the bedclothes, slid to her feet. Taking one
of Mae's hands, she said, "You're cold as ice!"

"I can't sleep." Mae drew closer, put her head on Fanny's shoulder.

Mae's hair was damp against the bed-warmed crook of Fanny's
neck; she shivered. "Get under the covers for a moment," Fanny said.
Leading Mae by the hand, she wrapped her under the summer quilt,
which didn't seem thick enough to ward off the chill. Fanny stepped
toward the casement, intending to close the window, but Mae said,
"Leave it open. I love to hear the sound of the surf."

The sea was unusually restless—dark rumblings and rolling
crescendos—Fanny could almost feel the salt spray in the night breeze.
She sat on the edge of the bed. "Shall I fetch you some milk?"

Mae plucked at Fanny's sleeve. "No, lie down." She lifted the quilt, urged Fanny under. "Tuck it in tight."

Fanny obeyed, making a snug cocoon for them both.

"I have a strange feeling," Mae murmured. She placed a hand against Fanny's sternum; the coolness of her skin seeped through the cotton chemise. Fanny slowed her breath, but it only made the thud of her heart stronger.

"It's as though there is this—" Mae sighed deeply, exhaled. Her mouth smelled of peppermint. "Hazy, unobtainable stairway to the stars."

In the distance, the surf crashed and hissed.

"But if reaching for something more material means that I must give myself away—" The last word was little more than a puff of air.

Fanny had learned to make sense of Mae's fanciful speech, as though they shared a private language. "You worry that you will be tethered," she said.

Mae's embrace was fierce, making plain her gratitude at being understood.

With her chin against Mae's dewy, lavender-scented hair, a palm pressed to her bird-wing shoulder blade, Fanny hugged her back gently. "You must find a way to keep your freedom."

Mae's face was burrowed into the quilt and Fanny's shoulder, her voice muffled. "We could be free together."

Fanny closed her eyes. A glow ran along her spine, something molten pouring through its hollow length.

"You have a way of drawing people to you, of becoming whomever you want to be." Mae rolled onto her back, trapping Fanny's arm beneath her slight weight. "We could be—" As she paused, she ticked softly, tongue against palate. "We could be rich heiresses, or young widows."

"We would be awfully young widows. And I have no money."

Mae squirmed, settling her warmth against Fanny. "Then perhaps we need to marry first. You could marry someone terribly rich and old and infirm."

Fanny smiled into the velvet darkness. "And in need of spectacles, I suppose."

"I think you are beautiful."

There was a tightness in Fanny's throat. "And whom shall you marry?"

From behind the closed door, the cat called out once, plaintively, then fell silent.

"Perhaps I shall not marry at all," Mae whispered.

"Then neither shall I."

Mae shivered.

With an arm wrapped around Mae's rib cage, Fanny gathered her closer. Tentatively she used her other hand to brush a damp curl back from Mae's cheek; she was surprised that the skin was warm to the touch, almost feverish, in contrast to her cold hands. "Do you truly believe we could run away together?"

Without speaking, Mae turned to face Fanny. She stretched out and pressed the length of her body against her, sliding a leg between Fanny's thighs as far as their nightdresses would allow. A burst of pleasure radiated from Fanny's groin; she let out a small gasp. Mae tilted up her chin and brought their lips to touch, the taste of salt joining the scent of peppermint. She pulled back a hair's breadth, her breath still hot on Fanny's face.

Fanny didn't dare to move as she felt the soft grope of Mae's hand, clumsy with the hindrance of tangled linens, brushing the side of her breast, traveling downward, coming to rest on her hip bone with a squeeze. Encouraged, Fanny kissed Mae again, holding her more tightly. Mae moved against her, and they became swathed, slow, sinuous wrestlers, fabric sliding against fabric, Fanny's breath shallow. Mae made a whimpering sound that pierced whatever defenses Fanny had left, and then fell away with a sigh. She lay still, seemingly in repose, while Fanny, still quivering, waited for what Mae would do or say next. She waited and waited, her heart slowing, cold air from the window drying the sweat on her brow. Mae's breathing deepened; she twitched, then rolled onto her side, away from Fanny, whose arm was still pinned under her.

Fanny lay awake and completely still so as not to disturb Mae, her hand prickling with pins and needles, her neck stiffening in an awkward tilt. She listened to Mae's quiet snuffle, the ocean, night insects. The curtains billowed gently. She balled up her fists, squeezed her eyelids shut tight until ghostly phosphorescence floated through a sea of blackness. She had a feeling like an itch—taut, almost unbearable, knowing a scratch would be delicious.

Full morning sun shone on faded curtains, a worn pine floor, frayed tassels of a sagging canopy. The pillow was bunched up along the headboard, the bedclothes twisted. Fanny still occupied the margin of the narrow mattress, safeguarding the now empty space beside her.

Memory of the night returned to her, and Fanny sat up abruptly, as if stuck by a pin. Blood bounded through her veins as her feelings battled—she both longed for Mae and wanted never to have to face her again.

She rose with a nervous drop of her stomach. Facing Mae would be even harder because she had neglected her duty by oversleeping. Hastily, she tossed and tucked the blankets into a semblance of neatness. As she doffed her nightgown, she wrinkled her nose at the musky scent of her armpit. A sponge bath would be necessary, just the quickest rinse.

Fanny took some deep breaths before tapping on Mae's door. As there was no answer, she pushed it open, took in the empty unmade bed, the pile of discarded clothes on the settee. No Mae. Panic rose like bile in her throat as she thought about why Mae had not woken her. She tried to calm herself, imagining Mae downstairs in her morning wrapper, having tea and scones, humming to herself as she often did.

But Mae was not in the breakfast room, either. The plates had been cleared; as usual, Winnifred had left the crumbs and crumpled napkins for the cleaning girl, whose wicker laundry basket was already stationed at the foot of the stairs. When Fanny saw the clock on the mantelpiece, she saw that she had slept much longer than she had realized—it was near eleven o'clock.

In the kitchen the fires were out, and Winnifred was sitting on a wooden stool by the open door, sipping a glass of iced cider. The wind from the night before was gone, the oven-heated cooking air trapped inside, stagnant.

"Is Miss Mildred at church?" Fanny asked.

Winnifred didn't bother to turn her head. "What do you think?"

Fanny ignored the bead of sweat she could feel trickling over her ribs. She pulled at the flared cuffs of her sleeves, straightening them. Winnifred had never treated her like Mae's cousin; she seemed to see through the ruse, and when no one else was listening, she spoke with scorn.

"And Miss Mae?"

"Gone."

Fanny waited for her heart to settle, cleared her throat. "Gone where, may I ask?"

The cook took a long draft from her glass, ice chips sloshing. "Best ask Miss Mildred, hadn't you?" She leaned against the doorframe, returning to her contemplation of the empty back drive.

Fanny retreated a few paces, then stopped. "Winnifred," she said. "Do fetch me a pot of tea and biscuits. I am famished." She caught a surprised glance hardening into antipathy. "I will take it on the terrace, thank you."

Winnifred's face was stony. Fanny forced herself to return the gaze with a neutral expression. When there was still no response, she raised her eyebrows, a silent question. A long moment passed. Finally, Winnifred made the slightest inclination of her head. Fanny acknowledged her acquiescence with an equally slight smile.

There was still no sign of Mae or Aunt Millie upstairs. Fanny pushed open the French doors to the terrace. The brassy sun was near its zenith, leaving only a sliver of shade along the wall of the house. There was not a breath of wind; the weary air settled over her, heavy with humidity, and Fanny regretted her choice to come outside. Nevertheless, her tea was on its way, and she would wait.

Fanny dragged a wrought iron chair a few feet back into the shade. The sun-warmed seat burned even through her skirt and layered petticoat, stinging the backs of her thighs. The terrace was bordered with pots of drooping begonias; beyond them a patchy lawn and row of cedars that partially blocked the view of the house next door. Toward the ocean, which was not visible from the house, ponderous dark clouds were massing on the horizon. Fanny tipped back her head, closing her eyes against the harsh light. The sounds of hammers and voices from nearby construction were loud in the torpid swelter. The surf could no longer be heard, as though the sea itself had succumbed to lethargy. As Fanny exhaled, her breath felt too hot on her lips, bringing back sensations from the night before.

"Well, hello, dear!" Aunt Millie, puffing and pink-faced, approached along the back walkway. She always went to church on foot; Mae said this was because she was too cheap to hire her own driver.

Fanny jumped up to meet her. Unsure how to help, she gingerly took the woman by the elbow to lend her support as she climbed the stairs to the terrace.

"Thank you, Kitty dear." Aunt Millie mounted each slow step cautiously, but she did not put any weight on Fanny's outstretched hand. "You are a sweet girl."

Fanny flushed, feeling useless. After a moment, she withdrew her hand.

"All the people come from the city—" Millie wheezed, lifting a leg with tortoise-like patience, ensuring a solid foothold on the stair before lifting the next. "—to escape these dog days." She paused and pressed a lace-trimmed handkerchief to her cheeks. "But even Newport can be inclement."

"I do hope the weather is not—" Fanny began, then remembered that the old woman was hard of hearing. "I hope it is not too oppressive for you," she said loudly. Too loudly, she thought, but Aunt Millie seemed not to notice.

"This too shall pass," she said pleasantly, plodding upward. "Soon, by the look of those clouds." Aunt Millie reached the terrace, leaned against the balustrade, and dabbed her upper lip with her handkerchief before tucking it into her sleeve. She sighed, smiled at Fanny. "How are you, dear?"

Fanny swallowed queasily. She felt naked without Mae by her side to lead the conversation with her aunt. "I am well, thank you," she said, enunciating deliberately. She fought the impulse to chew her lip. "How was the service?"

Aunt Millie continued to smile, looking slightly daft. Her hat brim tilted at an eccentric angle, the ruffles of her dress wilted in the sticky weather. The powder on her wrinkled face was grooved by rivulets of sweat. "It was serviceable," she said.

Fanny wasn't sure whether she was expected to laugh.

Winnifred appeared, carrying a small teapot. "Miss Mildred," she said, "I didn't expect you so soon."

"The Langstons insisted on bringing me most of the way home," Aunt Millie said, glancing at Winnifred. "I didn't argue too vociferously in this heat."

"I brought some tea." Winnifred sounded defensive. Fanny noticed that she never spoke above a normal volume to her mistress.

"I would think that cold Russian tea in the parlor would be more appropriate on a day like this."

Though Aunt Millie's tone had been mild, Winnifred stiffened. "Of course," she said.

After Winnifred withdrew, Aunt Millie said to Fanny, "It will be cooler inside, dear." Her watery eyes were hooded by sagging lids but alert. "Were you waiting for Mae out here?"

"I was wondering if she went to church with you."

The sound was somewhere between a chuckle and a wheeze. "I'm sorry, dear. She is out sailing with her new friends."

There was a bitter taste in Fanny's mouth. She dragged the chair she had been using back into its place.

"Though goodness knows, they won't get anywhere in these doldrums." Aunt Millie stepped carefully across the threshold, one tremulous hand on the tarnished handle of the French door. "It was quite an unexpected invitation," she added in a mildly apologetic tone.

Fanny followed, shutting the door behind them.

"From Tabitha Marshall, of all people." Aunt Millie shuffled down the corridor. "They have that enormous yacht."

It would have taken only a dozen strides for Fanny to reach the parlor, but she trailed the old woman politely with awkward, mincing steps.

"What is the name of that boat?" Aunt Millie mused, clucking, as she approached a sagging armchair. The parlor was furnished with relics of a bygone era, worn purple satin with yellow tuftings, gilt vitrines with warped glass. "Is it *Eos*?"

Fanny remembered Mae telling her about the Marshalls and their boat, giggling, a cupid pantomime. *"Eros,"* she said.

Aunt Millie huffed, deflating as she settled into her seat. "An uninspired name."

Fanny took the settee next to her. "Where have they gone?"

"Doubtless bobbing somewhere off the coast." Aunt Millie sniffed dismissively. "Rich people don't have destinations, dear." With fumbling hands, she pulled out her silver hatpin and laid her floppy leghorn on a footstool. She patted her hair, which did nothing to tame the wreath of gray wisps, then clasped her gnarled fingers together. There was a stillness, an expectant air about her steady gaze that demanded attention. "You are obviously clever, dear girl," she said. Her rheumy eyes were disconcertingly keen. "And I believe that you may have ambition to elevate your stature in society."

Fanny wanted to say, *You are thinking of Mae*, but instead she said, hesitantly, "I am grateful for your succor. You and your niece have been such a blessing to me." Even inside, the air was hot and humid; she pulled at her skirts, which stuck to her legs.

Aunt Millie shrugged impatiently. "You need an opportunity to lift you out of your current predicament."

Predicament? Fanny had flown from a precarious childhood, escaped being caged in a brothel, landed in the lap of unimaginable privilege, even if this all hinged on her continued deceit.

"You have nowhere to go after this summer. Mae, most probably, will not return to Cleveland."

The ground shifted for Fanny, her physical surroundings reassembling in unaccountable ways. The parlor took on a dreamlike quality, fractured sunlight and sharp shadows.

"Your relatives have cast you out." There was a dryness that Fanny had not heard before. "You need a plan."

Winnifred entered, set down a rattling tray on the side table. "Your cold tea, ma'am," she said, pouring from a pitcher. She placed a glass on a doily next to her mistress's elbow, the other out of Fanny's reach.

In the distance came the sound of children bawling, a woman scolding.

The old woman picked up her tea. "Have you thought about becoming a nanny, dear?"

Fanny watched Winnifred's retreating back. "Mae will return."

Aunt Millie's smile was tinged with sadness. "She didn't even tell you that she was leaving. That is not the behavior of someone who has your best interest at heart."

Despite the stultifying heat, Fanny felt chilled.

"I suspect that a domestic post is not what you had hoped for." She sipped her tea. "But one must be realistic, dear."

An ache tightened like a band around Fanny's temples.

"My neighbor, Mrs. Wells, is seeking a new nanny for her three little ones." Aunt Millie blinked slowly. "She met you at the luncheon and was quite impressed."

Fanny had no recollection of her.

"I told her that you come from a good family but had fallen on difficult times." A drop of tea dripped onto her bodice. "Mr. and Mrs. Wells cannot afford to pay handsomely, but they could offer you a comfortable home, dear."

The ticking of the clock was loud. Fanny looked down at her feet; the carpet was worn but still elegant. It had probably cost a fortune. For an elderly woman, alone in the world, money was a great protection.

"This may seem harsh—I do not intend it to be—but you could do worse for yourself." Aunt Millie's expression conveyed nothing but kindness.

Fanny rubbed her forehead; she was feeling increasingly sick to her stomach. "I am sure that Mae will be able to keep me on." Only after she said it did Fanny realize her mistake. She had spoken as a servant, not as a cousin.

With a shake of her head, Aunt Millie said, "I could be wrong, dear, but I suspect that little Miss Mae will find her way to New York." It seemed that she had not registered Fanny's slip. "I am fond of that girl, but she is a flighty young thing."

"I could return to Toledo," Fanny ventured weakly.

Aunt Millie raised her hand, creased palm toward Fanny. "Let us dispense with fiction, dear."

Sunlight disappeared from the window at the same moment that thunder rumbled in the distance. Fanny looked to Aunt Millie, wondering what to say.

"Just say that you will meet with Mrs. Wells, child. You don't have to make any decisions right now."

Fanny bowed her head. Outside, the clouds unleashed a deluge.

CHAPTER 19

Fanny didn't know how to occupy herself without Mae's direction, didn't know how to behave. She tried to be inconspicuous, spending her days reading in her room or walking by the shore. Thankfully, Aunt Millie's treatment of her was unchanged; she still spoke to her as Kitty, Mae's cousin from Toledo. Fanny was grateful for her benevolence, even if she didn't understand it.

At suppertime, Fanny always asked for news of Mae, but Aunt Millie merely shrugged and muttered philosophically about the fickle ways of young folk. Over leathery pork chops or chalky fish, Aunt Millie talked about her travel to India, charitable work, and music—she had been an avid piano player before her arthritis set in. Despite her disquiet, Fanny was drawn to the stories, and she filed away details of a genteel, if slightly shabby, single woman's life.

The muggy, dreary summer days dragged on, and Fanny grew increasingly worried about Mae's absence. She tried to stay hopeful, but Aunt Millie's prediction that she would have to fend for herself weighed heavily on her. As promised, Fanny met with the neighbor about the nanny position. Mrs. Wells, a tall woman with a wan, heart-shaped face, greeted Fanny with an air of vague confusion, even though Aunt Millie had prearranged the meeting. Fanny introduced herself and explained why she had come, but once seated in the stuffy parlor, Mrs. Wells seemed to have forgotten who she was; for a long time, she just looked at Fanny absently, brow slightly furrowed. The curtains were drawn against the heat of the afternoon; in the filtered light, dust motes that had been disturbed by the sweep of their skirts swirled ever more slowly. There was a musky scent, like the faint whiff of a kennel, and something sour, like spilled milk. From a distant room came the shouting of children, followed by the wail of a baby.

Fanny waited, her heart heavy, as Mrs. Wells maintained a dull silence. Finally, Fanny said, "Ma'am? Miss Millie sent me about the nanny job."

The woman blinked rapidly, lifted her pointy chin. "Yes, of course. Bitsy, is it?"

"Kitty, ma'am."

There was a rushing patter of footsteps down the staircase, and a pair of small boys dashed past the parlor door, stifling laughter. Upstairs, a woman yelled something unintelligible. A door slammed shut.

Mrs. Wells seemed not to notice. Her eyes were glassing over again. Fanny remembered the same look on the face of a girl at the brothel, her pupils swallowed by the brown of her irises, eyelids drooping, lips loosely parted. She felt a prickling on her scalp. The smell of the room choked her. From the corner of her eye, she thought she saw something move in the shadows; when she looked, there was nothing there, but the back of her neck still tingled.

"I completely forgot that we have visitors arriving at two o'clock," Fanny said, gesturing toward the clock. "I do hope that you will forgive me, Mrs. Wells, but perhaps we could find another time for me to stop by?" She was already rising from her chair.

Blinking again, Mrs. Wells said, "Of course." She sank back, resting her messily coiffed head against the velvet wingback.

"I will see myself out." Fanny forced herself to pause for the sake of politeness, but Mrs. Wells had closed her eyes. Fanny left quietly but quickly.

Escaping into the sunshine, Fanny gulped the air, as though she had been holding her breath. She didn't know what she was going to do, but she knew that she couldn't return to that place.

To purge her lingering nausea, Fanny took a long walk on the bluff overlooking the ocean. She welcomed the blinding dazzle of light on the water to banish the darkness in her mind.

When she returned to the house, there was a carriage parked in the driveway. As it turned out, Aunt Millie did have a guest, a Mr. Harold Warren, the younger brother of Aunt Millie's late companion, Frances. Aunt Millie invited Fanny to join them for tea, and lacking a ready excuse, she said yes.

Warren was a small, neatly dressed man, with a closely trimmed gray beard. From the gleam of his shoes and golden shine of his watch fob, he appeared to take great care in his appearance; Fanny imagined that he had been quite a dandy in his earlier years. Fanny sat demurely, sipping her tea, and listened to the pair banter and make occasional good-humored gibes, a side of Aunt Millie she had not witnessed before.

Through the conversation, Fanny gathered that Warren was from Pittsburgh, and that he owned grocery stores. He spoke of the trouble he was having with spoiling produce, saying, "Back in my father's day, when we only had a fruit and vegetable stand, it was no trouble to get the inventory right. Now with three stores, it seems that something always has to be thrown away."

"Have you thought about giving it back to the farmers?" Fanny had been silent until then, and Warren looked at her with mild surprise and disapproval, as though she was a child bursting in on adult discussions.

"To the farmers?" He examined her over the rim of his spectacles, lips pursed.

"It makes good feed, especially for pigs." Fanny found the man's haughtiness amusing. "You could ask for better prices in exchange." She returned his gaze with an innocuous smile. "It would certainly be better than throwing away something that holds potential value for others."

Warren rubbed his thumb on the bearded underside of his chin. "Who did you say she is?" he asked Aunt Millie.

"Kitty can tell you herself," the old woman said, setting down her cup with a shaky hand.

"I am Mae Garth's cousin," Fanny said. "My family is from Toledo. My father was a banker, but he died several years ago. I recently lost my mother as well, and Aunt Millie was kind enough to take me in for the summer."

"I am sorry to hear that, young lady," he said.

He hadn't sounded very sympathetic, but Fanny cast her gaze down for a moment, her hands balled up together against her corseted waist. "Thank you for your kind words."

"How do you know about livestock?" Warren asked.

"My mother's family owns a farm." Despite not having a plan for what she would say next, Fanny was calm. She had no stake in the conversation. She wondered if she had a stake left in anything at all. "Also, I am curious. Like a cat. I like asking questions. For instance, how much do you pay the workers in your grocery stores, Mr. Warren?"

"Kitty is indeed a curious girl," Aunt Millie said dryly. "Curiosity killed the cat, dear," she said to Fanny.

Warren looked surprised but not offended by Fanny's question. "I happen to care about what the people in my community think about me," he said. "So I pay a fair wage."

It was Fanny's turn to be surprised. She had not expected to be taken seriously, and she had certainly not expected an honest answer.

"Why don't you run along, my dear," Aunt Millie said. "We don't want to pester Mr. Warren with impertinent questions."

Warren smiled. His teeth were yellowed and crooked, his long canines wolfish, at odds with his tidy, compact exterior. "I am not troubled at all by questions," he said. "I quite enjoy witnessing the machinations of a young, astute mind."

Fanny wasn't sure whether to follow Aunt Millie's instructions or try to make more of the man's apparent interest, to discover what might be gained. She chose a middle path. "I should be on my way, as I do have letters to write, but I hope that I will see you again, Mr. Warren?"

"I will be here through the end of the season," he said. "We will doubtless cross paths again."

Mae had left without warning, and she reappeared the same way. She swept in like a zephyr, her eyes bright, her glow burnished by sun and salt air. Fanny nearly wept with joy at her return, but Mae's mind was still elsewhere, preventing the reunion Fanny had dreamed about. Her chatter was all about the Marshalls, their properties, their parties, their influential friends, their invitation for her to go to New York. When they were finally alone in Mae's room, she showed Fanny a silly sonnet Charles had penned, extolling Mae's beauty. "He is quite smitten with me," she said with a laugh.

Fanny's heart was lacerated by Mae's pleasure. "Are you smitten with him?" It was difficult to say the words.

Mae shrugged. "Look what I pilfered from downstairs," she said, pulling a bottle of brandy from her bag. "We can go out on the roof and toast my future."

The sunset was fading, leaving the sky a bruised purple. Mae pushed the window fully open and clambered through, pausing to disentangle her skirt from the latch. "Come on, you." Her smile beckoned. "I can already see the first star."

Fanny crawled out after her. The rough tiles were warm under her hands, the breeze soft. They sat with their shoulders touching, facing the ocean. Mae uncorked the bottle and took a swig, then passed it to Fanny. "There's the star." She pointed. "Make a wish."

The brandy burned Fanny's throat. "I wish . . ." She paused.

"You mustn't say it out loud." Mae poked her with her elbow. "It won't come true."

Fanny gulped more brandy, though she didn't like the harsh taste. She closed her eyes, listening to the song of cicadas. Her only wish was the one she already knew she shouldn't say out loud. She handed the bottle back. "Okay, I've got it."

"Me too." Mae took her hand, interlacing their fingers. "What a beautiful evening."

Fanny looked up at the sky. There was already more than one pinprick of light. She said, "Are you going to marry him?" Tears blurred the stars.

Mae squeezed her hand. "I hope so."

"But—" Fanny paused to steady her voice. "I thought we would go to Paris together."

"We will!" Mae turned to look at her. "Oh, don't be upset, my poor Kitty." She put her head on Fanny's shoulder. "Once I am married, I will insist on hiring you into the household. Then we will have all the money we need to travel the world."

Objections and questions crowded Fanny's mind, clamoring like unruly children, but she didn't have the strength in that moment to speak. She breathed in the scent of Mae's hair, listened for the surf, and watched as more stars pierced the darkness with their cold light.

A week later, Mae was gone.

CHAPTER 20

Aunt Millie said that Fanny could stay until the end of the month, and Fanny assured her that she would have gainful employment back in Cleveland by then. She hoped desperately that Mae would give up on Charlie Marshall and return home, and she could have her old job back.

Fanny's days were blank and disorienting. Waking without a task in front of her, she remained in her room until the rattle of the cleaning girl's bucket chased her out. She took tea from the hostile Winnifred, tried to dodge Aunt Millie, and continued to walk for hours along the shore. She felt like a mouse scurrying along a skirting board, exposed, praying not to be noticed before she found a safe hole to dart through.

As promised, Warren returned frequently to the house. Fanny decided to exert some effort to charm him, as he apparently had a lot of money, and money meant opportunities. He seemed to enjoy the sound of his own voice, so she pretended to be fascinated by what he had to say, and when he began to wind down on a particular topic, she wound him back up with a fresh question.

In truth, she did actually find his little lectures informative, as he possessed a lifetime of insights into culture and capitalism. Had she been in a better frame of mind, she would have enjoyed learning from him, but as it was, she was glad that he did the talking and asked few questions about her. When the subject turned to Fanny's past, she answered sparingly, and Aunt Millie swiftly redirected them to town gossip, or commentary on the weather.

One evening, when she returned to her room, Fanny found a small newspaper clipping on her bedside table. The title was "Mr. Charles Marshall Engaged to Marry Miss Mae Garth." Fanny couldn't read any further. She curled up on her bed, fully dressed, and hugged a pillow to her chest. Sickening hollowness was relieved by fits of sobbing, which subsided into hollowness once more. Like a vessel caught in a storm, she was thrown from trough to crest to trough. By the time the sun rose, she was spent, and she went to breakfast in a stuporous state. Aunt Millie was kind enough not to remark on her bloodshot eyes and swollen face. "Have some tea, dear," she said, pouring her a cup.

Fanny didn't think she could swallow anything, but she tried to sip to be polite. The warm porcelain in her hand was comforting.

Aunt Millie watched her with a look of sympathy. "Kitty, dear, I have something I wish to discuss with you."

"Of course," Fanny murmured, though she only wanted to be left alone.

"It's about Mr. Warren."

Fanny pressed a hand to her aching head.

"He wishes to marry you."

Her mind distracted and senses dulled, Fanny barely registered the words. "He wishes . . ." She trailed off.

"I think it would be sensible for you to say yes," Aunt Millie said from behind her teacup. "He would provide you with a comfortable life."

The idea seemed so preposterous that Fanny was unable to respond. She had thought that perhaps Warren could offer her a job, or introduce her to others who could, but a romantic liaison with the old man was ridiculous as well as repulsive.

"You seem to have captivated him quite effectively." When Fanny opened her mouth to protest, Aunt Millie raised her hand to cut her off. "I know that this is not what you had in mind, dear." She lowered her arm, shaking her head a little sadly. "I also know that you are clinging to the hope of an invitation to New York." After a slow blink, she said, "That is not realistic, dear."

In that moment, Fanny hated the old woman with her sagging jowls and watery eyes.

Aunt Millie sighed. "I am only saying these things to try to help you. The decision is up to you."

Like a somnambulist, Fanny carried on, outwardly maintaining her established persona as Kitty. She did not explicitly acquiesce to a relationship with Warren, but over time, their engagement was treated as a fait accompli. She told herself that she wouldn't have to marry him, that she would be rescued by a summons from Mae. And then summer was over.

Aside from an arm about her waist and the occasional dry brush of lips, Fanny was not subjected to amorous advances. She expected this to change once they moved to Pittsburgh and were married, but on their wedding night, Harry showed her to a bower of flowery brocade and chintz, and she crept into the cottony soap-scented bed alone. Fanny lay awake most of that night, first fearing that Harry would come back and then, as the wee hours of the morning rang from unseen clocks in the dark and otherwise silent house, brooding about her situation.

Why would a well-to-do man marry an impecunious girl of sketchy heritage and meager education?

This question had leaped fully formed into Fanny's mind as if from the pages of a novel—it haunted her.

What did Harry want?

"Companionship," Aunt Millie had said.

Fanny didn't believe it.

On the first morning, after a sleepless night, Fanny found her husband in the breakfast room behind a newspaper.

"Did you have a good night, Kitten?" He glanced over the top of the paper, his small dark eyes incurious under their beetling brows, then flipped it back up with a crisp *thwap* and went on reading.

"Yes, thank you." Fanny stood a moment, like a child in a game, waiting for the next cue. None came. She took her place at the table, in front of the remaining place setting. On a large serving dish there were crumbs and half of a scone. Fanny took it, nibbling. Her dry mouth was made more parched by the stale pastry.

Harry turned a rustling page of the newspaper.

"Excuse me, is there tea?" Fanny asked meekly.

A distracted grunt came from her screened husband. Fanny surveyed the tabletop; orange rinds and an empty cup delineated the perimeter of Harry's breakfast domain. A harsh squawk made her jump and drop the scone, raw nerves jangling. In a silver cage by the window, an exotic white bird twitched its tail and ruffled through its feathers with its beak. It shuffled on its perch and directed a baleful eye at Fanny. In the fog of fatigue, she had the sudden sense that she was dreaming. She closed her eyes, allowing herself to float for a moment in darkness. When she opened them again, she would be back in Newport with Mae.

Squawk! The bird tilted its ugly crab-claw beak toward the ceiling friezes, still glowering disapprovingly. She glared back at the supercilious animal, then at the wall of newsprint.

"Tea, please?" she called out louder.

Harry looked up sharply.

"Is there tea?" She held Harry's partial gaze, obstructed by the paper. "I am thirsty."

Harry sighed. "Annabelle!" he cried out. "Tea for the mistress!"

A servant peered around the door jamb. "Yes, sir?"

"Tea for the mistress, please."

In a few moments, a silver pot appeared. Harry nodded, and the girl poured a cup for Fanny.

"Where is the milk and sugar?" he said.

Annabelle nervously straightened her cap, disappeared, then reappeared with a creamer and sugar bowl, which she set down next to Fanny. She hovered. "Anything more for you, ma'am?"

"No, thank you, Annabelle." Fanny poured a stream of milk into her tea, where it swirled as a wan cloud. She watched the girl leave, wondering how old she was. The silver spoon made pleasing clinks against the china cup as she stirred; again, the absurdity of her position as mistress of the household struck her. It was like being transported into someone else's life. Well, she decided, she might as well learn her role. "What is on the calendar for today?"

Harry ignored her question.

Fanny set down her spoon and sipped her tea. "What is my duty today?"

Harold Warren lowered his newspaper with an aggrieved air. "Since you ask, your only duty is to choose a suitable gown for the twentieth, three weeks hence." He pursed his lips. "The housekeeper doesn't have anyone to take you shopping, but my neighbor, Mrs. Caldwell, will send someone to help."

"And what is the occasion on the twentieth?"

The corner of Harry's lip twitched in a half-smile. "The kickoff of my campaign."

A rosy-cheeked middle-aged domestic from next door, whose name was Colleen, knew all of the best shops and dressmakers in Pittsburgh.

"Well, I should know my way around; I took care of four girls at the Caldwell house," she said. "All married now." Colleen squinted at Fanny; a light hand on her shoulder signaled her to turn from side to side. "With the right sort of neckline and some pearls, you could be very elegant." She smiled, patted her cheek. "God gives beauty, but a nice gown helps men see it."

Colleen's motherliness loosened the knot in Fanny's stomach as she tried to navigate her new situation. She seemed to accept Fanny's story—that she was a guileless, marginal member of the upper class who had married an old man out of economic necessity. The reality—that she was a guile*ful* member of the lower class who had married an old man out of economic necessity—seemed an unimportant distinction. As the matronly woman ushered her from shop to shop, Fanny fell into her role with Colleen as into a feather duvet.

Colleen huffed about the short timeline for procuring a gown, but she made quick work of finding one. "No time for fancy embroidery," she said, "but that's no reason it can't be grand." They settled on ivory lace over lilac satin, and Colleen argued the dressmaker out of charging extra for the rush. "You have to be firm with them, or they will rob you blind, Kitty dear." Her eyes scrunched to jolly half-moons when she smiled.

"You have been so considerate," Fanny said as they exited the shop. "Please allow me to take you to lunch."

Colleen blushed furiously, and Fanny worried that she had made a faux pas. Still, with a shy glance, Colleen said, "There is a nice pub at the Grand Depot. I could take you there if you wish."

Colleen grasped her knife like a dagger, stabbing at her pink pork chop, smacking her lips and licking the juice from her thick fingers as she ate. Fanny's own sensibilities surprised her; in less than a year, she had gone from blithely eating with her hands to daintily carving off tiny bites. Made queasy by her lunch companion's lack of manners, Fanny felt a jolt of guilt as she averted her eyes.

The restaurant was nearly full, the clientele boisterous. After a while, Fanny no longer noticed the noise or the yeasty, sticky smell of beer mingled with the scent of grilled meat and tobacco smoke. Her plate was piled startlingly high with mashed potatoes and greasy sausages, which she picked at, never seeming to make a dent.

The other patrons paid them no heed, and the cheery, pimply serving girl was polite but not deferential. Fanny remembered Aunt Millie's oblique comment that she would find Pittsburgh "more convivial than Newport." It was indeed a relief to let go of the pretense for a while.

"You have lived with the Caldwells for some years now?" she asked Colleen.

"Almost thirty," Colleen said through a mouthful of food. She swallowed, then took a sip of ale. "I started out in the kitchen."

"How long have you known Mr. Warren?"

Colleen guffawed, and slapped a freckled hand over her mouth after a particle of food escaped. She was still smiling when she took her hand away. "I don't *know* Mr. Warren, child."

Perhaps it was the pint of beer or Colleen's affability, but Fanny wasn't worried about the reminder that she was navigating uncharted waters. With a self-deprecating wave of her hand, she said, "Of course. I meant, how long has he been your neighbor?"

The laugh had turned into a cough; Colleen pressed her palm to her breast and drank a swig of ale once it had passed. "Round about twenty years, I would say." She cleared her throat. "He moved in with his first wife, a Catholic." Though Colleen's eyebrows were so pale and sparse as to give her face a look of perpetual surprise, she managed a convincingly acerbic arch. "To church every morning and twice on Sunday. Always dressed like a nun, that one." She placed her forearms on the table and leaned in. "No children came from that marriage." When Fanny didn't register a response, she said, "If you ask me, the woman was frigid as an Eskimo."

Fanny wasn't sure that she understood, but she saw Colleen's blush returning, so she too leaned in, arranging her features into a look of complicity. "A man has certain expectations," she ventured.

Colleen nodded, her expression brightening. "Poor thing died. They say it was pneumonia. She always did seem sickly." She looked around the busy restaurant, as though someone might overhear. "After that, the lights burned long into the night at Mr. Warren's house. Carriages came and went at odd hours." Catching herself, she said, "I don't mean to gossip, ma'am." She fiddled uncertainly with the salt cellar.

Fanny lowered her voice. "It's just us ladies here."

Tentatively, Colleen smiled back. "What I tell my girls is, we got to stick together." She glanced across the table, then back at her plate. "It's a man's world, there's no doubt."

"There is no doubt of that, my dear." Fanny said this in all earnestness and added a world-weary sigh. Observing Colleen's response, she saw that she'd succeeded in asserting her social rank while still drawing her close. "I may be mistress of my household, but men are masters of us all."

"That's what I told my girls." Colleen shook her head. "Rosie thought she could influence her husband." The finality with which she ended the sentence made it amply clear that Rosie had failed.

"I am not so bold," Fanny said. "But as one who has helped to launch young ladies into society, how might you counsel me?"

Colleen lifted her chin, and Fanny could almost see her chest feathers swell and then settle. "Mr. Warren is running for the office of state senator, as the whole city knows. He needs a dutiful bride by his side." Her brow puckered in thought. "Fashionable, most certainly, for the upper crust. But also kind and humble." Her gaze flicked back to Fanny, troubled. "Not, of course, that you aren't kind and humble, ma'am! I am only talking of appearances."

"Of course." Fanny balanced her fork between her fingers, noting the cheapness of its construction. "His campaign will be officially announced on the twentieth."

"I suppose, ma'am."

"You will help me to be a grand success." Fanny beamed at her.

The pleasure in Colleen's soft-cheeked face was unmistakable. "I've a good deal of experience, ma'am. And the Caldwells have been good to keep me on, but I've not enough to do now that the girls are gone. I'm at your service."

CHAPTER 21

A seal fur redingote would turn heads," Fanny said, examining her nails. She remembered poring over the artful French fashion plates of *Peterson's Magazine* with Mae, one featuring the prized Canadian fur. The thought of owning a luxury item from her home country tickled her fancy in an ironic sort of way, but she knew that Harry would never pay for the extravagance. He was, in fact, frowning, though whether at her or at some unrelated thought in his head, she could not tell.

Fanny tilted her head submissively, and smiled at her husband. "Meanwhile, given that it is still autumn, I am sure that a velvet cape would be perfectly acceptable."

"You will look lovely in whatever you wear," Harry said. "I am merely reminding you that it will be an important occasion."

A crow cawed raggedly from the tall pine tree in the yard, where strong gusts of wind made the boughs shiver and thrash. Dead leaves swirled against the slate sky and tapped wearily at the window. Fanny turned back to the cozy parlor, where a tea service of Baltimore silver gleamed by a warming fire. "Of course, dear," she said. "They are all important occasions."

Harry's campaign for state senate was faltering, but as he said to Fanny, raising his profile in Pennsylvania was a first step, and if he had to try again for political office, that was not a real setback. "A single defeat is not a final defeat," he told her.

Fanny did not mind accompanying Harry to his stump speeches. He was an uncharismatic speaker, and she sometimes cringed at his inability to connect with audiences, but she appreciated his self-confidence, the way it reassured listeners that he was up to the job. He was a small, gray man with slender, childlike fingers and a light tenor voice. He had a tendency to gesticulate when he imbibed too much. He was not imposing, not brilliant, not remarkable in any obvious way, but he commanded respect because he believed that he deserved it—and he was rich. Affluence was a golden key that unlocked access to worldly approval. Heritage certainly mattered, but Fanny was learning that it might not be as all-important as Mae had imagined. Wealth seemed to be the prime determinant of social value, and that gave Fanny hope. She could not improve her parentage, but she had already vastly improved her financial standing, and that could be a path to the security and freedom she increasingly craved. It could also be a path back to Mae, whom she still longed for with a fierceness that she could not fully admit to herself, a fierceness that swallowed the sisterly affection from Betsy or the friendship from Grace that once would have been enough.

"Should I be mindful of anyone in particular at the event?" Fanny was taking note of those who held influence, those whose opinions were of consequence.

He sighed. "I don't think so." The wind whistled through the eaves and made the heavy oak door shudder in its frame. Harry glanced at the fire as it huffed a plume of smoke into the room. As an afterthought, "But every citizen is important, of course."

Pittsburgh crowds did not intimidate Fanny, despite her rural upbringing. She felt at home among immigrant coal miners and the nouveaux riches. The concerns of the working class were familiar to her, and because she had learned about the East Coast elite and Parisian fashion from Mae, the upper class of Pittsburgh did not seem so sophisticated.

Harry, who had been born into modest wealth, was dismissive of Pittsburgh's high society. "Pretending at Continental manners and finery" was how he put it. An exception was his worship of Andrew Carnegie, the Scottish bobbin boy who had risen to dizzying heights of industrial success in steelworks. "A genius," Harry said. "An example of man's intellectual powers." That Carnegie was unmarried and childless seemed to heighten Harry's admiration. "When a man channels his energy into productive work, God rewards him," Harry told her. There was no mention that the "champion of the working man" built his empire on the bent and bloodied backs of the poor. This was just one more example of society's glorification of the rich and utter disregard for how their money was made. Given her secret background, Fanny nursed anger at Harry's unwillingness to see the truth, but it also made her determined to never again be one of the backs they climbed upon.

"Did Mr. Carnegie respond to your request for an endorsement?" Fanny asked, knowing the answer. Harry could not have contained himself, would have needed to confide in someone, even his wife, if he had received a letter from the Scottish bobbin boy himself. She knew that it was foolish to poke at her husband, but the lemony tartness of subtle barbs was one of the few pleasures of her faux marriage. That Harry did not perceive the barbs did not diminish her admittedly petty gratification.

Harry stroked his beard. "Not yet," he said.

"Maybe you should pay him a visit."

Staring into the fire and sipping his hot cocoa, Harry ignored her.

A windborne twig slapped against the window, startling them both. "I hope the weather will cooperate for your event," Fanny said.

Harry didn't answer. A log in the fire collapsed, sending up a shower of orange sparks.

"I'm sure your speech will be a great success," she added.

The bare trees at the edge of their property swayed against a sooty sky. A raucous flock of crows wheeled and dropped, their caws like croaking laughter.

That Harry wasn't interested in her as a woman had been immediately apparent to Fanny. That she was needed as a social palliative dawned on her soon after. It was a marriage that benefited them both, and though he treated her as no more than a pet animal or practical acquisition, she felt a sort of loyalty to him. He'd given her a life of comfort and a platform from which to observe the machinations of society, and she would fulfill her end of the agreement.

Fanny questioned Harry about everything she could think to ask: Pittsburgh society, his grocery business, politics, the Pittsburgh Stock Exchange, steel factories, even Latin conjugation. She didn't know what knowledge would be useful to her, so she tried to learn as much as she could. Harry was loquacious on the rare occasions when he was in a good mood, and she did her best to keep him talking, roaming over a wide terrain of subjects. After these conversations, she retired to her bedroom and pulled a thick notebook from the bottom of her storage chest. In a neat, tiny script, she recorded details for later reference. She also made notes from newspaper articles she read, or tucked clippings between the pages. The back of the notebook was reserved for forgery practice; she took whatever samples of Harry's handwriting she thought he wouldn't miss, and worked diligently on reproducing it. His signature, in particular, might come in handy.

The couple had no joint social life beyond political functions. Harry held parties late at night, after Fanny had gone to bed. Tobacco smoke wafted up the stairs, along with male voices laughing and the cacophony of amateur performances on the piano, often accompanied by singing. In the morning, she found the parlor gamy and littered with bits of detritus, like the shore at low tide. At first, Harry gave her explanations for the gatherings—fundraising, a friend's birthday, an evening with the lads. Fanny made her expression bland, her few words as smooth and glassy as sea-washed pebbles. *It's none of my business*, her demeanor conveyed. Harry seemed content with her indifference. Once, a bleary-eyed guest stumbled down the stairs at breakfast time, his wrinkled, half-open shirtfront fastened with a large imitation pearl. Harry made no comment to his wife as the man disappeared through the front door. She concentrated on the soft-boiled egg she was carefully decapitating with a silver spoon.

Harry offered to get Fanny a lady's maid, but Fanny had no interest in inviting a stranger into her life. She cultivated Colleen from next door, who lamented that she had too much time on her hands "with all my girls married off." Her employers were only slightly known to Harry, and they never bothered to introduce themselves to Fanny. They didn't seem to keep track of Colleen, who came over to help with household affairs, unpaid, on a regular basis. While she pointed out problems with overstarched linens and unpolished floors, she also informed Fanny about local concerns, scandals, gossip, and the trajectories of the ill-fortuned and the ascendant families. Some women in the community came from "antique stock," as Colleen disparagingly put it, wives who had grown up overseas and "put on airs." Others met Colleen's approval as "good, wholesome folks." Fanny kept a list in her notebook and updated it with comments she overheard from Harry or his visitors.

Colleen told Fanny that she should hire a house manager, but she also told her how to handle Annabelle, the maid, and Nancy, the cook, herself. Nancy had staked out her kitchen domain in the absence of oversight, and she ruled it like a petty monarch, frightening the other help and cooking what she saw fit. Harry never complained; he didn't seem to care what he put in his mouth.

"*You* set the meal plan," Colleen said. "If Nancy needs to go to the market three times in three days to find quails, that is her job, and not for you to worry about."

"She always has an excuse," Fanny told her. "But I don't know whether she is telling the truth when she says that the cream is spoiled, or the eggs were sold out."

Colleen shook her head, clucked her tongue. "You just tell her to figure it out, and stop bothering you with trifles."

"I think she might leave if I do that." Fanny rubbed the lump of scar on her thumb. "I've heard that good help is hard to find."

"Bad help is what's unaffordable, ma'am," Coleen replied dryly.

About the two girls who worked in the mansion weekly, Colleen advised a light hand. "They're naught but children. If the bed corners are crooked, you should leave it; Mr. Warren won't notice."

Fanny learned that she could be exacting with servants while also inspiring loyalty by setting out clear expectations and rewarding results with sweet treats, days off, hand-me-downs. The cook did need to be replaced, but Annabelle became a staunch ally and purveyor of information. Her cousin worked for the mayor, a former miner and champion of the working people. The nuggets of gossip provided by Annabelle were gold for trading with Harry when he was being taciturn and uninclined to converse with his wife. Fanny offered little bits of hearsay, like a handful of seeds to a skittish bird, then delicately prodded for details about his business, his banking, his investments. Over time, she began to understand the concepts of collateral, interest, the distributions of loans. She learned of his contacts in New York and tried to convince him to take her there, to no avail. He did not care to travel more than was necessary and was not tempted by the cosmopolitan offerings of the big city. Fanny wondered whether he was intimidated by New York, but there was no easy way to test her conjecture; Harry lived inside a hard, smooth shell.

Harry was not an avid reader of books, only newspapers, but he did have a full library, and Fanny spent many hours ensconced in the bay window, half-hidden behind velvet drapes. She read John Stuart Mill's *Principles of Political Economy* and smiled at the fairy tales by Horatio Alger. She inhaled the novels of Dickens, Jane Austen, Sir Walter Scott; plodded through Ruskin, Plato and Xenophon, Cicero and Horace. With no instruction, no framework within which to house the ideas on the pages she read, she built her own unique understanding. Fanny did not have a particularly high opinion of her own intellect, but she had never met anyone whose intellect seemed to exceed her own, and so it didn't occur to her that there might be matters beyond her capacity to understand—she absorbed it all.

CHAPTER 22

Harry was a wealthy man, but he kept a tight grip on the purse strings. For many years, he had allocated stipends not only for salaries but also for household expenses; there were fixed budgets for groceries, cleaning supplies, coal, garden upkeep, house repairs. Even in the absence of a wife, his domestic sphere had operated both smoothly and frugally. When Fanny came into the picture, Harry gave her a clothing allowance and little else—she had no access to his bank accounts and only limited discretion to alter prearranged payments. It became apparent to Fanny that she would need her own funds if she was to achieve any sort of independence.

Over a dinner of leek soup and tri-tip, Fanny floated the idea to her husband that she might seek out a job. "I would like to feel useful in some way," she said. "I have no real role now that your campaign is over." Unsaid was an acknowledgment that Fanny would never be a mother. Not that she minded—she equated childhood with unhappiness and was in no way eager to bring another child into the world. Some part of her also understood that motherhood would be an unbreakable tether, a sticky web she might never escape.

"You could volunteer at the library. Mr. Carnegie said that there is no better use of money or time than public libraries." Harry mopped up the grease from his plate with a piece of bread, and popped it into his small mouth. Oil glistened on his mustache. "I know you like to read."

"I had rather hoped to earn some money."

Harry snorted. "You are such an amusing girl."

Fanny resisted the urge to chew on her lip, the word *unladylike* floating in the periphery of her consciousness. "Surely there is some sort of employment that would advance the interests of our household?"

Harry sat back in his chair and felt in the pocket of his vest for a toothpick, the sign that he was finished with his meal. Annabelle whisked his plate away and brought out a decanter of brandy with a crystal glass.

"If you are bored," he said, not looking at Fanny, "a volunteer position should suit you just fine." He set down his unused toothpick on the tablecloth and sipped from his cup. "Unless you have some need for money that I don't know about." His tone was mild, but Fanny felt the cold blade of a warning.

"I just want to be helpful," she said, arranging her expression in what she hoped was a pleasant smile. "The library is a fine idea."

The Pittsburgh Stock Exchange was something Fanny had learned about in bits and pieces from Harry, from the newspapers, and from listening in on the men's discussions. Companies had certain valuations, which Fanny struggled to understand—they spoke about money, debtors, creditors, investments, dividends, assets, loans, stocks, bonds, and most of all, profits, profits, profits. Some of these companies were well established, and Fanny recognized the names. Others seemed to be brand new, and their contributions to industry were unclear. Fanny wondered whether the worth of these companies was intrinsic or a perception created by the views of those who wanted to believe in prosperity. Perhaps there was no difference.

That the perception of success *was* success made sense to Fanny. If she had learned anything from her time in Cleveland, it was that so-called high society was ruled by seemingly arbitrary valuations of social worth. She had not yet learned all of the rules of the valuations, but it was abundantly clear to her that they could be manipulated. She had done so herself, under Mae's tutelage.

Fanny's interest was piqued when she overheard a conversation about the Occidental Silk Import Company selling stocks on the exchange. She knew from her conversations with Colleen that they sold high-quality fabric, water-smooth and thick, not the "flimsy, puckered trash" that Colleen said was the usual merchandise available in the local shops. The men who smoked cigars with Harry had other views. "Sure to fail," they said between puffs. "Orientals who think they know about finance." There were half-hearted guffaws before conversation turned to other subjects.

Fanny had a reserve of cash in her lingerie drawer, money she had skimmed from her shopping budget. On a humid, overcast spring day, she put on her most conservative walking suit and hat and took a hansom cab downtown, clasping an embroidered purse containing her savings. The coal smoke thickened as they descended toward the city center, irritating her throat, and the roadways grew more crowded, populated increasingly by men. She had chosen her staid tweed outfit as a form of armor but regretted her choice almost immediately; it felt like steam from her body was trying to escape through the tight collar, and the scratchy fabric chafed her skin.

When she recognized the Pittsburgh Exchange building, she rapped on the roof for the driver to stop, eager to escape the confines of the carriage. A faint drizzle dewed her face as she descended to the sidewalk, and she was grateful for it; it seemed the one fresh note in a teeming street redolent of manure and decaying food scraps. After paying the driver, Fanny got her bearings. At the end of the block stood the ugly sandstone exchange building with its superfluous pillars and bloated facade; in front, scatterings of individuals were stationed in ramshackle arrangements, on stools or crates, some with tables, one with a hand-made sign that read "BEST RATES HERE." Around them clustered men in various attire, looking over papers, vociferating, carrying on animated discussions.

Through the hubbub cut a call: "Hello, m'lady, what can I do for you?"

Fanny looked about, trying to locate the speaker. A pair of scruffy youths who had been approaching her retreated under her glare, slinking down an alley, chortling and jostling one another. A man sitting on stacked crates lifted a pudgy hand, beckoning. When Fanny moved to get a better view, checking whether he was beckoning her, he gestured faster, more energetically.

Fanny approached. The man's stiffly starched collar seemed to dig into the fold of his thick neck; his ruddy face was topped with an oily-looking tall hat. "Ignore the ruffians," he said, twisting his fingers about the heavy gold watch-chain that crossed his waistcoat. "What is it that you seek?"

Fanny wasn't sure what to make of him, with his old-fashioned attire and eccentric diction. "Do you work here?" she asked.

The man smirked. "Indeed." He pulled a large white handkerchief from his pocket and wiped his bulbous nose. "Welcome to my curb-stone office."

Though she worried that she was being mocked, Fanny persevered. "Do you know about trading stocks?"

His head jutted forward over his barrel chest. "That is what I do, missy. I am a broker."

She looked back in the direction from which she had come, where businessmen strode purposefully with briefcases and a black stream of carriages flowed over the cobblestones, weaving in cross-streams at the intersection. She cleared her throat. "Do you have a desk?"

His jet-black eyebrows drew together. "If you can afford deluxe service, please do proceed inside and to the upper floor, m'amselle." He made a flourish with his handkerchief, then shoved it back into his trouser pocket, from which, like a magician, he pulled out an improbably large flask. He took a swig. "Or, you may parlay with me, should you deign to stoop so low."

Fanny clutched her handbag nervously. "I wish to buy stock in the Occidental Silk Import Company."

The man nodded, the flesh above his collar bulging. "New stocks, those," he said. "Trading at four and an eighth."

There was no way to hide her ignorance. "What can I buy for twenty dollars?"

His smile was almost kind. "Well, at four and an eighth, you can buy four stocks."

Fanny reached into her bag, but before she had produced the cash, the man whistled loudly, and one of the scruffy youths appeared next to them. "Buy for OSIC, four times four and an eighth, maximum four and two eighths." The words were rapid and clipped. The boy saluted sloppily and loped off at a slow run.

It was not at all clear to Fanny what had just taken place, but a thrill rolled up her spine. This was a world she had imagined, where money could change hands without one's pedigree or male ownership coming into the equation. She had placed an order, and once she handed off her crumpled fistful of cash, she would own a tiny part of a new company.

Fanny tipped her face up to the sky, savoring the scattered drops of rain that had begun to fall like tiny benedictions. She could hear orders for the purchase and sale of securities hoarsely shouted down from the windows of nearby brokerages, with the execution of the sale then barked back up. It seemed to her a market where the ordinary man belonged, no different from the cattle sales back home. She belonged here.

The boy came trotting back with a certificate.

"Your shares in the Occidental Silk Import Company, m'amselle," the broker said.

Fanny held out her hand. Rather than give her the stock paper, the broker took her hand and shook it firmly. "Welcome to the worldwide commercial market," he said.

Fanny returned his handshake warmly before taking the certificate.

"We can be partners," Fanny said.

Colleen looked at her suspiciously.

"All you need to do is purchase the silk you were already planning to buy. You love the occidental silk!"

"Then in what way are we partners?" Colleen put the end of the thread in her mouth before passing it through the eye of the needle. Despite a slight tremor, she succeeded on the first try.

"You're still very close to the Caldwell girls; you can tell them about this first-rate fabric. If enthusiasm for the new silk goes beyond the four of them, well, that's money in your pocket, because I will pay you ten percent of any profit I make from the investment." Fanny leaned forward, pushing her teacup to the side, but Colleen did not look up from her work. "It's just about getting people talking," Fanny continued. "The dresses will be perfectly beautiful, so of course there will be talk."

Colleen grunted softly, rearranged the fabric in her lap. "I don't know that silk will be to everyone's taste," she said. "We aren't *Parisians* here." The word *Parisian* sounded like an insult.

"But you said yourself that it will be the event of the season! And that Marjorie has a new rope of pearls—how better to show them off than with silk?" Fanny hummed a bar of music, and then in a mincing voice said, "Dancing ever so gracefully, sumptuous silk gowns gleaming by candlelight, the Caldwell girls are the toast of Pittsburgh . . ."

Colleen rewarded her with a grudging smile. "I suppose it wouldn't hurt to take a look at the merchandise." She peered over the rim of her smudged spectacles, her deft fingers still stitching, and said pointedly, "No promises, mind."

It did not take much convincing on Colleen's part to get "her girls" to agree to the silk, which was, after all, of excellent quality. Fanny's next move was to visit Pittsburgh dressmakers and inquire after the gowns she had "heard so much about." She said that she had just returned from New York and that all of the most fashionable shops were displaying clothes made from the "exquisite Occidental Silk Import Company fabrics" prominently in their windows. It was almost impossible to buy the popular cloth in New York, she said, as it was perennially sold out. She hoped to be able to purchase enough locally to take back with her for her friends when she returned to the city next season. She used her entire clothing allowance to have silk dresses made at two of the most prominent ladies' tailoring shops.

Before long, the shops in Pittsburgh were displaying the silk in their windows. The much-anticipated ball caused a run on the fabric that exceeded Fanny's expectations; the price per yard more than doubled. Even better, when she buttonholed one of Harry's friends in the hallway, he admitted that he had heard about the Occidental Silk Import Company from his wife, and thought it was a sound investment. She decided that it was time to cash out. Fanny went back to the stock exchange, and when she bade farewell to the curbstone broker, she had almost two hundred dollars in her purse. It was a start.

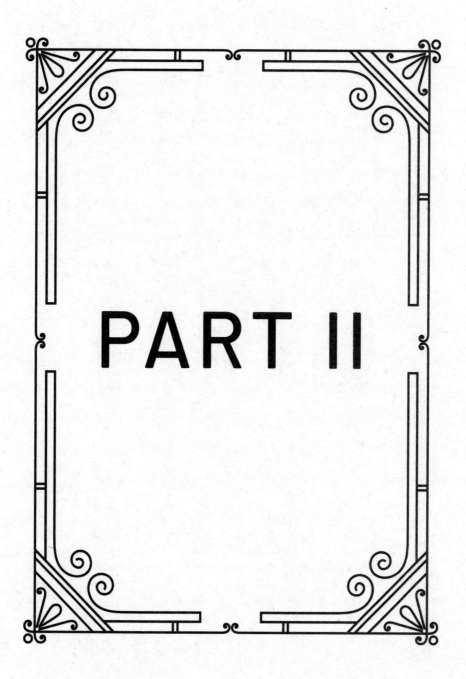

PART II

CHAPTER 23

Joseph Carrow, cousin of Mae Marshall

Whenever you feel like criticizing anyone," my father told me, "just remember that privilege is not doled out equally at birth."

I have long been inclined to reserve judgment on my fellow men. This has sometimes been to my detriment—uneasy souls seem to be able to sniff out my unwillingness to impose moral standards on others, and they draw me into uncomfortable confessions. While I try to avoid such uninvited intimacies, I do consider this habit of mind to be a matter of hope.

Yet—and yet. This habit of mind came under strain during my time in New York. There, superficial probity glazes over a morass of moral relativism which, in the end, made me yearn for the clean lines of upright behavior I learned in my youth.

It is a great irony that the only new acquaintance whom I admired in New York was the one who should have been most deserving of my opprobrium, Mrs. Kitty Warren. It cannot be said that she behaved with moral rectitude, but if a character is built through aspirations and actions, then she was a North Star. More than anyone I have met, she was sensitive to the promises of life and to the gift of hope. She may not have been born into riches, but she had the rare quality of one impelled by passion; it was the foul dust that floated in the wake of her dreams that soured me to her gilded entourage.

I recognize my own good fortune—my family have been prominent, well-to-do people in the Middle West. I attended Yale and Oxford, then wandered Europe for a year. Upon my return to the United States, I moved to New York, where I read law and was given a desk in the office of a respectable firm.

By any reasonable standard, mine is a life of great privilege. Yet, in New York, I came to rub elbows with a whole other class of individuals, beginning with my second cousin, Mae Marshall. I had only a glancing acquaintance with Mae when we were younger, but she married a classmate of mine from Yale, Charlie Marshall, and it was natural that our social lives should intersect once we all lived in the same city. Of course I was no denizen of Washington Square, where the moneyed New Yorkers lived; I made my home farther uptown and to the east of fashionable Fifth Avenue. It did not take me long to realize that, despite my "privilege," I was a nobody in the Empire City.

I was nervous on my first visit to the Marshall mansion. Their house was even more elaborate than I had anticipated, built from ivory-tinted stone—modeled on the residences of Parisian aristocracy—instead of the sedate brown sandstone that was de rigueur for wealthy New Yorkers, proper and plain as frock coats in the afternoon. The gardens also had a continental flavor, with sculpted topiaries, a glass orchid house, and a pool of white marble with water jets and cavorting cupids.

Charlie met me in the cool, expansive foyer, shooing his butler away as though he had no need for such formality. He was broader than I remembered, his powerful shoulders filling out his smoking jacket, but his arrogant gaze and hard mouth were instantly recognizable. At Yale, though Charlie had been respected for his wealth and athletic prowess, his patronizing attitude of noblesse oblige had made him few friends.

"Joe! Good to see you, cousin," he said, taking my hand in a vise grip and grinning broadly. At more than six feet tall with a dark, drooping mustache, Charlie had been one of the most eligible bachelors in New York; apparently debutantes in the city had not forgiven an interloper from Cleveland for snatching him up.

"Good to see *you*, cousin," I replied, though utterance of the familial title caught in my throat. "Thank you for the invitation."

He chuckled in a way that was meant to be companionable but wasn't. "Mae has been so impatient for your visit."

This seemed odd to me, since I hadn't seen my cousin in many years.

"What do you think of the place?" He glanced about as though he was the one visiting for the first time. "We brought in the pink marble from Italy." With a light slap on my back, he said, "Let me show you around."

Off the main entrance was a conservatory of flowers, with French windows that opened like doors instead of sashes that pulled up; beyond that, a sitting room filled with pre-Revolutionary furniture. He opened the door to the gothic library and invited me to step in; it smelled of linseed oil and was entirely paneled with carved oak. To be polite, I pretended to admire one of the leather-bound books, then noticed that the joined pages had not been cut. I quickly returned it to the shelf.

In the next room, the windows went almost from ceiling to floor, diaphanous curtains stirring gently. Mae reclined on a window seat, the skirt of her white frock trailing to the floor; she appeared as some Grecian goddess. I was stilled for a moment, taking in the tableau. She twirled a loose strand of golden hair, gazing toward the sky with an enraptured air. When Charlie spoke her name, she turned slowly and made a movement as if to rise, an earnest expression on her face. Then she laughed, a silvery sound, and fell back. "I am too happy to move," she said in lilting tones.

"Please do not disturb yourself," I said, but by then she had risen, and she took my hand.

"It has been far too long," Mae murmured. In her lovely face was both brightness and sorrow, and beneath it all an eagerness that flattered me beyond reason.

I told her that I had seen some of our people in Cleveland before coming to New York. She smiled vaguely but didn't ask after anyone.

Charlie, who had been hovering, clapped a hand on my shoulder. "What are you doing, old chap?"

The anglicism struck me as affected, his voice too booming.

"Reading law," I said.

He chuckled. "Not much money in that." He offered me a cigarette box, which I declined. "When you are ready for me to introduce you to the world of finance, do let me know. There is always room for another young man to make his fortune in banking."

"It is just too dull to talk about business with our guest." Mae made a charming moue.

"My dear, banking has bought you everything you care about." The hardness in Charlie's voice did not seem to affect his wife, who clapped her hands together when a servant brought in a tray of glasses.

"Do let's take that champagne on the balcony," she said, smiling. "The light is so beautiful at this time of day." Without waiting for a response, Mae moved languidly toward the open French doors, shoulders back, a jeweled hand perched on her slim waist.

The servant looked to Charlie inquiringly, who nodded. We all followed Mae outside.

"I heard a nightingale—I'm sure of it," Mae said. She turned to me. "Do you suppose it made its way here all the way across the ocean, on the White Star Line?" She turned away again, shielded her eyes against the setting sun, her skirt flaring in a puff of wind.

Charlie pulled out a wrought iron chair with a loud scrape against the stonework and asked where I was living. When I told him, he said, "Nobody lives above 40th Street!" He chortled. "You might as well live in Canada!"

Mae kept her face to the garden, with its blooming azaleas and splashing fountain. There was longing in her pose, the way she reached out a hand to the balustrade, bending toward the pink horizon.

Charlie grabbed a champagne flute before the servant had set down the tray. He drained it in two gulps and handed the glass back to the man. "A whiskey sour," he commanded. He consulted his watch, snapped it shut, polished it on his waistcoat.

I hesitated, not having been invited to sit or pick up a glass.

"There, did you hear that birdsong?" Mae's voice trailed off softly into a sigh, as though she had spoken only to herself.

The sounds of the city were all around us, and despite the expanse of their lawns, I found it difficult to imagine that she could pick out the chirping of a particular bird.

When Mae turned and noticed me standing awkwardly near the door, she bade me sit, rebuking her husband with a sidelong glance. "Cheers to my dear cousin," she said, lifting a flute. She held it aloft until I raised mine.

"Thank you," I responded. "Cheers to you both." I took my seat next to Charlie, while Mae leaned back against the balustrade, a faraway look on her lovely face.

Charlie drummed his fingers on the onyx table and shifted restlessly in his seat. He told me about his plans to build a new row of orchid houses and to purchase race horses. After craning his neck toward the door, he sat back again and told me about his planned cruise to the West Indies on a new steam-yacht fitted with tiled bathrooms.

The whole while, Mae gazed into the middle distance, sipping champagne.

"My wife says that she will only join me on the yacht if it has a proper boudoir."

Mae gave him a heavy-lidded look.

"Where is that drink?" Charlie heaved his considerable bulk out of the chair, and paced toward the door.

Mae watched him cooly, then said, "Why don't you just bring out a bottle of bourbon?" The acerbity was coated in honey, but Charlie glowered before making his way indoors.

Mae tipped up her empty glass; the setting sun shone through it, scattering shards of light. The last drop of champagne slid to the rim, glittering for an instant before falling into her mouth. She laughed. "One must never waste."

I was struck once again by her beauty.

"You know, Charlie has a woman uptown." Mae set her glass on the table and sat down beside me. "He pretends to despise the hinterlands, but really, those are his hunting grounds." She said this flippantly, but there was an edge to her voice.

I searched for a response to her sudden revelation.

She laughed. "When will you settle down, Joe? There's always talk about one woman or another, but the engagements never materialize."

I must have sputtered, trying to dispel rumors while also digesting what she had told me about her husband's infidelity. Meanwhile, Charlie reappeared with a bottle and a glass filled with amber liquid. "Reinforcements," he said with a grin.

I begged off, citing a nonexistent prior commitment, and retreated. Their interest in me was flattering, but in the hansom cab, I had the sense of escaping something that smelled sweet only because it was rotten. I preferred the mingled soot, manure, and grilled food odors of working New Yorkers, along with the blooming honeysuckle closer to home. I alighted at my modest townhouse, next door to one of the newest mansions in the northern reaches of the city, owned, I was told, by a Mrs. Kitty Warren. I stood for a while in the gathering dusk, gazing at a pale freckling of stars through city glow and lingering twilight. Springtime is lovely, even in a metropolis.

A clatter of hooves announced the arrival of a carriage; instinctively, I stepped back into the shadows. In the splash of light from streetlamps, a team of bays appeared, their metalled harnesses gleaming, the coachman proud on his tall perch. A footman jumped down from the Victoria, a bundle of fabric in his arms; as he waited for the carriage door to open, I did too.

A cat on silent paws crept past my feet, its bones sinuous beneath ebony fur.

The footman straightened as a woman emerged, stepped lightly down, back turned as she was swathed in the satin cape. She glanced over her shoulder, and though I was sure that she could not see me in the darkness, she seemed to smile at me. For an instant, I hesitated, wondering if I should introduce myself. She swept the cloak around her shoulders with élan. In a brief moment of indecision, I averted my eyes, and by the time I looked back, she was gone.

CHAPTER 24

Banks had money, and that was where Fanny needed to turn. In Pittsburgh, bankers would be familiar with her husband and his family, so she decided that it was time to make a trip back to Cleveland.

"I would like to visit with friends," she told Harry.

He nodded without looking up from his dinner plate.

"I will need money for the train and a hotel."

At this, he set down his fork and placed his hands on the table. "For how long?" he asked.

Fanny shrugged. "Only a few days."

He might have asked about the friends she wished to visit, or why she wished to go now, or even where she planned to stay, but Harry's complete lack of curiosity was a blessing. "You can take the funds out of next month's allowance" was all he said.

As a conductor in a neat uniform placed Fanny's baggage in a compartment, she thought back to her first trip to the city, what seemed like a lifetime before. She had been little more than a skinny child, ignorant and afraid, shrinking from the gaze of strangers. Now she straightened her shoulders and stood taller in her mint-colored suit, cut in the most modern silhouette to accentuate her fuller figure. She absorbed the glances of fellow passengers like strength tonic.

"I hope you have a good trip, miss," the conductor said with an ingratiating smile.

"Thank you," she murmured, pressing a coin into the gloved hand. How little it had really taken to become someone new, someone who deserved to be treated with deference and respect. She almost laughed.

From her handbag, Fanny pulled a sheaf of newspaper clippings. Harry had given in to her request to have *The Cleveland Plain Dealer* sent twice each month, along with his New York papers. She had obsessively kept up with Mae's life, as documented by the press, but since Mae had moved to New York, there had been little to read about her Cleveland family. What did appear in the newspapers were advertisements for Grace's hair care products. She had full pages praising the benefits of scalp ointments, hair growers, vegetable shampoos, and salves of many kinds. Grace had also become an example for aspiring local businesswomen. In an interview for *The Christian Recorder*, Grace spoke about Booker T. Washington and the importance of faith, education, and entrepreneurship—which Fanny took to mean as survival and advancement through whatever means available. Between the lines of the article, she read that funds were scant and banks unforthcoming with loans.

Fanny tucked the clippings away and took out her wallet. In the weeks leading up to her trip, she had been hard at work in her "art studio," the room Harry had allowed her to fill with papers, pigments, writing implements, glues, drafting tools, and even a camera. Through the use of ink transfer and painstaking hand drawing, she had turned one of her husband's First National Bank checks she had pilfered into Bank of New York checks, ostensibly issued to a Miss Catherine Buchanan. She pulled them from her wallet and looked at them for the hundredth time. She had no way of knowing what the actual design of Bank of New York checks looked like, but she was counting on Cleveland shopkeepers having no idea, either. Aside from that rather significant detail, she thought her handiwork satisfactorily convincing. Fanny forced herself to stop looking for flaws; there was nothing more to be done on that front. She put the forgeries away and mentally went over her plan once more.

At the Hollenden Hotel, Fanny swept past the doorman, her head held high. The clerk had just finished checking in a guest; he made a notation and set down his pen with a flourish. But as Fanny stepped toward the desk, the clerk looked right through her, smiling at a man behind her. Like a rooster in a hen yard, the man pushed obliviously past, dropping his valise at her feet. There followed an exchange of demands and responses, after which the gentleman left without a backward glance at Fanny or the bellboy struggling in his wake with his luggage.

Fanny moved as close as she could to the clerk. "I am meeting my uncle," she said.

The clerk scribbled something in his book and began flipping through a file box.

"Harold Buchanan," Fanny said more loudly. "My uncle. Could you please tell me what room he has reserved?"

"I am not authorized to give out such information." He sounded bored.

"But he is my uncle."

The clerk shook his head dismissively. "Our guests are afforded privacy."

Fanny leaned in, gloved hands gripping the varnished counter. "I do not have patience for this," she said. "I have come here at my uncle's behest. I am Miss Kitty Buchanan, and if you make this difficult, I will tell my uncle about your obstructionism."

The clerk regarded her for the first time. "Buchanan, you say?" He opened his leather-bound book.

"Yes." She drew out the sibilance. "Of the shipping Buchanans."

He ran his fingers down the page, stopped. "Harold Buchanan." His face pinked. "The Embassy Suite, madam."

Fanny knew this already, since she had called to make the reservation. "My uncle was unexpectedly delayed," she said.

The young man scratched nervously at the sparse hairs of his side whiskers. "I am sorry to hear that, madam."

Fanny leveled a disappointed stare at him. "My uncle *did* send a telegram to let you know?"

Blushing redder, he rifled through papers in a drawer. "Oh yes, here it is." He pinned the telegram to the desktop with long fingers. "Mr. Buchanan will not arrive until Tuesday, but you are welcome to use his suite in the meanwhile." His eyes darted about, as though he expected someone reassuring to appear and help him out of his faux pas. "Our hotel extends you every hospitality, Miss Buchanan. Your uncle is an honored guest." A pair of long incisors gave the clerk a look of rodent-like eagerness when he smiled. He hurriedly waved a bellboy over to take Fanny's bags.

Fanny signaled her thanks with the slightest inclination of her head. "Would you send up some champagne." A statement, not a question. "And a light snack. Oysters, perhaps?" She loathed oysters, but the request had the desired effect—the clerk took a posture of deepening deference.

"Of course, Miss Buchanan."

The bellboy lifted Fanny's bags onto a brass cart with silk tassels. He could not have been older than twelve, and he had a drawn, hungry look. Fanny made a mental note to tip him extravagantly. She followed the boy, but then slowed and looked over her shoulder, as though she had forgotten something. "You have my uncle's billing information?" she said, flicking at an imaginary speck on her coat sleeve.

"Just one moment, miss, let me be sure." The clerk consulted the large, leather-bound record book, flipping to find the page, running a long finger from top to near bottom. "Yes, we have everything we need here."

His gopher smile made Fanny want to smile in return, but she resisted. She nodded solemnly in acknowledgment, walked away at a stately pace.

"If you need anything at all, we are at your service!" he called after her.

The door to the suite opened with a satisfying dry click and swoosh against the plush carpet. The bellboy brought Fanny's baggage inside and set it next to a mahogany table bearing a silver urn choked with sweet-smelling lilies. The bellboy's eyes widened when Fanny dropped a heap of coins into his hand; he appeared ready to object, but with a stern look, Fanny wordlessly shooed him away. She explored the rooms of the cream and gold suite and tentatively bounced at the edge of an unwrinkled expanse of bedspread. With a small smile, she fell back, arms wide, picturing Mae's reaction to such an enormous bed. She made imaginary snow angels on the down-filled satin.

Voices from the corridor brought her back. She stood and pulled her clothing straight. In a gilt-framed mirror, she tidied loose strands of hair and checked that her suit was still neat. She nodded smartly to her reflection. It was time to go shopping.

The concierge pointed Fanny in the direction of nearby luxury shops. As she walked, Fanny adjusted her stride, taking dainty, clipped steps; she lifted her chin, kept her gaze forward. She had become Kitty in much of her life, but she still needed to focus, to immerse herself in Kitty's personality when she was nervous. Once she felt Kitty settle and seep into her bones, everything became easier.

"An evening dress," Kitty told the busty, petite saleswoman. "And a stole." Kitty didn't care that the woman pursed her lips sourly at her imperious tone. "I would not normally shop ready-made, but I assume that you have good tailors on the premises?"

With narrowed eyes, the woman said, "I haven't seen you here before, madam. Are you from out of town?"

Fingering a velvet cape, Kitty frowned. "I don't know about this quality." She glanced back at the saleswoman and, as if remembering her manners, smiled. "My luggage was lost." She shrugged with a sigh. "I will have to make do with what I can find here."

"We have a wide selection of the finest garments," the saleswoman said stiffly. She showed Kitty to the displays.

Cuts and fabrics were no longer a mystery, and Kitty seemed to know even more than Fanny about the latest fashions. "Have you no Josephine gowns?" she asked.

The saleswoman brought out a dark blue silk with a narrow band of pearls caught up under the bosom by an oversized clasp. In the other hand she held a chemise of ivory lace.

Kitty laughed with a light but deprecating air. "A tucker?" She put a finger to her lips, pretended to erase her smile. "How quaint."

The woman colored and flashed an unmistakably hostile look, but Kitty said, "I will be glad to take the gown. Do you have other colors in this style?"

"We have something in ivory, and an emerald green."

"I'll take those too. If you could have them delivered to the Hollenden Hotel, to Miss Kitty Buchanan in the Embassy Suite, and send a tailor tomorrow?"

Blinking, the saleswoman said, "Yes, of course, Miss Buchanan. And the stole?"

"Oh, whatever you have, fox, rabbit, mink, I don't mind," Kitty said. "As long as it keeps the chill off my shoulders." She glanced impatiently at the watch pinned at her waist. "I must be going."

The saleswoman beckoned to a shopgirl stocking shelves. "Fetch the new fur stole from the back, please." She ushered Kitty to the cash register.

"I apologize for my hurried visit," Kitty said breezily, looking toward the door, as though someone was expecting her.

The saleswoman's demeanor had softened, presumably at the thought of a fat commission. "We aim to serve our valued customers," she said with an ingratiating smile.

Kitty reached into her handbag. "A personal check will do?"

"Of course, madam" was the unctuous reply.

"I am in need of cash," Kitty said. "You do not mind if I make the check out for one hundred dollars more than the purchase price?" She brought out a sleek modern fountain pen; the silver casing flashed in the light of a chandelier.

A hint of wariness entered the woman's expression; momentarily, Fanny's worry broke the surface of Kitty's calm, like the breaching of frightened ocean prey. Then Kitty took over again. "You do honor checks, do you not?" The haughtiness of her voice impressed even Fanny. She arched her eyebrows.

"Oh yes, madam," the woman said, coloring again. "Of course we do."

The salesgirl brought the stole, deposited it lovingly by the register; before leaving, she gave it a surreptitious stroke with her babyish hand.

Recovering her composure, the saleswoman said, "This is the latest fashion, Russian mink fur."

Kitty flipped up the edge, examined the underside. "The finish is not what one would see in Paris."

The woman coughed, pressed a fist to her bosom. "I am told—"

"But no matter, it will do." Kitty placed her check on the counter. "What do I owe?"

Next, Kitty visited the jeweler. She requested a temporary account; she was staying in the Empire Suite of the Hollenden Hotel, and would they please lend her a fake diamond or pearl necklace for the evening, as her luggage had been lost? It needn't be anything too fancy—she had packed a Chaumet that had belonged to her mother, and she would just die if it was lost. But any simple necklace would be fine. She was frantic not to embarrass her uncle, Harold Buchanan, of the Buchanan Freight Company. His wife was ailing, and she, his favorite niece, was to accompany him to the award ceremony—had they not heard that he was being awarded for his philanthropy? Crippled children all over America had benefited from his generosity. Oh, yes, crystal would be perfect. She left fifty dollars cash to open an account and asked that the borrowed item be sent to her hotel. She would return it herself in a day or two, and she would love to look at some of their inventory then, when she would have more time.

As she left the jeweler's shop, an exhausted Fanny felt used up, like the bit of gristle left on the plate at the end of a meal. Her eyes stung, her body sagged. She wanted nothing more than to lie down, but the important part of Kitty's plan had yet to be executed.

Back at the hotel, Kitty imperiously demanded that the senior manager come to her hotel suite in an hour. She mounted the stairs energetically, but once the door to the hotel room was closed, she leaned back against the solid wood, removed her hat, and sank to the floor, her heart pounding. She had laid her plans carefully but could not entirely control how they unfolded.

There came a timid knock at the door. She stood, brushed off her skirt, took a deep breath.

"The manager sent these up for you, miss," a uniformed boy said.

There were at least two dozen roses. She stood aside, let him deposit the huge vase on the table next to the lilies as she dug into her handbag for a tip. "Will the manager come up presently?" she asked.

"I don't know, miss." He smiled gratefully, pocketing the money. "At your service."

After the door closed, Fanny glanced about wearily. The evening gowns she had purchased were already hanging from a brass coat rack, the stole presumably in the pink striped box next to it. She had to prepare for the next act.

She stripped down to her undergarments and put her folded suit in the closet. In the bathroom mirror, her face appeared sallow. With a warm washcloth, she rinsed her armpits, then dusted with powder; she pinched her cheeks, applied lip salve, and quickly pinned up her hair, finishing with mother-of-pearl combs.

The blue gown fit well. When the necklace arrived, along with a matching bracelet, her breath caught—they sparkled like real diamonds. She clasped the jewelry around her neck and wrist and stood before the mirror. She was transformed.

When the knock came, Kitty hoped that it would be the hotel manager. It would be easier to keep him in her suite until the banker arrived than the other way around. She had done her best to arrange for their visits to overlap, because she knew that two men vying for her attention would both bolster her perceived worth and, more importantly, obscure what she was really seeking from both—trust. Nothing buttressed a man's confidence more than observing the credence of another man.

Though she hadn't planned it, she was grateful for the heady mingled scents of roses and lilies near the entrance.

She opened the door. A bald, bearded man stood before her, and a small, white-haired man carrying a briefcase was rushing down the corridor toward them. Before the manager could get a word in, the banker, slightly breathless, pulled up beside him. She could not have had better luck.

Kitty looked from one to the other, apparently flummoxed. "Mr. . . . ?"

At once, they introduced themselves:

"Nicolas Malochev—"

"Francois Rimbaud—"

They turned crossly to one another, like hansom cab drivers negotiating an intersection.

"You asked—"

"The bank—"

Again they both stopped.

Kitty laughed affably, opened the door wider, and ushered them inside. "Monsieur Rimbaud, je suis désolée," she said. Her French was limited but her accent impeccable. "I thought that the bank had forgotten me, and I sought your succor."

The hotelier stroked his beard, looking at once flattered and confused.

"Mr. Malochev, as I told your assistant at the bank, I tried to reach you earlier, but as my travel was unavoidably delayed—"

The men murmured words of understanding.

"I haven't much time . . ." Kitty flattened the crystals of her bracelet against her wrist, all the while aware of how the faux diamonds of her necklace flashed. "I requested a modest loan from the bank"—she threw a judgmental look in Mr. Malochev's direction—"but apparently nobody was available this afternoon to approve it." With a half-amused, half-exasperated laugh, she turned to Mr. Rimbaud. "I am sorry to have involved you, monsieur, but I felt that the bankers were not taking me seriously." The pout she had rehearsed was slight, a mere tightening of her subtly varnished lips. "As an unmarried woman, I sometimes have to rely on knights in shining armor to come to my rescue."

"I am sorry, madam—"

The manager cut off the banker. "What can we do to make this right?"

Kitty held up her hand, feeling the bracelet slide, the heft of its stones and metal. "It is such a tiny thing," she said. "A trifle. I need a small loan of five thousand dollars to tide me over."

Malochev looked relieved. He glanced at Rimbaud with a small smile. "That should not be a problem, Miss Buchanan."

"But you see," Kitty said, "I will need to close this matter now." She leaned closer to Malochev. "My uncle will arrive soon, and he is very old-fashioned. He will not approve of a lady—" Her half-cough conveyed that nothing more needed to be said. "I can give you this necklace as collateral—" She lifted her hand toward her neck, but Malochev stopped her with an indignant gesture.

"No collateral is necessary, madam!" He smiled, showing his crooked teeth.

"Thank you, dear Mr. Malochev. And thank you for coming, and for the flowers, Monsieur Rimbeau. I can count on both of you for your discretion?"

With alacrity, both replied in the affirmative.

The next day, with a cashier's check, Fanny went to see Grace. The sign above the door was newly painted "Miss Grace," in fancy cursive. Beneath that, "Hair and Skin Products for the Discerning Customer."

In the sunlit storefront were hairstyling chairs and equipment. Fading posters on the walls showed Black women with waved sidelocks, straightened hair gathered in loose topknots, French-twisted hair shiny with pomade.

A girl sweeping the floor looked up with suspicion. "May I help you, ma'am?" she said with a faint lisp.

"I'm here for Miss Grace."

The girl peered at her more closely, then set her broom against the shelving. "I can see if she is available," she said, a hand on her hip. She seemed in no hurry to leave.

"Thank you," Fanny said. She dug into her handbag. "Would you like a peppermint?"

Clouds dimmed the sunlight streaming through the window. The girl frowned. "I will try to find Miss Grace." She disappeared through the curtained door in the back of the salon.

Fanny blotted a damp palm on the lapel of her felt coat, wondering why she was nervous. She was just there to see a friend, after all.

The bell above the door jingled, and a customer entered. She took an expectant step forward, but seeing Fanny, she fell back to examine the jarred products on the shelves. Outside, a loud, invective-laced dispute erupted between two cart drivers. Fanny cast a glance, meant to be friendly, toward the woman who had just arrived, but she remained studiously engrossed by the products on the wall.

"Yes?" Grace stood before the curtained door. She had always been pretty, but with the loss of childish contours and dressed so fashionably, she was beautiful. "May I help you?" She looked back and forth between Fanny and the other woman, who smiled broadly.

"You are a miracle worker!" the woman said.

Grace's face lit up. "Let me see," she said, striding over to look at the woman's hair. "This has filled in so nicely!"

They traded pleasantries and made plans for a future appointment. As the woman left, Grace's warm smile faded to one of mere politeness.

"Hello, Grace," Fanny said.

The smile remained, but behind her eyes was puzzlement.

"It's me."

Still nothing.

"Fanny?" She clasped her hands together. "You took me in at the Garth house?"

Understanding crept over Grace's expression. "Fanny!" Her eyes opened wider. "Well, I—" She put a hand over her mouth, looked Fanny up and down. "Whatever—"

Fanny rubbed at the scar on her thumb. "It hasn't been so long, after all!"

"But you look so different—"

"I suppose that I have gained some flesh—"

"Where have you—"

They both laughed awkwardly—a beat of silence as they each offered the other an opportunity to speak.

"You have quite a business here," Fanny said shyly. "I knew that you would make something of yourself."

"I suppose this is something." She swept her arm, taking in the room, and smiled in a self-deprecating way.

"This is a good location, and you have made it so inviting." Admiring Grace's appearance anew, she added, "You always did have an instinct for fashion. Those pleated sleeves are perfection."

Grace glanced at her sleeve. "Would you like some tea?"

Grateful for something to do, Fanny accepted.

Grace ushered Fanny into the back of the shop, which was filled with samples, bottles, wigs, unopened boxes. "Please, make yourself comfortable," Grace said, motioning toward a divan.

Fanny perched on the balding velvet. Her foot tapped against the hardwood floor; she stilled it when she registered the staccato sound.

On an enameled tray, Grace brought a teapot and two cups. She set it on the ottoman in front of Fanny. "Ginger," she said.

The pot steamed between them with a faint scent of spice.

"It's been so long," Fanny said.

Grace nodded and murmured, "It has."

"I've thought of you often, though." So clumsy.

"I forgot to bring the honey." Grace turned abruptly, her back—spine straight, shoulders square—a blank wall.

Fanny's heart sank further.

After what seemed an eternity, Grace placed a jar of honey with a spoon on the tray, along with a plate of cookies. Her nails were manicured, filed to oval tips, her hands smooth and unblemished. She sank back into her chair.

"I want to help you with your business!" Even to Fanny's ears, this exclamation was too eager, but she persisted. "I have some funds, and I can only imagine what you are up against."

Grace poured the tea.

"I know that being a negress is a disadvantage in business." She toyed with the mother-of-pearl buttons on her sleeve. "Being a woman is such a disadvantage anyway." When she glanced up, she saw that Grace was holding a porcelain cup out to her, her face impassive. Fanny took it, along with the matching saucer, and settled it on the flat, upholstered arm of the divan. She pulled the check from her handbag apologetically, held it delicately between thumb and forefinger.

Leaving the offering hanging, Grace picked up her teacup. "Do tell me about yourself," she said. "It has been so very long."

Fanny lowered her hand to her lap, placed the check in the folds of her skirt. "There isn't much to tell."

"You followed Mae to Newport?"

Fanny took a sip of tea; it burned her tongue, and she set the cup down with a clumsy clink against her saucer. "Yes."

"How was that for you?" The smile on Grace's face was lovely, but Fanny couldn't help but feel there was reproach behind it.

"Newport is a beautiful place," she said defensively.

Grace sipped her tea. "Cookie?"

Fanny shook her head. Looking at them made her realize how dry her mouth was.

"It seems that you have done well for yourself." Grace's gaze swept over Fanny's expensive attire. "I'm not surprised. I always knew you were ambitious. I hope that you have gone about it all the right way."

Fanny's throat tightened. She put her cup and saucer back on the tray and dropped the check next to them like it was a used napkin. "I must go," she said, rising. "I had quite forgotten my other appointment." The lameness of her excuse brought a flush to her face. "You must be very busy."

"Oh, for heaven's sake, Fanny," Grace said. "I'm sorry if I'm being a little prickly." She took a long breath, as if summoning patience. "I don't mean to be disagreeable, but you simply disappeared, after I made quite an effort on your behalf."

Fanny sat back down. "I suppose I did," she said, her voice small.

"Tell me about what you did, where you went." She watched Fanny's hands as they folded and rearranged themselves. "You're married?"

The girl Fanny had met in the front of the shop peeked through the door.

"Yes, Flora?" There was a gentleness in Grace's voice that Fanny had longed to hear.

"You have two customers waiting, Miss Grace." The girl ducked her head shyly. "Mrs. Bethany, and one who doesn't have an appointment."

"Please fetch them refreshments, and tell them that I will be there shortly." She smiled. "Thank you, Flora."

Fanny swallowed back the embarrassing lump in her throat. "I shouldn't be taking up your time."

Grace looked at her with sympathy, which brought Fanny even closer to tears. "Truly, I bear you no ill will."

"I thought I could help you," Fanny said. "To thank you for what you did for me." She indicated the check on the tray, and this time Grace picked it up. Her eyes widened when she saw the dollar amount. "I can't accept this," she said.

"But I want you to have it."

"Where did you get so much money? Is it your husband's?"

Fanny didn't reply.

"A long time ago, I thought that we might go into business together. That we might carve out our own space in the world." Her expression was inscrutable. "I suppose you found your own way."

At this, Kitty raised her head, pushing Fanny aside. How dare anyone judge her, after what she had endured? "Playing by the rules of men is no way for a woman to succeed in this world," she said.

Grace frowned. "I follow the rules of God."

"Since when does God save women?"

A hard look passed between them. "I certainly don't need saving by you," Grace said.

"I suppose not." Kitty rose. "You have customers waiting, and I shouldn't keep you." She refused to take the check back from Grace. "You may change your mind about the money."

"I won't."

"Thank you for the tea." Grace had risen also, and Kitty held out a hand to her. "I wish you the best of fortune."

The women shook hands like men.

"I will leave my card for you," Kitty said, and she departed without a backward glance.

CHAPTER 25

F anny paced restlessly in front of the marble fireplace in her hotel room, chewing at a ragged cuticle. Her dry skin itched; changing into a robe only made it worse, both hot and itchy. She pulled her hair off her sweaty neck, stabbed it full of pins. The champagne she ordered sat untouched; it turned tepid, lost its fizz.

Later at night, when the glow of embers was fading and street noises had given way to the spatter of rain, she poked ashes through the grate and huddled in a quilt, shivering by the dead fire. She stared into the darkness, thinking of her mother for the first time in a long time. Sleep remained elusive until slight fingers of dawn reached through the damask drapes.

When Fanny rose, her face bore the evidence of poor sleep, but she ignored her appearance in the mirror and practiced her Kitty expressions, one of confident directness, and another of pleasant openness. She always felt foolish starting out, but as she watched Kitty appear before her, her spine grew stiffer and her limbs looser.

When she was ready, she put on her Kitty armor, in this case a smart maroon walking suit which fit snugly, drawing attention to her feminine shape, but had clean lines and simple detailing.

Fanny had arranged a meeting with Patrick Armstrong, a private investigator. He had made a name for himself in the newspapers when he found the missing daughter of a congressman—the reason for her disappearance was never revealed. He said that his office was undergoing renovations and suggested meeting in the restaurant at Fanny's hotel. It was quiet in the midafternoon, much of the snowy linen barren, the chandeliers glinting forlornly, the occasional clang from the kitchen faintly audible. Armstrong, a lanky man with a gloomy countenance, ordered only coffee and a biscuit, making Fanny suspect that he couldn't afford to eat there. She ordered tea for herself. With an expression of disdain, the waiter told them that tables were for diners only. Fanny looked pointedly around the mostly empty room, and said, "Your invisible patrons don't seem to be very hungry, either." She smiled sweetly. When he didn't seem inclined to leave, she sighed. Tapping her finger on the table, she said, "I am a guest of this hotel, and if I have to complain, it will not end well for you." As the waiter walked stiffly away, she said, "One never knows the best way to dispatch them."

The hint of a smile appeared beneath Armstrong's drooping mustache. "What is it I might do for you, madam?"

"It's a small thing." She wanted to distance herself from the request, while also impressing upon him her value as a client. "But of course I will pay generously."

His expression remained bland.

"I'm doing a favor for my maid, Fanny Bartlett," she said. "She is loyal and industrious, and I am sorry for the plight of her sister."

"Your maid?" His voice hardly changed, but Fanny could detect the uptick of curiosity and skepticism.

She suddenly wished that she had come up with a better story, but she had learned that it was best to stick with a narrative rather than try to alter it mid-conversation. She looked at him archly. "Is that so surprising to you?" Then, as though to excuse his understandable ignorance, she said, "But I suppose you have never had servants."

With a somber nod, he said, "With all due respect, Mrs. Warren, little surprises me in my line of work. Please do continue." He had a pencil at the ready, to take notes. Fanny noticed that the end was deeply pocked with tooth marks.

"The missing woman is named Elizabeth Bartlett. She goes by Betsy." She looked out the rain-streaked window at rushing passers-by, their faces downturned, and wondered if one of them had crossed paths with her sister. "She grew up on a pioneer farm in Canada, and she was lured to Cleveland with the promise of marriage to a prosperous carpenter by the name of James Smith."

Armstrong stifled a cough, and it struck Fanny for the first time that "James Smith" was an obvious assumed name. How absurd that she had not realized it before. He scribbled something in his book.

"My maid tells me that Betsy may have ended up in a brothel run by a Mrs. Laporte."

With a *hmm* of acknowledgment, he said, "That woman deserves worse than jail."

Fanny reached into her bag and pulled out the small tintype she had of Betsy. She looked so pretty and demure in the picture, so innocent. Reluctantly, Fanny passed it across to the investigator. "It's very important that my maid gets this back," she said.

Armstrong looked at her with new understanding, and Fanny realized that she had blundered. "I will take good care of this," he said.

There was no point in attempting to recover the pretense. She thanked him and paid his advance, promising herself that she would never betray Kitty like that again.

The next day, Fanny set out for the jeweler to return the ersatz necklace and bracelet. She had already paid a hotel bellboy to unobtrusively deliver her bags to the train station at the end of his shift, so that she could disappear after this final errand without returning to the Hollenden.

The shop was the flagship store of Adair & Brothers, renowned for custom jewelry; buyers traveled long distances to purchase one of their original creations. The showroom itself was considered a departure for retail jewelry sales, le dernier cri, with its modern electrified chandeliers, stained-glass windows, and settees. It was sumptuous, but with an eclectic, studied disorder, creating a cozy ambiance.

Fanny found a clerk among the potted plants and flower arrangements and re-introduced herself as Miss Catherine Buchanan, from New York. "I am quite an avid collector, always looking for interesting pieces," she said to the clerk.

He looked skeptical, and she realized that she was probably too young to be convincing as a collector. "I inherited quite a sizable collection from my mother, you see." She smiled brightly. "I don't have quite her discerning eye, but I just acquired a Lalique. You have heard of him?"

"Ah, yes, madam." It was clear that he hadn't heard of Lalique, but he spoke and regarded her with deference.

"I wonder if I might speak with Mr. Paul Adair in person? I understand that he is quite involved in the creative process here."

The clerk disappeared behind a screen of cherry wood and plate glass, and when he reemerged, he beckoned Fanny to him with a small bow. They traversed a carpeted hall, and he ushered her into an office, where a rotund man with graying ginger curls and a warm smile waited.

"Mr. Adair, I am so glad to meet you," Fanny said. She sat in the leather-upholstered chair opposite him and took her time to remove her gloves.

"The pleasure is all mine, Miss Buchanan," he said. "Forgive me if I am being too forward, but the scent of your perfume transports me back to the West Indies, where my wife and I traveled just after our wedding—a bridal tour of sorts. It brings back happy memories."

"Ah, yes, I fell in love with the scent of jasmine when my husband and I visited Kerala."

Mr. Adair smiled vaguely.

"Southern India is so beautiful," she offered.

"Oh yes, of course! Southern India." He straightened the blotter and inkwell on his desk.

"I am sorry to take up your time, but I understand that you are the creative genius behind Adair's famous jewelry." She slathered her words with butter and leaned in, feeling the glow of her own expression.

He looked pleased. "We have produced some celebrated pieces."

"I collect for myself, but also for my friends. It's a sort of hobby for me." She paused to let him absorb this information and what it could mean for his sales. "So many women who have money to spend and love jewelry don't know how to recognize quality work." She pulled a photograph of herself, taken at one of Harry's campaign fundraisers, from her bag. In the picture, she was wearing costume jewelry, but there was no way to tell the stones weren't real. "For instance, these beautifully cut gems are worth a fortune, but the design is so boring."

Adair took the photograph and examined it with the magnifying glass he kept on his desk. "You are so right, madam," he said. He looked at her with the pleased expression of one who had recognized a fellow enthusiast. "I'm sure the gems are perfect, but what a dreary, old-fashioned setting—I could do so much better."

"I know it, sir."

He stood, something avian in the way he jutted his head on his thick neck. "Let me take you through the showroom, madam."

As they toured, Fanny commented on the artfulness of designs and on the trends in sales. She said that she would requisition some pieces, perhaps a set of ruby jewelry—necklace, bracelet, and ring—a lovely filigree mixed with pearls in an airy, fanciful design. Sadly, she needed to leave that day, but she would return soon. She bought a modest but tasteful pair of sapphire earrings with cash and promised to be in touch. Mr. Adair offered to create a more modern setting for her diamond necklace at no cost and told her with great enthusiasm that he was looking forward to her return.

CHAPTER 26

I hope that you have receipts from your trip," Harry said when she arrived home.

"Of course." Fanny shed her coat. "It cost near to nothing." She hovered by her husband, who was hunched at his desk. She waited to see if he would address her again. She had learned to be patient; if she left before he had his say, he could be peevish.

Harry jerked and shook his new stylographic pen like a mercury thermometer, trying to get it to flow; a dark blotch spread from the nib even as thick notepaper tried to drink down the ink. He scowled. Without looking up, he said, "I have a gathering tomorrow, an important meeting of business associates."

"I see." Fanny watched him wield the blotter impatiently. "Do you need me to arrange refreshments?"

"It's already done." He shoved the ruined note aside and pulled a fresh piece of paper from his drawer, shutting it with a bang. He waved the back of his hand at Fanny, indicating her dismissal.

Relieved, Fanny left, but before reaching the doorway, a strangled moan made her scalp prickle. She whirled around. Harry was attempting to rise from his desk, sagging, hands splayed on the glossy surface, arms shaking. His face was ashen.

Fanny rushed to his side, touched his back tentatively. "Are you all right, dear?"

He coughed. "I—" He coughed again.

She scanned the room, not knowing for what.

Harry managed to pull himself up straighter; he took a raspy breath.

Fanny's gaze alighted on the couch. "You should recline." She offered her arm and was surprised that he leaned on her so willingly and let her lead him.

Harry sat down heavily and loosened his collar, revealing a squiggly blue vein that pulsed near his jawline. He pushed his fist against his breastbone, then closed his eyes. His breathing, while not labored, seemed too rapid, as though he had come in from a brisk walk. "I'm fine," he said. "Just an odd palpitation."

With an uncharacteristic impulse, Fanny pressed her palm to his cool forehead, smoothed back his wispy hair. "Rest," she said. "I will fetch some tea."

Guilt chased Fanny on black wings as she rushed to the kitchen—was she really trying to help, or was she running away from responsibility for a frightening situation? She could have stayed by Harry's side and called for Annabelle to bring the tea. Or she could have told Annabelle to call for the doctor. She hurried back to her husband, her heart in her throat, the tea tray rattling. By the time she reached his study, Harry was once more at his desk, as though nothing had happened, frowning at the words he scratched on the paper in front of him. She waited until her arms ached from the weight she held, but he ignored her. She set down the tea tray and left without a word.

One evening the following week, Fanny sat in the parlor, leafing through newly delivered Cleveland newspapers. "Grift and the Hollenden Hotel," a headline read. The article didn't focus on the unknown woman who had left without paying for her room but on the firing of an employee who had allowed her to defraud the establishment. The picture showed a young man with a shaggy forelock and earnest eyes. Fanny recognized him as the clerk she had met, whom she had manipulated into giving her the suite. Where were his rodent-like teeth, his spidery fingers? He was so boyish in his photo. He seemed so innocent, almost handsome.

Fanny reached for her glass of brandy, wanting the fiery warmth, but she had trouble swallowing. A drop spilled on the boy's photo, a dark stain that spread. She turned the page, then folded the newspaper in half, then in half again. It resisted a third fold, so she took it to the fire, tossed it in. She watched as the flames leaped, devouring it. There was something calming in the heat of its destruction, as though burning the record could alter the past.

In the gray of dawn, there was a timid knock at Fanny's bedroom door. She roused, squeezed her eyelids shut against faint light, then opened them, unsure whether she had dreamed the sound. The door opened; Annabelle held a wavering candle. "Mrs. Warren," she whispered hoarsely, quivering. "Mr. Warren—" Her voice broke.

Fanny followed Annabelle to Harry's bedroom. The door was open, and Harry lay on the floor beside the bed, his legs twisted in sheets. That he was dead was apparent from across the room. His face was the awful color of paste, his mouth lolling.

"I was setting the fire downstairs—" Annabelle took in a sharp breath and let out a strangled sob. The candle in her shaking hand cast erratic shadows.

Fanny took two steps toward Harry but found that she could go no closer. It was not fright or repulsion. Nor, she concluded after she had gingerly probed her feelings, was it sadness. She simply felt that she had no business being there.

Annabelle sobbed again.

"Please call on the minister," Fanny said.

The inheritance Fanny received from her husband was not large; he had secretly been a profligate spender, and his balance sheets tilted heavily toward debt. The funeral would be expensive, and the house would fetch little if sold, both because it had fallen into disrepair and because the wealthy had begun to flee Pittsburgh for cleaner air in the outskirts.

Pacing from room to room in the quiet house, Fanny assessed her situation. She had no education or marketable skills, and even if she weren't loath to marry, she had no social standing to attract a man of any means. In Pittsburgh, she had no real friends; the company her husband had kept was exclusively male, and any wives she met had seemed wary of Fanny, as one might be of a stray dog. It was as though she carried an unfamiliar scent, and Fanny did not know enough to remedy the problem. Too late, it occurred to her that she had not tried hard enough to understand the rules of Pittsburgh's society, to try to fit in beyond the servants' quarters. After Harry's death, condolences arrived, but nobody called on her except Colleen from next door and debt collectors.

Fanny handled her husband's remaining correspondence at his desk. When convenient, she backdated letters and forged his signature, sent checks against empty bank accounts to give the illusion that Harry had meant to honor his debts before his untimely death. The appearance of good will could help soothe the irritation of creditors.

Fanny had several times withdrawn money at the bank using Harry's signature when her small monthly allowance had run out, but she had never taken so much from the account that her husband would notice. She thought no more of it than sneaking a snifter of Harry's brandy from his fancy decanter; it had been child's play. She realized that she had been lucky never to have emptied what dregs had been in the account at times.

Fanny's many hours of practice at counterfeiting had been a bulwark against an uncertain future, and that future had arrived, she decided. She had to consider what role forgery might play in her next act.

Harry's funeral was held at the Presbyterian church, which the couple had only occasionally attended. Harry had ascribed to the skeptical view of his hero, Andrew Carnegie, on organized religion, and he had done the bare minimum to keep up appearances. This did Fanny no favors with the churchgoing families in their neighborhood, and when she sat in the front pew, veiled in black, mourning a spouse she had hardly known, she cut a lonely figure. Afterward, Fanny continued to attend church at least weekly, always in her widow's weeds, head bowed. Slowly the women began to gather around her, their antennae quivering.

"Do you have good help at home?" they asked quietly.

"Probably for the best that there are no children," they sighed.

"Mr. Warren came from a good family."

"It is all so sudden."

"Such a shock."

"Tragic." A flutter of fans.

"Mr. Warren was—particular."

"A bit of a lone wolf."

"We never thought that he would settle down again after his first loss." There was a question implied, an invitation to fill in blank spaces, but Fanny only murmured her thanks.

One of the women was married to a prominent lawyer. Fanny had seen him with Harry, engaged in animated if hushed conversations, back when Harry still had political aspirations.

"Mrs. Kirkpatrick," Fanny said. "I believe that your husband was fond of my Harry."

"Oh?" The statuesque woman readjusted her stole. Her deep-set eyes were alert, but not unfriendly.

"They had mutual business interests, I believe—" Fanny looked away, blinked hard until she felt a tear escape. "I'm sure it was nothing important—" She made herself small, drawing her limbs in close. "But perhaps Mr. Kirkpatrick could look at some papers for me, see if anything can be saved."

"It must be so hard, poor girl." Mrs. Kirkpatrick began to reach out a gloved hand, then drew it back. "I will ask what George can do for you." Her expression was cool, that of a woman who wants to seem sympathetic but does not wish to be involved. "My husband is in New York for two weeks, but when he returns, I will be sure to inveigh upon him on your behalf."

"You are very kind." Fanny glanced up through her lashes, twisting the braided handle of her purse. As if in an afterthought, she said, "This might seem an odd question, but I wonder if you could recommend a New York hotel?" She took a quick breath, let it out. "I may need to visit to sign banking papers, you see, and—well, I have never been." She gave a nervous laugh. "I just thought, if your husband does business there, you might know—I wondered where your husband usually stays?"

○─┼─○

Fanny knew better than to wait for George Kirkpatrick to call on her. Mrs. Kirkpatrick might be genuine in her pity, but she was unlikely to expend wifely capital on behalf of someone she had no desire to admit into her sphere. Whatever influence she had over her husband's professional interests was doubtless best saved for more important subjects. Fanny would go to the city and take matters into her own hands.

CHAPTER 27

The thought of going to New York filled Fanny with turbulent emotions. One minute she was grazing the clouds with excitement at finally spreading her wings and being so close to Mae; the next she was despairing that she could exist in a city so much larger and more sophisticated than any she had ever known. She did her best to set aside her feelings and focus on finishing the tasks required to set her plans in motion. She had already spent long days producing documents and doing her research, but as the particulars of her stratagem coalesced, she needed to be sure of every detail.

Fanny was sleep-deprived and travel-worn when she arrived at Grand Central Depot. The structure was astonishingly massive, the crowds chaotic, the steam, smoke, banging, clanging, and screeching overwhelming. She soldiered through as Kitty, though, giving instructions to a porter, then a driver, and finally, at the Fifth Avenue hotel where Mrs. Kirkpatrick's husband was staying, a clerk.

"Mrs. Catherine Warren," she said curtly. "The Presidential Suite."

The Presidential Suite was occupied, the confused clerk told her, and he had no record of her reservation. Kitty was offended that he didn't recognize her, because she had stayed there only four months before. He apologized, saying that he usually worked the late shift and didn't see many of the guests. Kitty peered at the leather-bound book, asked if the Mr. Dubois staying in the Presidential Suite was the banker from Philadelphia, the one Alva Vanderbilt couldn't stand? He didn't know, and she cut him off, telling him that she needed to rest from her long journey, and the hotel's mistakes should not be her concern. There was nothing available on the upper floors, but Kitty agreed to take a corner room at a much reduced rate. She expected to be supplied with champagne and oysters. No—a selection of cheeses with fruit. She also wanted a hansom cab in the morning, as she had business to attend to.

As exhausted as she was once she got to her room, Kitty didn't think she would be able to sleep. The entry to New York had assaulted her senses; the city was bigger, louder, and more foul-smelling than she had imagined. As her carriage crawled through traffic and she craned her neck to take in the towering buildings, she had felt so small. Kitty shrank away, curling up small as a walnut in Fanny's bosom. The cool marble lobby of the hotel, with its gilt ornamentation and extravagant floral arrangements, its obsequious adoration of wealth, had summoned Kitty forth once again; it was Kitty who argued with the clerk, her instincts quick and motions languid. Kitty straightened Fanny's spine, asserted her will, and bent fortune in her direction.

But it was Fanny who pulled aside the lace curtains and watched the lights blink to life down the long street, slowly spreading a glittering net over the city. Her breath quickened. Somewhere out there, perhaps standing by a window too, was Mae.

As the pink light of dawn stretched across the polished floor of the hotel lobby, Kitty was already ensconced in an overstuffed armchair, a book open in her lap. Potted ferns and a broad-brimmed hat partially shielded her from the gaze of passers-by, but she had a clear view of the stairs, the elevator, and the street entrance. Casually, she flipped pages without reading, her eyes trained on guests coming and going. Near midday, she rose to freshen up and change her attire, in case anyone had noted her loitering in the lobby; a new hat and jacket would turn her into a different person. Nobody would look at her too closely; to the men who came and went, women were of no more interest than other lobby adornments.

Kitty pretended to scan a newspaper, to check her nails. She crossed and uncrossed her legs. She counted the tiles along the crown molding, softly tapped the rhythm of popular songs with her booted foot, imagined the thoughts that passed through minds of staff who served and flattered the pampered guests.

There was no sign of Mr. Kirkpatrick that day.

The next morning, Kitty was back at her post, nervous, wondering if she had chosen the correct hotel. Even with discounts, her bills would mount quickly. Perhaps Kirkpatrick's wife had been mistaken, or maybe he had changed his mind about where to stay. Maybe she had missed him when she stepped away. It seemed too risky to ask the clerk whether Kirkpatrick was registered, but maybe—oh. There he was. Alone.

Kirkpatrick hooked his glasses to his waistcoat with the air of someone who did not relish the day ahead. He had a sallow face, with bushy eyebrows and a drooping mouth.

Kitty leaped to her feet. "Why, Mr. Kirkpatrick!" She put a hand to her cheek, made a surprised and timid smile. "I did not expect to meet you here!"

He was taken aback, seemed unsure how to respond.

"Kitty." She gave him a demure glance. "Kitty Warren," she said. "Harry's wife?"

A glimmer of recognition showed in his eyes. "Kitty?"

"Yes! You do remember me!" She clasped her hands together, then looked away, bashful.

"Oh." He pulled at his lapels. "Oh, yes." He cleared his throat. "You are Harry's widow."

She bowed her head.

"Yes, oh." He swallowed, looked to his left, then his right. "I am sorry, Mrs. Warren." There was a falling note to his words, closure, but Kitty stepped a little closer.

"I wonder if I could ask a favor of you, Mr. Kirkpatrick?" She peered up with the most doelike expression she could muster.

"I should be going." He pawed at the air. "An engagement—" He rubbed the back of his neck, his gaze averted, but then something seemed to occur to him. "Might I ask, why is it that you are in New York, dear lady?"

Like a lofted blanket, calm settled over her. She had his attention. "As you know, my husband died quite suddenly."

He shifted uncomfortably.

"I came to the city to settle certain—" She covered her mouth, turned away briefly. "I have some unusual business to attend to, and I wonder if I could impose upon you for a small favor?"

Kirkpatrick glanced toward the entrance, then at his pocket watch. "What might I do for you?"

"I hate to impose, but would you be willing to accompany me on a necessary errand?" She bowed her head. "It is my first time in New York. I am all alone, and—" Her voice dropped to nearly a whisper. "Well, it doesn't seem safe to take public conveyances." When she looked back up, she could picture her own eyes, brimful, glistening.

His resistance seemed to crumble; he smiled wanly, took on a more agreeable air. "Certainly, Mrs. Warren. I have a carriage at my disposal, and would be honored to help you."

"It will not take long." She brightened with gratitude. "I promise not to inconvenience you too much."

With a shallow bow, he took her elbow, and they walked to the curb. He waved and called to his driver, who was leaning against a lamppost, smoking. The carriage pulled up, missing a parked barouche by inches, and Kirkpatrick helped her with the step. He sat across from her, lowering himself with a grunt, and set his walking stick against the door. "What is the address, Mrs. Warren?"

Kitty saw his brows draw down when he heard just how far north they would need to travel. "I cannot tell you how much this means to me, sir," she said. "You have a heart of gold. Truly, my husband thought the world of you." Vague, even clichéd statements were surprisingly effective, Kitty had discovered. Everyone can see themselves reflected in a generalized compliment.

Indeed, Kirkpatrick's shoulders went back ever so slightly. He gave the driver instructions. The horses snorted, and the carriage jolted forward. He sat with a stiff spine; the white silk écharpe wound tightly about his throat seemed to hold his chin aloft. "What might this errand be, Mrs. Warren?" he asked.

"I—" She faltered, leaned in. "I have a certain matter, a matter of a personal nature, to attend to." Self-consciously, she wrung her hands.

"Of course." He picked up his walking stick and bounced it in his hand, as though estimating its weight. "This must be a difficult time for you." He set the stick down again.

Kitty smiled her timid thanks. They sat in silence, gently jostled by the movements of the carriage. The buildings of Fifth Avenue went from densely packed to sparse; long tracts of green opened up. The quality of the road diminished, and the ride grew bumpier. Kitty gazed blindly out the window, avoiding her companion. The trip was coming to an end, and the closer they got to their destination, the more her stomach clenched.

The carriage clattered to a stop. Before them was an ivy-covered three-story building spanning nearly a city block. The gardens and rolling lawns were immaculate; the brick and stone facade would have been almost modest in its simplicity had it not been so enormous.

Kirkpatrick sat forward, peered out the window. He turned back to Kitty, his face suffused with sudden understanding. "Isn't this—" He gripped the silver head of his walking stick, his knuckles blanching. "This is Mr. Carnegie's new mansion." His tone was flat, but his eyes wide.

"I won't be a moment, sir, if you do not mind waiting." Before he could answer, she was stepping down from the carriage with a flourish of her skirt. She strode toward the house, heels and heart beating a syncopated rhythm.

A servant answered, his manner cool, edging on hostile. He observed her with narrowed eyes.

Kitty's mouth was dry. "I am the head housekeeper for Miss Emily Thorn Vanderbilt at the Triple Palace." She hoped that her outfit, somber enough for a widow, too fine for a servant but sedate in its refinement, would strike the right note.

His nod was slight; the sun from the open door glinted off his pomaded hair.

"As you must already know, the family is notoriously selective when it comes to help." She said this in a low voice, leaning in with a comradely smile. "I need to speak with your housekeeper about a prospective hire." She shrugged to convey her amused acceptance of the whims of the wealthy. "The girl is a maid who used to work here."

"Go around to the back entrance." His hand was on the door, ready to shut it in her face.

"My employer is an adherent to Mr. Carnegie's beliefs," she blurted. "She told me that I would be treated as a proper ambassador of the family."

There was a moment of silence, then, with an exasperated sigh, he opened the door wider and stepped aside to let her pass.

She kept her step light, her expression pleasant.

"Take those stairs down one level, through the door of leaded glass," he said. "The housekeeper's office is the first room on the right."

She could feel his gaze on her, like a hand propelling her down the hallway, until she passed through the door, shutting it quietly behind her. It was dim and faintly musty in the stairwell; the steps were carpeted, absorbing the sound of her boots. She stopped partway down the short flight, a hand against the wall, watchful, listening. The only sounds came from far off, faint thumpings and scrapings. At the base of the stairs was a short corridor with high transom windows at the far end. There couldn't be more than a few rooms in that part of the house, and she judged her chances of being seen quite low. Kitty opened the drawstring of her handbag and felt for the sheaf of papers inside. She left the bag open; if someone did happen by, she could pretend to be searching her purse.

The time on her watch ticked by. She heard a woman coughing, probably the housekeeper in her office. Kitty weighed the choice between knocking on the office door and staying on the stairs, and she decided that there was no advantage to engaging with another person in the household. She might be ejected faster from a conversation than by remaining unseen in the shadows.

She shifted slowly so the stairs wouldn't creak, relieving the cramping in her leg. A sharp bang came from nearby; she started, tensed, then focused on calming her breath. A moment passed. Then another. There came a rustling sound, then nothing. She checked her watch: only eight minutes had passed, not enough. The door opened.

"Yes? May I help you?" The woman in the doorway was plump as a pear, with a broad, ruffled collar that set off her aging but pretty face.

"I am here to see the housekeeper," Kitty said. "I am looking for a reference."

"Ah." The woman waved her hand in a welcoming gesture. "I have little time to spare just now, but please come in." She opened the door to her office; a warm shaft of light spilled out.

Kitty followed her, surprised to find the room cheerful, with comfortable-looking furniture, bright, quilted cushions, a fern hanging over the bookshelf.

"What can I do for you?" The housekeeper's voice was a husky contralto.

Having prepared for prickliness, Kitty was caught off-balance. "I am here about a potential hiring, a girl who worked for you."

"And where is your post?" Her cheeks rounded when she smiled.

"At the Triple Palace. The northern section." She was unsure what attitude to strike. "For Miss Emily."

"Oh, then you know Paulette?" Her appraising eyes flicked over Kitty's face and attire as she seemed to try to place her.

Kitty pressed on blindly, cautiously, like an anxious sailor in thick fog. She inclined her head, smiling, hoping this could be taken either as an acknowledgment that she knew Paulette or a polite denial, whichever made the most sense. "The domestic, a Carlotta Jones, is seeking employment with us," she said. "She gave your name as a reference."

"Carlotta Jones, do you say?" The housekeeper looked at Kitty with a worried expression. "I don't wish to disappoint you, but I am afraid that I know of no such person." She rubbed her wrinkled brow. "No, I am quite certain that nobody by that name has worked here. Though perhaps Jones is her married name. What did she say that she did for us?"

Kitty had been taking in the photos on the wall. A young boy in a train conductor's hat looked sternly at the camera, a toy engine clutched in his hand. A woman with a parasol, her face swallowed in shadows, shrank behind a man who squinted into the sun. "I believe she worked as a governess in Boston before moving back to New York," Kitty said affably. She tried to think of how to draw out the conversation without raising alarm bells. "Carlotta told me about those New England sewing circles—do you know about them? They sound so tiresome, so provincial." Raising a hand to her mouth, she said, "Of course I don't mean to say anything against Boston society!"

The housekeeper rewarded her with a knowing look.

"And the master of the house was, purportedly, a bit of a bully to his wife," she said in a quieter voice, as though someone might overhear. "I forget the name of the family—" She opened her bag, rifled through some papers. "I have notes somewhere—" She laughed with a self-deprecating shake of her head. "I can never find anything in here!"

"I am so sorry to disappoint you," the woman said again. "I don't recall anyone who fits that description." She looked genuinely pained to have to give Kitty the bad news. "I do hope that you are not being taken advantage of in any way!"

Kitty drew in a quick breath, put a hand to her throat. "Goodness." She paused as though letting the information sink in. "Do you think she may have been lying to me?"

With a sympathetic sigh, the housekeeper said, "You are young. I can tell that you are eager to prove yourself to your employers." Her eyes were kind. "You must learn that there are unscrupulous people who will misrepresent themselves. You mustn't assume that everyone is as honest as you."

"Oh dear." Increasing distress seeped into her words. "I hope that—I wasn't—Oh, what you must think of me!" Kitty clutched her bag closer. "Barging in on you, and being such a fool!"

"It is fine, truly. I am glad that I could prevent further trouble for you."

Kitty reached for the back of the chair beside her, leaned on it for a brief moment, then pulled her hand away with feigned embarrassment at her lapse in manners.

"Would you like a glass of water, perhaps?" With a concerned look, the housekeeper motioned at the carafe on her desk.

Kitty shook her head as if to decline, but then said, "If it isn't too much inconvenience, perhaps it would revive me."

"It is no trouble at all." The woman poured water, watching solicitously as Kitty slowly sipped it. "If you need help learning the ropes, please do call on me. I have been managing a household for some time now." She took the glass back with a gentle smile. "I am sure that you will do very well, dear."

Kitty approached Kirkpatrick's carriage at a brisk pace. The door was already open, and he watched her with undisguised curiosity.

"I'm so sorry that I took so long!" Holding up the front of her skirt, she bounded up the step, caught her foot on the bottom rail, and sprawled into the carriage, grazing Kirkpatrick's leg with her shoulder, striking the edge of the locker painfully with her knee. The contents of her open bag scattered across the muddied floor.

"Oh no!" she cried breathlessly, scrambling to her knees, sweeping at the strewn documents with sullied gloves. "Oh dear!"

After a brief, startled recoil, Kirkpatrick sprang into action, helping Kitty to her feet even as she clutched at papers, anxiously stuffing them into her bag. He bent down to gather the spilled pages, but as he moved to hand them back, he froze, a curious look on his face. His bushy eyebrows drawn together, he peered more closely, then leafed through the rumpled sheaf he held. "What—?" He cleared his throat, pushed his eyeglasses up the wide bridge of his nose. "Pardon me, but may I ask—?" His lips remained slightly parted, as though the link between thoughts and speech had suddenly disconnected.

"I'm *so* sorry about this!" Kitty took the papers from his hand, wiping ineffectually at specks of mud and dirt before sliding them into her bag. "I am so clumsy!"

He picked up the remaining documents from the floor. "I don't mean to pry, but aren't these stocks in the Scottish Caledonian Railway?"

"Why, yes," she said, taking them from him. "Among other stocks and bonds."

"But—" The unruly eyebrows went up, then down, like a pair of agitated caterpillars. "But these must be worth millions!"

Kitty pulled the drawstring on her bag closed and arranged herself in her seat, smoothing out the skirt of her dress. Kirkpatrick stood stiffly for a moment, then his legs seemed to buckle. He sat opposite her abruptly, like a marionette whose strings had gone loose. He stared blankly ahead. Kitty waited; when he didn't move, she knocked on the window herself, signaling the driver that it was time to go.

The two passengers swayed in unison as the carriage bumped over the Belgian block road. Kitty glanced intermittently at her companion, who stared steadfastly out the window.

"I am truly discomfited," she said in a small voice.

He turned his questioning face slowly to her.

She clasped her hands tightly over her bag. "I cannot imagine what you think."

The carriage ran over a rough patch, and they both bounced inelegantly in their seats; Kitty threw out a hand to steady herself. When the road smoothed again, she said with quiet vehemence, "I must beg of you, Mr. Kirkpatrick, never to speak a word of this." She lifted her chin enough to give him a beseeching look.

"Of course, madam," he said. "I am nothing if not discreet."

"I am sure of it, sir, but this is a matter of some—delicacy." She let the word linger in the air.

They were further downtown; the shouts, thumps and clanging were back, as were the pungent scents of swarming humanity. The carriage moved by starts and stops.

"Secrets are part of the very nature of my profession, I assure you." He straightened his jacket cuff.

"Well, you see—" She bit her lip. "I don't know how to say this."

He leaned closer to catch her quiet words.

"You see . . . well . . . Andrew Carnegie is my father."

CHAPTER 28

After her return to Pittsburgh, Kitty waited several weeks for the news of her illegitimate parenthood to spread. There was some chance that Kirkpatrick might have kept the secret close to his bosom, but given her late husband's temperament and the character of his friends, she doubted it. Information was a form of currency, and money was most of what Harry and his former companions had cared about.

A few Sundays later, as church bells rang to gather the faithful, Mrs. Kirkpatrick approached Kitty, the foam-green veil on her periwinkle-blue hat fluttering. She issued a cordial, almost fawning, invitation to tea. She would be most honored to welcome Kitty to her home, and she hoped that the pain of the terrible blow of her husband's death was easing. Mrs. Kirkpatrick smiled solicitously as she offered her hand, and Kitty knew that her assumptions had been correct. She had magically become an exalted and desirable person as the daughter, however misbegotten, of a very, very wealthy man.

Through Mrs. Kirkpatrick, Kitty arranged an introduction to the secretary-treasurer of Aims Park Banking Company, Joseph Pettigrew.

As a dear friend of the Kirkpatricks, Kitty was to visit him any time in his office; the door was always open.

Kitty wore her finest promenade ensemble to the bank, including the heavy ostrich-feather chapeau that required three hatpins to keep in place and made her head ache. True to Pettigrew's promise, she was immediately ushered to his office. He met her at the door, a tall, beefy financier with a barrel chest and thick wrists protruding from starched cuffs. He consulted his gold watch, making it clear that he was a busy man, and snapped it shut with an air of authority. He bowed his head slightly in greeting. "It is lovely to see you, madam."

His big, shepherding hand hovered near the small of her back, as though the path from door to chair might be too much for her feminine wit to navigate. He rounded the polished desk, lowered himself into his own chair with a satisfied smile, clapped his palms together, and interlaced his stubby fingers. The light from the window behind him, filtered through smog, cast a sickly halo. "Now what may I do for you, dear lady?"

"I have heard that you are a gentleman of the utmost discretion." Kitty moved slightly so that sunlight from the window fell directly on her face, knowing this would make her eyes bright. "I hope that I can entrust my affairs to you with full confidence."

He rubbed his cleft chin. "You may trust me completely."

"I have been advised to place my—well, these securities—in the hands of a third party." The word *money* beat silently in the air.

"Very good advice." He cleared his throat, watched her expectantly.

Kitty opened her bag. She withdrew an envelope, slid it onto the desk. "You may be—It is possible that you will be surprised by what you see here." She nodded her permission for him to open the flap.

With great concentration, Pettigrew examined the sheaf of documents. His mouth opened to form a small pink *o*, and he drew in air audibly, his forehead puckering. There was a note for two million dollars, which Kitty explained was in return for a block of stock of the Caledonia Railway of Scotland. Her father had gifted the stock to her, and later, on a trip back to his homeland, he had offered to cash it in for what he said would be a favorable rate. The note covered that transaction.

Pettigrew's eyes darted from the papers in his hand to Kitty and back again, but he asked no questions about the provenance of the note.

Kitty talked him through more securities, made up primarily of stock in Carnegie Steel Company and gold bonds. The total came to more than five million dollars.

"I am newly widowed," Kitty said with a tone of soft regret. "If anyone knew about this fortune, I would be in a vulnerable position." She lowered her face, fiddled with the lace trim of her cuff. "I would not wish to be quarry for an unscrupulous man."

"Of course not, madam!" His baritone voice was comforting. "You are in good hands here." A broad smile spread across his face.

"And—" She lowered her voice almost to a whisper. "My father is a private man. He is honorable and would never forsake me, but you must understand that my parentage—his youthful indiscretion—must be forever hidden." Kitty pressed her hands against the edge of the desk as if to steady their trembling. "It would kill me if a mere breath of this conversation were to leave this room." She looked at him imploringly. "I hope that I am not asking too much."

He shifted in his chair, shoulders back, laced his fingers together over his brocade-vested belly with a reassuring nod. "It is my pleasure to serve you."

"I would like to put these papers in your safekeeping for a few years, at which time I hope to be in a better position to—well, to use them, I suppose."

"We can certainly offer you a safety deposit box, but you understand that we cannot pay interest on illiquid assets." He stopped himself, chuckled. "I apologize, Mrs. Warren. I am not used to dealing with the fairer sex. I mean that all we can do is guard these like we would jewelry or such." He beamed at her benignly. "Once you exercise your right to cash these in, we could then give you a small amount of money each year as a sort of thank-you for using our bank."

"Oh, of course, Mr. Pettigrew, I don't expect any sort of payment. I am indebted to you for taking these off my hands. I feel lighter already." She smiled timidly. "I have made a list here of everything in the envelope." Kitty shuffled through her bag. "We can seal these papers up until, perhaps, five years hence?"

His face fell. "Five years, you say?" With a fat finger, he tapped the documents. "I should think you would want access to these funds earlier."

She laughed and shook her head in a self-deprecating manner. "I am a woman of modest habits," she said. "Five years will be fine." Kitty handed him the inventory. "Will you seal it now, and write the date on the envelope?"

With some reluctance, Pettigrew did as she asked. "The package cannot be opened until the designated date," he warned her.

She nodded solemnly. "I understand."

He dripped wax onto the envelope and pressed it shut with the bank's seal. "Very well. It is bound by the seal for five years."

The next day, Kitty rushed back to Pettigrew's office in a state of alarm. Her hat and coat were mismatched to a degree that might not be noticed, but she also let a messy tendril of hair float free, and made sure that the collar of her dress was askew. "Dear Mr. Pettigrew," she said. "I am so relieved that you could see me so soon!"

"Mrs. Warren, I hope that all is well?" He stood up with a worried look.

"Oh, Mr. Pettigrew, I am such an idiot!" She fixed the tilt of her hat, succeeding only in tilting it too far in the other direction. The diaphanous veil swung loose; she brushed it back ineptly. "When I brought my papers to you yesterday, I forgot to make a copy of the memorandum for myself!"

He raised his eyebrows quizzically.

"What if I died, and nobody knew about my assets here in your bank?" She put a hand to her cheek; the handles of her purse slid to her elbow, and her bag bobbed against her skirt. "I have been ever so sloppy!"

A look of amused understanding appeared. "Why, Mrs. Warren, it is no trouble to have one of our clerks write up a copy of the inventory for you." With a smile, he extended a gracious arm toward the door and moved to escort her out.

She stepped into his path, standing close enough to capture his full attention, though not so close as to make him uncomfortable. "Dear Mr. Pettigrew," she said, looking into his eyes. Her veil and hat were suddenly properly arranged. "I do hope that I am not being impertinent, but could you possibly take care of this yourself?"

His gaze slid to the door and back again. "Of course, madam." Disengagement seemed to require effort; he took a breath, withdrew a slow inch, moved backward a pace.

"Jeffries!" Pettigrew barked.

The young man posted outside his office jumped to attention, and rushed in as fast as his limp would allow. He nodded at the instructions, quickly left.

Pettigrew invited Kitty to sit, and returned to his desk. He withdrew a blank sheet of thick, creamy paper from the stack on his desk; at the top was a lithographed heading and embossed insignia of the Aims Park Banking Company.

The boy returned with Kitty's package, and Pettigrew examined the attached list of documents as though seeing it for the first time. He straightened the paper on his desk, and with his gold pen, he meticulously copied out the list of her forgeries. She watched, hardly daring to breathe, as line by neat line, the copy of the memorandum grew. Finally, with a flourish and smile, he handed her the receipt, signed by him, on the official letterhead of the bank.

It was important to carefully choose which banker to approach first for a loan. Ideally, it would be someone senior enough not to need oversight, well enough known to instill confidence in other lenders, and sufficiently old-fashioned to operate purely on the basis of personal trust. Kitty studied her options and decided on a Mr. Francis Beckett, a man of about sixty years with a neat white beard and sterling reputation in the city. He had started his career as a cashier at age eighteen, and had worked his way up to become president of DePaul Bank.

She started small, forging a letter from an independent bank in Kittanning, forty miles upriver from Pittsburgh. She wrote to the Kittanning bank, inquiring about opening a commercial account, and thus she received correspondence with their letterhead. With a magnifying glass and the finest paintbrush made of sable hairs, she patiently covered the inked letterhead with melted wax. Once finished, she reheated the waxed paper with hot curling tongs and transferred the wax to a piece of limestone; from there, the addition of acidic gum arabic and a cleaning with turpentine resulted in her own lithograph, ready for printing bank letterhead. She wrote:

> *Dear Mr. Beckett,*
>
> *We at Kittanning Central Bank have had the pleasure of doing business with Mrs. Catherine "Kitty" Warren, an exemplary*

customer and charming person. She is moving her banking to Pittsburgh, where she wishes to arrange small personal loans. We hold five thousand dollars of her securities which we can assure you are gilt-edged, and she always repays her loans on schedule. You are fortunate indeed to have the opportunity to bring her on board as a new customer.

On a side note, as one banker to another, she has offered a good bit more than the going rate for bonuses on her loans. Bonuses are not the reason we do business, but they are appreciated!

If you have any concerns, please do not hesitate to reach out to me personally.

Yours with esteem,

Mr. Barnard Clews, President

Francis Beckett greeted Kitty cordially when she visited his bank. He was a small, somberly dressed man, his manner reserved and posture erect, his shining blue eyes made even brighter by his snowy hair and beard. His old-fashioned politeness endeared him to Kitty, as did his gentlemanly restraint when presented with her jaw-dropping list of five million dollars' worth of securities. She was almost sorry to borrow money from him. While other bankers hesitated to do business with a woman or treated her with condescension—an underestimation she used to her advantage—Mr. Beckett appeared to admire her and believe in her prospects. He kept her talking long past the end of their scheduled meeting time and seemed to take genuine pleasure in their exchange. It was a new experience for Kitty, one that made her uncomfortable, because more conversation meant more opportunities to slip up. It also gave her more opportunities to learn, she decided, and Mr. Beckett could prove to be useful on that front.

CHAPTER 29

THE CLEVELAND PLAIN DEALER, APRIL 1887

BROTHEL MADAM WITH TIES TO CITY COUNCIL ARRESTED

In a surprise raid, fifteen women allegedly participating in criminal prostitution at a brothel on Prospect Avenue were rounded up last night. Arrests were made by officers of the Third Police District, who have been accused by local residents of excessive leniency toward the so-called "ladies of the night" who ply their trade in the tenderloin. When asked for comment, Sergeant Roy O'Malley, the commanding officer, denied that brothels are routinely tolerated by law enforcement. He added: "Prostitution has always been and still is illegal in Cleveland."

Among those arrested was Mrs. Celia Laporte, the wealthy widow of former city councilman Dr. Steven Laporte. Mrs. Laporte owns several tenements in the downtown center; it has sent shockwaves through Cleveland society to learn that at least one of those buildings may have been used for illegal purposes. She is being charged with keeping a house of ill-fame, renting a house to be used as a brothel, and suffering an establishment to be used as a house of ill-fame. According to the prosecutor in this case, Mr. Adam Davis, Mrs. Laporte faces significant fines and likely imprisonment.

Police were made aware of criminal activity at the alleged brothel when a private investigator, Patrick Armstrong Jr., contacted them regarding the disappearance of a young Canadian woman, Elizabeth "Betsy" Smith. Mrs. Smith's relatives had hired the investigator to find the missing woman, and he ascertained that her last known sighting was at the Prospect Avenue address, where she may have died in childbirth.

In a generous act of philanthropy, Mrs. Catherine "Kitty" Warren, formerly of Euclid Avenue, has offered to pay the fines of young girls caught up in the raid. She will donate eight hundred dollars to the Young Women's Christian Association of Cleveland to aid the effort to reclaim those fallen females who are leading a life of prostitution. "It is the young," Mrs. Warren said, "who are dependent upon their own exertions for support; it is the tempted and fallen who need protection and assistance."

CHAPTER 30

Kitty did not move to New York right away; she took steps to solidify her financial position and further her education on the ways of the wealthy, to fill in the fanciful outline she had sketched of Mrs. Catherine Warren, so that she might emerge a fully rendered socialite. She traveled to Paris, where she leased a suite in an apartment hotel on the Place de la Concorde.

Kitty took to the city immediately. It was sprawling but felt friendlier than New York, more quaint and open to the sky. Walking the neighborhoods, she admired the boldness and novelty of women's clothing, the jumble of colors on overflowing flower carts, rows of dainty, meticulously crafted petits fours behind gleaming plate glass, and tempting displays in front of fruiterers' shops. She lifted a pear to her nose and inhaled the sweet scent, which, delicate as it was in a cityscape of odors, still filled her senses.

There was a greater comingling of rich and poor in Paris than Kitty was used to, and displays of wealth lacked the earnest, ostentatious striving that Americans exuded. Parisian snobbery contained a faint note of humor, a nod to human frailty. This appealed to Kitty; she felt comfortable among people who understood that leaving the privacy of the boudoir meant stepping onto a stage. Americans pretended that the high-society show was real, whereas the French embraced the pretense.

Posing as a naive heiress to a little-known but fabulously wealthy steel manufacturer's fortune, she gained access to the designer ateliers for fashion and jewelry. With a magpie's attraction to sparkle, she gravitated to the artisanry, economics, and, most important, the illegal export potential of fine jewels. A long history of fine craftsmanship had made France a treasure box of splendor, and the changing fortunes of aristocrats, along with the sale of crown jewels by the government, flooded the small market for extravagant bijoux. Replicas of royal jewelry had become all the rage in New York; these sold in Paris at a fraction of the price they could command overseas. The American import duties were preposterously high, but Kitty knew that it would be easy to bring in something as small as a necklace or brooch unde-tected. Given the sheer number of transatlantic passengers and their mountains of luggage, it was astonishing that customs agents caught any smugglers at all. She bought both original pieces and replicas, and she would eventually hire a jeweler to make multiple copies of the same item at a discount. America was big enough to absorb four or five identical "unique and priceless sapphire bracelets that once belonged to Empress Josephine" without anyone becoming the wiser. In preparation for a return to America, Kitty sewed the jewelry behind the lining of fur coats and stoles, submerged it in jars of skin cream, even commissioned an oversized whalebone corset with inner pockets between the baleen strips. The hidden jewelry would make her look plumper than she already was from eating French pastries, but vanity was not one of her vices.

Kitty hired a tutor to teach her French and another for music; she attended lectures and art shows, and fed her voracious, omnivorous reading appetite at the library. At lunchtime, she frequented crowded, fashionable restaurants, sometimes observing from the shadows, other times peacocking in brightly colored gowns, a gold cigarette case dangling from her bracelet like a lure to other patrons who might wish to strike up a conversation and a smoke.

From her new acquaintances, Kitty learned to distinguish tourists from expatriates who made a home in the city and understood the intricate dance between foreigners and the French. The concept of new and old money was turned on its head in Paris, where mention of the *Mayflower* evoked nothing more than images of hawthorn shrubs, if that. To Parisians, all American money was new money—and the more, the better. She heard of women who lived in the faubourgs, surrounded by high garden walls beyond the Seine, Americans who had married into the French aristocracy and lived secluded lives of glittering elegance. For them, a Newport garden party would be as uncouth as a traveling circus.

A bored and relatively impecunious aristocrat, Comtesse Charlotte-Marie de Guché, took Kitty under her wing. She was a dignified spinster with a grave demeanor but keen appreciation for wit and irony. In a mix of French and English, Kitty regaled her with commentary on the people they met, conversations they overheard, the oddness of foreign customs. In return, the comtesse introduced Kitty at social gatherings and brought her to the opera and the theater.

It was with the comtesse that Kitty saw the actress Sarah Bernhardt play Phèdre, a performance that brought her to tears. She had never seen such passion expressed, and the tragedy of doomed love spoke to her bruised young heart. Kitty left the theater transformed.

Afterward, at the café, the comtesse nibbled strawberries and cream. "I will never understand this obsessive fixation on a particular man or woman," she said, dabbing her crimson mouth with her serviette. The gaslights cast a harsh light on her lupine face; when she smiled, the effect was vaguely sinister.

Kitty, still stirred by Racine's play, pushed aside her custard. "What could be more important than love?" She knew that her words opened her up to ridicule, but she couldn't stop herself. Gesturing at the crowded room full of well-heeled theater patrons, she said, "What is all of this ambition worth, this spectacle, if it is not in service of something greater?"

The comtesse raised her razor-thin eyebrows. "'The very substance of ambition is merely the shadow of a dream,' as your Englishman wrote." Her supercilious tone, normally amusing to Kitty, grated on her now.

"Isn't that just the point, though?" Kitty ignored her companion's disparaging smirk. "The dream is what lends purpose to our actions. Surely you have some dream."

With a Gallic shrug, the comtesse sipped her coffee. "You Americans are so charmingly childlike." She signaled the waiter for more chocolate wafers. "You cannot accept that life is without meaning, merely a brief interlude from the peaceful oblivion that bookends our petty struggles."

At that moment, as the older woman listlessly poked a silver spoon into her dessert, heavy rings sliding on bony, freckled fingers, Kitty decided that it was time to return to the United States. Watching Phèdre had cracked open something inside of her, something light and airy that would curdle in the astringent continental atmosphere. She would always come back to Paris, but her future was in America.

In New York City, Kitty kept a low profile at first. Between bank money and the smuggled jewelry, which she had begun to sell, she already had enough to buy an impressive house, but she chose to stay in hotels until she gained familiarity with the city.

Now that she was more established, it did not take long to learn where Mae's mansion was located, a patrician neighborhood that was becoming less fashionable as the wealthy moved north. In her peregrinations, Kitty studiously avoided the block where the Marshalls lived; she was not ready to see Mae, though her heart hammered whenever she imagined that she had caught a glimpse of her in the reflection of a window or strolling in a park.

In the new opera house, Kitty took a parterre box, a vantage point that allowed her to observe the characters who populated the society pages. She read all that she could about the city's prominent families, but seeing them in the flesh gave her some insights that could not be gleaned from snarky journalists. She noted that the young Miss V ignored the suitor her mother had reportedly selected for her in favor of a jovial-looking lawyer with a luxurious black mustache, and that Mrs. B was habitually intoxicated and clearly warring with her husband. Mr. S had a roving eye, but his brother appeared to be the more successful in seducing the fair sex.

Ivory shoulders emerged from under cloaks against the red penumbra of the background; through long-stemmed opera glasses, Kitty watched the coalescence and dispersion of waving fans, trembling plumes, twinkling jewels, along with the black-and-white-clad men who seemed to serve as mere foils to the brightly dressed women. Kitty recognized a chartreuse satin polonaise with jet buttons as a design from the Worth House on Rue de la Paix, noting that it fit its wearer poorly; it had likely been put away for a season or two, while the debutante grew. Why spend so much on a dress and not have it altered? Unsurprisingly, the girl's companion—probably a sister, as they both had ginger hair—wore an outdated gray and pink poplin that hung loosely on her youthful frame. No Parisian would wear something so ill-fitting.

Kitty followed the operagoers through her glasses as they took their seats, looking for familiar faces. She spotted a banker she knew had Cleveland roots, someone she was still debating whether or not to approach, and swung her gaze over to the other people in his box. A woman in ivory satin with diamond combs in her hair was conversing animatedly with a gentleman behind her; she turned toward the stage when the lights dimmed, and with an electric shock, Kitty recognized Mae.

As the opening strains of the opera filled the air, and the Egyptian high priest strode across the footlights, Mae sat still and erect, the crystal beads on her bodice glittering. She was not the girl Kitty remembered; her full cheeks had hollowed, her jawline was sharper, her hair darker. Prettiness had given way to a more haunting beauty.

The younger Mae had been in constant motion; this version was a statue. Kitty examined her, blood thundering through her veins; the hand holding the opera glasses shuddered ever so slightly with her heartbeat. Her eyes misted during Verdi's aria; Kitty was transported back to the cliff walk in Newport, when Mae laughed, full-throated, her head tilted back, their arms linked. Her spirit had soared then like the seabirds silhouetted against an enamel-blue sky.

The roar of applause took Kitty by surprise; it seemed a mere moment since the opera had begun. Mae, clapping lightly, glanced around, and Kitty dropped her opera glasses in a panic, as though Mae could follow her gaze back through the magnifying lenses. She grabbed her stole and rushed to the exit before the crush of the audience reached the doors.

Rain was pelting down, streaming off the awning, sloshing in the gutters; Kitty cursed and wove through the parked lines of private carriages, holding her hem out of the mud, looking for a hansom cab. She waved, but the driver, hunched under his slicker and broad-brimmed hat, ignored her; the carriage rushed past, its wheels spraying her with dirty water.

Kitty took shelter in a doorway as the opera traffic jostled away from the curb and into the roadway, drivers yelling, horses snorting, their ears pinned back in protest. Passengers were barely visible through streaming windows. As the street emptied, the rain let up; fog lingered over puddles and the air filled with the sweet scent of rot and a metallic tang. Kitty fastened the clasp on her stole, pulled her hat low, and headed on foot back to her hotel. It was time to emerge from hiding, she decided; it was time to make her mark in New York City.

CHAPTER 31

Kitty remained in close contact with her banker in Pittsburgh, Mr. Francis Beckett. When she first approached him, she had expected him to see her as a useful dupe; a naive young woman with a huge windfall that she did not know how to manage. This sort of attitude generally played in Kitty's favor. A banker sniffing out the opportunity to make easy money did not consider the possibility that he himself could be duped.

Beckett, however, did not conform to her expectations. He was avuncular, certainly, but he also took a keen interest in her thoughts and ideas, and he seemed to care about her success. Kitty was disconcerted by his curiosity at first, but he was so warm, so approving of her ambition to expand her fortune, that she decided to cultivate his good will and heed at least a portion of his counsel.

On Beckett's trips to New York, he arranged, when possible, for Kitty to join him at dinner, introducing her as his niece to head off prurient inquisitiveness. Beckett's companions were usually the shabbier sort of gentlemen, small twigs of old family trees who were raised with a tranquil disdain for earning money. They had opinions about wine and horses, and little else. Kitty did not learn much of practical value from the conversations, but she did develop an appreciation for old-fashioned values, the sort that did not distinguish between personal and business honor. Such quaint tradition could be exploited.

On one misty, gray evening, when the air smelled of wet ashes and the gaslights were shrouded in haze, Beckett escorted Kitty to a different sort of gathering.

"These are bankers, brokers, the sort of men who want to be part of modern New York City," he explained in the carriage. "Not the ones hoping for a small loan from a country bumpkin to tide them over."

"How dare you insult my dear Mr. Beckett by calling him a country bumpkin." She smiled with genuine affection.

His laugh was a short bark. "Ah, I am just a blacksmith's son who got too big for his britches." He looked out the window, pausing for a long moment before turning back to her. "You, on the other hand—" He pursed his lips and cleared his throat before beginning again. "You are a young woman of the world; you have education, vision. Your whole life is ahead of you, and I really think that you will make something of it." His voice was gruff, barely rising over the chatter of the wheels. "Now look at this old man making a fool of himself." He laughed again.

Kitty wished that he would stop talking.

"Well, now." Beckett pushed the brim of his hat up, then pulled it back down. He leaned forward, knobby hands on his knees. "You see, I never had the blessing of a daughter of my own. But if I had—" He cleared his throat again. "Well." He stroked his beard. "Well, I would want her to be just like you."

His words fell on Kitty like burning embers. Shame chased her through the chambers of her mind while she fled, slamming doors.

"Well, don't mind me."

Kitty could hear the smile in his voice but could not meet his gaze.

With a lurch, the carriage pulled to the curb, and the driver rapped on the roof.

"We have arrived!" Beckett pushed open the door and picked up his walking stick. He was slow to step out, as though his joints pained him, but he gallantly held out his arm to help Kitty down.

She took his gloved hand, squeezed it with gratitude. *I will treat this man with more care*, she resolved.

Though the restaurant was crowded, Beckett spotted their party immediately. Four men were seated at a round table, clothed nearly identically, down to the blue hues of their cravats and their overly tall starched collars with blunt little wings. They were speaking loudly and animatedly, already tucking into their supper.

"Gentlemen!" Beckett smiled widely. "I am glad to see that you did not wait for me. I apologize for my tardiness!"

Two of the faces turned to the newcomers while the other men continued their energetic exchange. The youngest-looking, who had hair the color of straw, pushed back his chair, but Beckett waved him down.

Now all four were looking at them, silverware settling on plates, eyes settling on Kitty.

"My niece, Mrs. Warren." Beckett introduced her matter-of-factly, ignoring or oblivious to their sour faces.

With a great scraping of chair legs and some heaving and muttering, they all stood. Beckett pointed to each man around the table, reciting their names and employment, but Kitty found it hard to concentrate under their cold gazes. Their scorn was palpable; she felt the feebleness of her thin arms, the flabbiness of her soft curves. She had landed like a fly in their soup, spoiling dinner.

Grudgingly, space was provided for Kitty at the table, and somehow a plate of roast beef and potatoes appeared in front of her, along with a small glass of claret. She hoped to make herself unobtrusive so that they would return to uninhibited discussions about finance; she kept her gaze down, taking in the aspects of her supper companions with furtive glances.

"Advantage is the only way to break away from the penny-ante returns you're getting," the broker with long, closely cropped side whiskers proclaimed. He put a fist to his compressed lips to cover a belch.

A portly man, his face bumpy and flushed with rosacea—was his name Walters?—laughed derisively. "What would you know? You make what, a quarter of a percent on par value when you sell?" He handed an empty wine bottle to the waiter, signaling for another.

Mr. Side Whiskers was not drawn in. "We could hold your stock on margin for a small interest fee. That way, you can double your buy."

Beckett looked at him with concern. "Isn't that risky, Elias? The market is so volatile."

Kitty focused on the lacquer tiles behind Beckett's head; the pattern was like fall leaves floating on a black pool.

"I think we're boring the little lady!" This came from a square-jawed, handsome man named Murray, who wore a gold tie pin and an excess of pomade in his dun hair.

"Mrs. Warren has an interest in finance," Beckett said mildly.

Murray guffawed, slapping his hand on the tablecloth like he'd heard a witty joke. "She doesn't look like one of those petticoated sharks I've seen on Wall Street!"

He had the attention of the whole table. The blond young man looked uncomfortable; he examined his nearly clean plate, speared a stray green bean. Walters patted his protruding stomach, took a tortoise shell cigar case from his pocket and passed it around. "The fat, ugly ones who swill champagne like it's ginger beer?" he said, egging Murray on.

Waiters gathered plates. Kitty didn't complain, though her food was hardly touched.

"The ugly ones I feel sorry for," Murray said. "It's those Cleopatras looking for a fool to play their Antony that I despise!"

Blue smoke curled up, enfolding them as more cigars were lit.

Beckett began to speak, but the man he had called Elias cut him off. "That characterization does not sound accurate to me." He enunciated well, laying his words down precisely, as a bricklayer sets bricks. "I share Mr. Darwin's view of the female sex. Women may be inferior to men intellectually, but they are generally superior in moral qualities." He accepted a large pour of cognac.

"Ha!" Murray rocked back in his chair, and Kitty had the sudden image of him tipping over, limbs flailing. "Clearly you haven't heard of Hettie Hawthorne and her dark Othello!" He threw Kitty a sidelong glance and smirk, then blew a smoke ring.

Beckett looked chagrined.

"Aren't you one for the Shakespeare references today," Walters said. "Showing off that fancy Harvard education, are you?"

The blond man turned to Kitty. "Perhaps we should ask Mrs. Warren what she thinks?"

Kitty kept custody of her tongue. She forced herself to look from one face to another, taking in their expressions, allowing each man to feel the weight of her attention. This was a strategy she had taught herself to create a large enough space in the conversation to insert her voice into the manly din. It also allowed her time to marshal her thoughts and project an appearance of dignity.

"I suppose that accomplishments speak for themselves, don't they, gentlemen?" She smiled warmly. "Mr. Beckett here was granted few advantages at birth, but he has risen to the position of president at his bank."

Beckett sipped his wine with a gratified air.

"And you, Mr.—?" She beamed her smile at the man with side whiskers.

"Cohen, madam." He seemed unsure where to look.

"Why, you seem to know all there is to know about the markets!" She infused her tone with admiration. "You *must* explain to me what you meant by short selling. It sounds fascinating! I am not sure that I would understand, but I do *so* enjoy hearing about the ways in which men can apply their analytical minds.

"Mr. Murray is obviously a hugely successful man of the world, as is Mr. Walters." Kitty turned to the youngest man. "You, sir, I have not heard enough about. I do hope that you will tell me more about yourself and what you do for a living."

He flushed with pleasure under her gaze. "It would be my honor, Mrs. Warren."

Kitty gave her attention to the whole party once more. "Dear gentlemen," she said, "I don't have a head for finance, but if you explain things to me simply, I feel that I will be better prepared to make some choices about the disposition of my wealth."

"Surely Mr. Beckett can take care of all of that for you," Cohen said.

"Oh yes." She tilted her head, sparkled at Beckett for the benefit of all of the men. "He is truly my savior."

Beckett did not contradict her.

"Now," Kitty said with her best coquette smile. "Do tell me about this short selling of stocks."

CHAPTER 32

As a widow without a new man in her life, Kitty feared that she would have trouble buying property in Manhattan. Beckett was not the sort of person who would agree to misrepresent himself, but she planted the seeds of misinformation with the sellers of an avant-garde mansion herself, telling them that her wealthy great-uncle, the owner of a shipping business, had asked her to take care of the purchase details for him. To Beckett, she said that she merely needed him to show up for the deed transfer so that she would be taken seriously, and that he would have to sign a paper to vouch for her solvency. He was only too pleased to be of use.

Kitty took great pains to furnish and decorate her new home in a style designed to impress. Gold was a dominant theme; she brought in gold clocks, gold figurines in gold cabinets, and a golden bird in a golden cage that sang when spring was touched. The floors were covered with jewel-toned rugs from Persia and India, and gilded chairs were topped with cushions sewn from medieval tapestries. She bought a Steinway grand piano, and an organ with 365 pipes—one for each day of the year. On the tables were cloisonné and Ginori vases, and in the lofty entrance hall stood two risqué Rodin marbles, one of nude

Orpheus and Eurydice, and another of Cupid and Psyche in a passionate embrace. Kitty also leaned on her Parisian experience to acquire works by the French painters Jean-Léon Gérôme and William-Adolphe Bouguereau and members of the Barbizon school, which she hung in ornate gilt frames.

The servants Kitty hired were mostly French; they appreciated her ability to speak to them in their own language, and she treated them with great generosity, buying them expensive clothing and giving them luxurious rooms. In return, she expected and almost always received absolute loyalty; the one time a girl tried to steal an emerald ring from Kitty, she was swiftly condemned by her fellow servants and immediately sacked. The kitchen workers were instructed never to turn away a beggar at the back door, and the female staff participated in buying and wrapping gifts for the children at the orphan asylum each holiday; this general largesse further endeared Kitty to her employees.

Breaking into New York social circles was a major campaign for Kitty. Without a husband or pedigree—she could not risk dropping Andrew Carnegie's name in his own neighborhood—she had to rely on charm and flamboyant displays of wealth to win over the cream of society. The highest echelons with proper lineage were well out of her grasp, but Kitty hoped to attract enough of the merely rich to eventually, through sheer will, make her home acceptable to Mae Marshall.

Kitty used knowledge gained through months of close observation to befriend women who operated at social nexi, people who lacked the genealogy of American royalty but who were nevertheless welcomed into their outer circles by dint of association with approved causes, charities, or institutions. In this way, Kitty insinuated herself into luncheons and teas and eventually had the opportunity to host small gatherings at her own house. She planned these functions down to the tiniest detail and coached her staff to attend to guests with attention to every cue. Watch their glasses, she told them, and be sure to refill them before they are empty. If a guest appears to be casting glances about the room, bored, tell her that I wish to have a private audience in the gallery—but of course warn me first. If anyone gets too tipsy, bring her to the conservatory to see our rare strains of roses, and be sure to serve something rich, like strawberries and cream, or chocolate pound cake, and, of course, a sobering cup of tea.

To flatter her guests' intellects, she arranged readings by writers and philosophers, or performances by musicians before the meal, and she always handed out lavish party favors, such as gold-framed miniatures painted on porcelain, or jeweled ivory boxes imported from China. She learned as much as she could about the women's husbands, and she finagled introductions to the husbands who sounded most useful. In this way, she met Thomas Murdaugh, a clothing manufacturer.

Kitty told Mrs. Murdaugh that she needed advice from a man about her finances, and since Mr. Murdaugh had a reputation for being both wholly honest and exceedingly charitable, she wondered if she might impose on him with her ignorant questions.

Thomas Murdaugh kindly invited Kitty to visit him at his mahogany-lined and leather-upholstered office on Madison Avenue.

"I am so appreciative of your generosity in giving me your time," Kitty said, settling herself into the wingback chair opposite his desk.

Murdaugh was a big man who stood with stooped shoulders and clasped hands, as though he didn't want to take up more than his allotment of space. "It's my pleasure, Mrs. Warren." He glanced briefly at a fly that buzzed and battered itself against the window, trying to escape, then sat down with an almost apologetic smile. He shuffled papers on his desk. "Ah, my wife said you needed help?" He made brief eye contact, then looked away.

"Actually, I have a financial opportunity to present to you." She looked at him bright-eyed, letting seconds slip by in silence, watching his discomfort mount. Just as he was about to speak again, she said, "Your wife is a wonderful person. When she found out that I am a widow new to the city, she was so welcoming. And she tells the most delightful stories about your adorable children."

Back on more familiar territory, the tension in his face eased. Kitty knew that he would let her talk for a minute or two, uninterrupted, to avoid further awkwardness.

"Mrs. Murdaugh said that you could help me with my investments," Kitty said warmly. "I do realize that you are not an expert in the stock market, but as a businessman with an unimpeachable reputation, you are just the person I need."

Murdaugh leaned back a little. After a desperate thwack against the sun-crazed glass, the fly found the opening in the window and hurtled away.

"You see, I have money to invest, but I need a gentleman partner, as the brokerages will not take me seriously. They refuse to take me on as a client." She caught the slightest downward twitch of his eyebrows, and quickly added, "There is no need to invest any of your own money, of course. Though you may choose to do so."

He gave a tentative nod.

"There is an underground rail system planned for the city of New York." Kitty paused, leaned in, and lowered her voice. "And the Bank of New York is planning to make a sizable investment."

"Ah." He looked confused. "Yes, there has been a lot of talk of an underground since that terrible blizzard." He shook his head sadly.

"Poor Ginny was hysterical. One of our neighbor's boys actually died in that storm." He clasped his thick-knuckled hands.

"The stock of the Bank of New York will rise in value, Mr. Murdaugh." She let this sink in. "It is the perfect time to buy."

Comprehension dawned on his blunt features, but he looked skeptical. "How could anyone be sure of this?"

"Oh, one can never be completely sure, of course." She gave a little laugh. "The nature of business involves risk, isn't that so, Mr. Murdaugh?" More solemnly, she said, "You could speak with your associates about how seriously the bank is considering backing the underground rail project. You are very well connected, I know."

He seemed pleased with her small bit of flattery. "I will ask around. Your idea is intriguing."

She reached in her bag and pulled out a check. "Meanwhile, if you would invest this on my behalf, I would be appreciative." She handed it to him across the desk.

He looked at her more intently when he saw the sum. "You must be very confident, Mrs. Warren."

She smiled. "I am." She snapped her bag shut. "And I thank you sincerely for your time, Mr. Murdaugh."

In this way, Kitty convinced a number of investors to buy Bank of New York stock. The price rose, and seeing this, investors convinced themselves to buy more. Once the ball was rolling, Kitty quit buying, and when the underground rail system was announced, and the stock price skyrocketed, she sold. Discreetly, she took a short position on Bank of New York stock, betting that the value would go down.

As anyone could have predicted, almost from the moment of groundbreaking, obstacles to the project were discovered. Kitty spoke worriedly about these problems to anyone who would listen. She told her acquaintances that the bank was overextended in its loans, and she was terribly concerned that their accounts would be frozen. She withdrew all of her own money and deposited it elsewhere. News spread of a possible run on the bank, causing more widespread anxiety about the bank's solvency and, more importantly for Kitty, a fall in its stock prices.

Kitty not only made a fortune on these transactions; she also gained a reputation for shrewdness—even clairvoyance—and the ladies at her luncheons thanked her profusely for her warning to empty their bank accounts before it was too late. Kitty accepted their gratitude graciously.

CHAPTER 33

Dear Fanny (or should I say Kitty),

I am glad that you left your card so that I might find you again. I have been thinking about you often since you visited, and I feel sorry that I was less than welcoming to you. By way of excuse, I was hurt that you seemed to forget about me when you started working for Mae, after I went out on a limb to befriend and help you. I also worry that you don't take the rules of man or God seriously enough.

That said, the Bible tells us not to judge our brothers and sisters, and I know that the money you gave me is your way of apologizing. Apology accepted, and thank you. I was being a prig to tell you that I wouldn't use it. It is so hard for me to get loans to build my business, and I shouldn't be too proud to accept money from an old friend.

My stipulation is that I will consider your gift a loan, and I insist that you accept my repayment in future. I hope that seeing my business thriving will make you proud, and I will be happy to be able to repay my debt. Meanwhile, Fanny, I wish you happiness in your new life, and please do visit again the next time you are in Cleveland.

Your friend,

Grace

CHAPTER 34

An apologetic letter arrived from Francis Beckett, urging Kitty to repay several of her bank loans. He said that the board members had become aware of the extent of her debt, and he was worried that they would resort to legal action if she did not submit overdue payments immediately.

Kitty's stomach clenched, and she asked her servant, Gisèle, for brandy. Gisèle looked worried. "Are you feeling ill, madame?"

Kitty was touched by her concern. "Your English has improved so much, Gisèle. Tout va bien, merci."

Gisèle, still frowning, poured a glass of brandy at the sideboard. Kitty took the drink to her study, where she wrote a carefully worded letter back to Beckett, assuring him that it was a mere oversight, and she would take care of everything.

She rang for Gisèle for more brandy. There was more than enough money from the stock windfall to fully pay off several of the DePaul loans, but she also had outstanding loans from a number of other banks, and if she didn't make at least minimum payments on those debts, those bankers, who were relative strangers, were more likely to come after her than Beckett. She would need to think it all through carefully.

Kitty opened another letter, this one from Patrick Armstrong, the private investigator. In it, he reiterated that he had high confidence that Betsy had been at Laporte's brothel, and although he could not prove it, he believed that she had died there too. He was grateful for her ongoing business, but he truly had exhausted all of his leads, and it would be unprofessional of him to accept any further payments.

Kitty had continued to retain his services even though he had not made any headway in years; it wasn't rational, but it made her feel like she was doing something for her sister. It seemed curious to her that Armstrong's greatest stated regret was not to be able to return a body to her for proper burial. In her past lifetime, on a subsistence farm in the wilderness, death had been a constant, for humans as well as animals. It wasn't that she hadn't loved the people, and even some of the livestock, but the flesh that was left behind after life was extinguished was not sacred to her. She imagined that wherever Betsy's remains were, she was already mostly returned to the earth and sky. This gave her some comfort. She raised her brandy glass to her sister's spirit and swallowed a burning draft. Betsy was free.

After several seasons of slowly building her reputation, working her way into ever more rarified salons, Kitty felt she might dare to organize her own party. She had taken a pair of young ladies from good families under her wing, just as Comtesse de Guché had done for her in Paris. The girls were not yet out in society and were dying to be entertained; their mothers were content for them to learn about music and art from someone as knowledgeable as Mrs. Warren, a decent widow with a Continental education. Kitty chaperoned them to galleries and concerts, regaling them with stories of famous artists and members of the nobility she met on her trips to France. She snuck them sips of champagne, introduced them to black truffles, and brought them silk stockings from Paris that they were absolutely not allowed to let their parents see.

When it came time for their debuts, Kitty suggested that the three of them organize a fancy dress ball to take place in her house. Her home was new and located uptown, where land was plentiful; it had a dedicated ballroom, unlike their parents' older, patrician houses downtown. Of course it wasn't as elegant, Kitty said modestly, but the ballroom did have enough space for a sizable orchestra, and they could spend as much time as they wanted on the decor—a theme of Venice, perhaps? It would be such fun!

The young women cajoled their mothers and ultimately gained their approval, and thus Kitty's ball secured the imprimatur of two respected New York families. Despite Kitty's relative obscurity, the three names on the invitations would ensure robust attendance. Kitty's co-hosts insisted on a theme of St. Augustine, a burst of subtropical warmth in late autumn. Kitty wasn't sure that the motif would inspire much in the way of costumes, but she agreed to it with feigned enthusiasm.

The custom in New York was to have one's own staff make food for a small affair at home, or to hire Delmonico's for a party in a restaurant. Kitty wanted the best of both, and turned to a new, little-known business started by a Mr. Louis Sherry, a French-trained cook who partnered with a talented assistant chef from Delmonico's to create a catering service. Mr. Sherry would not only supply a lavish feast but would also use his Parisian training to create equally impressive decor. Kitty told him to spare no effort or expense, and that the party would provide the best possible publicity for his new enterprise.

For a dramatic mise en scène, Kitty employed a set designer who had worked on Gilbert and Sullivan productions. For music, she hired a fine chamber orchestra, which came inexpensively in New York's crowded field of starving musicians. Sherry and the set designer created a miniature pond in the ballroom with Asiatic lilies and bowing ferns, copper-scaled fish darting in the dark reflecting pool, and iridescent globes floating on top. In its center was a fountain with spray that caught the many refractions of crystal chandeliers. Leafy palms and figs surrounded and overarched the water, giving it an aura of mystery; tropical foliage and blooms were spread throughout the ballroom and banquet room, turning the whole space into a garden paradise.

By six o'clock, the orchestra was tuning instruments—strings, woodwinds, brass—and shortly thereafter, guests began to arrive. Many came in fancy dress; tropical bird feathers and fish scales were popular, as were the miters and robes of Saint Augustine himself. The more poetically minded dressed as the ocean or a moonlit beach with cloth-of-gold and waves of blue satin bordered with pearls. Kitty stood by her fellow hosts near the entrance to receive them, her insides abuzz with anticipation and, increasingly, anxiety. The ballroom slowly filled with chatter and laughter; on a banquet table, the caterers set out cut glass bowls of Roman punch, canvasbacks, terrapin, chaudfroid of reed birds, aspic of foie gras en bellevue, pain de rillette, and baba au rum. The orchestra struck up the music, dancers swirled, and champagne flowed.

Mae and Charlie had not shown up by seven o'clock, and by then Kitty's nervousness had turned to dread. The prospect of seeing Mae again was suddenly unbearable. Seized by a terrible shyness, she excused herself, retreating to the darkened library. She slumped into a leather armchair and pressed her cold fingers to her warm cheeks, taking deep breaths.

Fanny, who had lain dormant for so long, crept back into Kitty's body, along with her memories of the farm, the brothel, her lost sister, the snug room she had shared with Grace. Kitty ruthlessly pushed Fanny back down, but an echo remained; the girl, barefoot in the attic room, hands on her skinny hips, stared up at Kitty with reproach.

Crescendoing strains of the orchestra and a burst of nearby laughter brought Kitty back into the moment. The door to the library swung open, letting light spill into the room, quickly followed by a flurry of tulle skirts. Kitty shrank further into the shadows as three young women giggled and hushed one another with loud, tipsy shushing. They closed the door most of the way, listening to the call of baritone voices in the hallway.

Kitty caught excited whispers of "Won't find us—" and "Looking for you—" followed by more stifled giggling.

"Oh, it's a library," one of the girls said.

From behind the wing of her chair, Kitty could only see half of her, but from the thuds, she could tell that books had been knocked to the floor. There came dismayed muttering, a whirl of activity, then Kitty heard her name.

"Warren. Somebody told me—"

The girls gathered closer together.

"Somebody told me that her husband was—"

A rumble of male voices in the hallway came closer.

"Shhh!"

"You stepped on my foot!"

There came a muffled snort of laughter, more shushing, then quiet.

A man called out names from the hallway, but from farther away. The girls began their whispering again.

"—that strike at the steel mill in Pittsburgh, where those people got killed, they say that was the Warren family—"

"No, this house was bought with railway money, I'm sure!"

"—all that booze—"

"—some kind of tycoon—"

"I have never once seen her!"

"Who here even knows what Kitty Warren looks like?"

"I think it's all gaudy, myself."

All at once, there came a raucous hue and cry, and the door burst open. Kitty jumped and nearly shrieked along with the trio of girls. The boys howled with mirth and were soon joined by the startled young women, who, when the hilarity died down, cheerfully followed their tormentors out of the library, shutting the door behind them.

Kitty remained still and silent for a moment, then she too burst out laughing. She laughed and laughed like a crazy woman, until her sides hurt. She felt herself grow lighter, until the great, clanking armor she wore every day fell away, and she floated, featherweight, above her boned, laced, swathed, primped body.

Kitty descended the stairs to the ballroom, where she took in the merriment, the costumes, the dancing. She circulated, unnoticed, among her guests, lifted a cup of champagne from a passing tray. To be a woman was to be invisible. It had always felt like a weakness, to inhabit a body so easily dismissed and overlooked. But it was not only a weakness, she realized. It could also be a strength. She could go wherever she wanted, be whomever she chose, wield her invisibility as a weapon.

The swirl of colors, the glitter, the changing light, seemed to have nothing to do with her, but delighted her still, like a beautiful sunset or rainbow. The ball was a success, and word would spread; she would throw more parties, attracting more of New York society. If Mae never came, no matter; she had already decided that an intimate meeting would be better. She also knew who could help her to set the plan in motion when the right time came: Joseph Carrow, her neighbor and Mae Marshall's cousin.

CHAPTER 35

Joseph Carrow, cousin of Mae Marshall

Summer in New York was always quiet, when the fashionable people fled to breezy seaside escapes, but in the fall, as the swelter and hot city stink abated, the social scene sprang back to life. Though the neighborhood I inhabited was hardly the most posh *quartier*, my next-door neighbor, Mrs. Kitty Warren, became a magnet for some of the Fifth Avenue and Washington Square crowd. She threw extravagant parties at her imposing residence—by far the largest house for several blocks in any direction—on Friday nights. A thick fog of wealth clung to the glittering guests, but it was whispered that they were not of the highest caliber. Rumor had it that they included opera singers, foreigners, even a papist or two.

Still, curiosity lured some of Old New York, who arrived in gleaming barouches, swathed in furs, noses in the air and eyes darting about for subjects worthy of gossip. They approached the brownstone-clad mansion on a velvet carpet that had been rolled down the steps by footmen, fatuously dressed in old-fashioned silk stockings. If the footmen struck a crass note, the ballroom apparently did not—Mrs. Warren did not stoop to the traditional practice of putting a crash on the drawing room floor and moving the furniture upstairs but had a dedicated ballroom, complete with gilt chairs, a dais for the orchestra, and chandeliers fit for a palace. Even with my windows closed, on Friday nights I could hear strains of "Blue Danube" or the melancholy "After the Ball," wafting through the night air.

One October day, a hand-delivered invitation arrived, white ink calligraphy on expensive pigeon-blood notepaper. Mrs. Catherine Warren humbly requested my attendance at "an informal soirée" the following week. I was stunned, as up to that time I had not more than glimpsed my neighbor, and we certainly did not belong to the same social stratum. I was itching to know more about the mysterious lady, however, whose provenance seemed unknown. Some said that she was a Continental transplant, used to "colorful" customs of those "wicked old societies," while others claimed that she was related to some Middle-West coal baron. I tried to suspend any notions of my own and arrived at the appointed time sporting my smartest evening attire. (The invitation said *informal*, but I guessed that my best clothes would scarcely measure up, and I was correct.)

There was no red carpet, footmen, or orchestra; the smiling servant who greeted me led me through an enchanting set of enfiladed drawing rooms, each decorated in a vivid hue—citrine, jade, claret—lit with a multitude of sconced candles, their flickers reflected by polished parquet floors. I could imagine partygoers clustered in each of the rooms, pulling on dancing gloves, the air alive with chatter and laughter, but on this night the chambers were deserted. Beyond the last drawing room was a conservatory; the servant left me at the entrance, where I had a moment to take in the scene. Fig trees, sword ferns, and palms bowed their fronds over gold and black furnishings; a table had been placed in the middle of the conservatory, cleverly arranged with nonflowering plants of variegated shades; the effect was of dining in a fairy forest graced by the quiet playing of a string quartet.

There were no more than a dozen guests milling about the conservatory, champagne glasses in hand. It was impossible to miss Kitty Warren, who wore a sparkling silver gown accessorized with diamonds—her *informal* diamonds, I presumed—vivacious and flushed, conversing with a mustachioed gentleman boasting a highly glazed shirtfront and silk ascot. When my hostess noticed that I had arrived, she excused herself to welcome me.

"Why, I am so delighted that you could join us!" She held out her hand in a strange way, not quite in the modern fashion lately adopted by young ladies, nor in the French fashion; unsure what to do, I took her gloved fingers between both hands as I bowed slightly.

"I was delighted to receive your invitation," I said. "And a little bit surprised."

On close observation, I could see that Mrs. Warren was beyond youth, but her face was still unlined; her round cheeks gave her a cherubic appearance. She was not beautiful, but her eyes held mine with an intensity that made it impossible to look away.

"It is only neighborly," she said lightly. Her eyes were an unusual color, flecked with blue and ocher. "I feel that we have met somewhere before?"

"Oh, no, I would certainly remember that!" I realized that I had been embarrassingly vehement. "I hadn't—" Flustered, I lost my train of thought.

She touched my arm encouragingly.

"I would not have thought that you had cause to notice *me*."

Her smile was kind but much more than that. It seemed to take in the whole of our circumstance, even—forgive my flight of fancy—the whole of our world. She seemed to see me for myself and approve of my beliefs, my objectives—my whole being. It was a moment of eternal reassurance that I do not think I will find again.

The dinner bell rang, and she said, "I have saved you the seat next to mine."

At supper, Mrs. Warren held forth on subjects as diverse as mayoral election campaigns and fruit tree grafting. She had a light touch, sprinkling her remarks with amusing anecdotes, drawing out commentary even from those with little knowledge of the topics. As the musicians played on, a feast was served by unobtrusive white-clad staff on silent feet, and listening to conversation, I did not once feel the urge to consult my pocket watch. In the moments that my host was exclusively engaged with other guests, I did my best to converse with the person seated to my other side, a kind matron in creaking satin, but it was like being banished from sunshine, the colors duller, the air colder. When at last Mrs. Warren turned the full warmth of her attention on me she said, "I have heard that you are a cousin to Mrs. Mae Marshall."

It did not take long for her to extract a promise of introduction from me. Indeed, I could think of little I would rather do than spend an afternoon in the presence of two such lovely individuals.

CHAPTER 36

Joseph Carrow, cousin of Mae Marshall

As we took a stroll in the park, I told my cousin that I had met my fabulously wealthy neighbor, Mrs. Warren. She smiled vaguely and nodded her pretty head, her thoughts obviously elsewhere.

"She wondered if I might reintroduce you," I asked.

From beneath her parasol, Mae glanced at me quizzically. "Do I know her?"

I had tried to discover Mrs. Warren's connection to my cousin, but she was elusive on that subject. "She's from Pittsburgh," I said. "After her husband died, she came here alone."

Mae lifted a hand in reciprocal greeting to a passing couple. "That was a mistake," she said.

"A mistake?"

How I loved to hear Mae's silvery laugh, even tinged, as it was, with weariness. "Her money won't open doors here."

With my walking stick, I pointed out a pile of horse dung on the path; she *tsk*ed and grasped my arm to step over the mess in her dainty boots. Though the sun was out, the breeze was brisk. I pulled my hat lower and puzzled over her statement—the rules of New York society were still Byzantine to me.

"I know what you are thinking, my sweet, earnest Joe," she said. "I am from Cleveland myself, a complete outsider. But I married a Marshall, and that makes all the difference."

Her wistfulness struck me again. Mae was more beautiful than ever, but there was a resigned sadness to her beauty, like a Lippi Madonna.

"I have never been to Pittsburgh," she said. "But perhaps I met her at some event in Cleveland. What did you say is her Christian name?"

"Catherine. She goes by Kitty."

There was a slight hitch in Mae's step; she looked at me sharply. "Kitty?" Whatever passed through her mind, she seemed to shrug it off. She resumed her pace, skirts gently swaying. "You never did finish telling me about your sister," she said.

I was not done with my subject; I had, after all, promised Mrs. Warren an introduction. "She does appear to have many acquaintances, though. Mrs. Warren, I mean. She entertains constantly. Were you not invited to her fancy dress ball?"

Mae's expression was blank. "Fancy dress?"

"The theme was St. Augustine. The Van Dyck and Christensen girls were companion hosts."

"Oh, that thing. Rather vulgar, wasn't it?" She twirled her parasol, then said, amused, "Is that woman really your neighbor?"

"Yes, and I think that she has done rather well for herself."

Mae sighed irritably. "You are too naive. Well-to-do arrivistes will of course attract the low sort of social climbers who sniff out money."

I confess that I bristled at this. "Catherine Warren seems to me a genteel, educated woman with a keen understanding of humankind." It occurred to me that she was likely about Mae's age, though her worldliness and manner made her appear older. "And I do not see how your choice of a husband makes you so much her superior that you wouldn't even give her the time of day."

We walked in silence for a time, then Mae said frostily, "If it is so important to you, I will meet your new friend. Why don't you invite us both to tea. I have not yet seen where you live, after all."

It was on the tip of my tongue to protest that my lodgings were far too meager to host the likes of Mae and Mrs. Warren, but I decided not to press my luck. "Of course," I said. "I will send you a note about the time."

She nodded curtly.

"And thank you for being so amenable," I said. "I don't believe that you will regret it."

On the day we had set for Mrs. Warren and Mae to come to tea, it dawned dull red against heavy clouds. A storm had swept through during the night; the bang of shutters and beat of rain kept me from sleeping despite several stiff whiskeys.

The walkway to my door was littered with soggy leaves; in my slippers and overcoat, I pushed them aside with a straw broom. The trees lining the street looked as disheveled and groggy as I felt, swaying like dazed drunks.

My cleaning lady had scrubbed and polished, and the cook had agreed to come early to serve tea, but my home and provisions seemed woefully inadequate to host my affluent cousin and neighbor. After a breakfast of soft-boiled eggs and tomato juice to settle my queasy stomach, I went to the shops in search of flowers and citrus fruit to spruce up my dim and somewhat shabby apartments.

I needn't have bothered with the flowers, because at two o'clock a large shipment of floral displays in ornate vases was delivered to my door courtesy of Mrs. Warren. The lady herself soon followed, hugging her fur coat tightly and looking peaky.

"Mr. Carrow." She nodded to me in greeting. "Is everything sorted?"

"Do come in, Mrs. Warren," I said, stepping aside. "The flowers are lovely. Thank you."

A small crease appeared on her forehead as my words seemed to slowly, slowly sink through whatever was occupying her mind. "Ah. Yes. I am glad to hear."

I gestured to one of the arrangements she had sent, a tower of white gardenias in the foyer.

She smiled politely, looked with unseeing eyes. "I hope that I am not too early."

"Not at all," I replied. "Though I expect my cousin will be fashionably late."

She remained stock still, her lips compressed in a thin line.

"May I take your hat and coat?"

Her hand gripped and released the fur; she looked down with mild surprise, as though she didn't know how she came to be wearing a coat. "Oh. Of course."

"I regret that I have no manservant for the customary niceties." My much stronger regret was that I had agreed to host the tea at all.

Mrs. Warren seemed to revive. Coins of pink appeared in her cheeks. "My dear Mr. Carrow, you are so kind to indulge my whim to reacquaint myself with Mrs. Marshall. I would, of course, have hosted you both myself, but it is doubtless a testament to her affection for you that she proposed coming here." She handed me her coat and hat.

"The parlor is just through that door," I said. "I will join you momentarily." The fatigue from a fitful night and weight of her fur made my arms leaden, my regret heavier.

When I entered the parlor, Mrs. Warren was stationed by the window, peering through the lace curtains. She turned when she heard me. "I suppose that the traffic coming uptown may be slow this time of day."

I murmured in agreement, invited her to sit. She perched on the edge of the divan, her back ramrod straight. Conversation deserted me. She smiled vaguely, worrying the brass nailheads on the armrest with her long fingers. She squinted at the book spines on my shelves, then seemed to lose interest. She chewed her lip like a nervous child.

The cook was clanging and banging in the kitchen; I was about to ask her to quiet down when I realized that the ticking clock on the mantelpiece also seemed deafeningly loud.

Mrs. Warren rose, went to the window again. "I suppose she could have been detained." In her simple gown, hair bunched at her nape, and her slim figure angled toward the slanting afternoon light, she made me think of a sailor's wife watching the restless sea.

I consulted the clock. "It is only a quarter past."

Just then, the bell rang; Mrs. Warren jumped, looked at me with wide eyes. I was struck by the greenish glow of her irises in the sunshine.

Overjoyed at the chance to move, I threw open the front door. Mae's amused smile, bright under the trailing veil of her hat, was a balm to me.

"So this is where you hide from society, dear Joe?" A lock of hair escaped in the wind, blown like corn silk across her cheek.

The warmth of her voice melted the ice that had stiffened my shoulders, my neck. I had a fanciful impulse to brush away the strand of hair; instead, I ushered her inside. "Mrs. Warren has already arrived," I said.

Mae nodded, her expression indulgent. "Your home is just so charming!"

I chuckled sociably at her kind fibbery.

She bent close to the arranged mass of gardenias, inhaling deeply. "Why Joe, who would have thought that you would have such an eye for fresh flowers!" Her small hand alighted on a bloom like a graceful bird. "These are exquisite!"

I almost said that Mrs. Warren was to thank, but something told me that she would not want Mae to know. "Even a blind squirrel finds the occasional acorn," I said.

The parlor was deserted. A small expression of dismay escaped me. My cousin seemed not to register my reaction; she lowered herself, with a pert swish of her skirt, onto the settee. Reclining, she looked about with a charitable eye. "You have made a fine nest for yourself here, dearest."

"I have tried—"

"I do adore the sconces. Cherubs? Or are those seraphs?"

I took in the plaster adornments for the first time. "I—"

"And the chandelier! That could be a Baccarat!"

Just then, Mrs. Warren appeared in the door to the library, a book clutched to her chest. I hadn't noticed the gold threads in her indigo gown before, but the beams of afternoon light caught them, glinting brightly.

Stillness descended upon us.

I looked to Mae; she was a graven statue.

"Mrs. Kitty—Mrs. Catherine Warren." I was embarrassed by my stumble. "I believe that you know Mrs. Marshall?"

There was a flash of dilated eyes, a whiff of what I can only describe as fright, and then Mrs. Warren gathered herself. "Why, Mrs. Marshall!"

Like a soldier called to attention, Mae stood.

The air vibrated around us.

Mrs. Warren stepped forward, into the full, sloping, amber rays. Her eyes glowed; she didn't blink in the light. She bowed her head slightly, then lifted her face, recapturing the shine on her curved cheek, her vivid irises. When she smiled, dimples appeared, lovely shadows I had not noticed before. "I recall that you have a fondness for mousse au chocolat," she said, seemingly apropos of nothing.

As if by magic, my cook appeared with a tray of tiny china pots filled with chocolate and cream. She set it down next to the teacups.

"Please." With a sweep of her arm, Mrs. Warren invited us to sit in my own parlor.

The cook crept away, gaze averted, her apron bunched in her hands.

Mae was a somnambulist. She looked about herself slowly, then focused on Mrs. Warren with the intensity of one trying to make sense of a dream.

"Should we sit for tea?" My voice was mortifyingly high.

"Kitty?" The way she said the name excavated layers of emotion.

"Dear Mae." Mrs. Warren extended a hand.

My cousin's beautiful face shifted only slightly, like a wind-ruffled field, but the room around us took on a strange vibrance.

"You must excuse me," I said quickly. "I must see to—" I hesitated, not knowing what justification to offer, but I realized that they had not registered my speech, or even my presence. They seemed transfixed, inert, facing one another like a pair of bookends. I backed away, muttered something apologetic, and softly closed the door.

I needed some air. Outside, the weary autumn sky was streaked with purple clouds. Rain earlier had left puddles on the road that reflected a ghostly version of the sky, as if the day was lying to rest in them. I walked several times around the block, my coattails flapping in the wind. Gutters dribbled, and a crow cawed from atop a streetlamp, emphasizing the unusual quiet; light faded without fanfare, the sun dunking toward a murky horizon.

I re-entered my home, making noise in the foyer, rattling the coat stand and throwing my boots down heavily. I clomped up the stairs and found the women seated close together in the parlor, heads angled toward one another. Mae looked up, and I caught a gleam of tears in her eyes, a slight trembling of her mouth. Kitty's face flared with something close to triumph.

"We are going over to my house," Kitty said.

"Oh." I looked from one to the other.

"You will come of course!" Mae's voice was tight, whether with grief or joy I was not certain.

"Are you sure that you want me—"

Both women interrupted, rising, surrounding me with tense chatter and motion. There was a concerted sweep of action toward the door and out, across the courtyard, and up the stately path to Mrs. Warren's mansion. Murmuring, Mae admired the imposing facade, the gardens, the scent of sweet alyssum. We mounted the marble steps, and inside, we wandered through a high-ceilinged, chartreuse-walled drawing room with pale brocaded furniture, immense mahogany bookcases, ormolu ornaments, rosewood consoles, and an arched fireplace with an ebony marble mantel. There was a library furnished with leather and malachite, a buttercup drawing room, a lavishly equipped music room and Restoration-era salon.

Upstairs, we peered into bedrooms swathed in floral damask, dressing rooms decked with silver and gold. In a pink parlor, Mae twirled and laughed with flashing gaiety.

We landed in a cozy lounge with a crackling fire, a tray of crystal tulip glasses on the polished table with a decanter of cognac. The servants must have been everywhere but were invisible to me; it was as though fairies had set the scene.

Mae took her drink to the divan, where she stretched out, brazenly kicked off her shoes, and tucked up her stockinged feet, her face pale, eyes burning with a guileless excitement.

I walked about the room, examining its contents. There were few personal elements. I pointed to a tintype of a girl with big eyes and a wistful smile.

"Who is this pretty young lady?" I asked.

With a quick glance, Kitty said, "My sister. Betsy."

"I didn't know you had a sister!" Mae rose eagerly to examine the image. "There is some resemblance."

"Unfortunately, she died." Had she not told Mae that she had a sister? Or had Mae forgotten?

"Oh dear! I am sorry." Mae's smile faded, but then she noticed a framed photo on the table. In it, Kitty stood in front of a train engine and beside a dapper gentleman wearing a top hat. "Is this you with Henry Clay Frick?"

Kitty waved her hand dismissively. "He was just an upstart back then."

Mae picked up a jeweled box. "How wonderful! Are these real rubies?"

Kitty nodded. She had not stopped looking at Mae the whole time, and I think that she saw everything anew through Mae's perception. Occasionally she seemed disoriented, as though her house and its adornments were materializing before her out of thin air.

"You may keep it if you like." Kitty seemed shy, something I had not seen before.

Mae beamed at her but put the box down. "Is that your dressing room?" With glass still in hand, she motioned to an adjoining space, what appeared to be a boudoir.

"It's one of them." Kitty went in, opened an enormous double-sided armoire. "I do most of my shopping on my trips to Paris." She stepped back, examining the contents. "I don't understand this American rule about putting away one's Paris gowns for one or two years. They are too lovely." She pulled one from the shelf, unfurled it from its tissue paper wrapping. It was thickly beaded, with an opaline sheen.

Mae gasped.

"I have standing orders for twelve a year, two velvet, two silk, two satin, and the other six of poplin and cashmere." Kitty handed the gown to Mae, who cradled it in her arms. "That would look beautiful on you."

Mae bent her head into the folds of fabric. When she lifted her face, her eyes were dewy.

"What is it?" Kitty asked, her brow furrowed.

With a tremulous smile, Mae said, "I have never seen such a beautiful gown."

By the time we returned downstairs, the evening was upon us, deep gold and indigo. Mae threw open the French doors, letting in the drenched air.

"Look at that," she murmured.

The wind and rain had died away, leaving the grass and trees jeweled with raindrops; big-bellied clouds blushed pink in the west.

Mae took Kitty's hand in hers. "Remember when we used to climb out on the roof at night." She beamed up at Kitty. "We used to imagine that we could fly."

Kitty's smile was tight, a neat rosette to keep her face from quavering.

"I'd like to jump and dance with you on those wonderful, beautiful meringue clouds just now!" There was something feverish about Mae's glittering eyes.

A shadow flitted across Kitty's expression; what looked to me like a shade of doubt. She seemed to brush it off and, moving closer, covered Mae's hand with her other palm. Leaning in, she whispered something I could not catch.

It was past time to take my leave; they had already forgotten me. Mae glanced at me and lifted her hand; Kitty looked through me. The space between them seemed a living thing born of their hopes and dreams. I went out into the soft twilight, leaving them there together.

CHAPTER 37

In Kitty's leafy conservatory, tucked into the garden at the back of her house, Mae looked up eagerly from the embroidery in her lap. "Dear one," she said, "of course I remember our talk of going to Paris!" She set her needle into the fabric with a jab. "My husband refuses to take me. A waste of time and money, according to him."

Kitty's laughter bubbled up, full of joy. "It is so much the opposite, dear Mae! It's called the City of Light for good reason."

"Can we go to the opera house?" She sat forward, pulled up her knees, a froth of petticoat escaping beneath her encircling arms. Her embroidery circle fell to the floor unheeded.

"*Le Palais Garnier—mais oui, bien sûr, Madame!*"

"And will we get to see the ballet? I do so want to see *Giselle*!"

Mae's passionate sigh transported Kitty back in time to the golden-haired fairy girl dancing barefoot in her bedroom, snowflakes swirling in through the open window. "You should have been a ballerina."

Mae sniffed. "Nobody here appreciates ballet. New York society deems itself superior to the louche Europeans, but really they are just provincial." She turned the full dazzle of her smile on Kitty. "You, on the other hand, know so much about continental life. You have become such a sophisticate!"

There was a tautening of Kitty's joy, a sail pulled trim in a spirited wind. "There is a new ballerina, Maddalena Aceto, probably from Italy, I don't remember—a friend writes to me that she is wonderful in *Giselle*."

"I simply cannot wait! And we will stay near the Champs-Élysées?"

"As you wish, my dear."

"And the art—you know so much about art!"

"It is said that American art is found mainly in Paris."

"Don't let my father hear you say that." Mae seemed too happy to deliver the sour tone convincingly.

A gray-haired servant entered with a tea tray and set it on an enameled table with the spindly, delicately bowed legs of a faun.

"Thank you, Manon," Kitty said. "How is little Evie doing?"

Carefully arranging the china on the table, Manon said, "Much better, madame, thank you for asking. And my daughter sends her thanks again for your help. She never could have afforded a doctor for the baby otherwise." She tucked the tray under her arm and took a step back, waiting for the signal to serve.

"It was no trouble at all. I am so glad to know that the baby is improving." Kitty waved her away with a smile. "I will pour the tea, thank you, Manon."

As though the interruption had not occurred, Mae burst out, "I simply cannot wait to meet Mr. Worth in person!"

"You may order as many gowns as you like," Kitty said, and was gratified by an expression of absolute delight. Mae leaped from her settee like a little girl, clapping her hands together. For a moment, the world blurred and pivoted around Kitty. The girl-woman seemed almost monstrous to her, a matron in the guise of an imp, a distortion of memory come to life. But then Mae threw her arms around Kitty's shoulders and peppered her cheeks with tiny kisses. A great, melting warmth spread through Kitty's body, and the world reverted once more to a glorious cornucopia of possibility.

"Mrs. Warren? Madam?" The butler's tone was tentative.

Mae released her, and Kitty turned to the butler, her face hot. "Yes, Felix, what is it?"

"There is a gentleman here for you, ma'am. He would not give his name."

His obvious discomfort filled Kitty with foreboding. "Did he say why he is here?"

"No, madam." Felix was studiously examining the polished tips of his shoes as though they were oracles about to speak.

Mae looked at her quizzically.

"Please tell the gentleman that I will be down shortly." Kitty was pained by Mae's worried, furrowed brow. "I am sorry, but you will have to excuse me." She wanted to say something to salvage the moment, to return them to a state of sparkling anticipation, but all she could say was "Do help yourself to the tea while it is still hot."

The man in the foyer was tall and stooped, with well-tailored clothes and a glossy hat that he held in his hands, slowly rotating it by the brim. He had placed his leather briefcase on the floor, where it slouched against his leg. When he looked up, Kitty was surprised to see how youthful his face was, clean-shaven, almost boyish. "Mrs. Warren?" he said.

She put on her brightest smile. "Why, yes. And you are?"

"Davidson. Leonard Davidson. From First Bank of New York." His expression was neutral, but his voice was cold.

"Pleased to meet you, Mr. Davidson." She stepped closer, still smiling, but this did not elicit a bow or handshake. "I normally deal with Mr. Trumble. I do hope that he is not ill?"

Davidson picked up his case and placed his hat under his arm. "Perhaps we could speak in private?"

Kitty followed his gaze to the butler, who was uncertainly hovering in the shadows. "Oh, I do assure you that I trust my staff's discretion completely."

The man just stared at her.

"But, of course, please follow me to the parlor where we can be more comfortable."

Distance seemed to expand with each step she took, her shoes tapping on the marble floor, the banker slouching silently in her peripheral vision, a half-pace behind. In the parlor, she positioned herself at a high-backed chair near a window, so that her guest would have to look directly into the bright sunlight. He waited for her to sit first, but she motioned for him to sit instead. After a slight hesitation, he did.

"So, Mr. Davidson. To what do I owe the pleasure?" She spoke in a good-natured but low voice, so that he would have to lean forward to catch her words.

He placed his briefcase in his lap and spread his fingers slowly and deliberately over its tanned surface, as though he was about to summon ghosts. "As you must already know, I am here about the loans you have taken from our bank."

Her heart pounded almost painfully against her rib cage, but she tipped her head coquettishly and said, "Oh, Mr. Trumble and I have sorted—"

"I am here only as a courtesy," he interrupted. "Our bank has received a subpoena from the federal government to turn over all of your records, which we are obligated to do." He enunciated carefully and expressionlessly, as if he was reading out the terms of the subpoena itself. "The timing of our compliance is not, however, set in stone."

Her tongue seemed glued to the roof of her mouth when she opened her lips to say, "I am sure, Mr. Davidson, that we—"

"We could delay, giving you time to repay what you owe us, and your payments would then be reflected in the accounting we turn over to the government. We would even be willing to renegotiate the interest rates, and credit you the amounts of the bonuses." He opened his case, handed her a sheaf of paper. "You will find the details here of what you owe."

"That is kind of you," she murmured, taking the papers from him. "I am sure this is all a misunderstanding that can be cleared up. If I could only speak with Mr. Trumbull . . ."

"Please come to the bank tomorrow morning to work out a schedule of repayment—though I must warn you that we have not got much latitude." He closed his bag and stood abruptly, moving quickly now that his business was concluded. "You may ask for me when you arrive." He handed her his card; without waiting for her to gather herself and rise, he nodded curtly and strode away.

Kitty took deep breaths, telling herself that she had escaped from tight places before, and would once again. A faint rustling sound gradually encroached on her consciousness; she looked down to see the papers shaking in her trembling hand.

CHAPTER 38

otes from the files of Miss Marija "Mary" Horvat, secretary to Mrs. Catherine Warren

- Reservations for Mrs. Warren and Mrs. Marshall at the Hôtel Continental, Rue de Rivoli
- Arrange for a private appointment at House of Worth (7 Rue de la Paix)
- On a separate day, private appointment at Parfumerie Toussaint (Mrs. Warren has already personally commissioned Baccarat perfume bottles)
- Arrange to attend the private showing, art exhibition of the Académie des Beaux-Arts at the Palace of the Louvre
- Jules Dalou has said that they may visit his sculpture studio on any day (Tea with Mr. Dalou?)
- The House of Paquin (3 Rue de la Paix) **meeting with Mrs. Jeanne Paquin
- Luncheons at Laurent, Fouquet's, and the Pavillon de l'Élysée on the Champs-Élysées

- Dinner first priority Maxim's, Rue Royale
- Second, La Tour d'Argent (canard à la presse for two), 15 quai de la Tournelle
- Other possibilities: Restaurant Prunier (Rue Duphot), Restaurant Drouant (Place Gaillon), Restaurant Lapérouse (Quai des Grands-Augustins), Bois de Boulogne (either Pavillon d'Armenonville or the Cascade)

CHAPTER 39

While arranging the itinerary for the Paris trip with her secretary, Kitty was giddy, almost feverish with excitement. She imagined Mae's wonder and delight as she took in each sight, sound, touch, and scent, all of the marvels that had so affected Kitty when she had lived in France. They would be alone together, just the two of them, anonymous, away from the prying eyes and wagging tongues of New York's claustrophobic and provincial high society. It was the apotheosis Kitty had hardly dared to dream about: complete freedom. It would be freedom from loneliness, freedom from the reach of creditors, and freedom from the ever-present judgmental audience that forced her to wear a heavy mask almost every hour of every day.

After Mary, the secretary, left, Kitty remained at her desk with her eyes closed, savoring the visions she had conjured.

There came a knock at the door. Kitty recognized the soft rapping as that of her maid Gisèle. "Come in," she called.

Kitty hadn't wanted to subject her servants to the tyranny of a housekeeper like Mrs. Williams, so she had made herself their chief manager. She was very fond of Felix, the butler, but she had hired him to be public-facing only, to deal with guests. The closest Kitty had to a second-in-command was Gisèle, a quiet, conscientious Frenchwoman who seemed to know what was happening in all parts of the house at all times.

Gisèle stepped in and gently pulled the sturdy oak door to the study closed behind her; she sat primly at the edge of the oversized leather chair that faced her employer's desk. The chair was meant to make its occupants feel small, even a little childlike, so that the sort of men who enjoyed looming over women had that particular pleasure denied. Self-possessed, tiny Gisèle, with her hands folded neatly in her lap, somehow looked like she belonged in that enormous chair, like a painting in its frame.

"Madame, I am concerned," Gisèle said. She was not one to mince words.

Kitty had the intense desire to remain with her visions, but she tamped down her frustration at the interruption and said, "Yes, Gisèle, what is it?"

"I hear the bankers who come to the house. I see the correspondence you leave unopened."

These gray, hard, ugly details about the present were not what Kitty wanted to think about. She wanted to return to the bright, gauzy future. "That's nothing to worry about," she said with a wave of her hand. "It will all be over soon."

Gisèle pursed her lips and took a deep breath. "Madame, with respect, a voyage does not solve any problems. With time, problems only grow larger."

Despite the warmth from the fireplace, Kitty suddenly felt cold. She swallowed and shook her head. Gisèle didn't know what she, Kitty, was capable of; she didn't really know anything of the truth. "It will be fine, my dear," she said. "You will see, we will all be right as rain."

CHAPTER 40

I n Mae's parlor, Kitty sat, petrified and ramrod straight, stone hands clasped in her lap. The only part of her alive was her heart, pounding.

A freshly laundered nurse led a little blond girl into the room. She initiated each delicate step with pointed toes. Kitty was dizzy, remembering her first encounter with Mae.

"Darling," Mae crooned to her daughter, holding out her arms. "How beautiful you look in your new dress!"

The girl untangled herself from the nanny and dashed to her mother, burrowing into her lap.

"Say hello to my friend, Miss Kitty," Mae said.

Lily glanced up, then dove back into her mother's skirts.

"Go on, ducky." The shove Mae delivered was more admonishment than encouragement.

Reluctantly, the girl inched across the parlor, eyes downcast. Kitty took the tiny, hesitant hand in hers. "Hello," she said, astonished that this doll-like replica existed.

"I learned a new song," Lily said in a hushed voice.

"Oh." Kitty glanced around, looking for guidance from she knew not where. "That's nice."

Mae shook her head, smiling. "You know what the best thing a girl can be in this world." Her face was a mask of porcelain fragility. "A beautiful little fool."

Kitty thought that she had heard or read those words somewhere before. They filled her with a great sadness.

Lily retreated to her mother and fluffed out her skirts in a curtsy. "Just a song at twee . . . light," she warbled.

Bright sun through wavering tree branches dazzled Kitty's eyes and made the walls seem to warp. The wispy, golden Madonna-and-child pair made her feel elephantine, clumsy, as though the air might shatter around her if she moved.

"Lovely!" Mae took her daughter by the shoulders and pointed her back toward Kitty. "How do you like Mother's friend?"

Lily's face was solemn. "Where is Father?" she asked.

Mae laughed. "Don't you think she looks like me?" She lifted her daughter's chin, turned it in profile. "She has my nose and the shape of my face."

The nanny stepped forward and held out her hand. "Come along, Lily," she said. "Mother has a guest, and we must go to bed."

"Goodbye, sweetheart!" Mae waved, curling her fingers like a child.

With a shy backward glance, Lily allowed her nanny to pull her away.

Charlie returned, preceding a servant with three whiskey sours balanced on a silver tray.

Kitty took her glass. "Thank you," she said, her voice strangled.

"You were a childhood friend of my wife's?" Charlie showed little interest in the answer; he stroked his mustache with his pinkie finger, his garnet ring flashing.

"Oh—yes," Kitty said.

"I hear that you have done well for yourself." The corner of his mouth turned up. "But I also hear rumors that all is perhaps not as rosy as it might seem."

"Kitty is very clever," Mae said in a small voice.

Kitty watched as Charlie leaned against the mantel, his broad shoulders straining the fabric of his jacket. He looked so sure of his rightness in the world. "I have done fairly well, yes," she said.

Charlie swirled his drink.

Kitty could feel her heartbeat in her throat, as though she had swallowed a moth. "I suppose that Mae has told you about our trip to Paris?"

His burst of laughter startled her. Kitty looked to Mae, bewildered. Mae would not meet her eyes.

Charlie shook his head, still chuckling. "Paris—the two of you!"

"But Mae wants to go. We have it all arranged." She tried to will Mae to look at her.

"Even if you didn't have this specter, this scandal, hanging over you, I would never consent to letting my wife gallivant off to Europe without me." The amusement was suddenly gone; his words were flat, cold.

A flare of fury made Kitty reckless. "Mae never wanted to be married, especially not to the likes of you! You bought her with your inheritance, because she couldn't afford to live on her own. And what did you do to earn your wealth? Nothing!" Anger poured from her mouth, hot, sulfuric clouds of it. "She would have gone with me to Europe years ago, but for want of money. That is all you are to her—a fat bank account!"

The silence following her outburst was profound. At first, Kitty floated on the propulsive power of outrage, but as the moment stretched on, her emotion cooled and congealed sickeningly.

Charlie strode over to his wife and yanked her by the wrist to her feet. He put a possessive arm around her waist. Mae was pale, and she still wouldn't look at Kitty. She held her chin high in the air, like she was in the deep ocean and afraid of drowning.

"You are no longer welcome here, madam," Charlie said.

"Mae, Mae, tell him about our plans," Kitty pleaded.

Though Charlie didn't move, he seemed to coil, menacing her in a way Kitty instinctively recognized. She flinched, but instead of advancing, Charlie looked down at his wife.

Finally, under the gaze of both Charlie and Kitty, Mae spoke. "We didn't have plans," she said. "Those were just silly daydreams."

This was said so placidly that, like the cut of a sharp blade, it did not first cause pain. Kitty stared at Mae, trying to reconcile this demure helpmeet with the woman who had held her hands, kissed her, whispered ardently about their future together.

Before she could respond, Mae said, "Perhaps it is time you were going, Kitty." Her eyes seemed focused on the garlanded French clock on the chimney-piece. "I am sorry for your troubles, but we cannot have Charles associated with any sort of legal complications." She drew in a shaky breath. "We must ask you not to come again."

CHAPTER 41

I t was a mercy that the police came to Kitty's house after dark, when none of the neighbors were watching. They swarmed like beetles in their black carapace hats, seizing assets, rousting the inhabitants, asserting their authority with swagger, sharp commands, and threatening hands on batons. They gave Kitty five minutes to dress before marching her to the front door, scowling officers flanking her, one of them jostling her and snickering when she stumbled.

The servants descended the stairs holding candles; some startled, disheveled, wrapped in quilted robes Kitty had given them, others still wide awake and indignant, muttering to one another about the indecency of it all.

"You can't just take the lady from her house in the middle of the night like this!" Roger, the cook's boy, called out.

Kitty hushed him, told them all that it would be fine, that they should go ahead and ready the house for the holidays if she was not back in time.

Maggie, Kitty's chambermaid, let out a sob and then clapped her palm across her mouth to stifle another.

At the threshold, one of the officers shoved Kitty outside. She skittered on the frosty flagstones, nearly falling, but she recovered her footing and drew herself up before the heavy doors closed behind them, shutting out light and warmth. The night was frigid and the wind stinging, but Kitty refused to shrink from the police or let them see her shiver.

"Shall we be off, then?" she said, extricating herself from her surprised escort and striding toward the prisoners' wagon. "No sense in wasting time."

The sounds of the Tombs Prison at night were more animal than human—howls, screeching, curses, retching, the clang of tin cups on metal bars. More sickening still were the meaty sounds of blows and slaps, of flesh-on-flesh, hissed breath, despairing moans. The air was swampy, dank, foul. Kitty was shut into a dark cell, left to find her way by touch in the squelching, ammoniac blackness. Snoring alerted her to a mattress that was occupied; as her eyes adjusted, she found her way to an empty, moldy, straw-filled bed. She took off her cloak and spread it out, lowered herself tentatively, flinching when something scuttled ticklishly over the back of her hand. A snort and grunt came from her cellmate, a flurry of rustling—Kitty sat still—then the rhythmic snoring resumed.

A welcome numbness came over Kitty; she felt distant from all that surrounded her. As a child, she had learned to seal herself up like a chestnut snug in its shell, buffeted and battered by the outside world but hidden, safe in her own way. Like a child, she hugged her knees to her chest, and she fell into an uneasy slumber.

"Well, aren't you the fancy princess," said a hoarse voice.

Kitty blinked in thin sunlight falling from a high window. Above her loomed a shadowy, lumpish figure that soon resolved itself into an emaciated woman wrapped in a tattered blanket.

"You are a regal sight yourself," Kitty said. Her tongue was thick, her mouth dry.

The laugh turned into a ragged cough. "How did the likes of you end up here?"

Kitty sat up, brushed back her matted hair, sucked on her furred teeth. "Probably the same way as you."

The woman made a sound like a crow's caw, coughed again. "I doubt that."

"Is there any water?" Kitty looked around. The cell was no more than twelve feet wide, both mattresses pushed against the back wall. There was a wooden bucket, an empty tin bowl, and a crock with a ladle.

Following her glance, the woman said, "It's empty. It'll get filled soon." She shrugged. "If we're lucky." She slumped back against the wall with a sigh, slowly sank down to a crouch. She stared vacantly at the wall across from her as time stretched on, seeming to have forgotten her new cellmate.

Kitty stood, briskly shook and brushed down her skirt. She had worn a cloak, a shawl and a fur stole the night before and had used them all for bedding. "My name is Kitty." She picked up the stole, deciding that it was the most dispensable, and held it out to the other woman.

"Inez," she croaked. She looked dazedly at the fur.

Kitty tucked the stole around Inez's shoulders. "How long have you been here?" On closer inspection, she realized that Inez was no more than a girl; the thinness of her face created sharp planes that made her look older. Her skin was pockmarked and mottled in places, but she had pretty dark eyes fringed with long, curling, black lashes. "What did you do to end up in prison?" she asked the girl.

Inez shrugged wearily, lifted a bony hand to touch the stole. She patted it cautiously, like it was a frightened animal. In the distance, a door opened and clanged shut; Inez froze, lifted her chin, head cocked. There came voices, banging, the high squeal of rusted cart wheels. Inez relaxed back into a slump. "Food," she said. "Or what passes for it here."

Thin soup with tattered bits of floating cabbage, bread too black and hard to be fed to pigs, tea like dishwater—this was both breakfast and lunch, according to Inez.

"Friday clam soup is the worst," she said. "The stink alone is enough to make you puke." She tore off small bits of bread and pushed them to the back of her mouth, chewing gingerly, like her teeth hurt. The nourishment seemed to revive her, and she grew chattier.

Inez had been waiting six months for her trial, she said, and there was still no date set. The arrest had been for prostitution, though at the time of the raid, she had just been washing her hair. The brothel had been her home for as long as she remembered; her mother had died when she was a baby, and she didn't know who her father was. When she got old enough, she started turning tricks—the madam was nice enough and let her keep a fair amount of her wages. She hadn't saved enough to pay her bond, though, so she was stuck in the Tombs.

Kitty was struck by how accepting Inez seemed to be about her lot in life. She sighed and made minor complaints, but didn't rail at the unfairness of it all. What curiosity she had about Kitty's presence was satisfied by her explanation—all of her assets had been seized or frozen by the government, so she had no way to bail herself out. Inez didn't probe any further, just slowly chewed on her crusts of bread. "I hope your trial comes up faster than mine," she said.

Time passed slowly in the Tombs. The women were allowed into the yard once each day for an hour, and that brief feeling of sunlight on her face, a bracing breeze, a snow shower, the crunch of gravel underfoot were what Kitty clung to, what she thought about when she couldn't sleep at night. It was important to wall off too many thoughts of the outside world. She fell back on survivalist ways of being; she took each day a few minutes at a time, focused on each small thing she could make better.

The keepers and guards ranged from cruel to indifferent, but one of the volunteers, Miss Elsa, spoke with real compassion in her voice. Inez said that she was known simply as "the Angel" and that she came from a wealthy family but spent her time caring for prisoners. She helped them write letters, obtain medicines, access legal counsel. She prayed with them and for them, sometimes even posted their bonds.

Neither Inez nor Kitty received visitors during the visiting hour, but Miss Elsa came to see them. She was middle-aged, dressed in practical but well-made clothes, a silver crucifix around her neck. Her roundness was a perfect match for her pleasant demeanor; like a snowman, she had a round head atop a round torso, her full skirt flaring out below a cinched waist.

From her hamper, Miss Elsa pulled out an apple and a smoked sausage for each of them, and held them through the bars. Her voice was barely audible over the cries and lamentations of visitors at other cells, some of whom carried on with the fervor of mourners at an Irish wake, but Kitty heard her ask if she could do anything more for them.

Inez grabbed the proffered food with surprising alacrity, shoving it into her pockets, while Kitty thanked Miss Elsa profusely and expressed admiration for the woman's good deeds. She could tell that her words were landing flat from the way Miss Elsa smiled wanly, refusing to meet her eye, angling her stance toward Inez.

"You are looking peaked, dear," she said to Inez.

Inez shrugged. "The extra rations will do me a world of good," she said. "Thank you."

Kitty tried again. "Please allow me to introduce myself, madam."

"Oh, I know who you are. I read the newspapers." She did not quite succeed in keeping the disdain from her tone. "The infamous Kitty Warren."

There was to be no sympathy for a rich woman brought low by her own misdeeds, Kitty realized. She switched her tack. "I, too, am worried for the girl," she said, handing Inez her apple and sausage, which quickly followed the matching pair into her pockets. "I am so grateful that you are here to help."

Miss Elsa looked at Kitty with mild interest.

"This cough she has is very concerning." Kitty shook her head. "Inez needs more time outside, away from this pestilent, damp atmosphere." She put a hand on Inez's shoulder. "She is so young, and innocent, too—a victim of dire circumstances."

As if on cue, Inez coughed again, a deep, wet rattle. "It's alright," she said. "I don't much like the courtyard; it's too cold."

"I think Mrs. Warren's point is sound, dear child," Miss Elsa said. "You need fresh air. I will make inquiries." She narrowed her eyes at Kitty. "You're right—this poor girl is a product of unfortunate circumstances."

Kitty ignored her implication. "I will walk with her outside myself if I am allowed," she said. "I am a sinner, and all I can do now to try to make peace with God is to extend whatever help I may to the less fortunate." She saw that Miss Elsa's expression had softened. "It is surely too much to ask—I know that books are hard to come by—but if you could find one, a book of psalms perhaps. I could read to Inez."

"Oh, no need—" Inez began, but the gong sounded loudly and repeatedly to signal the end of the visiting hour. The noise level rose and rose, with weeping, shouting, and groaning, drowning out her voice.

Jostling accompanied the noise, as keepers pushed and dragged out distraught family members. Miss Elsa nodded once in parting, and was gone, threading her way expertly through the crowd.

CHAPTER 42

STATE OF NEW YORK   )
)
CRIMINAL COURT THE COUNTY   )
OF NEW YORK   )
)
PEOPLE OF THE STATE OF NEW YORK)
) File No. 74-5569-P
        Plaintiff   )
)
        Vs   )
)
CATHERINE B. WARREN   )
)
        Defendant   )
)

DEPOSITION OF MR. PAUL THOMAS ADAIR

The deposition of Mr. Paul Thomas Adair, a witness and plaintiff in the above-entitled cause, taken before Mr. Ezekiel Fischer, a Notary Public in and for New York County, New York, at 52 Chambers St, New York, New York, on the 24th of February, 1906, commencing at 11 A.M., pursuant to the New York General Court Rules.

INQUIRY BY MR. MILTON TRULOVE, ESQ.

Q. Please state your full name and occupation for the record, sir.

A. Paul Thomas Adair, co-owner of Adair Brothers Jewelers in Cleveland, Ohio.

Q. What is the nature of your acquaintance with Mrs. Catherine Warren?

A. She was a customer of our store.

Q. Please describe your encounters with Mrs. Warren.

A. She introduced herself as Miss Catherine Buchanan, from New York, and said that she liked to obtain unusual pieces of jewelry for her well-heeled friends. It was a sort of hobby for her, she explained, as she was so fond of jewels but already owned more than she could wear in her lifetime. I did greatly admire her tasteful emerald earrings and matching cabochon ring. I never forget first-rate pieces. The amethyst—

Q. Please tell us what happened during her visits.

A. I guided Mrs. Warren through our catalog and took her on a tour of the showroom. She was visibly impressed and made astute comments about our inventory. It was clear that she knew a great deal not only about jewelry but about the business of selling. She made a series of requisitions, at first small, then larger ones.

Q. How did she pay for her purchases?

A. Mainly cash, and some credit. She provided her bank details, and I verified that she had an account in good standing. She refused to take any commission on the pieces she requisitioned for other women.

Q. The credit was under the name Catherine Buchanan?

A. Yes, sir.

Q. For the record, the real Catherine Buchanan was entirely unaware of Mrs. Warren's perfidy. Can you please tell us about your final encounter with Mrs. Warren, Mr. Adair?

A. On our last meeting, she persuaded me to loan her an entire set of diamond jewelry. I did so without qualms, as she had been such a good customer, and I knew her to be in excellent financial standing. You have to understand that we had a very good relationship. Forgive me if I wax poetic, but she can instill such confidence.

Q. Please just tell us what transpired, sir.

A. Unfortunately, when she failed to return the jewels, I discovered that Mrs. Buchanan of New York was another person entirely, and I had no way to trace the woman who had stolen from us. It was not until I was contacted by you people in New York that I realized I had been defrauded by Mrs. Kitty Warren.

CHAPTER 43

Kitty received several tattered books, including the psalms, and she also got permission to accompany Inez on an extended walk in the courtyard every other day. Besides reading, time outside was the only thing she looked forward to. It was peaceful when the other women went back into the jail, leaving the two of them alone for fifteen extra minutes of laps around the small walled-in area. Inez was passive at first, merely enduring her time outdoors, but she opened up to Kitty over time. Her hoarse voice turned to white puffs in the frigid air as she told of her life in the brothel. Kitty thought of her sister Betsy, wondering if her experiences had been similar. She delved into Inez's history and was surprised by how many cheerful memories she related, despite the harsh circumstances.

Kitty's trial began within a few weeks of her incarceration. Inez said without bitterness that rich people got the first crack at so-called justice. The trial did not start well; Kitty did not have access to funds to hire good lawyers. She felt the noose tightening around her neck as her misdeeds were enumerated, dissected, and scrutinized, and her character was flayed, laid bare to the judgment of all.

In the stone courtyard with Inez, snowflakes as big as moths fluttering down, Kitty said, "Did you ever want something badly enough that you would do whatever it took to chase it?"

With her characteristic hunched shrug and wave of a hand, Inez dismissed the question. "I never wanted much." She stopped, lifted her thin face to the sky with closed lids, and let the snowflakes melt to droplets on her pocked brown skin. "I like it out here after all," she said, taking a deep breath, which led to a fit of coughing. When it subsided, she whispered, "Thank you."

"Get a move on!" the guard barked. He stood under the roof's short overhang, scowling, shuffling from foot to foot to ward off the cold.

Kitty took Inez's arm, which through the threadbare sweater felt like skin and bone, and encouraged her to resume a slow walk. "I have been a fool," Kitty said, more to herself than to her companion.

"Everybody makes mistakes," Inez said. "You're only a fool if you don't learn from your mistakes."

Kitty laughed with surprise. "Wise words, my dear. I suppose I am a slow learner."

Inez coughed into her chapped hand. "You are the sort of person who will come out on top," she rasped.

There seemed no chance of that, but Kitty didn't see any benefit to contradicting her.

"Time's up!" The guard banged his cudgel on the railing that led down a set of stairs to the courtyard door; the metal vibrated audibly with each whack. "Move!"

Kitty led Inez toward the stairs, but too slowly, and the guard gave a shove. It was only hard enough to make Kitty stumble, but Inez was weak and slight; her feet skated out from under her. Kitty failed to recapture her grip on Inez's arm, and she felt the sweater sleeve slip from her fingers. The girl fell, tumbling forward, skidding on the icy paving stones, then went sideways down the stairs, her head making a sickening thud. She lay sprawled in the stairway, her skirt twisted around her hips, a leg bent at an unnatural angle.

For a moment, all was still. Kitty held her breath. The snow fell thick and silent, as if determined to blanket the ugly tableau.

With clomping boots, the guard descended the stairs and stepped over Inez's inert body. He wrenched open the door, shouted for help. Kitty stood watching, a hand pressed tightly to her mouth, not knowing what to do. Another guard, his gray wool jacket askew, hair mussed, face pink, arrived at the scene, and the two conferred in hushed tones. Ignoring Kitty completely, they picked Inez up, one by her shoulders, the other by her waist. Her legs dangled like a broken doll's.

Kitty sank to the top stair, and sat shivering as the imprint of a body and boots was slowly erased by the falling snow.

CHAPTER 44

COURT OF GENERAL SESSION OF THE PEACE,
City and County of New York, Part V.

THE PEOPLE OF THE STATE OF NEW YORK, Before: HON.
EMMETT R. CLINE, Judge
-against-
CATHERINE "KITTY" WARREN, née Fanny Bartlett

New York, February 11th, 1906
Indictment filed December 16th, 1905

Indicted for 7 counts of conspiracy against the government and conspiracy to defraud a national bank

Appearances:
For the People: ROBERT BOSTWICK and F. ADAM RUBIN,
ESQRS, Assistants to the District Attorney
For Defendant: MAX P. FULLER, ESQ.

New York, November 16th, 1906
TRIAL RESUMED

THE COURT: I understand both sides answer ready. You may call the next witness for the prosecution.

FRANCIS Q. BECKETT, called as a witness on behalf of the People, being first duly sworn, testifies as follows:

(The witness states that he resides in Pittsburgh in Allegheny County, Pennsylvania)

DIRECT EXAMINATION BY MR. BOSTWICK:

Q. Mr. Beckett, you are the president of DePaul Bank in Pittsburgh, Pennsylvania?

A. Yes, sir.

Q. How long have you known the defendant, Mrs. Catherine Warren?

A. About seven years.

Q. What was the occasion of your meeting?

A. Mrs. Warren borrowed money from my bank.

Q. She also borrowed some of your personal funds, did she not?

A. It depends what one means by personal funds.

THE COURT: Please answer yes or no, sir.

A. Yes, she did.

Q. Let us move to a time closer to the present day. When did Mrs. Warren first default in her payments?

A. The first time was three years ago, approximately. But after I met with her and helped her sort through some financial encumbrances, she promptly paid what was owed.

Q. Your bank has now joined three other banks in suing Mrs. Warren for damages in a separate civil action?

A. Yes.

Q. The damages you and your institution have suffered are catastrophic. There was a run on your bank and it has all but completely collapsed.

A. Inaudible.

THE COURT: Please speak up, Mr. Beckett.

A. Yes.

Q. When Mrs. Warren defaulted for the second time, what explanation were you given?

A. Mrs. Warren said that her securities were controlled by another party whose name was withheld, and as a result, she was unable to touch those securities.

Q. Was this truthful?

A. I do not know.

Q. Surely you must have suspected dishonesty on her part?

A. I did not at that time.

Q. In my notes here, I see that Mrs. Warren later claimed that a New York banking firm held power of attorney to manage her estate, and that shifting permissions would take time.

A. Yes.

Q. I see also that Mrs. Warren claimed to know a speculator who would take up the loan she had with your bank and let you out of the obligation entirely.

A. Inaudible.

THE COURT: Again, please answer so that the court reporter can hear you.

A. Yes.

Q. And you refused this proposal?

A. I did not think that such a person was trustworthy. He wanted absolute transfer of her property to him. I advised her against signing.

Q. Do you regret this decision now?

(Witness does not answer)

Q. I withdraw my question. When did your bank directors become knowledgeable about the extent of your loans to Mrs. Warren?

A. In the last year.

Q. One of your directors, Mr. Williams, said, "This was a ghastly overloan from a bank with our amount of capital."

MR. FULLER: Now, I desire, may it please Your Honor, to object to this line of testimony, on the ground that that is hearsay and immaterial to the subject matter in the indictment.

MR. BOSTWICK: It seems to me that that is all part of the res gestae, and in all the cases that have been tried all the details—

THE COURT: I will allow the witness to testify and overrule the objection.

MR. FULLER: I respectfully except.

BY MR. BOSTWICK: Q. Please proceed, Mr. Beckett.

A. I do not recall.

Q. Mr. Williams also said that Mrs. Warren was nicknamed "The Duchess of Diamonds," and that she met with visitors in her home with a "positively royal display of wealth," with caskets of gems and exotic libations.

MR. FULLER: I object on the grounds that my colleague's language is inflammatory and prejudicial.

THE COURT: Sustained. Mr. Bostwick, please reserve the pyrotechnics for your closing argument.

BY MR. BOSTWICK: Q. Mr. Beckett, is it true that Mrs. Warren's semiannual interest on ten million dollars in securities was long past due when you met with her?

A. That sounds about right.

Q. Yet somehow she still lulled you into compliance.

A. I take offense at this characterization, sir.

Q. How would you characterize the situation?

A. She wanted to secure her estate in such a way that no debts could be held against it. She had an annuity, but she needed more liquidity to properly organize all of her assets. There was still money in her trust that could bolster the reserve of our bank. Mr. Carnegie was obdurate in his position and wished to teach her a salutary lesson.

Q. You believed that Mr. Carnegie was her father? It says here, "A stiff-minded Scot."

MR. FULLER: I object. This is entirely irrelevant and bordering on defamatory.

THE COURT: Sustained. Watch yourself, Mr. Bostwick.

BY MR. BOSTWICK:

Q. Mrs. Warren had half a million of the bank's money and one hundred thousand of your personal savings. She paid you an unknown amount of bonus for a loan. Do you care to share with the court the value of that bonus?

A. I do not recall.

Q. I find that surprising. Was it larger than a usual bonus?

A. I do not recall.

Q. I am surprised that your memory is so faulty, Mr. Beckett, given how much damage you have sustained at Mrs. Warren's hands. This concludes my questions for today.

THE COURT: We will adjourn now until 12:30. Gentlemen of the jury, you are admonished not to converse among yourselves on any subject connected with this trial or form or express any opinion thereon until the same is submitted to you, not to talk about the case with anyone, or let anyone talk with you about the case.

CHAPTER 45

The next day, Kitty learned that Inez was still alive, but the keeper couldn't or wouldn't tell her anything more. She hoped that Miss Elsa would come during visiting hours, so Kitty could exchange information with her. She gripped the bars and watched intently, looking for her old-fashioned white bonnet, listening for her fluting voice in the cacophony. Instead, Kitty saw Maggie, her chambermaid, approaching, shouldering her way through the crowd, looking fearfully from side to side. When she saw Kitty, her face lit up with a smile.

Kitty's heart leaped at the sight of Maggie's familiar, almost painfully ingenuous face. She had to blink back tears as her servant clutched her hands through the bars of her cell.

"I am so sorry that I have not come sooner, Mrs. Warren." Maggie leaned in as far as she could, clearly shaken by the chaos and stench. "We kept aside as much as we could of the silver and jewels, and we raised enough for your bond."

Kitty felt faint with gratitude.

"My brother took what we could keep of the valuables without the authorities noticing and hid it safe. He sold in bits and pieces, so as not to attract attention. He had to sell it cheap, but it was enough, and there's still some jewels left." Maggie pressed her lips together and nodded, her gray eyes solemn, signaling her assurance that Kitty would come out of her predicament whole. "We posted your bail just now, and you should be free soon."

"I cannot thank you enough, Maggie." Kitty bit down hard on the inside of her cheek to stem her tears.

"The house hasn't sold. Bertrand said you could likely stay in the guest cottage without anyone noticing till you land on your feet. Françoise and Gisèle made sure it was habitable."

Kitty's throat was full, as though she had swallowed a plum. She didn't trust herself to speak, so she just squeezed Maggie's hands.

Maggie's cheeks pinked. "You've always been good to us, ma'am."

The gong sounded, and Maggie jumped. In a sudden tide of receding bodies, Maggie was swept away.

Kitty took up residence in the guest cottage behind her former home. The servants had outfitted it with all of the food, linens, firewood, clothing, pens, paper, liquor, and toiletries she could need. They took turns sneaking in at night with fresh supplies. She went to court when required, leaving through the back entrance that led into alleyways for stables and carriage houses. She always dressed plainly, with a veil covering her face; her picture was in all of the newspapers, and she did not want to be recognized.

Kitty wrote notes to Miss Elsa, telling her she wanted to talk, and after numerous petitions, she reluctantly agreed to visit. Kitty told Elsa where to have her driver park the carriage, and she had Maggie meet her there with a dim lantern, to guide her through the alley and bushes and across the dark back lawn.

"I'm sorry that you had to come in past the horses," Kitty said as she ushered the women in the back door. "I'm not really supposed to be living here, and I didn't suppose that you would want to be seen with me."

Elsa scuffed the soles of her boots on the mat, took off her cloak, and slung it over her arm. Her lack of an answer was clear confirmation that she had no wish to be associated with Kitty. Despite her soft features, there was something steely in her gaze and straight-backed stance as she waited for whatever Kitty had to say next.

"Maggie, help yourself to the pie in the kitchen," Kitty said. "Won't you please come into the sitting room, meager as it is, Miss Elsa? I can offer you brandy."

Elsa sniffed, seemed on the verge of refusal, but then she untied her bonnet, lifted it off with a sigh. "I can't stay, but I wouldn't say no to a dram," she said.

Kitty poured two stiff drinks into the crystal cups arranged on the sideboard. "We have more in common than you believe," she said.

"I doubt that." Elsa took the glass from Kitty with a weary smile.

"We have Inez in common."

"Indeed." Elsa tipped back her glass and took a manly swig of liquor without grimacing or coughing.

Kitty hid her surprise. "How is Inez?"

"Not long for this world, I'm afraid." Elsa drank again. "I can't find a decent doctor to see her. They haven't set her leg properly. Fevers, rigors, constant pain. Delirium is a blessing, and God forgive me for saying it, death will be a greater one." A look of anguish passed over her face so fleetingly that Kitty wondered if she had imagined it.

"Are you sure you won't sit down?" Kitty said.

Elsa didn't seem to hear the question. She was staring pensively into her tumbler. "So much unnecessary suffering for women who are just too poor to buy their way out of jail."

Kitty felt this as an accusation, though the other woman's tone had been impersonal. "Is there nothing else to be done?"

After downing the rest of her drink in one large gulp, Elsa placed her glass back on the sideboard. "I should be going."

"But you just arrived."

Silence communicated all of the reasons Elsa needed to be elsewhere. She donned her cloak and bonnet like a soldier's uniform.

"I want to make arrangements for Inez to get a proper burial," Kitty said. "I know the poor girl has no relatives to claim her body, and I hate to think of her dumped in the lime bed on the hillside." In her mind's eye, Inez's bloodless face was suddenly replaced with Betsy's. Her mouth went dry.

Elsa gave Kitty a long, level look. "That is kind of you."

"I don't know whom to contact."

"Bring me paper and a pencil, and I will write a couple of names down for you," Elsa said.

Kitty handed Elsa what she requested, and she fetched Maggie to escort her guest back to her carriage. As she watched the women recede across the lawn, a swaying spot of yellow light growing fainter, she folded the paper and tucked it carefully into her pocket.

CHAPTER 46

Joseph Carrow, cousin of Mae Marshall

O n the night of the fire, in early spring, I was staying with friends in the countryside. I returned home the next day to the sight of police and firemen swarming my block; the air still smelled of smoke, and I could see charred debris piled in Mrs. Warren's driveway. The street, puddled with dirty snowmelt, was cordoned off, and an officer tried to stop me from entering, but when I pointed out that I needed to get to my house, he allowed me to pass. I asked him what had happened.

"Cottage burned down to the ground," he said, spitting a wad of tobacco on the wet cobblestones for emphasis.

"Was anyone hurt?"

He sucked on his teeth, looking bored. "They're still going through the wreckage, I guess."

I asked other officers for information, but they either didn't have any or were staying closed-lipped. From my lawn, I could see that one side of Mrs. Warren's house was scorched and soot-stained, and two gables had collapsed. The roof of the cottage, which should have been peeking out from behind the main building, was gone. A sadness washed over me. The damage to the house was an echo of the suffering of its owner. I held out hope that Mrs. Warren would be cleared of charges and reclaim her glittering life, but the destruction I saw reminded me that those prospects were dimming.

Later that day, there came a knock at my door. I opened it to a middle-aged policeman with gold stripes on the sleeves of his uniform; he introduced himself as Captain Connor. "I need to ask you some questions about your neighbor," he said in an Irish brogue.

"I don't know what I can tell you, but please come in," I said, opening the door wider.

"Thanks, but it won't take but a minute." He pointed a thick thumb at the scene behind him. "What have you noticed about the comings and goings there?"

I was only in my shirtsleeves, and felt chilled when the wind blew. "I'm not home during the day, usually." I crossed my arms tightly across my chest, hoping that he would take the hint and come inside. "There have been a lot of carriages and big moving crates. I heard that all of the contents of the house are being sold by the government."

He grunted his acknowledgment. "Have you seen Mrs. Warren?"

I was confused. "I am acquainted with Mrs. Warren." As he seemed to be waiting for more, I said, "Of course I haven't seen her since she was taken to the Tombs."

He frowned. There was something walrus-like about him, with his muddy little eyes, bushy mustache, and receding chin. "You didn't know she was out on bail?" He indicated her house with his thumb again. "We think she was holed up in the cottage there."

"She—" I couldn't quite marshal my thoughts. "She wasn't . . ."

"We're still investigating." He paused, making a slight rocking movement back onto his heels. "Well," he said gruffly, "I suppose since the reporters already found their way here, I might as well tell you. We found a body."

It was like a blow to my stomach. For a moment, I couldn't fill my lungs.

The policeman narrowed his eyes. "You knew her well, then?"

I leaned a hand against the doorframe. I had forgotten all about the wintry wind, but my fingers felt numb. "I—I admired her" was all I got out.

He made a quiet huff of derision at my remark before he got back to business. "We're trying to determine the cause of the fire. Did you see anything suspicious on the street last night?"

I shook my head.

"You look peaky." He sounded vaguely accusatory. "Were you a particular friend of Mrs. Warren's?"

Collecting myself, I said that I had met her a half-dozen times, no more, and that I had been out of the city the previous night. It was just such a shock to hear of her death. He seemed to consider this, then said, "Well, if you remember anything that might be useful, or hear anything new, I'd appreciate you coming down to the precinct." He handed me a card. "Ask for Captain Connor." He tipped his hat.

"Good day," I said. I felt faint as I shut the door.

I slept fitfully that night, and I was awake in the predawn quiet when I heard the thud of the newspaper hitting the porch. I rushed down in my robe to grab it and spread it out on the table. By the light of my lamp, I read the headline: "Notorious Bank Swindler Found Dead in House Fire." I despised the editors' money-grubbing sensationalism, but read on.

> The nation has been transfixed by the arrest and trial of
> Mrs. Catherine Warren, a career criminal believed to be

responsible for defrauding banks of millions of dollars, smuggling jewels into America from Europe, and manipulating the stock market to her own advantage. Mrs. Warren was facing the possibility of a decades-long prison term for her crimes.

After her release on bail, Mrs. Warren is believed to have returned illegally to property she once owned, which was for sale by the government. At midnight on March 10th, the fire department responded to a blaze in a cottage behind the main house. While they were successful in preventing the fire from spreading, they were unable to save the building or its sole inhabitant. The cause of the conflagration could not be determined, but authorities have stated that Mrs. Warren appeared to have been fleeing from the second story of the cottage when she fell down the stairs and broke her leg. The severity of the fracture found at autopsy would have rendered her immobile and helpless to escape a fiery death.

I am not ashamed to say that I shed some tears upon reading this. I was already mourning the loss of my charismatic friend—yes, I did consider her a friend—and the thought of her trapped in a blaze with a broken leg caused me almost unbearable heartache. I wished fervently that I had been home and had seen the fire, because I might have been able to rescue her before it was too late.

I kept an eye out for any familiar faces going to Mrs. Warren's house that day, hoping to ask about her funeral, but I saw nobody I recognized. Then I remembered that her butler, Felix, frequented a nearby tavern on his days off. I made my way to the Crown and Anchor, and once my eyes adjusted to the indoor darkness, I was not surprised to find Felix at the bar. He was slumped, a gray forelock dangling in his eyes, unheeded, his hands cupping a whiskey glass.

There were few other customers, and the bartender was nowhere to be seen. I took the seat next to him, my empty stomach roiling at the sour-sweet odor of beer-drenched floorboards and tobacco smoke.

"Hello, old fellow," I said.

Felix turned his head, and looked at me blearily. "Oh, hello."

He was usually so proper, so erect in his posture and crisp in his diction, that he seemed like a completely different man from the one who had opened the door to me at the mansion. I wanted to put a sympathetic hand on his back, but I sensed that he would not welcome it. "It's a very sad day," I said.

He turned away and sipped his drink.

I waited, but he seemed to have forgotten me. "Look here," I said, "I thought a lot of Mrs. Warren."

Felix nodded, and roughly wiped at his cheek.

"I'm just wondering if you know anything about a funeral, or if you know whom I could ask about it. I want to help."

The bartender shuffled out from the back room and asked me indifferently what I wanted to drink. When I told him I wasn't staying, he yawned, sat on a low stool behind the bar, and picked up a book.

"Next Saturday, at Saint Mark's," Felix muttered.

I was surprised that the funeral was already organized. "Who's in charge?"

He pushed the hair out of his eyes with a shaky hand. "A colored lady. Hope, or Grace, or something. Came in from out of town. Seems she's rich."

I was even more surprised. "How does she know Mrs. Warren?"

"I've no idea." He snapped his fingers at the bartender, who didn't ask what he wanted, merely refilled Felix's glass. Felix hung his head again.

I tried to think of something comforting to say, but I was feeling bleak myself. I stood to leave, and before I could say goodbye, Felix grabbed my arm and looked at me intently. Suddenly, he didn't seem so drunk.

"Make sure you come on Saturday," he said fiercely. "She died alone. Don't let her be buried alone."

"I will be there." As I put on my hat, I added, "Please take care of yourself, Felix."

I called on Mae three times that week, and each time was told that she wasn't feeling well enough to have a visitor. I asked the servants to tell Mae that the visitor in question was her cousin Joe, but still she would not see me. I left her messages about the funeral, and wished her a speedy recovery.

On the day of the funeral, the weather was appropriately dreary, and the church was empty except for Mrs. Warren's loyal servants. The wealthy female stranger who had put this all on was not in attendance. I nodded to Felix in the nearby pew, and he nodded back solemnly, once more the sober, respectable butler. There were two massive flower arrangements flanking the closed casket; floral scents mingled with linseed oil and incense. I whispered to Felix, asking who sent the arrangements, hoping they were from Mae. But they were from the out-of-state benefactor, Grace, he said.

From my pew, I kept an eye on the misty, wet road, hoping that some of Mrs. Warren's many friends would come. The minister seemed to be hoping for the same thing, for he delayed the service, praying silently behind the altar. Nobody came.

At the graveyard, the rain fell listlessly but relentlessly, and I was soaked through by the time the casket was lowered into the ground, with water dripping from the brim of my hat and trickling inside the back of my collar. I tried to concentrate on Mrs. Warren, but her brilliance, her spirited conversation, her effervescent laugh, none of it seemed to have anything to do with the body being interred in the cold, sodden earth. I dropped a flower on the coffin, as did the few others present. I noticed that several of the women were crying. I couldn't help but think that Mae should have been one of them.

CHAPTER 47

Joseph Carrow, cousin of Mae Marshall

Soon after Mrs. Warren's death, I moved back to the Middle West, to fields of snow like fresh linen, gossipy neighbors bearing warm-from-the-oven oatmeal cookies, and a church steeple around every bend. My memories of New York took on a surreal quality. Like a half-remembered night of bacchanalia or a fever dream, their remembrance evoked queasiness. I liked the clean simplicity of my new life; I found a lucrative job, met a nice girl, and got married.

After the wedding, my bride and I took a leisurely tour of Europe, and my mother informed me in a letter that the Marshalls were in Paris. I had not seen Mae or Charlie in some years. As we were in Tours at the time, and planning to visit the City of Lights, I sent them a telegram with our travel dates.

I purposefully chose a time to meet the Marshalls when my wife was otherwise occupied; I told myself that she, in her small-town innocence, would find the New Yorkers insufferably pretentious. A part of me wonders, though, if I feared my wife might seem diminished in Mae's company.

As it turned out, Charlie begged off, so I made a lunch reservation for two. I saw Mae sitting at the table before she noticed me and had a moment to observe her. She was no less radiant than I remembered, but the radiance was constrained, like a flame trapped under a lamp's dome. Her hair, with a few strands of gray, was pulled back in a simple style, smooth and neat; her attire was somber and elegant. There was a stillness about her that spoke of sadness.

When she caught sight of me, Mae rose. "Why, cousin, how contented and hale you look." She gave me her hand. "Marriage suits you." She was thinner than before, her cheeks hollowed, making her blue eyes look bigger.

"You are perfection itself," I said. I was rewarded with one of her silvery laughs.

"Always the charmer, dear Joe." Her smile was broad, but it animated only her mouth.

"Please." I indicated that she should sit.

As we took our places, champagne and oysters were delivered by mournful black-suited servers.

"I hope I wasn't presumptuous in ordering these," Mae said. She thanked the waiters in what sounded to my inexperienced ear like fluent French.

"Your timing is impeccable, and these look delicious." In truth, I didn't care for oysters, but I swallowed one to be a good sport, then chased it with a sip of champagne. "Are you and Charlie having a nice time in Paris?"

She used a long, two-pronged silver fork to delicately scoop an oyster from its shell, and I was embarrassed that I hadn't known to do the same. "I've been looking forward to coming here for so long." She closed her eyes, savoring the oyster, then examined the mother-of-pearl appreciatively, before returning the empty shell to its bed of ice. "I hired a tutor to learn the language, read up on French artworks, and even learned French history. But Charlie, he doesn't really care about any of it. You'd think it would kill him to go to the ballet." She twirled her champagne flute, watching the bubbles float to the top. "I've begged him to let me go on my own, but he's so stodgy about it. He can't have his wife going out unchaperoned." She surprised me by tipping up her glass and finishing her drink in two long swallows. When she set the flute down, one of the silent waiters was already at her elbow, refilling it. If he noticed her crassness, it did not show on his lugubrious face.

"I don't know why we even came to Paris," she said darkly, this time spearing her oyster with the sharp tines. The mollusk slipped off, and she speared it again. "Charlie is such a wet blanket." She gave up on the oyster, and took another swallow of champagne instead. She reached across the table and placed her hand on the back of my wrist. "Dear Joe," she said earnestly. "I am so glad that you are here."

I was flattered by her warmth, but also concerned. "It really has been far too long," I said. "I hope Paris hasn't been entirely disappointing. Maybe my lovely bride and I can be companions on your outings."

She squeezed my wrist and gave me a tender look. Then she lifted her glass and polished it off.

I tried to hide my disapproval of her dipsomania. "We ought to get some real food in our stomachs," I said, perhaps a bit too primly.

Mae seemed about to protest, but then inclined her head, her cheeks tinged with pink. In a subdued voice, she said, "Do you like coq au vin?" When I answered in the affirmative, she turned toward a waiter, who glided over, as if on casters. She said something to him in French, and he murmured back to her, bowing respectfully.

I felt that my beautiful cousin's formerly irrepressible spirit had been broken, and I couldn't help but blame Charlie, the bully. "My sweet Mayflower," I said, using a childhood nickname. "You seem unhappy. What can I do?"

When she looked back up at me, her eyes shone with tears. "I was supposed to come here with her."

"With whom?"

"I don't think you need to ask." Her mouth grew small, and her chin wrinkled like a walnut shell.

Kitty Warren, of course.

"We had a whole plan, down to the last detail." Mae kept her gaze averted, twisting the silver salt cellar to and fro.

"I—I wasn't aware." The conversation had taken an uncomfortable turn, and I wished to banish her tears, so I said, "Have you been to the Orangerie art show with all of that cubist nonsense? The posters and pamphlets are everywhere. I wonder what you think of it?"

"Kitty and I were going to stay at the Hôtel Continental," Mae said, as though she hadn't heard me. "We were going to have dresses made by Mr. Worth, attend a showing at the Académie des Beaux-Arts . . ." The tears spilled over, and she just let them fall. She reached for her water glass, but set it down again. "Do you know, I thought I saw her last week."

I had been pulling my handkerchief from my pocket to give to her and stopped.

"You think I'm crazy." She sighed heavily, her breath hitching, then took a sip of water. "But I could swear it was her."

I held out the handkerchief and tried to think of how to respond.

She ignored my offering. A dark spot had appeared on her bosom where her tears had fallen. "I was crossing the road, on Rue Pasquier," she said. "There was a crowd." She briefly closed her eyes; her long, damp lashes fluttered. "I had my head down, and when I stepped onto the curb, I looked up. She was there, just turning the corner." Her voice was soft but steady, tears sliding down her cheeks. "I called out to her. I tried to go after her, but it was so loud, and so crowded. I lost sight of her." Mae gave me a watery look of dismay. Somehow I knew it was about losing sight of her, not about seeing a dead woman in the first place. "I've been going back there every day since, walking through the streets . . ." She put her head in her hands.

Clearly, my cousin was in a state of emotional delirium. I had been angry with her for abandoning Mrs. Warren when fortune turned against her, and I had thought Mae's behavior quite selfish and shameful, but her fragile mental state frightened me, so I spoke to her gently, as one might to a sick child. "You must miss your friend."

She lifted her face again, which crumpled alarmingly. "I *loved* her!" She was weeping in earnest, her shoulders shaking.

I looked around, but mercifully, the other customers were carefully ignoring us. I leaned forward, covering her hand with mine. "Mrs. Warren was an extraordinary person." I gently patted her hand, waiting for the storm to pass. "She lived life to the lees." I was talking to soothe her, but I meant it, too. "I don't think she cared about anything in this world as much as she cared about you." As soon as the words left my mouth, I was certain of two things: The statement was true, and it was the worst thing I could have said at that moment.

To my astonishment, Mae blinked back her tears, and looked at me with eyes as azure as sky after rain. She used my handkerchief to dry her face. She made a girlish little hiccup, then said, "Thank you, Joe. You're right. Kitty must still care about me. She must."

She had taken complete leave of her senses.

"Ah, look, our coq au vin has arrived." She smiled tremulously and sat up straighter, with her shoulders back, as though trying to be brave. "After we finish, will you take a walk with me? Perhaps we will run across Kitty somewhere."

What was I to say? She was an unhappy woman determined to cling to her fantasy. "Yes, Mae," I said. "Of course I will take a walk with you."

ACKNOWLEDGMENTS

The seed for this novel was planted when I heard a podcast about the Gilded Age con artist Cassie Chadwick, who enjoyed a brief moment of notoriety when she was tried for swindling banks out of millions. In an era when the daughter of a poor farmer had few options in life, she rewrote the playbook, much like the fictional Jay Gatsby in the Roaring Twenties. This novel does not attempt to faithfully reproduce the details of a life story, which, like the lives of most, if not all, real-life con artists, was sordid, parasitic, and petty, but I did borrow her most successful con: She pretended to be the illegitimate daughter of Andrew Carnegie.

In writing this novel, I received a lot of help along the way. I would like to thank my brilliant author friends: Liese O'Halloran Schwarz and Pooja Bhatia Agarwal for their support and thoughtful comments on the manuscript, Sarah Ladipo Manyika for challenging me to create the character Grace, and Kathy Wang and Shaili Jain for propping me up during the often discouraging quest to find a publishing home for *Forged*. I would also like to thank Leslie Wells, Adrienne Davich,

Michael Mungiello, Jimmy Cajoleas, and the members of the Stanford physician writing group, Pegasus, for insightful critiques of early drafts.

My other early readers include my dear friend Jennifer Bird, my amazing husband, and my wonderful father. Thank you. A special shout out to the incomparable Michelle Kauffmann who is not only my unofficial publicist, along with my husband, but whose help in brainstorming plot points was invaluable. Thanks also to Angela Rogers for parallel writing with me by the sea.

I feel so lucky to be able to work with the talented Jessica Case and her great team at Pegasus Books, including Julia Romero, Maria Fernandez, Ally Purcell, Victoria Wenzel, and Lisa Gillam. Big thanks also to Beth Parker of BPPR, Lori Paximadis at Pax Studio, and to Faceout Studio for the gorgeous cover.

My greatest gratitude goes to my agent, Michael Carlisle, who relentlessly advocated for my work in a crowded marketplace, enduring disappointments with me, but never faltering in his belief that *Forged* would find its readers. This book could not have had a better champion.